Ace Books by Dawn Cook

The Truth Series

FIRST TRUTH
HIDDEN TRUTH
FORGOTTEN TRUTH
LOST TRUTH

The Princess Series

THE DECOY PRINCESS
PRINCESS AT SEA

Princess at Sea

Dawn Cook

ACE BOOKS, NEW YORK

THE BERKLEY PUBLISHING GROUP
Published by the Penguin Group
Penguin Group (USA) Inc.
375 Hudson Street, New York, New York 10014, USA
Penguin Group (Canada), 90 Eglinton Avenue East, Suite 700, Toronto, Ontario M4P 2Y3, Canada
(a division of Pearson Penguin Canada Inc.)
Penguin Books Ltd., 80 Strand, London WC2R 0RL, England
Penguin Group Ireland, 25 St. Stephen's Green, Dublin 2, Ireland (a division of Penguin Books Ltd.)
Penguin Group (Australia), 250 Camberwell Road, Camberwell, Victoria 3124, Australia
(a division of Pearson Australia Group Pty. Ltd.)
Penguin Books India Pvt. Ltd., 11 Community Centre, Panchsheel Park, New Delhi—110 017, India
Penguin Group (NZ), 67 Apollo Drive, Rosedale, North Shore 0632, New Zealand
(a division of Pearson New Zealand Ltd.)
Penguin Books (South Africa) (Pty.) Ltd., 24 Sturdee Avenue, Rosebank, Johannesburg 2196,
South Africa

Penguin Books Ltd., Registered Offices: 80 Strand, London WC2R 0RL, England

This is a work of fiction. Names, characters, places, and incidents either are the product of the author's imagination or are used fictitiously, and any resemblance to actual persons, living or dead, business establishments, events, or locales is entirely coincidental. The publisher does not have any control over and does not assume any responsibility for author or third-party websites or their content.

PRINCESS AT SEA

An Ace Book / published by arrangement with Cold Toast Writings, LLC

PRINTING HISTORY
Ace mass-market edition / August 2006

Copyright © 2006 by Dawn Cook.
Cover art by Katarina Sokolova.
Cover design by Annette Fiore DeFex.
Interior text design by Kristin del Rosario.

ISBN: 978-0-441-01424-8

ACE
Ace Books are published by The Berkley Publishing Group,
a division of Penguin Group (USA) Inc.,
375 Hudson Street, New York, New York 10014.
ACE and the "A" design are trademarks of Penguin Group (USA) Inc.

PRINTED IN THE UNITED STATES OF AMERICA

11 10 9 8 7 6 5 4 3 2

To my dad,
who not only taught me not to fear the water,
but to love it as well.

Acknowledgments

I'd like to take the chance to thank both my editor at Ace, Anne Sowards, and my agent, Richard Curtis. Anne, for her patience and efforts in helping me bring this one back in line with the rest, and Richard, for everything else.

One

I kept my eyes on my cards and my breath slow when Duncan slid the red king I had discarded two turns ago under his sleeve, draped over the narrow table between us. His left hand holding the fan of cards moved in distraction, his right gripping the raised rim of the table when an especially big wave rolled under the boat. Behind him, the stacked tin plates from our lunch slid down the polished ash and into the wall with a *plink*. The light coming in down through the hatch glinted on them, drawing my eye.

From my peripheral sight, I saw a bare movement as Duncan hid his cheating. His brow was tight in pretended worry when I looked back, and his mussed bangs hid his eyes. Lower lip curled between his teeth to make his narrow chin narrower, he discarded. "Your turn, Tess."

His voice was as guiltless as the rest of him, and I stifled my ire. He didn't know I'd spotted his cheating; few could. That I learned to play cards with a cheater as good as he helped.

Pretending ignorance, I drew a black priest, sitting straighter on the bench built into the side of the boat. The faint sounds of an argument came stronger over the creaking of wood and hum of wind in the sails vibrating up through my feet. One voice was high and excited, the other low and coaxing. They were at it again. I caught the accusing word "slavery" and winced.

I laid down the priest with a soft snap, taking a moment to tidy the discard pile and wedge it where two sides of the railing about the table met. The tilt of the deck had strengthened, and the rhythmic surges had become more pronounced. From above came Captain Borlett's confident call to reduce sail. The *Sandpiper* was a fast boat—especially with the wind coming from the angle it was—and the two accompanying warships were likely struggling to keep up.

Duncan picked up the priest with a casual slowness. His thumb rubbed the side of his second finger, telling me he was close to going out. My pulse quickened, and I watched his long, unmarked hands move. They were deeply tanned and strong, having no calluses whatsoever: the hands of a thief, though he claimed he wasn't. Twin rings of gold glittered on one hand. They were new additions. "Purchased," he had claimed last week as he proudly showed them off to me, and I believed him.

There had been many such changes lately as Duncan took the opportunity to remake himself, and I couldn't help but silently applaud. His slow shift from vagabond to settled wealth had left me pleasantly surprised as Duncan developed an unexpected sensitivity in his appearance, which was amusing since I could see that parting with a coin so clearly pained him. I only hoped a smidgen of respect would come with it. Not that Duncan wasn't worthy of respect, but his history showed an appalling tendency to be—ah—inventive in the ways he kept food in his belly and a pillow under his head.

A new bit of color swirled through his brown trousers and long-sleeved shirt: soft golds and deep greens to match Costenopolie's new colors, changed to reflect the addition of the Misdev line by way of marriage of their prince to my sister. I thought it looked grand. His boots were brand-new—and in my eyes, gaudy—picked up at one of the first ports we had called in and still smelling of the red dye he had insisted they rub into it so they would match his hat. The wind had left his hair tousled, but it was newly washed, and his cheeks were freshly shaven, thanks to the harbor we'd left this morning before sunrise.

Duncan had always looked good—having a roguish mien that went well with his slight build, wide shoulders, and narrow waist—but now he'd accented it with a modest show of wealth that made him downright attractive. And even worse? He knew it.

The self-proclaimed cheat met my eye, his lips curving into a sly smile when he realized I was watching him again. "Pay the table or fold," he said, his casual voice matching the soft teasing in his eyes. Flushing, I pushed one of the sweets we were using as wagers to the center with the rest. Taking up a card, I stifled a start when I realized he hadn't discarded into the pile but somewhere on his person. *Chull bait, I missed it.* If I lost now, I deserved it.

The sound of my sister and her new husband's argument suddenly grew louder, and I jumped at the loud bang from the stern of the boat. They grew muffled again, and a shadow came from the depths of the back of the boat, the confident, swaying movement telling me it was Haron. Going sideways in places to navigate the narrow aisle, he entered the small common room at the base of the hatch's stairs. Sun-weathered face creased in irritation, the *Sandpiper*'s first mate stomped up the ladder, his shadow briefly eclipsing Duncan's and my game. From him came a steady, irreverent mutter about it being damn foolish to have women on the water and how we were all going to die for it and that it wouldn't be his fault.

The soft touch on my bare foot as Duncan stretched his long legs jerked my attention back. In the instant I had been distracted, Duncan moved the card under his sleeve to a more secure location. I didn't see it, but I knew that was what happened when he made a show of stretching, proving there was nothing under his arm at all. His cap had shifted position, though, and I would bet all my caramels that was where it had gone.

Irate I'd missed it, I nevertheless kept my face impassive. Having allowed Duncan to distract me like that was inexcusable.

"Are you going to discard, or not?" he asked, a hint of exasperation hiding his deceit.

Eying the inculpable man, I slowly put one of my sweets into my mouth.

"Hey!" Amusement lifted the corners of his lips. "You aren't supposed to eat them unless you win them."

I arched my eyebrows. "Or I catch you."

For an instant, surprise showed, then his jaw clenched. "Burning chu pits," he swore, hunching into himself and looking away. With abrupt motions, he began gathering his cards.

"Duncan, wait," I said, suddenly sorry when he snatched the cards from me. "I only saw it the once. Just the one you put under your sleeve. Everything else was perfect. And the only reason I knew to look for it was because you kept distracting me."

His brown eyes pinched. "You *saw* me move it?"

I nodded, wishing now I had swallowed my pride and kept my mouth shut.

"It's the cold," he said, looking at his left hand and flexing it. Thin lips pursed, he jammed the cards into the hard-leather box he kept them in. I said nothing, feeling guilty. It wasn't the cold—the warm current that bathed the coast kept snow from lingering, especially here on the water—it was the poison that still remained in his hand.

The not-so-long-ago prick from my hairpin had been an accident, but I still felt as if it had been my fault. I had been fleeing a palace takeover, and as a cheat running with me intent upon regaining a portion of the coins I had fairly tricked from him, he hadn't known I carried poison, the weapon of choice in the ancient sect of hidden power I belonged to. He was lucky to have survived it, actually, seeing as he was overly sensitive to punta venom.

I reached to touch his sun-browned hand. I didn't know why. I hated his cheating, and here I was, telling him it was all right. My father would have said it was because I cared more about Duncan's feelings than what was right and that I shouldn't allow myself to be charmed like a fishwife or I'd end up one. A fine ending for a Costenopolie princess, even if she had been bought into the royal family.

Yes, bought as a decoy, unknowingly raised thinking I was the crown princess until a suitor bent on claiming everything some damned Red Moon prophesy promised brought out the ugly truth prematurely. Looking for answers, I had fled, finding not only the real heir, but that the kingdom's chancellor, Kavenlow, had secretly raised me to succeed him in his position as player. My crushing disappointment that I wasn't to rule the people I loved had easily slipped into delight when I found I'd rule them by stealth as Kavenlow now did in a continentwide game of hidden conquest even the royals did not suspect.

The prophesy, incidentally, had been fake, concocted by Kavenlow to ensure his successor would be raised knowing the protocol and studies of a princess, and it had been so full of romantic tripe as to choke the most quixotic daydreamer. Lord love a duck: A child of the coast destined to rule and conceived in the month of the eaten red moon will make an alliance of the heart to set the mighty as pawns and drive out the tainted blood rising in the south. There was no wonder my neighbors wanted to kill me.

My sister had quickly, albeit reluctantly, married to forestall any more assassination attempts. She had gone further to make my royal status irrefutable, so whereas my breeding was from the streets, I was still a princess. I no longer had to marry whoever was best for the kingdom, and in the few months I'd been free of the kingdom's demands, I'd found that freedom was heady, taking more strength to rein in than I was sometimes willing to exert. Especially when it concerned attractive, clever, bad-for-me men like Duncan, who liked to scheme and was as good at it as perhaps even Kavenlow.

Seeing him now in his mix of worry and anger, I reached out as he stood to go. "Please stay?" I asked, taking his damaged hand, and he hesitated, his shoulders easing. It looked fine, the injury so deep that it only showed when he needed the greater finesse to move his cards.

Duncan leaned against a support post to balance against the boat's motion, his red hat brushing the low ceiling. Pulling from my grip, he watched with me as his hand moved in a gesture as smooth and even as royal silk, pulling a card from under his hat with two fingers and tucking it in the box with the rest. "It's the cold," he said, knowing it wasn't.

I made a face to try to break him out of his mood. "Don't think so," I said saucily. "I've always been able to spot you cheating." I playfully reached out and took one of his sweets, popping it into my mouth and arching my eyebrows.

"Hey!" he cried in mock distress. "I spent half a purse on those."

My tongue ran over the inside of my teeth to get every last bit of sticky amber. "Nuh uh. I caught you. I deserve at least three."

Lurching in time with the boat, he sat beside me on my side of the table. His brow smoothed when I didn't shift away, and his hand went out to take mine. Unlike my sister's, my skin was as dark as his, my fingers having faint calluses in places most people had smooth skin. A soft smile took me, seeing how small my hand looked within his. He was so close, I could smell the dye from his hat. I should have moved, but I didn't.

My pulse increased, and I watched his eyes. An eager feeling of daring lifted through me, and my breath caught. I let him turn my hand over, and he dropped a handful of caramels into my palm. "I bought them for you," he said as he curled my fingers over them.

I met his solemn expression with a smile that was probably besotted. "Thank you." I dropped the sweets into a pocket and shifted closer under the excuse of a wave, reaching to check the topknot my long curls were in. It was a nervous habit that brought a knowing glint to Duncan's eyes. He leaned closer, and my eyes widened. *Oh heavens, he's going to kiss me. It's about chu-pits time!*

Another bang from the royal apartment brought my head around. "To get some air!" came a furious shout. It was Contessa, one hand on her gathered skirts, the other reaching like a blind man as she struggled to make her way up the narrow aisle to the common room. I reluctantly eased away; my sister had the timing of an aunt with nothing to do but play chaperone.

Alex was behind her, managing the rocking boat well in his shiny boots, snug-fitting breeches, and long-tailed coat of a rich green lined in gold. In his grace, he even managed to keep his sword, at his side despite the security of the boat, from smacking anything.

"Let me help you, Contessa," he said gallantly, a devious smile about his thin lips as he nodded first to me, then Duncan. His light dusting of freckles, fine blond hair, and trim, small-waisted figure brought to mind his murderous, power-crazed brother—the one who took over my palace and murdered my adopted parents. The similarities of the two brothers had bothered me greatly until I realized that apart from their outward appearance, they were as different as salt and sand. *Thank God.*

"I don't want your help," Contessa muttered, red spotting her pale cheeks as she tottered to the steps. "I'm trying to get away from you."

"Contessa, love . . ." Green eyes sparkling, he reached to help her, and she jerked away, jewelry chiming. Giving him a potent glare she must have learned at the feet of the nuns who raised her, she struggled up the steps. The wind whipped her unbound hair into her eyes and made her skirt flare out. I'd have a wickedly hard time getting the yellow strands untangled tonight. Steadying herself, she stomped in her tiny boots to the railing and out of sight.

Tempting fate, Alex ran a hand over his clean-shaven cheeks and followed the petite woman up. The quick-minded prince was bored, and teasing my sister was apparently the only thing he could find to do. Unfortunately, Contessa's provincial temper made her an easy mark.

The mood broken, Duncan slid down the bench a smidgen. He took three cards from his deck and practiced moving them in and out of hiding, the motion intentionally slow as he stretched and strengthened muscles. I was fascinated in that I could have sworn that he put the sun card in his sleeve but it was the huntsman he took back out.

Both our heads rose when Haron stomped downstairs and to his bunk, still grumbling. The first mate had the night watch, and I knew it was too early for him to be up. The faint sounds of Alex alternately trying to calm down Contessa and drive her to distraction grew louder over the creak of rope and wash of water. A sigh shifted my shoulders.

"Are you going to stop him?" Duncan asked when the sharp click of Haron's door shutting came to us. "She sounds ready to slap him."

Weary of it, I shook my head. When I had accepted the position of Costenopolie's ambassador at my sister's request, I had thought it would mean I would be smoothing great political problems, not acting as nursemaid and arbitrator between my sister and her new husband.

"No," I said, folding my arms on the table and dropping my head onto them. "I told her he's doing it to see her stomp her feet and put a blush on her cheeks, but she doesn't listen."

"Maybe she likes it."

"That's my guess." I tilted my head to see him past my brown curls. Contessa was anything but even-tempered. Despite being a mirror copy of our deceased mother, one would never know she was a queen by the amount of caterwauling she did. That's why the nuptial holiday. Under the advice of Kavenlow, I was trying to instill the provincial woman with some polish as she met the people for whom she was now responsible. It wasn't working. And though I liked Prince Alex, he wasn't helping.

The word "execution" and "hungry thief," quickly followed by "barbaric" were a veritable feminine shriek, and Duncan shifted uncomfortably. The argument about changing Costenopolie's policy on suspected criminals had started this morning when we slipped from harbor. I should step in—if only to get them to stop talking about executing thieves where Duncan could overhear. He wasn't a thief; he was a cheat. There was a difference. Sort of.

"Maybe you're right," I said, gathering my skirts to rise, pausing at Duncan's hand on my shoulder. Surprised, I turned, blinking at the worry and the hint of pleading in his eyes.

"Tess. You don't owe her anything. You owe Kavenlow even less. Why won't you—"

Pulling from his hand, I stood, cutting him off and catching my balance at one of the support planks over which the deck was built. "I owe her everything. I owe Kavenlow my life for pulling me from the gutter. Nothing is keeping you here. If you want to go, that's fine, but she needs me. Costenopolie needs me." Frustration at the old argument made my words harsher than I had intended, but I wouldn't drop my eyes.

He made a scoffing bark of laughter, slumping back. "God save you, Tess. Costenopolie won't fall if you leave it," he said bitingly, then pinched his brow to soften his words.

I flushed. Actually, it might. Eventually. But I couldn't tell him that. He had no inkling that a continentwide game of hidden conquest swirled under the veneer of royal power. Very few did. I had been raised in the palace, and even *I* hadn't known until Kavenlow told me of the magic for which he had been secretly building my strength.

I said nothing while the frustration shifted behind his eyes. He knew he was welcome to stay at court as long as he wanted, but as a player, I couldn't allow myself to get close to anyone lest he be used against me by a rival. All Duncan knew was that I wouldn't allow more than a fleeting kiss, and I knew it confused him when he saw my willingness in an unguarded moment. Things had been a lot easier when I'd been the crown princess.

"I'm not leaving her," I said, stepping from behind the table. "For you, or anything." Grabbing the ladder, I started up, hiding behind my responsibilities as ambassador. I felt like the bottom of a chu pit for my lies of omission and my lack of trust in him.

A confused anger at myself warmed me as I held my skirts with one hand, the ladder with the other. It wasn't fair. None of it. Whom I gave my heart to was no longer linked to the crown, yet I was still ruled by it. I left him with his cards, as silent and as frustrated as I was.

The wood framing the hatch under my hand was warm from the sun, and I lurched onto the deck. Like a blow, the wind struck me, pushing me and making my skirt flare. It wasn't cold, but so strong a force took getting used to. My toes gripped the wood, polished by sun and sliding ropes. Squinting from the glare, I held back the brown curls that had escaped my topknot.

I was facing the stern, and the clouds behind the tilting horizon were blue with rain. The waves were choppy since the wind was blowing against the current, tearing the wave tops as tonight's storm grew closer. At the wheel, Captain Borlett gave me a sympathetic nod, looking stiff and uncomfortable at his unintentional overhearing of the royal argument. I thought he looked inexcusably relieved that it wasn't his responsibility to put an end to it.

A welcoming nicker pulled my gaze to my horses, standing tethered against the wall of the galley shack at the bow. The black animals were here only because Alex's horse hadn't taken to the water, and Contessa had rightly insisted they should have matched animals.

I didn't mind riding borrowed horses myself when we went ashore to assure the populace that they really did have a queen, and she had our mother's elegant, regal beauty even if I didn't, but the royal couple should be on horses in which we were confident. Jy and Pitch were well behaved, and had been trained for water travel even before Kavenlow had given them to me. The gelding was my favorite. I had named him Jy, short for Jeck's horse, which is what I had called him before knowing he was really mine.

Contessa's voice pulled me to the railing where Alex had nearly pinned the white-clad woman. Her fair skin was even paler in anger, and she had taken a defensive stance, with her hands on her hips, looking like a fishwife despite her wearing enough silk to make a tent. Alex, too, had lost his teasing air, having a stiff attitude with his chin high and his jaw set. His freckles were lost behind a red tinge. My mood of exasperation shifted to one of bother. She must have insulted his honor. It was the only thing that could arouse the fun-loving man's slow temper.

Setting aside my thoughts of Duncan, I went to the railing, then forward across the sloping deck. "Contessa," I called, but neither of them heard me over the wind.

My sister drew her heart-shaped features tight, pushing herself away from the railing and boldly into Prince Alex's space. The two of them made a handsome couple in their finery despite their anger. "You're wrong," she said, loud enough for the sailors below to hear, and I cringed. "You may have wiggled your foul way into my palace, but your Misdev cruelty will not gain one foothold in Costenopolie as long as I breathe!"

"And you are a silly woman who has no inkling of how the world works," he said. From the wheel came Captain Borlett's audible intake of breath.

"You chull!" Contessa shrieked. "And you're a royal snot who can't see the ocean for the waves. The power to chop the hands off thieves will *not* be given back to harbormasters and village leaders. Kavenlow will hear every complaint before sentence is cast. I don't care how much it pulls from the coffers. I will see your sword broken and you slinging chu before I let you convince me otherwise!"

"The sword of my grandfather will not break," Alex said, setting a hand atop the handle.

I came abreast of them, not sure how to interfere without

ending up publicly reprimanded. It was embarrassing, and I didn't like it. "Ah, Contessa?" I started, tension slamming the air from me when she lunged forward and pulled Alex's sword.

My hand went to my topknot where I usually kept my poisoned darts. "Contessa!" I shouted, lurching to stand between her and Alex as she struggled to hold the heavy sword.

The point dipped as the fiery woman looked from me to Alex in frustration. "If your sword won't break," she threatened, "then I'll be rid of it."

"Contessa! No!" I cried, reaching out even as she twisted her body and threw Alex's sword out over the water. I held my breath, watching in a horrid fascination as the hazy sun glinted on the highly polished metal. Alex's green eyes went wide in disbelief; he was too shocked to move. Soundless over the wind, it cut cleanly into the water—and was gone.

She had thrown his sword into the waves. She had thrown his grandfather's sword where none could find it. Suddenly frightened, I tore my gaze from the gray waves laced with froth. I could see the new Misdev/Costenopolie alliance that I had worked so hard to foster shred like cotton. Her temper had dealt a blow more severe than had I murdered the prince in his bed.

Contessa's color was high, and she met my horrified look and Alex's expression of shock with absolutely no repentance. Her satisfaction melted into surprise when Alex swooped around me, and before I knew his intent, picked her up, and dropped her over the side. Her shriek of surprise cut off with a splash.

"Fetch my sword, wife," he whispered, his jaw tight in anger.

"Contessa!" I shrieked when the call for man-in-the-water went up from three different throats. Panicking, I pulled three knives from my waistband. The first I threw to thunk into one of the twin lines holding the mainsail. One side of the massive sheet fell in a sliding sound of canvas amid shouts of distress. The second went thunking into the lead of my black gelding, freeing him. I had a third knife which I wanted to stick into that fool prince Alex, but instead I used it to rip my outer dress off. My heart pounded and my fingers fumbled in fear. *Contessa* . . .

"Where is she?" Alex said, his angry satisfaction dissolving as he peered over the railing and watched the waves.

Slowly, he moved to the stern of the boat to stay with the disappearing bubbles. "She hasn't come up yet."

"She's drowning," I said, shoving my dress into him so hard he almost fell back. *Stupid landlubber. Doesn't know a bloody thing.* "Her skirts are pulling her down. Congratulations. I think you're the new king of Costenopolie."

His mouth opened, and his face went ashen under his blond bangs. I had no time to spare for him. Whistling for my horse, I ran to the stern, and as Captain Borlett reached out in alarm and protest, I scrambled over the railing and fell ungracefully into the water.

Captain Borlett's call cut off with the shocking, swirling cold. A second, muffled whoosh of sound shook me as I pushed to the surface. It was Jy, having jumped the railing right behind me. Pulling in a huge breath of air, I dived. The sounds of organized panic vanished.

Salt water burned my eyes as I looked for a shadow in the murky dusk the clouds had made of the ocean. Nothing. I came up, gasping. Jy was nearby, his feet darting down as if trying to trot. His neck was arched and his eyes wide in excitement. I thanked God I had spent the last three months training him to follow my whistle. Kavenlow had thought it was a vain, silly, woman thing to have a horse come when called. I wished he had been right.

From above came the sound of Duncan shouting my name. The boat had slipped farther away despite the remaining sails having been dropped. I went to dive again, pulling in so much air my lungs hurt. I upended myself and went down. *Oh God. What if I can't find her?* My parents' deaths, allowing a prince of Misdev to wed my sister; what would it all be for if I lost the only person I had a tie with?

My breath slipped out in a trail of bubbles at the gray shape darting past me, my first fear of sharks dying when I realized it was a stingray. It was followed by a painful strike of hope as I followed its motion to a wildly struggling shadow.

Contessa! I thought, striking out for her, feeling that my arms were too slow and my motions useless. She was deep underwater, almost lost in the gloom. Panic showed in her violent motions. Fire burned in my chest. I had to surface.

I clawed my way up, breaking the surface in a fear-laced

breath. The boat was far ahead, stalled in the mounting waves. Beyond were the warships, their heavy momentum making it harder for them to turn. Jy had begun to follow them, my call forgotten. I dived again.

The numbing rush of water filled my ears, making my pounding blood a goad, driving me down. Her shadow grew. Fingers stretching, I grasped her wildly waving hair. Face to the surface, I kicked myself upward. Her weight held me down. Too slowly, the surface brightened.

A muffled sound of bubbles, carrying her sob, urged me upward, pushed by my sister's last breath. Arms aching, I pulled us to the soft smear of sky made gray by too much water. I broke the surface, gasping. My limbs trembled as I pulled her up. She burst out in a panic-driven gasp of air. I managed one good breath before she pushed me under, frantic to escape.

The influx of air gave her the strength to keep her face above water, and I kicked away and surfaced. Her eyes were wide and unknowing in terror, the blue of them shocking in the depth of fear they showed. "Tess," she managed, water slipping past her mouth, and she reached out to push me under again.

The sounds of a distant rescue vanished in a swirl of inrushing water. Breath held, I went passive, letting her get a full gulp of air while she unintentionally drowned me. My thoughts were screaming in a shared panic, but I walled them off. I had to call my horse back. There was no chance if fear ruled me. If I couldn't get him to return, Contessa would drown both of us.

I exhaled, sinking out from under her. My sister's motions grew violent as my support dropped away. The muzzy gray of the world's water surrounded me, insulating me from her terror. I fell deep into my thoughts, willing my magic to surface. My left leg throbbed, and my head pounded as I pulled on more magic than I was capable of. I had to call my horse. I had to find Jy's thoughts.

As my lungs burned and my reason screamed to surface, I sent my awareness out, slow and cold from the surrounding water. The quick thoughts of the stingrays were distracting, their mirror-bright minds like flashes in the dark. Desperate, I searched more carefully, following a faint emotion of cold water making limbs slow and unresponsive. It had to be Jy.

Fastening on feelings that weren't mine, I slipped my thoughts into the intelligent animal's, the way made easy by frequent practice. Air slipped past my lips and ran a fast trail to the surface in relief. I had found him.

Immediately, I struggled to the surface lest our joined thoughts make Jy think he was drowning. *Here*, I thought, relief flooding me as the levelheaded horse obediently turned and headed away from the *Sandpiper.* From the deck came Duncan's hail. I caught a glimpse of him, standing at the stern beside Captain Borlett, leaning halfway over the railing.

Contessa clutched at me when I surfaced, reason clearly having broken through her panic. Strands of blond hair were in her face, and fear had twisted her expression—but she wasn't panicking anymore. "Tess," she sobbed, the water seeping past her lips. "I thought I killed you. I'm sorry. I'm sorry. I've killed us both. I can't stay up. They won't get a boat to us in time."

"Jy is coming," I said around a cough. "Grab on to him."

Her eyes widened, and the hint of hope made her look like an angel, downtrodden by the ignorant rabble of humanity. "Jy?" she said, sinking as she exhaled.

I pulled her up, going under myself. The sound of Jy's splashing was muffled, and when I shook the water from my eyes, he was there.

Contessa was coughing violently, sinking lower into the water with her motions. I grabbed Jy's mane, pulling her hand to lie beside mine. Her thin, pale fingers trembled, then clutched the horse's mane with a frightened, white-knuckled strength. Sobs mixed with her hacking coughs as she hung on, the thin muscles of her arms showing under the sodden silk.

Draping one arm over Jy's back, I hung low in the water, content to do nothing as my body shook, and exhaustion made its claim on me. Contessa wouldn't stop crying. The *Sandpiper*'s momentum had left us far behind, and if it hadn't been for Jy, we would have drowned. The two heavy warships had finally gotten themselves turned about and were heading back in wide angles against the wind.

I couldn't see him yet, but I heard Duncan's voice come strong over the waves; he was in a dinghy. Jy's ears pricked in recognition, and the slap of waves against wood and the concerned voices of crew members grew audible.

"Tess!" Duncan exclaimed, when the shadow of the low-slung boat came alongside Jy, still swimming toward the *Sandpiper*, his ears pricked at the memory of hay and mash. "Tess, are you all right?"

"Get her in the boat," I said, coughing when an errant wave smacked into me. "Hurry. I don't know how long she can hold on with the water pulling at her."

Still crying, Contessa grasped for the wiry, sun-browned arms reaching for her. With a great deal of noise, they pulled her in. The boat rocked violently, and she hit the planks with a sodden thump. Her coughs turned to retching, and she pulled herself up to vomit seawater over the far side of the boat.

I was next. The grip about my wrists was painfully hard, and my front scraped the side of the dinghy as they pulled. I landed at the bottom of the boat with a shoulder-hurting force. The wind cut into me, chilling me through my wet underthings. Duncan put a coat about me, and I clutched it closer. Pulling my legs under me, I sat up and wiped my face, not yet fully cognizant that I was alive, and Contessa was alive, and we were both going to see the sun set tonight.

"Quick. Turn around," Duncan was saying, though the able-bodied men had already done so. I pulled my head up to find Jy beside us, swimming strongly to the *Sandpiper*. There was a sling aboard one of the warships. He would not be left to die, no matter how the captain might fuss and bluster about the approaching storm and the time needed to get the animal back on board. Not after he had saved the life of his queen.

My pulse slowed, and I began to shiver. My sister was safe. My sister was alive to irritate me for another day.

Duncan touched my shoulder, and I met his eyes from around my soggy strands of hair. He took a breath, then with his brown eyes holding a defiant slant, he pulled me into an inappropriately public, crushing hug where everyone could see. To push away was not an option, and I let my head drop into the hollow between his neck and shoulder, shaking from the cold and exertion while I breathed in the scent of leather and soap from his shave yesterday. My eyes warmed with tears no one could separate from the dripping water.

How can I be so fortunate? I held myself apart from him, yet he cared for me still. That I had to keep my secret history from him was like a guilty thorn. Slowly, I pulled away, and feeling it, he let me go. His expressive eyes from behind his wind-tossed bangs met mine, forgiving me again for having sensed my acceptance before protocol pushed me away. Reassured, he turned to the *Sandpiper*, yelling out for clean water and blankets before we even got there.

I wiped the tears and salt water from my face, my gaze falling upon the Misdev warship nearing in a wide tack. My overwhelming relief at having saved Contessa turned to shame when I found the black and green of Jeck's uniform at the bow of the Misdev ship. Even from this distance, I could see his stance was stiff and tense.

My fingers trembled as Duncan took them in a more appropriate show of concern, and I pulled my attention from Jeck, my face warming in shame. Jeck would know. The rival player from Misdev would think I was a fool, rightly claiming I was unfit to play the game if I couldn't even keep my royal couple from killing each other. And as the crew began chanting to keep their strokes in time with each other, I wondered if Jeck might be right.

Two

I tugged at Contessa's clean but damp hair, yanking the pearl-inlaid brush through her waist-long yellow strands with an aggressive strength. And the queen of Costenopolie, ruler of the seas and the vast inland forests, took my tight-lipped abuse in a shamed silence.

From above the ridiculously small cabin came the noise of my horse being winched aboard. The room off the officers' quarters had once been first mate Haron's, but it was now swathed with so much silk and linen that the original lines couldn't be seen. It was mostly bed, actually, with only a small space for Contessa's drying clothes and the two of us while I made her presentable. The ceiling was just over my head, and I held my balance easily under the swells since the sails were down, and the deck remained reasonably level.

My foul mood had started the moment I had landed upon the deck of the *Sandpiper* in my sodden underthings amid a flurry of overdone excitement. Contessa had claimed most of the attention, which didn't bother me at all as I slunk belowdecks and into some clothes. Even her getting the bathwater first, and therefore hot, hadn't bothered me. Much. I had yet to bathe, and salt had dried on me and in my hair. Duncan's sweets were beyond rescue. But what bothered me the most was that Jeck had taken the opportunity to switch boats.

The powerfully built, pensive man was supposed to keep himself on the warship with the rest of the Misdev soldiers. Under the guise of making sure Alex was all right, he had gained my boat, and I felt his presence aboard almost as clearly as if he were standing behind my shoulder, his resonant voice muttering about foolish women and games and kingdoms lost from ignorance.

On the surface, Jeck was the captain of our neighboring King Misdev's guards, on loan until a new captain to manage the Misdev soldiers that Alex had brought with him could be arranged for. The reality was far more dangerous. Jeck was a rival player, and I didn't trust him, despite Kavenlow's assurances and the Misdev officer's claim of a temporary alliance.

It didn't help that Jeck had once tried to lure me from Kavenlow to be his apprentice. The memory and fear of the temptation still lingered. It was an odd balance we players existed in, with both a public persona always near the throne and a hidden status known only to other players. I publicly outranked him and could have him flogged, though he was too clever to give me the excuse. Privately, he was a master player despite being only a few years my senior, and I a mere apprentice, and it was my task to keep him from taking advantage of it. The delicate balance was one I was becoming reasonably good at, but he, again, was better at it. And as I tugged the brush through Contessa's hair, I spared a thought that perhaps Kavenlow had let the potentially dangerous man accompany me in the hopes of an impromptu lesson in humility.

Despite his physical prowess—which even I had to admit made the man ruggedly attractive—Jeck was the only player who could use his magic to heal or kill with his hands. I had the potential as well, but since Kavenlow couldn't teach me how, I was stymied, my loyalty to Kavenlow keeping me from reaching my full potential. It wasn't as if I could safely teach myself. As Jeck had been quick to point out when he unearthed my ability, healing and killing are different sides to the same knife—and a knife will kill you if you make a mistake.

I was sure Jeck was with Alex right now, filling his ears with propaganda under the guise of arranging for a new sword for his sovereign's youngest son. Until Alex had married into the Costenopolie family, he had been one of Jeck's pieces and was certainly conditioned to heed Jeck's counsel both because Jeck was the captain of his father's guard and because of Jeck's magical abilities. That Alex was now Kavenlow's piece to manipulate probably didn't mean gull spots to Jeck. He was up to something. I couldn't believe that he would voluntarily leave his playing field for this amount of time if he didn't think it would benefit him in some large fashion.

Alex had been properly frightened for his wife when we finally got back aboard, his lost sword forgotten in the fear he might have killed Contessa. I knew that the emotion would pale when time put distance between his fear and the memory of her throwing his grandfather's sword into the drink. If pride kept Contessa from admitting she'd made a mistake, Alex might listen to the first person in the devious royal courts who saw a chance to gain personal power by setting the young prince actively against her.

Worried, I yanked the brush through Contessa's hair. She silently winced when I found a knot and the brush jerked to a stop. "Sorry," I muttered, remembering how it hurt when Heather, my childhood friend and handmaiden, took her frustration out on me in a similar fashion. Immediately, I set the brush down to pick out the snarl.

"You're hurting me," Contessa complained, sounding fearful about what I might come back with. In public, she was the queen, and I was her sister-by-law and respected member of her court. Privately, she took counsel from me and sometimes-harsh criticism as I tried to teach her a lifetime of political grace before she stuck her foot in her mouth so far she choked us all.

"You were a fool," I said, thinking it would be easier to cut the knot the salt water had made of her hair than continue to pick it out. "Wars have started over less."

Her fingers trembled as she picked up the small hand mirror and watched what I was doing. "He can't start a war with his wife."

Lips tight, I dabbed the barest hint of fragrant oil on my fingers to try to loosen the snarl. "Yes he can," I said, and her eyes met mine in the mirror. The deep blue of them were frightened. Good. She should be. She might be back on the boat, but her head was barely above water, and I think she had just realized it.

"What should I do?" she asked. "Apologizing will make me look weak. I'm a queen."

"You should have thought of that before you threw his sword into the sea." Taking up the brush, I roughly continued untangling her hair. The faint smell of fish rose from me, and I grimaced. "What were you thinking?" I accused. "It was his grandfather's sword. It protected the royal family through every battle. He can't replace it. And from a practical standpoint, what is he supposed to do for the rest of the trip? Swords of that quality are not commonplace. He'll have to rely upon another man's blade. Do you have any idea what that means to a man? To a prince?"

Her face miserable, she set the hand mirror down so I couldn't see her tears. "I will publicly apologize and give him a new sword," she said, her voice low.

My breath escaped me in a tired hiss. "You will do no such thing. You will publicly tell him that you stand by your decision to require royal approval for any mutilations of thieves. And tonight, you will apologize profusely in the privacy of your room. On your knees with all the humility the nuns taught you. You will tell him you're a fool, that what you did deserves a flogging, and you will give him the strap to do it."

"No!" she cried, a hand rising to her mouth. "I can't!"

I edged past the chair holding her washed dress to stand in front of her. My brow was pinched enough to give me a headache, and my stomach was tight with worry. "You will."

"I can't!"

"You threw the sword of a prince of Misdev into the sea. You will."

She closed her eyes, a tear slipping from her dark lashes. I stifled my jealousy at how much she looked like our mother: small, graceful, and pale, someone strong of will but needing to be protected. I was too tall to be delicate, my skin dark and my womanly curves merely suggestions. That I could ride like a man and protect myself was often small consolation.

Contessa nodded, eyes still closed as she accepted my counsel. Immediately I softened. "But, Contessa?" I said, and her eyes opened. "I can guarantee that if you are truly sorry, he will see it, and he won't be able to lift a finger against you. Most likely he will beg for your forgiveness for nearly drowning you. Not that you deserve it," I added sourly.

"But what if he does? What if he hits me?"

It was a frightened whisper, and I frowned. "Then he didn't hear the sincerity in your voice, and you deserved it." She blinked violently to forestall more tears, and exasperated, I knelt to take her hands in mine. They were very cold. "You handled the situation very badly," I berated her gently. "Word will go out at the next port that you can be goaded into a mistake by anger. Tonight is a pause on the balance point, the sole chance for words to be said and heard clearly before others cloud Alex's judgment." *Unless Jeck already ruined it.* "Don't make an entire kingdom suffer for your pride," I said, trying to meet her eyes. "He's a good man. You shamed Mother and Father by bringing his honor into question."

Her gaze dropped, and I thought how easy it was for me to be spouting advice. Me, who almost sent my kingdom to war over my pride when I vowed to kill Alex's brother for murdering our parents. I almost did, but Jeck convinced me not to. Jeck—who still harbored a lust for Costenopolie's ships and forests, who was probably whispering in Alex's ear this very moment.

"I'm sorry," Contessa whispered again, a single tear sliding down a well-marked trail. She reached up to wipe it away, her deep blue eyes flicking to mine.

I stood, handing her a soft cloth. "You should be." Going behind her, I gathered her hair, relaxing now that it seemed I might be able to keep everything intact another day. "Here," I said. "I'll put your hair up like Mother kept hers. You can at least look nice while groveling."

A worried sound came from her, part relief but mostly worried resignation. "Some of this is his fault," she said petulantly. "I left, and he followed. I said stop, and he didn't."

"Most of it's his fault," I agreed, and she started, clearly surprised.

"But you told me to . . ."

I nodded. "His fault for goading you beyond reason. But you did throw his sword into the sea. You outrank him. The fault lies with you." I divided the silky mass of her hair into three strands. "Me? I probably would have punched him in the belly and tied him to the mainmast. There would have been no way to make amends for that."

She laughed, though it was decidedly forced. It ended in a sigh, and I began braiding her hair, weaving silk rings into the plait as I went. I'd make her look like an angel. Alex didn't have a chance, no matter what Jeck was telling him.

Technically, Alex was my piece to play with, and Jeck shouldn't be here, but there were only six rules to the game, and this situation wasn't covered by any of them. *Why did you let him come, Kavenlow?* I thought, wondering if I was keeping Jeck busy while my master set other plans in motion. If so, it was a very dangerous game. "You know," I said as I worked, "you shouldn't be so harsh on Alex."

Her head dropped to pull the hair from my fingers. "He doesn't like me," she said.

"Yes, he does," I answered. "That's why he teases you."

"Well, I don't like him." Her lips pressed into a thin line. "I love Thadd."

Oooooooh, I thought, eyebrows rising and my fingers faltering as I finally understood the unending arguments of the last three weeks. Contessa liked him, and she had taken to being disagreeable in order to remain true to her first, childhood love.

Deep in thought, I pulled her braid up and around, weaving it through the rings to secure it. I couldn't bear it if Contessa's and Alex's paths turned against each other when there was the chance for a real marriage, not snatches of comfort taken from someone else in palace corners amid shame and fear of gossiping tongues. A royal marriage bound by love could create an empire. It *had* created an empire. And it could easily be sundered by the love of another man.

My throat tightened in the memory of my parents. Forcing the lump down, I dropped my hands from her hair to arrange the lace about her collar. "Alex came into this knowing it was a marriage of convenience," I said cautiously. "That you have no affection for him. Has he . . . Has he touched you? Is that why you're so disagreeable with him?"

Contessa flushed a red to rival the sunset. "No."

I remained silent for a moment, hearing the lack of completeness in her confession. "Do you want him to?" I finally asked.

"No!" she said, a shade too quickly. "I love Thadd."

My jaw tightened at the bitter tinge my thoughts had taken. I, too, had been worried about my husband-to-be when I thought I was Costenopolie's crown princess. And I hadn't the complication of a preexisting relationship to deal with. She had been raised by nuns, never knowing who she was and expecting a provincial life with an apprentice sculptor.

"I don't want to talk about it," Contessa said abruptly, taking up the mirror and trying to see what I had done with her hair.

"Give him a chance," I whispered, my hands falling to my side. "He left his mistress behind when no one would have said anything should he have brought her with him. He has stayed silent about you and Thadd though you have shown a callous disregard for Alex's feelings, flaunting your relationship. Alex doesn't want a loveless marriage, and you're trampling his feelings like flowers in the mud, ignoring that he's trying to start a new one with you. He has accepted his loss and is showing more honor than you have a right to expect."

"I'm aware of that," she almost snapped, and I knew I had struck a sore spot. The fiery woman sat with a stone-lipped stillness. I couldn't tell what she was thinking. I had only known her for a few months, and I had found that when she turned like this, she could do anything from burst into tears to tackle me and try to tear my hair out. It had happened before.

Slowly, I reached up to my own simple topknot and pricked my finger upon one of the poison darts I had started wearing since hearing Jeck had boarded. The sharp prick of pain was familiar, and I felt my vision lose its focus while my body fought the poison off. It was the same toxin that almost killed Duncan, but Kavenlow had laboriously built my natural immunity to where it became a benefit, not a drawback.

This was what made the game possible. This was how a chancellor, a captain of the guard, or a child taken from the street could secretly manipulate thousands. The toxin slowly built up in the body, imparting some of the magical abilities of the animal it came from.

My slight headache vanished as my magic swung past its usual limits and into a temporary extreme by the dose of venom. I'd need the extra boost to sense Contessa's emotions. Giving oneself a dose of venom to increase one's magic wasn't advisable since it also put one closer to death until it wore off, but I was reasonably secure. Jeck was more likely to steal my limited stash of venom than try to kill me with an overdose of his—Kavenlow would be furious. Building an apprentice's tolerance to venom was expensive and risky, but he'd be angry because he loved me as the child the venom prevented him from having.

A flush of warmth from the poison swirled through me, and I sent my thoughts out to find Contessa's current state of emotion. This was a magic I had found on my own, completely by accident and shocking Kavenlow speechless.

We had been building my ability to find a rival player when he or she was trying to avoid detection, an extreme game of palacewide hide-and-seek. It wasn't taking me nearly as long to find him as it should, and when I innocently told him that I was following his emotions of tension and anticipation, he had stared at me for a good fifteen seconds, which may not sound like much, but it's an eternity when you think you've done something wrong.

Rubbing his hands together in delight, he immediately sent me to find Jeck. That was harder, but after a week's practice, I was able to find him as easily as anyone else unless he was sleeping or intentionally keeping his emotions quiet. Kavenlow said sensing people's feelings was probably born from my uncanny ability to manipulate animals by finding their emotions and playing upon them. I just thought it was fun to sneak up on Jeck, catching the young, stoic man doing something scholarly like reading a book or penning a letter. He would much rather I think of him a muscle-dense lout who got his position by strength not cleverness. I had quickly run out of excuses for stumbling in on him, and I think he suspected I had been using him to hone my skills when he stopped trying to hide from me, making it harder to stretch my abilities. By comparison, finding Contessa's emotions was easy.

Slowly our breathing synchronized as Contessa's emotions mingled with mine. It wasn't a pleasant sensation, and

I searched my feelings, finding the ones that didn't fit. Over-whelming, almost debilitating worry crashed through me, and I held my breath, dealing with it.

Pulse pounding, I turned to shake out Contessa's drying dress and the underthings strewn about. Contessa was worried. Worried about Thadd. Worried about the bed she slept in and the hammock that Alex had voluntarily consigned himself to, waiting until he thought her asleep before even entering their small cabin. Worried that she might like the clever, fun-loving man who could make her laugh as easily as frown. Worried that she was an inconstant woman and weak of will if she found her-self attracted to him as well as her slow, predictable Thadd.

Her confusion was deep, directed inward by a wedge of shame. There was no anger at Alex or me. Relieved she wasn't upset with me, I let my shoulders slump, surprised when Con-tessa's did the same. A flash of worry pulled me upright. There was the potential here to direct her emotions, to manipulate her by making her feel things she really didn't, and the idea that I could twist her so easily left me with a strong feeling of wrongness.

Immediately I worked to find the emotions that were en-tirely mine, separating myself from my sister. We simulta-neously took a cleansing breath, and I wished Kavenlow were here.

"You like Duncan," she said softly—as if the thought had just occurred to her.

My mouth dropped open. She met my startled gaze, and I wondered if she was commenting on the obvious camaraderie between us or if she had picked the more-certain emotion from my thoughts. Had she seen a smidgen into my feelings as I had seen into hers but labeled it intuition? *What have I ac-cidentally learned to do?*

She met my worried smile with the confidence of shared secrets between sisters. A tap at the door startled us both, and I ran my hand down the dress I had thrown on so I wouldn't be running about in my underthings. "Come in," we said together, me sounding relieved.

It was Duncan, his gangly frame halting in the door. Con-tessa saw my flush, her smile going knowing. "Water's hot again," he said, his expression unbothered.

"Thank you," I said, hoping he hadn't been eavesdropping. Eyes down, I edged about the chair to get to the door. I was so desperate for a bath that I would have taken it cold, but I had to get Contessa presentable first. And water was easier to heat when we were stalled in the sea. Through the deck came the call for sails to go up. Even fainter came the signal horns from the two warships. Though we weren't actually moving, we were under way. It was going to be harder to wash up, now, but I'd done it before.

"Thank you, Tess," Contessa said, when I reached the door, her voice precise, every syllable carefully pronounced as she adopted a formal air in the presence of someone besides the two of us. "You may go tidy yourself."

I jerked to a stop, her altered tone reminding me of our public relationship. Duncan grinned, catching a glimpse of my frustration before I hid it. "Thank you, Your Majesty," I murmured, managing to elbow Duncan in the ribs as I curtsied in the doorway.

"Would you please see that Jy is given an extra ration of grain tonight," she added. "And have Captain Borlett free enough water from the cisterns to rinse his coat."

"Thank you, Contessa," I added, grateful she had remembered my horse. I'd been planning to use all my wiles to get Jy something. Now all I would have to do was say Contessa wished it.

The young woman met my smile with her own, reminding me that for all the temper and the provincial fishwife at her core, she was an intelligent woman who naturally thought more of others than herself. *Perhaps,* I mused as I shut the door behind me and followed Duncan through the boat, *I should remember that more often.*

Three

❖

The wind from the nearing storm had become aggressive, but it felt wonderful in my curls, a few brown strands pulled from my topknot to blow artfully about my shoulder while they finished drying. My bath had been short since the waves had grown higher, but the salt was gone, and there was no better feeling than standing at the rail of a ship with the wind in your hair, the balance of power between the wind and waves vibrating up through your feet. I didn't care that the crew members were surly and bad-tempered. None of it was my fault.

Because of Alex's dumping Contessa overboard, we weren't going to make the next harbor before twilight. Normally it wouldn't matter since Captain Borlett and the captains upon the two accompanying warships could sail at night as well as day, but the approaching storm had added a dimension of uncertainty. I knew everyone was blaming me for the delay through some twisted male logic. They couldn't blame Alex, and because women were bad luck on ships, the thought to toss her over had probably occurred to every one of them at some point or other. I had even overheard Haron grumble, "Our first mistake was goin' back for 'em."

My fingers upon the railing tensed when the wind gusted and the light boat slowly heeled. Hair blowing into my face, I turned to look behind me to Haron at the wheel, his feet spread wide so his short stature could better control the boat. His bearded features were lost in the gathering dusk, but his stance said he was glad to be moving again. Near to him were Captain Borlett, Duncan, and Jeck.

A frown pinched my brow. They looked deep in discussion, and immediately I headed over. My stomach clenched as I snuck glances at Jeck. He stood a head above everyone else and looked trim and elegant in his tidy Misdev uniform of black and green. The wind tugged his severely black, gently curling hair about his small ears. He had taken recently to shaving, and his cheeks had tanned to the same dark, well-oiled wood sheen the rest of him had.

The black-silk sash about his waist was the only sign of his higher rank since the official, overdone hat with the drooping feather had gone over the side the first day out. I knew Jeck had lost it on purpose, rightly thinking it looked ridiculous on him. He was not much older than I, his hidden status of player having pulled him higher in rank faster than was customary. But with his square jaw and muscular arms, it was obvious it wasn't just his status of player that had gotten him his captain's appointment. The man had enough muscles to force what he wanted when his magic failed him. It was this last I didn't trust.

The sword hanging from his belt was different, and I imagined Alex had Jeck's best blade, now. Jeck saw my eyes on the new hilt as I approached, and he moved his powerful shoulders in a small shrug. There was a wisp of amusement in his brown eyes directed at me even while he discussed something with Captain Borlett. He thought it had been funny. Contessa's almost death had been funny to him. What a chu slinger.

"Good evening, gentlemen," I said, boldly interrupting them by forcing myself between Captain Borlett and Duncan. I touched my still-damp topknot to reassure myself my darts were there where they would stay as long as Jeck was on board.

"Ma'am," the squat captain of the *Sandpiper* said, accepting my presence as an equal. It was refreshing, and my bother eased.

"Hey, Tess. You look good," Duncan said, making a show of taking in the dress I wore when we were in harbor, where impressions were important. I knew I was embarrassingly over-dressed, but it was the only clean, dry thing I had to put on.

"Thank you." I gave him an honest smile, flicking a glance at Jeck to see him drop back a step and sigh in exasperation. "When do you expect we will make harbor, Captain?" I asked, fishing to find out what they had been talking about.

The squat man curled his lips inward upon themselves to make his graying mustache stick out. His hands went into the pockets of his sun-bleached, long, blue coat, and he squinted at the top of the mast. "That's what we were just discussing, ma'am. We can make it all right, but it seems unnecessary to risk Yellow Tail's sandbars when we can hunker down in the lee of Midway Island. Because of—ah—our delay, we would hit Yellow Tail at low tide. The *Sandpiper* can handle the shallow draft. It's those damned heavy tubs we're dragging behind us. They're likely to ground at the bottom of a wave if we try it at low tide with high seas."

Duncan gently sucked at his teeth, fidgeting. I never would have noticed it but for our frequent card games. He liked anchoring every night somewhere new, more often than not slipping over the side for a spot of carousing to come back satisfied and with his pockets heavier than when he left. Someday, his desire for money was going to get him caught, and all his pride for being a member of the palace court wouldn't be worth fish entrails. "So we'll be anchoring tonight at Midway?" I prompted.

I followed Captain Borlett's gaze past the bow and to the approaching island, a thickening presence on the horizon. "That'd be my advice," he said.

The trace of hostility in his gravelly voice brought my attention back. Jeck's brown eyes were pinched in concern, and I arched my eyebrows, shifting a step so I could hold the boat for balance when an especially big wave lifted and dropped us. I didn't know where Jeck stashed his darts, though I knew from experience his dart pipe was tucked somewhere inside his leather jerkin. "You disagree, Captain Jeck?" I said boldly.

The man's square jaw clenched and relaxed at the tart challenge in my words. "There's a ship already at anchor there," he said, taking a firmer stance, with his feet spaced wide and his hands laced behind his back. The wind shifted his short black bangs. It was the only thing about him that was moving, his well-made, heavy boots planted firmly on the deck.

I shifted my gaze back to the island, now seeing a pair of lights. "It looks like a small ship," I said, imagining they put one at the bow and stern like everyone else. "We have two warships full of well-trained men, Captain. What on earth are you worried about?"

Duncan chuckled, and Jeck's eyes narrowed.

"I'm not questioning the abilities of my men," the dark man all but growled.

"Then there should be no problem anchoring beside them."

Captain Borlett was bobbing his head. "That's what I've been saying. The shoals are the real danger. I'm more afraid of them than of a merchant ship. Besides, I recognize her flag. That's *Kelly's Sapphire*, or I'm an innkeeper on the plains of Misdev."

Jeck's gaze went distant and unseeing. I recognized his mien as that which he gave stupid people making stupid decisions that he had to deal with. It was annoying, and whereas I might have sided with him, I trusted Captain Borlett when it came to tides and water levels. If the big warships couldn't make it past the sandbars by the time we reached Yellow Tail, then we should anchor at Midway Island.

"Why don't we invite the ship's captain for dinner?" I said suddenly.

Duncan caught his balance with a soft hop step.

"No, really," I protested, when Jeck gave me a blank stare of disbelief, but Captain Borlett bobbed his head eagerly. "What better way to judge a man's character than over a plate of food?" I added. "We'll all sleep better tonight for having met him."

"Capital idea." Captain Borlett smiled in anticipation. "I haven't seen Captain Pentem for over a season. He'd be interested to see what's become of my boat." His pride in his new position of captaining the ambassador's boat was obvious, and I thought that it wasn't Captain Pentem's possible interest in his boat but that Captain Borlett wanted to show off.

Jeck shifted his hands. One settled atop his hilt, and I saw a flicker of surprise from the unusual feel of the new weapon. Captain Borlett was nodding, and Duncan fingered the rings on his hand, clearly eager for the chance to take the innocent captain of *Kelly's Sapphire* for all he was worth. "Dinner?" Jeck said, not a clue to his thoughts in the short utterance.

"Dinner," I affirmed. "It will give Contessa a chance to work on her etiquette before meeting with our neighbors down coast next month."

"Heaven save us, yes," Jeck muttered. "I'll see to the seating arrangements."

"Contessa will do that," I said quickly. "She needs the practice."

Jeck frowned, straightening to look aggressive somehow. The coming dusk made his dark complexion darker, and the military captain's insignia on the black sash about his middle seemed to glow. "It's a matter of security. I'll not leave it up to a nun," he said.

I put my hands on my hips, too, irate that I had to look up at him. "She's not a nun," I said tartly. "And I'll help her. She'll learn nothing if none of you let her *do* anything." This was my playing field, and I didn't like his interfering.

His breath came from him in a tired sound, his entire chest moving as he exhaled. It was a clear conflict of interest. His captain duties demanded he obey his distant king and ensure Alex's safety until his sovereign called him home, but his player status required he minimize his influence over Alex. The prince had married into Costenopolie and was clearly my piece to manipulate and protect. "Fine," he said, clearly peeved. "But if she puts me too far from Prince Alexander, I'm moving. The woman has as much political savvy as a duck."

Duncan laughed, and I smacked his shoulder with the back of my hand. "Be still," I warned. "She's trying."

"Give it up, Tess," the cheat said, when Jeck nodded to everyone and walked away. "The woman is hopeless, and you know it."

Captain Borlett touched the brim of his salt-grimed hat and started to the wheel, probably to tell Haron we would be anchoring off the island. Duncan started to hum in anticipation, his hands moving in what I recognized as his traditional warm-up preparation for a game of cards. Trying to ignore him, I watched Jeck make his confident way across the moving deck. The tall man moved with a balance and confidence I envied, his pace measured and slow. Duncan's humming stopped, and I looked to see him eying me in question.

"You're going to get caught," I said, and a devilish grin came over him. Frowning, I headed for the galley hatch, not nearly as graceful as Jeck though I tried. Contessa would need some coaching, and I wanted everything to be perfect if Jeck would be there, evaluating my growing skills at being a player.

Four

❖

The yellow light from the lamp overhanging the narrow table made short arcs, sending beams across the cramped officers' common room to mix with the pleasant talk and warmth instilled by food and the close quarters. Candles supplemented the usual light, glinting off the china that Contessa and Alex dined upon. Above came the sound of the crew enjoying their ale now that the threatened rain had failed to appear. The approaching storm had broken upon us with little more than wind and high seas and was likely to stay that way.

I pushed my plate of nearly untouched food away, finding the motion of the *Sandpiper* uncomfortable now that the smooth rolling of waves had been replaced with short awkward bobs at the end of a tether. The warmth of perfumed bodies was cloying, and I couldn't decide if it was better or worse than the stench of the unwashed crew.

A soft laugh brought my attention up from the glass in my hand, and I smiled as if I had heard the jest. Good Lovrege wine had loosened the tongues of our visiting captain, but Contessa had become depressed and silent. Most of her evening had been spent trying to meet Alex's eyes at the opposite end of the table. The proud young man would have none of it. His windburned and suntanned hand was ever on his wineglass though he had drunk little, and he looked every bit the noble as he sat with a casual grace in his best coat of Costenopolie gold and green, gold glittering in a subdued show of wealth at his collar and cuffs. Alex had a good heart, and that Jeck had hardened it to Contessa infuriated me.

I turned my accusing gaze to the captain of the Misdev guards. The dark man's glass was almost full since he had sipped only what was polite. He was sitting between me and Alex, as if protecting his efforts at turning the man against Contessa. His uniform made him look refined and respectable despite my knowing otherwise, and his low voice rose and fell with a mesmerizing cadence. I liked it, even as I thought myself a foolish woman for finding something as simple as the sound of a man's voice attractive. The man was a skilled player. If I found him attractive, it was because he was trying to lull me into a false sense of security.

Contessa was at the far end of the table, Captain Borlett to her right and the visiting captain—a Captain Rylan, not Pentem—on her left. Apparently, *Kelly's Sapphire* had been drydocked last spring to undergo repairs only to have the company that owned her fall on hard times and be forced to sell her for taxes.

Captain Borlett didn't know Captain Rylan, and I wasn't happy about having an unknown sitting that close to Contessa, but I couldn't say much, seeing as the entire dinner was my idea. I had made sure that Contessa put me on his other side to help ease my faint jitters, a precaution I now felt silly for after having spent a good three hours beside the man.

Captain Rylan had a kind voice with a familiar, though perhaps affected, noble accent. Quick with his jests and motions, he entertained us with stories of customers who tried to take advantage of him and lost. His occasional outburst of an infectious laugh had set Jeck visibly on edge, and I was smug about it. The smallish man was well dressed if somewhat flamboyant for a merchant, with a long-tailed green coat that was all the fashion last year. It might have once rivaled Prince Alex's more subdued attire with its gilded trim and flamboyant cut, but now the vibrant reds, golds, and greens were muted with age and showed wear.

The man actually had bells on his boots, bells that chimed

softly with every shift of feet. I had found it charming at first, but after a good three hours of it, it was annoying. He had a habit of touching his small mustache and trim beard. The original black was heavily silvered with gray, and I think it bothered him as he kept looking at Jeck's very black beard and mustache. The gray made him look just within his fourth decade, but his clean, unmarked hands put him younger.

Captain Rylan's first mate had come with him. He sat across from Jeck and me, eating quickly and with little regard for manners. His gaze was perpetually distant, as if more interested in the noise from atop the deck than our conversation. A frown crossed my face when I realized I didn't remember his name, then eased. *Smitty*, I thought. *That's what it was.*

Bothered I had forgotten, I pushed my plate away, trying not to get involved in Captain Rylan's latest story. They had lost their appeal a good half hour ago, as they all revolved around sums of money and how he had gained it. Jeck leaned close as if for a private word, and I stiffened when our shoulders touched. Immediately he pulled back, bother showing in his brown eyes. "I was only going to ask if you were all right," he said, and I stared stupidly at him.

All right? Why? Do I have soup on my dress? I looked to see, and he prompted in exasperation, "Your swim?"

"Oh. Ah, yes. Thank you," I stammered, thinking that the only good thing to come of it was that I had gotten a bath. Wanting to avoid the visiting captain's conversation, I turned to give Jeck my full attention.

Jeck gave me a raised-eyebrow look, and my gaze dropped to his strong fingers manipulating the tarnished silver fork, twirling it with a surprising dexterity. "That was quick thinking with your horse," he said, and Alex flushed, focusing on Captain Rylan's conversation instead. "How did you get him in the water? Did you jump him over the side?"

I hesitated, wondering if he was asking from a professional interest, and if so would it matter. "No. I went in first. I've trained him to follow my whistle," I admitted, spearing a potato chunk and placing it delicately in my mouth. I wasn't hungry, but I had to do something.

His vacant focus sharpened. "You were lucky he didn't jump atop you, then."

Swallowing, I gave him a dark look. "Jy is smarter than that," I said, thinking smart or not, I had been lucky not to have four hooves and several hundred pounds land on me.

Jeck's elbow bumped mine, and my next fork of potato hit the edge of my mouth. I wanted to believe it was an accident but knew better. The situation was preposterous: I outranked him in polite society, he outranked me in player tradition. I think I had just been rebuked—which wasn't his job to begin with—yet he couched it with enough flattery that my royal standing would have trouble finding fault with him. Annoyed, I snuck a glance at him, thinking he was unnervingly good with this dual nature we were both afflicted with.

I set my fork down with a restrained force. Having this conversation at the table was risky but better than having it alone on deck somewhere. "Leave Alex alone," I muttered from behind my napkin. "You have no right even to be here, much less interfering."

Our shoulders touched, and I couldn't help but notice it was like running into a post. A sturdy, strong post that gave slightly and smelled like leather and horse.

"You should unknot your bodice and take a good breath, Princess," he said, lips hardly moving as he raised his glass in Captain Rylan's impromptu toast to greedy men and their poor choices. "I said very little to Alex, just listened. I want this alliance to prosper as much as your master, which is why he asked me to intervene if necessary. He trusts me; why don't you?"

I sipped my wine and set it down, hearing the conversation rise anew around us. I didn't trust Jeck. I didn't think Kavenlow did either. But there was a reason Kavenlow was forcing this close association. I should take the opportunity to study him for his failings. He was cold. That was a start. Impersonal. And annoying in his almost compliments of me and my skills, and clever, though that wasn't a fault unless it spilled into overconfidence.

"You did well," he said, laying his napkin on his plate so the cook would take it away. "Saving your sovereign's life and convincing her to apologize? She will, and so will Alex. Now close your mouth or say thank you."

"Thank you," I said, reaching for my wine with the intent to spill it on him.

"You're welcome." The man's powerful fingers gently encircled mine, and he set my glass on the table, "They're going to come from this with respect for each other, not hate. You are an appalling judge of character, but you play matchmaker very well." He inclined his head. "Potential disaster turned to opportunity. Kavenlow may be right—you have some value after all."

Wondering if there was a compliment in there, I pulled my fingers out from under his, thinking they were warm. "I've had practice. My childhood was one disaster after another."

He laughed. It was loud and surprising, and I think it shocked him as much as me since he abruptly cut it short.

Immediately Captain Rylan leaned to the center of the table, his eyes bright from too much wine. "Tell us!" he demanded. "You two have been very quiet among yourselves. What has Madam Ambassador said to make such a distinguished gentleman of valor laugh?"

Gentleman of valor? I wondered, bothered. "Nothing," I offered. "I was simply telling Captain Jeck that my life seemed to be one disaster after another."

"Disaster," the visiting captain said. "Tell us!"

Contessa looked pleadingly at me, clearly wanting me to intervene, and I was glad smooth dinner conversation wasn't my responsibility anymore. I directed her gaze to the wine, and she reached for it. "Mr. Smitty," she said softly. "Would you like some more wine?"

Barely breaking from sopping the last of his gravy with a chunk of biscuit, he pushed his tin cup to her. She blinked, and in the awkward silence, filled it. Not even glancing up, Mr. Smitty reached for it and downed it.

I stared, appalled, matters made worse in that he didn't wipe what spilled from his beard. The bells on Captain Rylan's boots chimed, and Mr. Smitty wiped his face. "So," Captain Rylan said as if to distract us all, "Madam Ambassador, how did you and your sister meet? I've heard you were raised apart, not knowing of each other until recently. I think how two people meet is telling, casting shadows on their entire relationship."

My attention jerked from Rylan's first mate, who had stretched halfway across the table to reach another biscuit.

His overcoat had a tear in the armpit that showed a vivid red undershirt. "Um," I started, glancing at Contessa. A short thirty seconds after we had met, I had knocked her down and pounded her head into the ground. She had tried to pull my hair out and ended up giving me a black eye. "Nothing special," I murmured, watching the lamp swing.

Captain Rylan's thick eyebrows bunched. "How about you and Captain Jeck, then? It's obvious you're well acquainted. *That* must be a fascinating story."

Jeck and I exchanged looks. I was sure mine was tinged with panic. My parents had just been murdered, and Jeck had been the one to carry me kicking and screaming to my room, dropping me on the rug as if I had been a slaughtered pig. *Fascinating* didn't seem appropriate.

I opened my mouth while I tried to think up some lie, but Jeck set his glass down with an attention-getting thump. "We met in the palace," he said, his voice rising and falling in a soothing cadence, his faint Misdev accent making him sound exotic. "There isn't much to say. She was the crown princess at that time. I was a guard. We met. We parted."

"Ah!" the flamboyant Captain Rylan exclaimed, gesturing. "But you were the captain of the guard. Romance blooms with chance meetings of forbidden pairings."

I gave Jeck a wry look, stifling my snort. "You're a romantic, Captain Rylan," I said, as Contessa blushed. "I've never found that how two people meet has a bearing on their future."

My mind drifted to how Duncan and I met. I suppose that could be considered romantic, especially from his point of view. He had been cheating a table of merchants and laborers. I had needed money to escape the capital and so forced him to lose the entire table's winnings to me or I'd turn him in. I wouldn't have, though. They would have cut off his hands, and I would have been recognized and recaptured.

"No, no, no," Captain Rylan insisted, the wine he had drunk making him louder than he ought to be. He accidentally knocked over a candle in reaching for his glass, and it went out, spilling white wax. My shoulders slumped. I would probably be the one to have to scrape it from the oiled wood tomorrow.

"That's where your youth betrays you, my dear lady," the slightly tipsy man was saying. "The wiser—the old man or woman—would agree with me."

He turned to Contessa, the fragrant smoke from the extinguished candle rising between them to tickle my nose. "Your Majesty," he said, "how did you and your husband meet? I'm sure *that* is a romantic story. You are both so obviously fit for each other. Such a finer-matched royal couple I have never heard of."

The table went silent. Contessa dropped her eyes, and Alex stiffened. Stomach tightening, I wondered if I should say something, even though it wasn't my place.

Captain Rylan glanced between them, the widening of his eyes telling me he had realized there was a problem. I was sure the small man was perceptive enough to know something unsaid was shifting through the air smelling of chicken, boiled potatoes, and extinguished candle.

Alex moved his wineglass but didn't drink. "It was an arranged affair," he said, and my shoulders eased. "We met at a political function organized for the occasion."

"Yes, yes," Captain Rylan encouraged. "But wasn't she the most beautiful woman there? Did you dance? Did she step on your foot, spill a drink on you, flirt with the other men and drive you mad with jealousy?"

Contessa grew even more despondent. She had been beautiful that night, her color high and her every move beyond reproach. She hadn't flirted, but all eyes had been on her, and many strove for her attention. She had given it all to Alex, though reserved and modest in her shy awkwardness. She had forgotten her childhood promise to Thadd that night, caught up in the elegance and circumstance of the evening.

Only now did Alex seem to soften, looking almost pained. "She was the most exquisite woman there, in a dress as black and soft as a midsummer night, her skin as pale as the moon. I remember how kind she was to the serving girl who dropped a spoon and soiled Contessa's hem."

I remembered, too. Contessa had been so nervous, frightened. Seeing someone make a mistake and survive had given her the strength to risk making a mistake herself.

"I think it was at that moment that I vowed a woman that kind should have the opportunity to find love in her marriage, especially one forced upon her," Alex said.

The table was silent. Contessa flushed, and even I was embarrassed by the man's admission. From above came loud shouts followed by bare feet thumping as the crew was distracted, and they crossed the deck following some new amusement. Jeck's face was empty of emotions and closed when turned to him.

"There, you see?" Captain Rylan said into the awkward silence, filling it with a voice surprisingly loud for a man so small. "Romance, even in arranged marriages."

Mr. Smitty finally stopped eating and pushed his plate away. Wiping his hands upon his pants, he gave Captain Rylan a wary, expectant look.

Contessa stood with a frantic quickness, her face frozen in a heartbroken expression. Immediately, the men stood as well, Mr. Smitty rising slowly and last of all. The more I saw of him, the less I liked, though he had said no more than three words to anyone all evening.

"Excuse me," Contessa warbled, miserable. "I need some air, gentlemen."

I shifted myself over the bench, hands gripping my skirts as I rose. "I'll come with you."

"No, allow me." Captain Rylan graciously extended his arm. "It would be an honor to escort you. Permit me some small show to repay you for your hospitality."

I wondered if going on deck might not be a good idea since the shouts coming through the deck had grown louder, more instant. I caught the word *fire*, and I froze.

My gaze shot to Jeck, my heart pounding. *We were on fire?*

Jeck was poised, staring up at the deck as if he could see through it. "We're on fire," he said softly. I followed his gaze to where the candle had extinguished itself, the smell of the burning tar and rope on deck disguised by its fragrant smoke.

A sudden clatter of boots at the open hatch drew everyone's attention. "Captain!" a frantic crewman stammered as he all but fell partly down the stairs. "Fire. At the bow!"

Captain Borlett leapt to the hatch, jerking everyone else into motion. Jeck was halfway up the stairs and gone before I had even reached for a handhold. Heart pounding, I took Contessa's elbow and helped her forward. I could smell the sharp tang of burning tar now over the candle. *Heaven preserve us. We were on fire.*

Contessa's boots slipped on the wide stairway. Alex appeared from nowhere, catching her other elbow and keeping her from going down. Jeck was standing on the deck already, his eyes on the bow as he extended a hand to everyone to make their exodus faster.

I followed Contessa up into the black night. Immediately, the cool wind struck me, and the bobbing of the deck seemed more pronounced. Holding the hair from my eyes, I squinted into the dark, looking through the scattered, frantic crewmen for Duncan. A thick, oily scent caught in my throat: the scent of half-burned oil seeming to be the very night burning.

My gaze shot to the bow, where a small fire sent orange-and-yellow shadows against the railings. As the wind cut through my lightweight dress, my first panicked reaction faltered.

From the reaction of the white-faced crewman, I had expected to see flames in the lines and half the boat gone. What I found was a small spot of orange where the bow light had hung. The fire had been spotted by the other vessels, and their railings were full of calling men. Behind them, the island loomed, a darker black against the cloud-darkened night. It was a single point of stability in the moving night. The *Sandpiper* rose and fell with the waves in the lee of the island. Nearby were the lights from the two warships and Captain Rylan's own smaller vessel, lit up with what looked like half a dozen torches.

Captain Borlett's squat figure was outlined by the orange light. I recognized Duncan's lanky silhouette beside him. The crew had been organized to beat the fire out with rags. Two men were throwing empty sacks out of the fore hatch, and more men were starting in with those.

"It's bad luck!" Haron called as he slapped at the oil fire, making my lips purse. "Bad luck for bringing them women. The bow light has never fallen before."

"Shut your mouth, Haron!" Captain Borlett demanded distantly, swooping forward to take the sack out of his hands and beat at the flames himself. "You two! Leave off there. Keep the fire off the anchor rope and the foresail. No, you fools! Get that bucket out of here. You can't put an oil fire out with water! You want to set the entire boat aflame?"

Alex touched Contessa's shoulder. "I'll be back," he murmured, his green eyes on the flames. He started to the bow with quick steps, and Jeck boldly took his arm, jerking him to a stop. Alex stared at him, pulling out of his grip.

"I'll go, Your Highness," Jeck said. "I'd ask you to remain here."

Grimacing, Alex dropped back to us, looking frustrated as he tossed his short bangs from his eyes and took a protective stance beside Contessa. My eyes smarted when a gust of wind sent smoke over us. Contessa started to cough, and Alex took her arm in concern. She waved him away, which he ignored, taking off his silk-lined coat and draping it over her shoulders.

Jeck gave me a warning look before he started to the bow at a fast pace. The hair on the back of my neck rose, and unnerved, I spun to find Captain Rylan and his first mate behind us. "Captain," I exclaimed, pulling the hair from my mouth. "You gave me a start."

"My apologies, ma'am." His face was unseen from under his hat in the absolute dark of the deck, and I wondered if I had heard his bells over the wind or just sensed him behind me. Mr. Smitty beside him had his hands clasped at the small of his back as he balanced easily against the boat's motion. Eyes tearing from the oily smoke, Captain Rylan waved a ringed hand at the bow, and asked, "Was it your bow light?"

"I think so," I said, worried. Arms clasped around myself, I held my breath when Duncan handed his sack to another and jogged back to us. My pulse increased as he halted beside us, breathing hard and bringing the smell of burned oil with him.

"The knot holding the bow light slipped," he said by way of greeting, eyes red and tearing. "It hit the deck and shattered. It's the oil that's burning, not the deck."

"Thank goodness," Contessa whispered.

"We'll have it out in a moment," he said, turning to watch the flames. His hands were on his hips, and the light reflected off him. He didn't seem at all worried, and my shoulders eased.

A twang reverberated up through my feet, and I hesitated, wondering what had happened. The wind pushing me shifted, and the island began to move. Eyes wide, I looked to Duncan.

"We're adrift!" someone shouted faintly, sounding panicked. "We lost anchor!"

"Chu pits," Duncan breathed. He tensed, clearly not knowing what to do.

"We're drifting?" Contessa clutched my arm, and I nodded, thinking it odd the rope would have burned through. It was nearly as thick as my wrist.

Alex gave her elbow a squeeze and jogged to the bow and Jeck, his boots unheard over the turmoil. Duncan bolted after him.

"Haron!" Captain Borlett shouted. "Get to the wheel! Raise sail. Keep us off that reef!"

"Sir!" the spare man exclaimed. I pulled Contessa out of the way when Haron thumped across the deck, pushing past us to get to the wheel. He threw off the loop holding the wheel unmoving and spun it. Orders came nonstop from him at a bellow. I could do nothing but stare as half the men abandoned the fire, scrambling to lines. Tied to the wall of the galley, my horses pulled at their tethers, the scent of fire instilling fear as the men grew frantic.

Gray blossomed in the dark night when sheets rose up masts. The wind coming off the island billowed into them, and the boat's motion changed.

"No!" came a faint shout from the bow. "Not the fore jib! You'll catch her afire! You bloody fools! Drop the fore jib!"

Gasping, I spun to the bow. The shadow of sail had risen halfway up the front forestay. Orange firelight reflected off it, showing men battling the fire. "Watch out!" someone shouted "She's caught!"

A frightening whoosh of sound sent Contessa and me staggering back. Orange fire raced up the front sail. My mouth dropped open.

"Cut her loose!" someone screamed. "For the love of God, cut her loose!"

I stood, shocked. The wind pushed the flames back, filling the sail like a visible wind. In an instant, the entire sail was aflame. Haron spun the wheel. The deck leveled out as he turned us into the wind, and the sails emptied. Noise beat at me. Empty sails clashed against each other. Men shouted for buckets, their fear of fire putting an ugly, high sound into their voices. Captain Jeck was trying to cut the heavy salt-laden rope and free the sail.

Frightened, I pulled Contessa to the stern. Her eyes were riveted to the fire, and she was trembling. My eyes went to the ships surrounding us. Both warships were working to get their dinghies in the water. It was too late for them to reach us otherwise since I was sure we were already over the reef. The tide was well out, and the depth was too shallow apart from the pocket of deeper water near the shore that we had been resting in until the morning's high tide.

I pulled Contessa out of the way when a smoke-marked, thin sailor ran to us. "It's Alex," she protested, pushing my hand off her.

"I don't think they can stop it," he said as he came to a breathless halt, his youthful face grim and marked with soot to stand out harsh and shocking against his fair skin and hair. "Captain Jeck wants her in a dinghy as soon as one gets here. I agree with him."

Contessa clutched at me. "No!" she exclaimed, terror making her eyes wide. "I can't! Tess, I can't get in the water again. I won't!"

My eyes searched the crowded, frenzied deck. Everyone was trying to put out the fire or cut the sail free without getting burned. Haron had abandoned the wheel, his place taken by another. The front jib was again on the deck, the fire climbing the ropes even as the men tried to put the heavy canvas out. The flames had jumped to the first mainsail's lines and were creeping down to the crumpled sail. We were still drifting, the tide and the wind pushing us out over the shoals and farther from help.

"Careful!" I cried, reaching for Contessa when the *Sandpiper* shifted out from behind the lee of the island and the first of the storm-driven waves hit us. Cold spray from nowhere shocked through me, soaking me in an instant. Contessa shrieked when the deck dipped, and the horses whinnied, terrified.

Alex and I steadied Contessa, the dark and the moving deck making everything a confused chaos. I cowered when the deck swooped and another spray of water took us.

A sharp whistle drew my attention, and hope made my pulse pound. Captain Rylan's ship, *Kelly's Sapphire*, was headed our way, her booms swinging even as I watched, filling her sails with wind. Captain Rylan was standing at the railing of the *Sandpiper*, the slight man gesturing and bellowing out orders over the distance. His smaller vessel had a shallow draft. It could reach us where the warships couldn't.

"Come on, Contessa," I said, pulling her to the railing.

"Alex!" she cried, resisting. "Alex?"

"It's all right," he soothed, calm and smiling. "I'll help you make the jump."

"Jump?" she warbled, her face going terrified.

In a smooth motion, the merchant vessel sailed alongside of us, coming in so the wind would push her away and not into us.

"Hooks!" Mr. Smitty shouted, and I stood amazed when three or four clawed hooks were tossed in near unison. They hit the deck and were pulled in tight. The rolling deck lurched, and I staggered as the two vessels started to move as one.

"Point her into the wind!" Mr. Smitty shouted at the man at the wheel on Captain Rylan's ship. "Are you daft? You want that she swamps and takes us down with her?"

My pulse quickened. *The* Sandpiper *was going down?*

Alex had heard the rough man as well, his eyes meeting mine behind Contessa suddenly carrying a deep concern tempered with resolve.

"Here!" Captain Rylan called from the railing, with Mr. Smitty, gesturing. I started forward with Alex and Contessa, slipping on the wet deck though Mr. Smitty climbed the rail of the *Sandpiper* and jumped to his brightly lit ship as if it was nothing. Another wave came over the side, and Contessa fell, taking me down with her. The hard deck of the ship smacked into my hip, bruising me. My horses called again, and I looked at them from around my blowing hair.

"I can't do that—" Contessa said, looking lost under Alex's coat, her eyes on the railing. Alex pulled her up, and I rose without help, looking between her and my horses. "I can't do that!" she said again, her voice high and panicked.

"Grapples tight!" Mr. Smitty shouted over the wind and the noise of rattling sails and calling crewmen trying to put out the fire. "Hands stay to release and come about!" .

"I can't do that!" Contessa cried, clearly panicking as we dragged her forward.

"Come on, Contessa," I coaxed, angry and frustrated. I

pulled her to Captain Rylan. Crewmen had swarmed aboard in a motion so quick, it took me by surprise, securing lines and making the two vessels rise and fall as nearly one. "They're closer. See?" I said, eying the rough-looking men. "And I'll be with you. It's either this or a dinghy."

"But if I fall, I'll be crushed between them!"

Another wave hit us, chilling me and sending my feet slipping. "I won't let you fall," I promised. "Contessa! Please!"

Her frantic expression in the reflected firelight eased, and she nodded. Her emotion was short-lived as a thunderous boom reverberated up through my spine, shaking me. Contessa screamed, and the *Sandpiper* groaned. I thought I heard wood splintering. My eyes went to the dark masts. Something had hit us.

"What was that?" I exclaimed, and Duncan staggered across the deck, his eyes wide.

"We hit bottom," he said. "Hold on. We're likely to—"

We hit again. This time, I felt the sudden cessation of motion as the *Sandpiper* descended upon a wave, halting in a jarring motion that sent the sailors shouting and Contessa to clutch at me. It was the most frightening sensation I'd ever felt. My horses nickered in fear. We lifted off the reef as a wave rolled under us. I held my breath for the next hit, but it never came.

"Jy!" I called, my sore hip now the farthest thing from my mind. I glanced at Alex, then my horses. "Get Contessa off the boat," I said. "I have to get my horses."

"No!" Contessa said, gripping my arm. "Tess, I can't do it without you!"

I stood frozen as Captain Rylan gestured brusquely. Alex's eyes pleaded with me, and from the bow came Jeck's angry shout, "Get them off the boat, Tess! Before we break apart!"

"My horses!" I shouted back, not liking the fear in my voice.

We hit bottom again, and Contessa made a muffled scream, clutching me.

"Your chu-ridden horses will be fine!" Jeck turned from the fire long enough to gesture angrily at me. "Get the royals off the boat before she tears apart on the reef!"

Duncan pulled at me, his eyes bright from reflected firelight. "Come on, Tess. I'll help."

I nodded. Taking Contessa's elbow to keep her upright,

Alex and I got her to the railing. Her smooth-soled boots were almost useless. Captain Rylan was waiting, impatient and curt.

"Jump," he said, pulling her roughly from me and lifting her to the railing.

She panicked, screaming and twisting until she fell. Captain Rylan cursed, bending to pull her upright. The bells on his boots rang, almost unheard over the wind and clashing sails.

My face tightened. "Stop it!" I demanded, grabbing his arm and pulling him from her. He spun, shock and anger on him. Alex stepped between us, and I turned to help Contessa up as she was now sobbing. "Here, Contessa," I said. "Watch me."

Taking a breath, I gathered my skirts. Duncan's hand filled mine, and with his help, I got onto the railing. Rough hands reached for me, and I gasped when they yanked me onto the merchant's deck, yellow with torch and firelight. I fell sprawling, and I spun, pulling the hair from my mouth to see Contessa. Duncan stood over me with his hand extended, having made the jump somewhere between me hitting the deck and getting the hair out of my face.

He pulled me up and I looked at the *Sandpiper*. "Contessa!" I called, holding my hand out to her. Alex was standing with one leg wrapped around a stay to keep his balance as he helped her up onto the railing. Captain Rylan was holding her other hand from the safety of his deck. She met my eyes, and fixed on them, she stepped forward, lips moving in silent prayer.

Captain Rylan's men grabbed her, and with no more reverence than they had shown me, pulled her aboard. I reached for her as she shrieked, easing her descent so that she only fell to one knee. Alex was next, making the jump by himself and immediately going to Contessa.

"Contessa!" he called, ignoring everything else. My sister's head rose, meeting his eyes. My breath caught as she reached for him.

"Free grapples!" Mr. Smitty shouted when Captain Rylan's feet hit the deck beside me.

Free grapples? What about the crew? What about my horses!

I stood aghast when several crewmen jumped nimbly aboard the *Sandpiper*. Each had a metal bar to unwedge the grappling hooks. Faster than I could breathe, they ripped the claws from the railing of the *Sandpiper* and were back aboard. More men pushed the floundering boat away with long poles. It was a well-rehearsed dance that left me shocked and stunned.

"Fill sails!" Mr. Smitty shouted, demanding more authority than he had the entire night.

My heart pounded. *What the devil is going on?* "Captain Rylan!" I demanded, pulling the short man around to see me. "The *Sandpiper* is going down. We have to get everyone off!"

The man looked me up and down in a quick motion of disdain. "Get them below," he said to no one in particular, and two crewmen stepped forward. From behind me, the rattling canvas finally ceased as the ship turned and the sails filled. There was a series of thumps when the canvas filled, the sails landing firmly against ties already in place. The ship began to move, and I shifted to adjust to the new balance.

I looked at the *Sandpiper,* flames yellow and red at the bow. Men were shouting, beating at the flames spread by the thin film of water that had sprayed aboard. She was going down, one sail burned beyond recognition and the hull being slowly knocked apart as she found the shallower spots of the reef. It struck me like a slap from the dark what had happened.

"We're being taken," I whispered, my stomach twisting and panic striking deep into me. They had been lying in wait for us, timing it so the tide would prevent the warships from following, then burning my boat to keep it from following as well.

I brought my eyes up, meeting Alex's. He saw the knowledge of what had happened in my face, the firelight reflecting off the water in orange and black. His smoke-marked face was empty and his fingers were on his sword hilt. His blue eyes looked hard from his grimed face, and as I watched, his slight build tensed muscle by muscle. He knew it, too. God save us. We were fools. "You take the men on the left," I whispered. "I'll take the right."

Contessa, who knew what I was capable of, took an audible breath, holding it. Alex blinked. He didn't know I had eight venomous darts in my hair, three throwing knives, and, around my waist disguised as a belt, a bullwhip that would scare a bear.

Three crewmen were approaching, eying Alex's sword with a casual cautiousness. "Aye, Your Royalship," one said with a mocking respect. "Come take a wee bit of a walk with us, and I'll show ya the boat, I will."

The man with him chuckled. He reached for Alex's sword arm, and the audacity of someone touching him broke through Alex's shock. "Stay back, Contessa!" he shouted, pulling his sword in a sound that would forever terrify me.

I retreated to protect Contessa, stumbling when she pulled me to kneel beside her.

Laughing, the three crewmen paused at the sight of the slight, bookish prince with a blade in his hands. They didn't see his feet in the first position. They didn't know he had been schooled until there was no fear. They had no clue that the lean muscles under his silk shirt were used to swinging a blade with no effort, and he would react without thinking, his movements instinctive and deadly.

Hunching in anticipation, the surrounding men dropped their hands to their own swords. My stomach clenched, and my hand rose to my topknot as if I was nervous. I plucked several needles, putting one in the dart tube that had bisected my hair like an ornament. The first man to touch Contessa or me would go down.

Duncan fell back to me, grasping my shoulder protectively. From around us came the hooting calls of the crew, most of them turning to watch, apparently eager for some sport.

Mr. Smitty's rough shout came from the wheel, jerking my attention to the stern. "Get his bloody sword away from him and get them the hell belowdecks!" he demanded. "If they jump the railing, you can by bloody God-well believe you're going in after them!"

"Shouldn't take more than a moment, Captain," a thin, quick-eyed man said, grinning as he came forward, naked blade swinging.

Contessa made a muffled shriek. Looking magnificent, Alex met his strike with his own, twisting to send his blade within inches of the man's side. The pirate leapt back, surprised. Face going ugly, he lunged forward with a yell.

I brought my hand to my mouth and blew a dart at him. It struck him perfectly in the neck, right where his pulse lay. The man took a huge breath as he raised his arm, faltering when the venom hit him. His eyes went wide, and a strangled gurgle came from him.

Alex swung in the instant his attacker faltered. The *thunk* of steel into flesh struck horror in me. I had killed that man as surely as if I had swung the blade myself.

Choking, the man fell to his knees. Alex unhesitatingly followed him down, frighteningly silent as he ran his blade into the man's chest, down between the man's ribs to suffocate him in his own blood. With only a grunt to mark his efforts, the mild-seeming prince killed a man while everyone watched in slack-jawed amazement.

An ugly noise gurgling up, the struck crewman slowly fell to the deck in an awkward sprawl. A dark puddle seeped from under him. Alex gave a final push to his blade. Setting one foot against his downed man, he yanked his sword from him and tossed his hair from his eyes.

"By all that is holy," Duncan whispered at my elbow, clearly shocked.

He was a prince of Misdev. What did they expect?

With an outraged shout, the surrounding crewmen pulled their blades and started forward.

"Don't kill 'em!" Captain Rylan shouted from beside Mr. Smitty at the wheel, his courtly accent gone. "You kill 'em, and you get nothing! Hear me? Nothing!"

I didn't think they cared.

Alex rolled the dying man over and took the pirate's blade. "Here," he said grimly, sliding it across the deck to Duncan. The cheat picked it up. He glanced at the length of steel, then shifted his grip tighter, his face drawn and frightened. The two men fell back to surround Contessa and me. *Why?* I thought. We couldn't take the ship. We couldn't save ourselves. But to give up was never a consideration.

"Look out!" Contessa cried, and I spun. Two were coming up from behind us. I downed them with a dart each before Alex or Duncan could kill them. My darts they would survive. Alex's blade they wouldn't. Duncan looked to see them fall, then turned with a shout as a man jumped at him.

Two men had attacked Alex simultaneously. The prince was holding his own, fighting silently but for the sound of his feet and blade. Duncan was sadly lacking, being driven back to us.

"Duncan!" I cried when the tip of a sword found him, ripping his shirt.

He sprang back, fingering his shirt, anger pulling his face

tight. "I just bought that!" he shouted, following it up with a
curse and a furious attack that beat the man back a step.

I darted a man with a bare blade at the outskirts waiting for
an opportunity to enter the fray. Groaning, he fell into his com-
panions. They caught him, their faces going terrified, not knowing what had brought him down. The call of witchcraft went up,
and I palmed my dart tube before they could see.

"It's the woman!" Captain Rylan shouted, and my brow
furrowed in dismay. "She's got poison darts. Get the woman!"

My stomach twisted. At Mr. Smitty's rough gesture, three
men circled to our back. Alex and Duncan were too busy to see,
but Contessa trembled and clutched my arm. Her breath came
fast, and a small sound of fear slipped past her. Torn between
being angry and afraid, I pushed her arm off me. "Don't," I
warned, and one grinned to show yellow teeth in the torchlight.

Taking one of my last daggers, I flipped it, ready to throw,
warning him again. He glanced at the knife, then leered, beckoning me closer.

"Prick me with your little knife, love," he taunted. "I've got
my own dagger I'll be sticking you with."

Repulsed, I threw it, gagging as it hit him in the throat.

I never saw him go down. The other two men lunged, arms
outstretched.

I backpedaled. My heels found Contessa, and shrieking, I
fell. Feet kicking, I rolled, my hand pulling my whip free from
my waist as I rose.

Contessa screamed. Pulse pounding, I spun. She had gone
back to Duncan and was unhurt. "You won't touch her!" I
shouted, uncoiling my whip and sending it to crack in the air.

A sharp cry from Alex jerked my attention. A man had
scored on him, and the prince was down on one knee. "Alex!"
Contessa exclaimed, lurching past Duncan. I jerked her to a
halt, pushing her to Duncan, then flicked my whip at the two
men approaching. They fell back at the sharp sound, their ugly
looks worse for the flickering torchlight.

"Tess! There!" Contessa cried, and I followed her gaze to
Alex, down with a man grappling with him. Heart pounding, I
sent the whip to strike his attacker.

The man howled, rolling off Alex. Duncan swooped forward to drag the prince to us. Contessa knelt beside him, her

face pale. I spared them a quick glance. He seemed all right, his words soft and reassuring as he got to his feet, his free hand never leaving Contessa's grip.

I flicked the whip to coil behind me, looking over the deck to find the pirates had fallen back to the limit of my reach.

"You afraid of a woman with a bit of string?" Captain Rylan shouted from the safety of the wheel. "Get them below you sons of chulls. What am I paying you for?"

One of the men took a step forward. I spun the whip over my head and brought it cracking down before him. The man retreated, his face ugly. "Captain?" one called, sounding almost frightened. A satisfied smile came over me. The waves lifted the deck, and I rode the swells easily, my feet spread wide. Maybe. Maybe we had a chance.

From behind the wheel, Mr. Smitty frowned. The torchlight landed on his face, showing me his ire. Never taking his eyes from mine, he spun the wheel.

"Coming about!" he shouted, with enough force to carry over storms.

The pirates sent their eyes to the rigging. I followed their gaze. The sails started to flutter, then rattled as the ship turned into the wind. Under my feet, the deck evened out.

"Tess!" Contessa cried, looking over my shoulder. "Look out!"

I turned. Out of the dark came the boom carrying the bottom of the mainsail. It swung with the force of the wind, unstoppable. Gasping, I ducked. White-hot fire exploded. I cried out, not hearing it. I didn't remember falling, but the deck struck my cheek, cold and bruising.

"Tess!" I heard my sister cry, and the sounds of renewed battle.

A belled boot slammed into my middle, and I caved in on myself, unable to breathe, unable to think, drifting in the neverworld on the edge of consciousness.

"Now that," I heard Captain Rylan say, "is the proper way to bring down a sea whore."

Five

❖

I think it was the smell that woke me, a rank, back-of-the-
throat stench that caught in my nose and carried the scent of rat
urine and wet moldy burlap sacks to my tongue. The gentle
rolling and the sound of booted and bare feet on the deck
above me had long ago become familiar—too familiar to wake
me. And I knew it wasn't the pain that pulled me from unconsciousness. Pain had been a part of my existence for so long, it
no longer had the power to tell me something was wrong.

My stomach hurt, and my lower ribs ached when I breathed
too deeply. There was a raw feeling where the air hit my wrists,
and when I cracked my eyelids, the dim light hurt them. My
neck was stiff, my lips were cracked, and my head was a massive ache of agony. I took several slow, shallow breaths and
tried to remember.

It was the sound of the bells tinkling upon Captain Rylan's
boots that brought it all back.

My ribs hurt because Captain Rylan had kicked me. My
head hurt because Mr. Smitty had swung the boom into me,
and I had been too stupid to duck. Squinting, I could see that
the skin had been rubbed raw from around my wrists, probably by salt-laden ropes tied about them. They were gone now,

and I was thankful for small favors. I didn't know why my stomach hurt, except perhaps because I was hungry. And my neck was probably sore from lying atop a moldering pile of wooden floats and rotting nets.

Wedging an elbow under me, I tried to rise. My head thundered in time with my pulse, and I very slowly lowered myself back down, breathing shallowly and staring at the low ceiling, willing myself not to vomit. There had been a clink of metal, and the heavy weight about my ankle gained meaning. I was chained to something.

"Tess?" warbled a voice from the other side of the low, long hold. "You're all right!"

"Contessa," I breathed, wanting to look but not trusting myself yet to shift my head.

"You're awake!" she said, hushed but intent. "They hit you so hard. And you didn't wake up. I thought you were dead. And they wanted to kill you. They wouldn't stop hitting you, and you didn't wake up!"

"Contessa," I whispered, as her frantic voice seemed to scrape the insides of my eyelids and make my head hurt even more. "Please be quiet."

"Alex tried to stop them," she said, the sound of tears heavy in her babbling. "It took three of them to bring him down. And they forced him to kneel and Mr. Smitty took his sword. Oh, Tess, I thought they killed you!"

"Contessa," I breathed, staring at the black mold on the ceiling. "Shut up. You're hurting my eyes."

She gasped, her next outburst dying. Her breath came out in a sob, and she held the next.

Feeling bad now for having told the queen of Costenopolie to shut up, I tilted my head to find her, wondering why she hadn't rushed over and given me a good shake to finish killing me. Tongue scraping the inside of my mouth for any hint of moisture, I found her sitting in a shifting patch of sun about two man lengths away.

I sat up slowly, the thick mat of nets under me making an uncomfortable surface. The soft clink of metal drew my attention to my filthy bare ankle, wrapped in a shackle that looked as if it was used for wrists, not feet. I followed the length of

chain to where it was bolted to the wall, red and white flakes
of rust and salt making an ugly knot.

Taking another shallow breath, I tried to clear my head,
cataloging my new state with a numbed acceptance. My underskirt was badly ripped, and the overly elaborate dress I had
worn to dinner was stained by salt and brown smears of old
algae. My shoes were gone, and my hair was down and tangled. Needless to say my whip, dagger, and what darts I'd had
left were absent.

The stench of mold and burned oil hung thick in my nose, a
black, greasy film covering most of my exposed skin in smears
between the bruises. Rubbing my sore palms together, I looked
across the low-ceilinged hold to Contessa. She looked better
than I felt, her dress still in one piece and her useless boots on
her feet. Her blond hair was lank about her face, and it had
fallen to hide her features as she sat in her beam of light. A soft
murmur came from her, and I realized the monotone of rhythm
haunting my pain-filled dreams had been her prayers.

The light was becoming tolerable, and I shifted a body width
closer, breath held against the hurt. A cold feeling shocked
through me as I realized the slump of green-and-gold fabric before her was Alex, his fair head in her lap. "Contessa," I whispered, "what happened?"

She brought her head up, staring at me with blue eyes
forced wide so she wouldn't cry. "After the boom hit you?"
she asked, her voice wavering.

I nodded, then wished I hadn't as my stomach threatened
to empty itself. I slowly worked my way off the pile of nets,
finding the damp sacks beside them marginally better. At least
the ceiling wasn't quite so close. It was the limit of my leash,
and I wasn't sure I could get to her. It was stifling, but I felt
cold, not hot—and sticky from old sweat.

Contessa looked from me back to Alex, her face screwing
up in dismay, unable to speak. From where I was in the shadows, I took in the new bruise on Alex's face, visible under a
thickening growth of blond and red stubble. His clothes were
bloodstained and torn, all the ornamentation gone. A clean,
well-applied bandage showed from under his open shirt, tied
to his front shoulder. He was flushed, and when I stretched to

the limit of my reach, I found I could put a hand to his forehead. My eyes rose to Contessa's. He was burning in fever.

"How long was I unconscious?" I asked, not believing this happened overnight.

"A night," she said, her voice unusually low and flat. "The following day and night, and then up to now."

Appalled, I counted. A full twenty-four hours, and then some. Almost two days.

Contessa sniffed loudly, wiping her hand under her nose in a very unqueenlike motion. I followed her gaze to Alex, shifting the empty sacks smelling of moldy flax to try to find a more comfortable position. "Contessa," I prompted softly, not wanting to push her too far but needing to know. "What happened? Where's Duncan?" My heart clenched. *Why isn't he down here?* "Is he . . . Is he dead?" I asked, not liking how my voice rose to a squeak at the end.

"He will be if I ever find him alone," she said.

The bitter hatred in her voice pulled my head up. Seeing my shocked look, she added angrily, "The chull bait is up on deck with the rest of those foul bastards—playing cards. I've been alone all this time, not knowing if you or Alex were going to live or die. And he's been swilling ale, playing cards, and laughing at us, the chu pit of a man."

Stunned, I stared at her. *Duncan? He wouldn't do that. He couldn't!*

"Why didn't you tell me he was a thief!" she accused hotly.

My cracked lips parted. "He's not a thief, he's just a cheat," I said, not knowing anymore if the difference meant anything. Confused, I drew back, her shrill voice making my head pound. Alex, too, stirred, and I think that, not my pained look, made her lower her voice.

"He has a thief mark, Tess," she said. "I heard Captain Rylan say so. The lying bastard said he owed Costenopolie nothing and that he'd rather live a free pirate than be a dead man upholding a name he owed no allegiance to."

"No," I protested, feelings of betrayal pulling at me. "Duncan wouldn't do that. He's lying so he can stay free and help us."

My voice was low in case someone was listening. Duncan wouldn't do this. I had to believe he wouldn't leave me—leave us—to die. He had proven his worth a hundred times over. He had shown his feelings for me before he knew I had ties to the palace, helping me find Kavenlow when Alex's brother had taken over the palace last spring, knowing there was likely no reward but death at the madman's hand. He had willingly risked death to retake the palace after I told him not to. He could have stolen from the palace and run hundreds of times in the past, and he hadn't. He hadn't betrayed me then, and he wouldn't betray me now.

"Contessa," I said, leaning forward to make my chain clink. "He had to lie so he can help us. Having him chained to a wall beside us doesn't help anyone."

"He's a lying, cheating, filthy dog," she said bitterly, "leaving us here to rot while he schemes. The only one benefiting from him being free is *him*."

"Sometimes scheming is more powerful than a blade," I said, thinking of my lies necessitated by the game that manipulated her like a chess piece. Duncan was probably more honest than I was. "He doesn't know how to use a sword. He has to rely on his wits. He hasn't left us," I said, an ugly sliver of doubt sliding between my heart and reason.

"But I heard him!" she exclaimed softly. "He called you a fool and said Costenopolie would fall before an heir could be conceived, much less born, and he was done with it, having gained all he could. He has betrayed you, Tess. He's cutting his losses and moving on."

Contessa's voice, though low, was hard. Alex stirred. "Rooo?" he murmured.

"No," Contessa whispered, her ire falling from her like water. She brushed her pale hand over his hair and tried to arrange his tattered collar. "It's Contessa, Alex. I'm Contessa."

I watched her soothe him, wondering if he was about to wake but deciding he was delirious. Faint in the back of my pounding head was the memory of him calling out for his "Rose, Sweet Rosie" while I had been unconscious.

Contessa's breaths became harsh, and she seemed close to tears again. Apparently this had been happening a lot. My heart went out to her. She had been here alone for almost two days, chained to the wall, tending her husband and unable to reach me, not knowing if either of us was going to survive. But Duncan was free, and with that, came hope.

"Contessa?" I said softly, and she pulled her head up. Her eyes behind her long, greasy hair were red-rimmed and swollen. "I'm sorry. I knew about Duncan's thief mark. I should have told you. It's not his. He took it for another, and he's ashamed for having it. That's why I never said anything. He isn't betraying us. I have to believe that."

The fire was gone from her, and she slumped, looking beaten, her hair falling to hide her face. Her hands on Alex never ceased. My chain clinked softly as I tried to move closer. "Tell me what happened," I said.

The sun caught upon her hands, now empty of rings as they moved over his forehead, gently pushing his hair back. Her fingers were chapped from salt and looked sore. "The boom knocked you out," she said, and I could hear the tightness of her throat in her emotionless words. "The sailors attacked you when you fell. Alex tried to keep them off you. I was so scared. He couldn't do it, even with Duncan's help. They hurt him." She took a deep, shaking breath. "They drove a knife into his shoulder to make him kneel. He wouldn't even then. They cauterized it this morning after I told them it was infected. It took five men to hold him down."

I swallowed hard and reached out to her, imagining her down here listening to that, unable to help and not knowing what they had done to him until they brought him back to her.

"I don't know if he's getting better or not," she said, her voice deceptively level. "He won't eat, and the small bit of water I've gotten into him just burns up in fever."

"Water?" I said, my cracked lips suddenly unbearable. "You have water?"

"Oh, I'm sorry," she said, twisting to reach behind her. Leaning over Alex, she held a water sack out, the bloodstains under her nails looking ugly as her hands passed through a narrow beam of light.

I stretched for it eagerly, my soot-blackened hands just meeting her white ones. The sack was almost flaccid, and I sucked greedily at the tepid water tasting of hide. Three gulps almost emptied it, and I reluctantly pulled it from me, thinking

I could have downed it all, but not knowing if they would ever give us any more.

"Thank you," I said, passing it back to her for safekeeping.

Contessa took it, her hands resuming their motion over Alex. "We're taken, aren't we," she said.

My gaze dropped in guilt. "I'm sorry, Contessa," I whispered. "I never should have made you leave the *Sandpiper.*"

She didn't look up, watching Alex's breath slip in and out of him like fire. "He said it was his fault. Before he went delirious, he said he should have known by Captain Rylan's grip that he wasn't a merchant. That he deserved to lose me. That he was sorry," she whispered. "But it's really my fault."

"Yours!" I exclaimed, then winced when Alex stirred.

She finally met my eyes, her face miserable. "I'm so useless, Tess. I was so frightened. I should have been able to do something. You did something. You almost got us free. I should have jumped into the water when we realized we were being taken. We might have survived the water, but this?"

She gestured helplessly, and I reached over Alex to take her hand in mine, stilling its incessant motion. "No," I said firmly. "If you had gone over the side in the black of night, you would have drowned. We all would have. They knew who we were. They're taking care of Alex's wounds. They'll ask for ransom, and Kavenlow will pay it or rescue us. I never should have let that man on my boat."

Contessa was silent. *Guilt?* I wondered, then changed my mind. She was apprehensive, fearful. "What is it?" I asked, not liking her air of bad news yet unsaid.

"They only want Alex and me," she said, not meeting my eyes. "They don't care about you. That's why Duncan turned pirate. They were going to kill him if he didn't join . . ."

"Contessa?" I asked, a sliver of fear for the hesitation at the end of her words.

"You killed some of them," she said, without the barest hint of recrimination or distaste. "Alex did, too, but he's a royal."

"So am I. You sent notice to all our neighbors. Until you have children, I'm the third in line to the throne. Everyone knows it!" Kavenlow and the player community weren't pleased I was still in line for the throne, but as long as I didn't take it, they wouldn't try to kill me. And now the pirates wanted to kill me because I was too far away?

"You aren't royal in their eyes," she said, her words seeming to fall over themselves in her pity. "I told them that Kavenlow would pay as much for you as for me. I promised them everything, but all they see is a gutter trull who killed their mates. It was all Captain Rylan could do to keep them from raping and killing you right then. They want revenge from you, not money."

The moist, clammy air under the deck set an unbreakable chill in me. Somewhere in the back of my memory, I could remember the agony of being beaten, and the fear in Contessa's eyes as she watched. *I'm alive,* I told myself, stomach quivering and arms starting to tremble. *I am alive, and I will stay that way.*

But it didn't help.

"Tess?"

I jerked, finding her expression pinched in worry and fear. "You would have woken up tied to a hook in the crew's quarters if they hadn't started arguing over who was to have you first," she said. "Half the crew is claiming blood-rights, and the other half is trying to buy you."

My face started to twist, but I quickly sealed my expression to nothing when she started to cry.

"I'm sorry," she sobbed, the racking sounds bringing laughter from the men above. "But I had to tell you. They're going to kill you, and all my money and royal name won't stop them."

Six

✦

"Rosie?"

Alex's dry voice was featherlight, but it woke me where the steps of the sailors above us and the snap of the sails no longer did.

"Hush, Alex," Contessa whispered, and I cracked my eyes. It seemed to be noon, by the angle of the sun slipping in through the few cracks, but I was still cold. I didn't move, lest my stiff muscles remember how sore they were. I had been drowsing, almost asleep, but something had changed.

Curled up with my knees almost to my chin, I lay on the rank, moldering nets and listened. I could hear waves on the shore and gulls. The wind in the canvas was gone, and the deck was flat. There was a rhythmic rise and fall and the soft slap of waves hitting a stationary hull.

"Mr. Smitty." I heard Duncan's faint call, and I listened intently. I couldn't believe he had betrayed us. This aligning himself with the pirates had to be an attempt to help us.

"Mr. Smitty?" he called again, closer. There was a splash, and a rising of catcalls. A gentle bump thumped through the hold. I think the dinghy had gone in. A shiver went through me, and my stomach clenched. We had arrived somewhere. There was no sound of civilization, no hint of commerce or the noise of women calling. Just water and wind.

"Aye? What you want now?" came Mr. Smitty's rough voice from right atop me, and my eyes widened. I stared up at the underside of the black planks.

"Mr. Smitty," Duncan said breathlessly. "Should I get the royals up on deck, sir?"

"What for?" It was a belligerent accusation. "They're fine where they are."

"It's Prince Alex," Duncan continued, undeterred. "He's in a bad way. The fresh air—"

"Won't do him any more good if he gets to it an hour later. And what the hell do you care for?"

"Money, sir." His response was quick, and I could almost see his sideways grin, sly and contriving. I prayed it was an act. "Two ransoms are better than one. Three are better than two."

"Greedy chull," Mr. Smitty responded, and I could hear his booted feet shift overhead. "I only have to keep him alive for another week. He won't die of a fever for at least that. After that, I don't care.

"Hey!" Mr. Smitty shouted suddenly, and I stifled a jump. "Don't roll that sail up! It's wet, you damned fools!

"I know you got eyes for her," he continued to Duncan. "But she killed three men, and I can't take away their want for revenge. Hell, I don't want to. It'll give them something to do."

Three men? I thought, appalled as I put a hand to my mouth. I hadn't meant to kill any of them. And that I had become a thing to "give them something to do" was sickening.

"I want her first," Duncan persisted, and I gritted my teeth, refusing to believe the worst of him. "I've been almost a year trying to get under her skirts. She's a tease, promising one thing with her eyes, then turning me away with her words. I want what she promised me before she dies, and I want her all fire and spit, not weepy and slack after another man has broken her."

I couldn't look at Contessa, though I knew from the sound of her breathing that she was listening. Mr. Smitty grunted. "You got the same chance at her as any man. Bring them over on the last boat."

From above came the sound of him walking away, shouting

orders. I didn't move on my moldy sacks, my heart aching and my hope dying to a sour lump. Duncan wasn't betraying me. I had to believe that.

Depressed, I ran a finger between me and the rusting band of metal about my ankle. I was cold and sticky from old sweat. My hair was greasy, and I was bruised and stank. I wanted to cry, but daren't. Holding my breath, I bit my lip until it hurt.

"I'm sorry, Tess," Duncan whispered, and I wondered if he knew I could hear him. "I won't let you die like that. I promise."

His boots slowly moved away, and my eyes grew hot. The tears pricked, and my head started to pound.

"Night crew ashore first!" came Mr. Smitty's shout. "The rest of you, lock her down!"

Good-natured catcalls rose high, giving evidence that the crew was widespread over the small vessel. Feet padded to the railing, and after a moment of confusion and thumps of bundles, the dinghy rowed away. It grew quiet, and it seemed I could feel the motion of the ship easier.

"Rosie?"

It was Alex again, and I closed my eyes. *God help me, I was going to die at the hands of men. How could a dinner party turn into this?*

"I'm Contessa, Alex," my sister said softly, the hurt clear in her voice. He was delirious again. There had been only one brief interlude of rationality this morning where he apologized for being such a bother, his dark eyes wide and unseeing and his pale fingers around hers.

I ran a hand across my eyes. It left a clean spot on the back of my hand where my tears had wiped the grime away. Duncan was trying. I would be ready when the time came.

"Rose?" Alex said, his tone gentle with a loving chastisement. "You promised me you wouldn't come."

"Please be still, Alex," Contessa said, a hint of desperation in her.

I cracked an eye to see them together as before, Alex with his head in Contessa's lap. Alex sent a bandaged hand up to touch her cheek, and her head drooped, her hair falling to hide her face. "Don't cry, love," he said. "You promised me you would find a man who would love you, who would give all of

himself, not the half-life and polite insults a concubine has at
court. I love you too much to see you suffer like that."

"I'm Contessa," she pleaded. "Please stop. . . ."

I could hear the tears in her voice and see the love in his
touch as he cupped her cheek with his hand. So could Contessa.

"No tears," he whispered, his cracked lips barely moving.
"You understood too well. To say you didn't would be a lie.
My father needs me, and I will follow his wishes."

"Shhhhh," Contessa urged, pain clear in her soft pleading.
"Be still."

It was obvious the poor woman didn't want to hear any
more. I didn't either. It hurt, and it would tear him up if he
knew the torture he was putting his new wife through.

"But I met her, Rosie," he said, and Contessa shook. "And
as much as I didn't want to, I think I might grow to love her."

"Please stop. . . ." she begged.

"Hush. I will always love you, Rosie. Never think I won't.
But I must set aside our wants for the greater good of Misdev.
I am a prince of Misdev first. You know that. It's what you
loved about me from the start."

"Please. Please don't," she whispered, tears glistening wet
upon her cheeks, and I felt my heart breaking.

"She's nothing like you," Alex said, strength entering his
voice for the first time, heavy with excitement and the thrill of
discovery. "She's nothing like you, and exactly like you. When
I met her, I almost sent for you despite our vow. She seemed
so frail, so soft-spoken, mild and easily swayed. A woman not
worth the food on her plate. But she isn't, Rosie. And no one
sees it. Her fire is deep within her, hidden where it grows strong
and bright."

Contessa took a gulping gasp of air. Her hand went out and
her pale fingertips covered his lips. "Alex. Stop," she begged,
barely above a whisper.

A bandaged hand crept upward, and Alex took her fingertips in his hands and kissed them. "Don't cry for me. I'll be all
right. She is as wild as the wind before the rain, made more so
because she can seem so soft and pliant. She fights for what
she believes in, and she's not afraid of a royal title, having no
regard for any but herself and her God. I think . . . I think I
might love her if she can find some way to love me."

My throat tightened, and I held my breath lest they know I was awake and listening. I clutched a fold of a sack to me, desperate to be silent. It wasn't fair, what royalty was forced to endure. To live a life without love, forever to set aside passion or mix it with the fear of being found and shamed. I had escaped it, only to find myself snared in it again with Duncan.

Contessa gave up all pretense of restraint and openly began to weep. "What if she doesn't love you, Alex," she said between heaves for breath. "Will you send for me then?"

"No."

Her sobs grew harder, and I looked to find her thin shoulders shaking, her head bowed over him and her hands imprisoned in his. "I can't, dearest," he said, "though I'd give almost anything to. It would destroy her. For all her strength, her heart is as fragile as new ice. I vowed to be true to her, and I will whether she believes it or not."

"But what of you?" she asked, her voice harsh with pain. "Will you live without love because she remains true to her heart? Should she leave her man just to make you happy?"

It was a bitter accusation, and Alex smiled softly in his delirium. He reached up again to touch her face. Eyes closing, Contessa tilted her head so that his hand fit her perfectly. "As a prince of Misdev," he whispered lovingly, "I will wait until I know she won't be swayed."

"How long?" she asked, barely audible. "How long will you wait?"

"I don't know." His voice had gone wispy. He was growing tired, and his voice was starting to slur. "But you must leave, Rosie. I don't want her to see you. I don't want word of your being here to mar any trust she might have in me."

"I want to stay," Contessa said faintly, "to hear your voice gentled in love."

My focus sharpened, thinking this was a dangerous game she played.

"Shhhh," Alex whispered. "Come here."

His bandaged hand pulled her down to him, and she settled against him, crying softly.

"Don't cry," he murmured, his hand moving atop her hair. "I want you to promise me you'll go back to Misdev and find a man who loves you for your fire, not your beauty or how many shops your father has. Marry for love, Rosie. Live it for me in case I don't find it."

"How?" she mumbled into his shirt. "How will I know if his words are only pretty words? I've only loved one man. I've nothing to gauge another's words against."

"His kiss." Alex's words, though soft, were clear over the gentle slap of water. "You can feel it when he holds you."

"But I don't know what love feels like. . . ." she stammered as she sat up into the beam of sun. It glowed around her, making her a downtrodden angel.

My cracked eyes saw him smile, and as I clenched into myself, I felt the tears start at the love he held for his Rosie. "Then one last kiss, Rosie. Look tight. Remember it. And when you kiss another, measure it against this one to know if his words are true or just words."

Contessa was silently crying, the tears slipping from her. Slowly, hesitantly, she bent to him. A sheet of her hair fell between us, and my head pounded as I wanted to sob right along with her. It was beautiful and tragic. An honorable man saying good-bye to the woman he loved so that he might be true to a woman who might never love him.

And I knew why Contessa had given in and played the part of Rosie. She had stolen a piece of Alex's love for herself. In her words to Alex, she admitted she had found herself able to love him, though her loyalty to Thadd held her back. If Alex ever kissed Contessa again with that same passion, she would know that he loved her, too.

I closed my eyes and turned away, thinking it had been wrong to have overheard such a private moment. It had filled me with a bitter envy. No man would ever love me with that depth, that purity. And if one ever did, I would somehow have to find the strength to walk away to keep him safe and alive. The game had taken that away from me. I could not afford to love anyone, or a rival player would use it against me.

I took a shaky breath as they broke apart.

"I'm sorry," Alex said, his voice a thin ribbon. "I don't feel well. I think I'm going to go to sleep. I'm sorry, Rosie. I'm so tired."

"Go back to sleep, love," Contessa whispered, and I heard

a gentleness to it that had never been there before. "I'll watch over you until your Contessa comes."

"Be nice to her, Rosie?" Alex asked, his words hardly more than a breath. "She's frightened, despite all her bluster and fire."

"I will. Shhhhh, go to sleep."

"Promise?"

"Promise," Contessa said, her words choking.

I waited, listening until his breath went slow and deep. Under me, the ship rose and fell. The remaining crew readied to leave, unaware and uncaring of us. Past the soft sounds of them was Contessa silently weeping, and I huddled into myself, trying not to do the same.

Seven

The sailor coming up the stairway behind me gave me a shove, and I stumbled over the last step. I fell sprawling onto the deck amid rude catcalls and jeers. From belowdecks came Contessa's cry of protest. My knees had taken most of my weight, the dull ache shocking me out of my numb stupor. A chill wind from the coming sunset shifted my lank hair about my face, and I looked past it, squinting. I took a grateful breath of fresh air, then fell to coughing.

I was faint from hunger, but with the threat of someone helping me, urging me on, I got up. It was harder than usual as my hands were tied before me with a cruel tightness, and I was stiff from having not moved much the last few days. The salt-laden ropes burned, adding to my misery. The thought of the fickle nature of men flashed through me. They were afraid of me, so I was a subject of ridicule and persecution.

"At least the air is fresher," I breathed, and someone cuffed me. I staggered, almost going down again, the unexpected pain bringing a gasp from me. From the railing, Duncan tensed, watching, though it seemed he was more interested in the dinghy rope he was coiling up. I took my eyes from him lest I give his interest away. It seemed unlikely he had planned an escape from here, surrounded by half a dozen men.

Before me was a subtropical island, like hundreds that dotted the southernmost reaches of Costenopolie. We were anchored in a small bay, the water dark and gray from the coming dusk. A thin ribbon of smoke trailed up through the trees. There was a small beach between the trees that grew right down to the high-tide mark, and I could see the scrapes from where the dinghy had landed earlier. There wasn't a cloud in the sky, and it was cold, the wind cutting through my tattered finery as if it weren't there.

I stood and watched with the rest when two crewmen brought Alex up, cradled between them as if he were a drunk. He was unconscious, and that worried me more than his being lost in a delirium. Contessa came up after him, blinking into the late sun and looking begrimed and filthy as she hastened to Alex, checking his bandage and trying to get him to open his eyes even as he hung in the sailor's grip.

Seeing her in the sunlight, I felt a wash of pity. I was hurt and filthy, but her heart was being torn, and it marked her as my physical hurts didn't. But even though her face was streaked with old tears, there was a new strength in her. Her hand clutching Alex's was protective, not fearful. The pirates, with the exception of Captain Rylan, perhaps, didn't see it, but I did. It was the tightness to her lips, the subtle flash in her eye when the sailors mocked my torn dress. She had set her thoughts to protect him, and that's what she would do down to her last breath.

Slowly, my headache lessened, and I found it easier to bear the light. As the bundles going ashore were dropped to the man in the dinghy, I tried to meet Duncan's gaze. He would have none of it, and it seemed Captain Rylan was keeping a sharp eye on him. Remembering his derisive words about me, I thought it might be worth my effort to further the deception.

I took a deep breath, and, praying I wouldn't faint from lack of food, I kicked the man holding me in the shins. He shouted in surprise, and twisting, I broke away.

"You chull bait!" I screamed, lunging at Duncan. "You murdering chu pit of a man. Thief, cheat, liar! You're filthier than a chamber pot!"

Someone grabbed me, spinning me back with a tight grip on my shoulder. I flung the hair from my eyes and lurched, stretching for Duncan with my bound hands as if wanting to claw his eyes out. Duncan's eyes were wide, looking properly shocked. The expression in his dark eyes shifted then to amusement, only slightly shamefaced at the outpouring of good-natured ribbing the surrounding sailors gave him.

"I'll kill you!" I shouted, wiping the spittle from me. "I'll kill you if I get free. You hear me? I'll kill you myself!"

Tears had started somewhere. I didn't care to know how much of it was real and how much of it was acting. It was hard to go hungry in the hold of a ship while someone you knew and trusted was drinking ale and playing cards. Heart pounding, I went slack in the man's grip, my muscles shaking. I was so weak with hunger, I could hardly stand up. Contessa gave me a shared look of misery, and I wiped my eyes, but the tears wouldn't stop dribbling out.

Captain Rylan made a satisfied-sounding grunt, eying both my frustrated tears and Duncan's shrug. "Get them in the boat," he said, sounding bored with it all, and someone shoved me forward.

It was the last boat to the island, and I was surprised we all fit. They made me sit on the floor at the feet of three men. None of them had shoes, and their feet were ugly. I sat and watched the ship shrink. Seeing it in the sun, I cursed myself for twice the fool. It was clearly not a merchant vessel. There were far too many men on it to be a merchant crew, and too many catapults for lobbing flaming tar. The woman on the bowsprit had her eyes burned out.

Slowly the sound of surf and birds came louder. The scraping of the dinghy's keel on the sand-and-shell shore was a shock vibrating up through my spine. Several men got out, and before I could move, one picked me up and dropped me just over the side.

I gasped as I fell into the water. A wave sloshed over me, knocking me down. Cold water filled my ears and eyes, and I struggled to get up before I drowned. A hand grabbed a fistful of hair and pulled me upright. Sputtering, I tried to breathe.

"Get her out of the water," Captain Rylan said from the middle of the small boat, seemingly more upset that I had splashed sand and water on his worn coat than anything else.

"Jest helping the lady pretty herself," the man said. Some-one snickered.

Contessa's eyes were narrowed, her temper starting to build. I shook my head at her to be quiet, then cried out when the sailor who had pulled me up pinched my shoulder and dragged me out of the surf. He left me there with my feet in the water so he could help unload the boat. I awkwardly rose, my hands still tied before me and more filthy than before. Skirts heavy with water, I staggered to remain upright, feeling the lack of food gnaw at me like a cur.

I didn't want anyone to touch me, so I followed the first of the sailors as they slogged across the narrow beach and onto a well-worn footpath. I was tired of being shoved and cuffed, and I had a faint hope that if I was cooperative, they would leave me alone. Contessa, though, had other ideas.

"I want clean, hot water immediately." She started in from behind me as soon as the greenery closed over our heads. "And a bottle of your strongest spirits."

"Planning a festival, Your Majesty?" Mr. Smitty mocked, and two sailors chuckled breathlessly from behind the empty water barrels they were rolling.

"And a knife if I request it," she added. "Something sharp. My husband needs attention. If he dies, nothing in this world or the next will keep you alive."

"You'll have what you need to keep him alive," Captain Rylan said from over his shoulder, pacing at the top of the line of men. "Just keep your skirts down, missy."

She huffed indignantly, but her voice went soft as she mur-mured encouragement to Alex, now awake enough to move his feet. The greenery abruptly gave way to a somewhat open area with three ramshackle huts and several community fires about which hammocks were strung. Larger trees arched over-head to block the ambient light. Sand and short, jagged-leafed scrub made a cool patch below. It was their land base, I would guess, and it was as foul as their ship.

Most of the men who had come ashore before us were gath-ered around one spot, all looking into a pit about twenty feet across. One of the sailors threw a stick, and an animal screamed. A shudder went through me. It almost sounded human. As one, the men fell back, cursing when whatever they had caught tried to get out.

I was so intent on trying to hear them that I stumbled when the man behind me shoved me away from the rest of the group.

"Tess?" Contessa called, panic in her voice when she realized I was being led away.

Twisting, I struggled to keep her in my sight even as my feet kept me moving forward. "It's all right," I called, stumbling when I was shoved again.

"No, it isn't," Captain Rylan said dryly. His courtly accent was utterly gone, and the bells on his boots chimed with his steps, a harsh discord to what I now knew he was.

Turning my gaze from him to the pit, my heart pounded. Close by was a small cutout in the surrounding forest. Limbs arched over it, and hanging from them were two lengths of chain. The metal was stained with old blood, black and crusty. Under it was clean sand marked with footprints. "God save me," I whispered, and Captain Rylan snickered. I stopped where I was supposed to under the formidable lengths of iron, determined not to show how frightened I was.

The sand was cooler here, and my begrimed toes sank into the rough smoothness of it. My mouth went dry as a second man took my bound hands and reached for the hanging shackles. Feeling weak and nauseous, I sent my gaze up the twin lengths of chain, seeing that they had grown into the trunk they had been there so long. It was a deceptively cruel position. If I stood, my arms would hang naturally at my sides. If I sat or knelt, my arms would stretch above my head. Lying down would be impossible. But I'd probably be dead before I needed to sleep again.

"Don't get too comfortable," Captain Rylan mocked, his attention half on the pit and the jeering men surrounding it. "I've got a little job for you before you meet my crew nice and personal-like. You're going to read back to me the queen's letter to be sure it's just what I told her to put down. And I know you were raised a princess, so you can read."

And you can't, I mocked in my thoughts, but pain had taught me how easy it was to hold my tongue.

Seeing my sullen capitulation, he lifted his brow in a cruel amusement. "If you read back to me exactly what I told her to write, you get to wear your dress when we decide what to do with you."

I swallowed, trying to stay upright when the skinny crewman jerked me, fumbling with the shackles he was trying to fasten about my wrists. They were rusty and scratched my skin, but that wasn't the problem.

"Captain Rylan," the man said, bringing his attention from the men about the pit. "The irons are too big for her. She'll just slip right out of them."

It was true, and I cursed the man for being so attentive.

"Then use a rope," he said, going to the pit and leaving him to work it out. His eyes went wide, his expression going slack in amazement as he stood at the edge and peered down. Hands on his hips, he exclaimed, "My God. It's magnificent."

"Use a rope," the crewman muttered, letting go of the shackles, and they swung from their momentum. "Of course I'm going to use a rope." He jerked my wrists, and a cry of pain slipped from me, unremarked upon as if I was worth no consideration. "Damn fool man." He gave another tug, and I bit my lip when pain flamed up my arms. "I'm so tired of listening to that white-gloved sucker fish I could slit his throat," he said, taking the loose end of my tether and flinging it expertly over a limb above me. "Use a damned rope. What else would I use? My mother's apron strings?"

Backing up with the tail end of the rope in hand, he squinted, his narrow gaze running up the length of rope and back down to me. Apparently deeming that I couldn't reach, he tied it off against a nearby tree, pulling my hands up over my head so I couldn't see to work the knots about my wrists loose. He gave a final yank on the rope, jerking me forward a step. The distasteful man ran his eyes down me, and back up.

"You ain't got much for a man to grab on to, but I've got a little sumtin put away. I was saving it for the whores at Long Beach, but you'd do. If Jake and I go together, we might have enough to buy you first. I'd be gentle with you, if you don't bite. Would you like that?"

"Go to hell," I whispered, feeling my face go white.

He laughed, and his foul breath slid over me. "Someday," he said, not bothered at all. "But not tonight, and not with you." He gave me another ugly look, then reached for me.

Frightened, I fell back, taking a wide-footed stance, my arms still over my head. "Touch me, and I kick you between your legs," I threatened, heart pounding.

The sailor hesitated then, thinking better of it, gathered up the hanging chains and looped them around a tree and out of my reach. "Women shouldn't be on the waves anyway," he said. "You deserve whatever you get."

I made a face, and he spat on me. It hit my jaw, and I jerked, saying nothing as he walked away. I waited until he was gone before reaching up with my shoulder and wiping his warm spit from me. Miserable, I looked for Contessa and Alex, but they were gone. Duncan was watching me from over the pit. I could see his hidden tension in how his thumb was rubbing his second finger. Seeing my gaze on him, he dropped his attention to the pit.

"What is it?" he asked Mr. Smitty, loud enough for me to hear him.

Mr. Smitty stood beside him, his hands in his pockets, as proud as if he had given birth to whatever it was. "Don't know," he admitted. "We caught it 'bout a month back. Been feeding it goats. It probably came ashore with the last hurricane. Whatever it is, it can kill a man. We found two dead last month in the interior. And Gilly. He got drunk and fell in." The man put a thick-knuckled hand to his upper chest in salute. "That thing down there outright killed him afore we could lasso him and pull him out."

"But what is it?" Duncan asked again, getting no answer.

Someone kicked sand into the pit and the creature screamed. A shudder rippled its way along my spine and goose bumps covered me, made worse by the sudden gust of wind. The men had all taken a step back at the sound, and a murmur of awe broke over them. I felt an odd kinship with whatever was down there. I wondered if either of us would escape.

Captain Rylan gave it a final look and started back to the huts, his steps jaunty despite the loose sand. Duncan jiggled on his feet. Glancing from me, to the animal in the pit, then to the captain, he nodded as if making up his mind and jogged to catch up.

"Captain Rylan," he called as he ran. "You know what you should do?"

"No, Duncan," the spry man said without turning around. "What should I do?"

"You should drop the ambassador down there with it."

My lips parted, and the captain halted with an almost comical quickness, his attention falling on me. "What a grand idea," he said. "If she is still alive after everyone is done with her, that's just what I'll do."

"No," Duncan insisted, his eyes wide and bright as if eager for it. "Now. If you sell her off, you'll only get the money from one, maybe two men. But if you drop her down there and take bets on how long she'll last, you'll get a portion of all of it."

My stomach grew light, and I thought I would have vomited if I had anything in it. *Why is he doing this? Why?* I had to believe he had a plan.

Captain Rylan's smile widened. "Duncan, my lad!" he said, clapping him companionably about the shoulders. "For a moment, I was wondering if you had gone native, but this? This I like. And you, knowing her the best, will tell me how long she's likely to stay alive, hummm?"

Duncan nodded, never looking back as he accompanied Captain Rylan to the huts. I had to believe this was Duncan's idea to give me the chance I needed, but fear still slid between my skin and my soul.

As if sensing my fear, the animal screamed, sounding like a wounded child bent on revenge. I had no idea what it was, and tonight, I would be fighting it.

Eight

❖

The sand had quickly gone cold under my feet after the sun vanished behind the thick overgrowth. I was cold through my torn dress, and my arms ached with every involuntary shiver. They had let me hang, ignored while they roasted the goat they had slaughtered earlier, and the air of a drunken festival was thick and depressing. Fatigue had pulled my head down, and though I tried to doze, the pull on my back was enough to keep me awake—the pain was a throbbing ache radiating from my shoulders with every breath.

That the warships would find us was a thin, impossible hope. We could be anywhere, and the warships had been trapped behind the shoals until the tide rose anew, giving our abductors hours of sailing to hide themselves.

All of the crew but the few minding the ship and the three sullen men with Contessa and Alex were carousing at the largest bonfire. They had lit torches, putting one in the holder tied to a tree next to me so they could watch my reactions as they tried to outdo each other's boasts of their plans with me and how they would extract their revenge for the killed crewmen. The smoke from the torch kept the early insects from biting me too badly, and for that, I was grateful.

I must have fallen into a doze as a spray of sand against me jerked my head up. Captain Rylan stood at the edge of my circle where the rough grass grew, the bells on his boots chiming. His hand was on my rope tied to a nearby tree, and a black bottle was in his grip.

His coat was undone despite the cold, and his eyes were red-rimmed and sharp. With his stubbled face and slumped posture, his faded finery made him look twice as repulsive as if he had been in rags. My gaze lingered on the new gold glinting in the torchlight upon his collar and cuffs. It was Alex's, and I prayed he was still alive.

The ship's captain had been to bother me once earlier just after sunset, tense and fidgety when he made me read Contessa's note. In my sister's careful script was my past and my future, telling Kavenlow that we had been taken and if he sought us out or attempted a rescue, the royal couple would die. A second letter would be following to tell Kavenlow where they would meet to exchange money for the royals. My name hadn't been mentioned.

Now, as Captain Rylan stood before me taking a long swig of his bottle, he seemed much more relaxed, but he was clearly a good distance toward being drunk. The source of his mood was obvious. If the warships hadn't found us by now, they wouldn't.

"Duncan is intent on saving your life," he said by way of greeting, his voice soft and precise, showing none of the rough street accent it had earlier.

A stab of hope followed by fear kept my mouth shut. I liked him better when he wasn't pretending to be anything but what he was—street filth.

He lifted the bottle again, and I licked my lips, eying it. No one had seen fit to give me water or food all day. Beyond him at the fire, the men became noisy. That Captain Rylan was talking to me had been noted, and they were turning to watch, shouting encouragement to bring me over and start the bidding.

"He says," Captain Rylan continued when I dropped my head so my hair hid my face, "that he's only out for revenge, but even our good Mr. Smitty can see he wants you."

Hungry, cold, and miserable, I shivered, and with that betraying me, I brought my head up and stared at him. Duncan was a good man. I wished I had trusted him with my secret. I wished I had said something so he would know it was my choice but not my desire to keep so much from him.

Captain Rylan pushed himself off the tree, and I twitched, a surge of fear bringing me out of my numb state. Pain radiated through me at the quick motion, and I gritted my teeth to keep from crying out. The bottle under his arm, he untied the rope from the tree and hauled on it.

My arms jerked straight over my head. The rush of pain made me gasp. Grunting, he pulled again. My heels went up, and my shoulders flamed. Panting, I refused to make a sound. I hung with my toes dragging in the sand, trying to get a good breath of air into my lungs. My sight darkened, then steadied. *God, please make him stop.*

Captain Rylan tied the rope off with a firm tug. "You wouldn't let him touch you," he said, bells jingling as he came closer. "Maybe it's the want of what he hasn't had."

My jaw clenched, and I tried not to twist as I hung. My shoulders were in agony, making tears start in my eyes. He stood before me, his ale-tainted breath reminding me of festivals at the palace. His beard was coming in white, and his tired eyes made him look old.

"It certainly isn't your looks," he said, his gaze traveling over me.

"Your breath stinks like a chu pit," I panted, breathing through the pain.

His expression never registered I'd spoken. "Oh, you're pretty enough," he said. "But you aren't soft, and you don't have enough for a man to hold on to properly." His eyes lingered on places that made a cold spot start in my middle. "Or maybe he likes 'em looking like boys."

I said nothing, fear warring with insult and winning.

He tossed his bottle to land upright in the sand. Reaching behind him, he pulled on the rope running from the tree to over my head. I rose another inch, gasping as I swung into him. Pain went through my shoulders, but I brought my knees up, trying to force him away from me.

With a silent, aggressive intent, he sent his free arm about my waist, pulling me too close to fight. Shocked, I did nothing in the instant that he forced his lips against mine. Rough and ugly, his beard scraped me.

Panic broke through, and I fought to get free. His lips muffled my shout as I wiggled and twisted at the end of my rope, pushing away and kicking. Immediately he let go, falling back out of my reach. He had released the rope, and my toes were again on the sand. I stared at him, knowing I was helpless.

"Must be the thrill of the hunt," he said, calm and unruffled. "It sure isn't you."

I spat the hair from my mouth, hating him. Hating feeling helpless. Glad I was going to die from an animal rather than at the hands of a man.

He bent to get his bottle, drinking it to make his Adam's apple bob. Finished, he threw the bottle into the scrub behind me and pulled on the tail of the rope. The knot slipped free, and I fell to the sand with a small groan. Pain spread through me so thick and heavy I didn't even know from where it stemmed. The sand was cold, and I wanted nothing more than to lie down on it.

"Make a good showing, girl," he said, jerking at my rope as if I was a dog until I wedged my knees under me and got up, trying to find my breath around the agony. "I've got half a year's money wagered on you," he finished, pulling me stumbling to the bonfire.

A ragged cheer went up when the men realized I was being brought forward. Most were staggering drunk or halfway to it. Slowly my muscles remembered how to move, the pained stretching almost bringing me to my knees. I found Duncan at the edge of the gathering, deep in the shadows from the moon and fire with a full bottle in his grip. It was clear the crew didn't yet accept him. He looked worried, and he tensed as if to say something, held back by his deception.

Sun-browned hands reached to prod and pinch as Captain Rylan yanked me through the outskirts and into the brighter light at the bonfire. I took it without comment, my limbs tingling with renewed circulation. "Get your hands off!" Captain Rylan shouted when one pulled me shrieking into him. "None of that. You want her first, you will bloody well buy her first."

Captain Rylan yanked me out of the sailor's grip, and I fell into his chest, forcing my first feeling of gratitude away. I would feel nothing. I had to feel nothing.

"Jest checking the goods," the sailor whined, gaining a

weak agreement from those nearest him. "We all gonna want a taste afore we buy."

"I already tasted her for you," Captain Rylan said. "She tastes fine."

"We saw that," a man with no shirt said, rubbing his lower chest and grinning. "She's kinda skinny. I like skinny." He leered, chilling me. The tingle in my arms had worsened, and I shifted my shoulders to try to find a position that didn't hurt.

"I'll give three coppers for her!" someone shouted, and my face went cold. I thought I was going to fight that animal in the pit, not be sold.

"Me and Nate, we'll share. We got five between us," another said, and my stomach clenched. *God help me, I can't do this!* I stared across the fire at Duncan, but he had turned away, terrifying me.

A thin, anemic sailor stood up, nearly falling. His neighbors laughed and propped him up until he found his balance. "I'll give you one for the sea whore," he slurred. "That's all she's worth. Stinking little whore in a pretty—p-pretty dress."

"She killed Garson," said a high voice from the back. "Killing her is worth all I got. That's eighteen. Any of you got more than that?"

A sound of awe rose. "Where'd you get eighteen?" someone asked, and was shushed.

Standing with my feet in the fire-warmed sand and my hands numb and bound before me, I struggled to catch Duncan's eyes. His head was still down, his long brown hair hiding his face. He hadn't enough money to save me.

"Now trench your anchors and drop your sails, all of you," Captain Rylan said, yanking the rope so my arms jerked and I almost fell. I submitted to it, vowing to remember everything. "I told you I tasted her, and she isn't much of a tumble."

The catcalls were loud, making the animal in the pit scream. I found myself balancing on the balls of my feet, but there was nowhere to go. My pulse hammered, and I dropped back down. *Not a man. I can't fight a man. Not bound and made helpless.*

Captain Rylan raised his hand, soothing them. "But what you all seem to want," he continued, "is revenge. You can buy a piece of lace at Mad Mary's for half a coin, so it must be revenge, yes? You all buying a chance to mete out the punishment?"

They roared their answer, and I cringed. The short captain buttoned his faded coat and took on a more respectable air, my rope drawn casually through his arm as if I were an obedient dog. *Full circle,* I thought. Bought in the streets, raised to wear silk, only to be sold again. My life had come full circle; it must be over.

"I can sell her to one of you, and the one with the most money will be satisfied, or . . ." He hesitated and the voices of the waiting men stilled. My heart pounded.

"Or we can put her in the pit," the man finished, a wicked, vindictive grin on his bearded face. My breath escaped me in a grateful heave. *God forgive me,* I thought when tears of relief started. There was something wrong in being glad to be thrown in a pit to die mauled by an animal. But I felt myself go white at the resounding shout simultaneously raised from every man but the one with eighteen coins. The call of "Put the cat with the cat" rose, was taken up, and repeated.

"And one of you," Captain Rylan shouted over the tumult, "can even make some money off her if you're right in how long it takes for her to get the shakes and die!"

If I had thought they were loud before, it was nothing compared to the tumult that rose, drowning out the scream of the animal in the pit. Most of the men had stood, and I found myself shrinking back until I was almost pressed against Captain Rylan. Terrified, I looked past the ugliness to find Duncan, seeing only his bowed back. Fear gripped my heart. It had been his idea. Was it a chance to escape or simply a better way to die?

"I give her two minutes!" someone yelled, shoving a coin into Captain Rylan's hands. "One coin for two minutes."

"I say thirty-eight," the skinny drunk sailor said, lurching to fall and disappear behind the mass of men unnoticed.

"She killed Tom," one missing all his front teeth said. "I say if you give her a sword, she'll last four . . . no, five minutes. Gilly lasted five, and he was drunk."

"She's half Gilly's weight," another protested, coming close and fingering my arm. I jerked away, and they laughed. "It will bring her down in half the time."

"It will have to catch her first," the first said. "I still give her five minutes." He shoved money into Captain Rylan's hands. The small man handed my rope to Mr. Smitty—who looked bothered by it all—and proceeded to take everyone's money. His eagerness and greed made me sick, and I recognized the new, businesslike glint as he mentally matched money to faces and estimates of the length of my life.

My knees started to tremble, and the wagers continued around me. They ignored me, since I had gone from something to abuse and torment to something they could make money from. Listening to the wagers get larger as the estimated time of my survival grew smaller, my pulse grew fast. I hadn't had much to eat in days, and fatigue made me light-headed.

"Enough!" Mr. Smitty bellowed, making me jump. His expression was cross, as if irritated by it all. "Let's get her in the pit and be done with it. I want those ransom letters to go out before one of them dies."

My thoughts flew to the dark, ramshackle hut that Contessa and Alex had been taken to. I prayed they were all right. I'd never know, and I wiped the hint of tears from me, steadying myself. They would survive. I had to believe it.

The crew made more noise than I thought was necessary as they plucked torches from the sand and followed Captain Rylan when he reclaimed my rope and jerked me to the pit. The sailors got there first, and the animal screamed, a raw, frustrated sound, when a few threw their torches down to light the hole. The sound struck my heart and I shuddered.

"Make a spot, make a spot. I can't get her in if you don't let me through," the captain complained as he pushed forward, and I stumbled after him. Duncan had forced himself a place directly across from me, the firelit pit between us. The harsh glow flickered up against the sloping walls as if it opened up to hell itself. I could tell by Duncan's empty expression that there would be no help coming from him. There would be no rescue. This wasn't a way to escape. All he had done was give me a more dignified way to die.

Panic crept up from my belly, settling in about my throat. Seeing my face go cold with the knowledge of my death, Duncan's jaw clenched, and he pushed to the front. "I put my entire take of ransom that she survives," he shouted. "But I want her. If she survives, she's mine."

I held my breath against a sob. Even now he was trying to give me hope. Not many heard him, but those who did, laughed.

"Never seen the cat in action, eh?" Mr. Smitty said, the first hints of amusement in the sour man. "I'll back that one," he called to Captain Rylan. He took an ornate watch from a pocket and reverently opened it. "She ain't gonna survive," he added. "No one survives the cat. Not even Gilly, poor bugger. No more than a scratch and he fell, twitching and jerking."

Someone shoved me forward. The sand was cold on my feet, and a sliver of hope drew my gaze into the pit. A cat? A cat had killed a man with a scratch, dying with convulsions? Had they caught a punta? Was that a punta in the pit they had dug?

Even as hope took me, it died. Even if it was a punta, it would make no difference. True, it was the punta's venom that players used as the source of their magic. And yes, Kavenlow had upped my natural immunity to where I could handle three times what would kill anyone else, but the amount of poison they inflicted was far beyond the limits of even players. It would kill me as easily as anyone else. Frightened, I peered over the edge of the lip, seeing nothing.

"Cat with the cat! Cat with the cat!" a man chanted, the litany taken up by angry voices.

Heart pounding, I held my bound wrists out to Mr. Smitty. He seemed to know more about the animal than anyone, in charge of the men though he wasn't the captain. "Give me my hands," I demanded. "If you want me to fight, you will give me my hands."

Captain Rylan glanced at me in mistrust. "Won't that change her odds?" he asked.

"No." Mr. Smitty pulled a dagger from his belt. "Won't make a chu pit of a difference."

As the men cheered, Mr. Smitty sawed at my bindings. They gave way with a snap, and a groan slipped from me. My hands felt like dead things, tingling painfully. Mr. Smitty eyed me in warning, and I closed my eyes in an understanding blink. I wouldn't attack anyone to get a weapon. My hands didn't work yet, and even if they did and I managed to get a knife, the men would have me.

Legs shaking, I moved to the edge of the pit. The torn hem of my dress hung over, hiding my bare feet. I shivered, feeling the cold wind off the water, shaking the tops of the trees and finding me. The men shouted, their faces ugly as they bellowed their approval. Trembling, I peered down, seeing the cat for the first time.

It was larger than I had expected, the size of my wolfhound at home, with a short sandy coat. It had pressed itself against the side of the pit, ears flat against its head and its stubby tail bristled to twice what I imagined it to normally be. Mind whirling, I tried to remember what Kavenlow had said about killing one: nets, snares, and deadfalls baited with an entire deer. Things that killed from afar. I took a slow breath. *Was there hope here, or was it a cruel jest?*

The cat's head jerked as if it had heard the sound of my breath over the noise. Cold, blue eyes met mine, and the animal screamed to show long, yellowed canines.

My breath caught. *I have to fight this? With nothing?* Frightened, I turned to Mr. Smitty since he seemed to be in charge of the beast. I wondered if he knew what he had. If it bit me, I would die. My voice trembled as I said, "May I take a moment to pray?"

The disregard in his eyes grudgingly shifted to respect. He gave me a curt nod and bellowed, "Quiet! Let her make peace with her god!"

Immediately the noise ceased. I stood, surprised when the rough, unkempt men went as still as the man who had passed out. A few even bowed their heads. Over the silence, I could hear the harsh breathing of the punta: three quick breaths, a hesitation, then three quick breaths. My toes in the cold sand, I closed my eyes and stood over the pit—thinking, not praying. I had a bare advantage over poor Gilly in that I could probably withstand a scratch, though a bite would probably kill me. I couldn't defeat it. Escaping the pit would get me nowhere.

A new despair crept up to smother my faintest glimmer of hope. I knew what it was, but I still had nothing to survive it.

"That's enough time," Mr. Smitty said, and the men burst

into a collective, savage shout. "In you go," he said, and with no more thought, he shoved me forward.

I couldn't help my cry as my feet slipped, and I fell. The shadowed torchlit ground rushed up, and I flung my useless hands out to fend it off. I hit the sand floor of the pit with a jar that sent shock waves of pain to reverberate through me. On my hands and knees, I looked past my fallen hair to the punta. Frightened, I tried to breathe quietly.

It was bigger now that I was down here with it, pressed against the sand walls atop a small rise. The air was markedly warmer, stagnant, and smelling of feces though I was sure the animal had been burying them as its smaller kin did. The top of the pit was about twenty feet across; down here it had shrunk to about fifteen. Bones with half-gnawed gristle and cartilage littered the sand among the confused tangle of webbed footprints the size of my outstretched hand. Black beetles skittered over the sand, scavenging. My attention went to its feet, seeing claws long as my fingers contract and extend in time with its breathing.

Ears back, it fixed its eerie blue eyes on me and growled so low that the sound seemed to resonate in me. I shifted to rise, freezing when its growl turned to a spine-tingling scream before falling back to a growl. The men shouted their approval, and the hair on the cat's stubby tail bristled farther. It didn't want to be here, and it wanted me here even less.

"Tess!" Duncan's voice cut through the noise. I only heard it because it was familiar. I risked a glance up, not seeing him. Above was only a black circle marked by the waxing moon. The men's jeers and shouts came down like the voices of unseen, angry gods.

I jerked at the sensations of tiny pinpricks atop my hand. It was a beetle the size of my palm, and I stupidly pulled myself upright to shake it from me.

Fire lanced through my upper arm. Crying out, I instinctively flung myself backwards. My back hit the sandy wall. The heady rush of venom scoured through me, and I took three quick breaths, walling it off. From above, the cheer of men sounded hollow through my venom-laced hearing. My heart pounded, and my skin tingled. It had scratched me. The punta had scratched me. I hadn't even seen it move.

Focus wavering as my body assimilated the poison, I looked to find the cat nearly in the same place. A new sheen of red was under its nails, glinting in the firelight as it moved its claws in and out of hiding. Empty blue eyes watched me. They were uncaring. There was no surprise that I hadn't fallen. No expectation. Nothing.

My hand had automatically covered the scratch. Slowly, I pulled it away. Under the tears in my dress were two long rips in my flesh. There would have been more but my arm wasn't as wide as its foot's spread. My skin was laid open in a soft welling of blood. The cat didn't seem to mind my moving now, probably thinking it had given me a killing dose and was expecting the twitches and jerks of a dying man. If I was going to move, now would be the time.

Breathing shallowly, I estimated the dosage to be three or four of my darts. Anyone but a player would be dead. One more bite or scratch, and it would be beyond even my limits.

The first cheer of the men faltered and died as they realized I hadn't gone down. "She's still up!" one said, as I stood and put a wavering hand against the wall of sand.

"It don't kill women!" another cried. "It don't kill women! She's a witch!"

He sounded panicked, and I spared a thought that if I survived, I would either be revered or stoned to death. Sailors were superstitious idiots. My focus blurred, then steadied. My left leg ached, and I knew it would drag if I tried to walk. It was where Kavenlow had desensitized me to the toxin, and the damage to my body showed there the most.

"Fool!" Mr. Smitty said, a tremor of fear in his voice. "It just missed her. That's all."

The cat screamed again, sounding confident, vindictive, and angry. Its whiskers bent forward, then back as it sniffed me, smelling my blood. From the back recesses of my mind came a faint tickle. Its eyes met mine, and I wondered if it was seeing me as something other than a warm body to take its anger out on, then bury to eat later once I stopped twitching.

The tickle in my head turned into a soft, insistent push. My eyes went to a still-burning torch. Maybe I could use it. But I'd have to reach to get it.

My attention flicked back to the cat, estimating the distance.

The men were cheering, shouting encouragement. I wished I could have said good-bye to Duncan, to ask him to take care of Contessa for me and see her back safely to Kavenlow.

Balance wavering, I stood with one hand on the sand walls for support and prayed the animal wouldn't move. "My whip!" I called up, knowing it was a lost cause. "For the love of God, give me something!"

Captain Rylan's voice came down, full of a self-satisfied dominance. "That will change her odds. She gets nothing, or all wagers are returned."

But there was a sliding clatter of an enormous sword as long as my leg falling to land closer to the cat than me. It was old and notched, as if having been used to cut wood. From above me came laughter. I couldn't even pick it up. All it did was enrage the cat further.

It started a low growl again, its tawny hide rippling when kicked sand fell on it. I couldn't fight it. But I had something that poor Gilly hadn't. I had my magic. And with venom from the large cat coursing through me, it would be strong. Perhaps strong enough.

Closing my eyes, I pulled myself straight. I settled my mind and sent a tendril of awareness to the back recesses of thought where my magic slowly accumulated, walled off from the rest of me so it wouldn't kill me. Reaching the mind of a wild animal was tricky at best. The reason I could manipulate Jy was from our frequent association and because he thought I was his lead mare. And the punta, whose poison was a natural part of its body, would be immune to all but the strongest of impulses, much as I was immune to a rival player's mental persuasion—to a certain degree.

"Fight it!" came the jeering call of a pirate. "I didn't give up my chance at ya to watch you die of starvation!"

The sound of spilling sand pulled my eyes open. They were trying to force the cat into action. Disoriented, I sent my thoughts out to the cat, hoping I could find it among the aggressive emotions of the crew. With a jolt, I found it was already searching for me.

Shocked, my breath came in a gasp and I shuddered. Time seemed to slow, and the rush of my blood paused. My heart beat once, the slow contraction of muscle as definite and sedate as a sigh. My eyes were fixed upon the cat, and suddenly the dead blue of its eyes lit with an inner fire that only I could see.

The jolt of connection fed back into me, rebounding against my soul and reverberating up my spine. Abruptly I saw it through its own perceptions: a force so free, it couldn't comprehend being any other way—untamed, trapped, insulted, chained, powerful, a killer, but not knowing what that meant or even thinking to justify it.

My heart beat again—a spasm of slow motion—and my thoughts were swallowed. Now his emotion flooded me, mixing in a slurry to make the clearest mind doubt its sanity. Anger, pure and honest, roared through me. Faint in the far reaches of my mind, farther back than even a race memory might even exist, I felt my own emotions of fear of the future, determination to survive, and a growing need to escape. But my desires weren't mine alone anymore. The cat was feeling them, too.

Again, my heart beat. My body sagged in shock. I saw myself, leaning against the wall. I seemed taller than I really was, a source of noise and fear, something I was unable to understand. All I wanted was to be free of it. If I could bring myself to get closer . . . if I could sink my teeth into it, it would stop moving. *Why?* I thought. *Why wouldn't it go away?*

A fourth beat of my heart, and I gasped, finding myself back within myself. The punta was in a crouch, shaking its head and biting at the air, screaming in his inability to comprehend.

Above us the roar of the men, thinking he was going to attack, beat down like a wave. I could see his confusion now as clearly as if I had raised him from a cub. I cowered at the noise, as did the cat. Wonder and fear joined my confusion when I realized what had happened. We had shared too deeply, becoming each other for an instant.

My heart raced for what we had done. The cat howled in pain, and with that, I realized we were still connected. I understood what had happened and had been able to find and reclaim my thoughts and emotions. The cat was still floundering, still existing in that insane, maddening mix of selves. The fervor in his eyes told me he was ready to break. His natural fear, multiplied by my own, had pushed him to where he would brave his instincts to attack me.

Immediately I forced my panic down. I had a chance. There was something here I could use. And when the cat calmed in response, I almost lost the thin link we had from excitement.

They are nothing, I thought, focusing on the idea that the men screaming down at us were beneath notice—and the cat panted, his fear receding. I listened for the sound of the wind in the trees, hearing it in my memory, if not for real—and the cat's ears came away from the sides of his head, and his eyes grew less intense. I recalled the feeling of clean water, the taste of it, the cool silky sensation across me—and his claws eased in and stayed retracted.

I slipped myself deeper into his mind, the way easier for having done this so many times with Jy. I knew the paths to take so I wouldn't be noticed and could nudge inattentive thoughts: the memory of tall grass, of sun on one's back, of a full belly and soft sounds of stable mates. I closed my eyes, and when I opened them, I was seeing through the punta's.

The jolt of confusion was muted. My pulse was slow, my breathing sedate. I took three breaths and held them, breathing as the punta did and finding it natural and comfortable. I could see myself, still standing with one hand against the wall. I willed myself to drop my hand, and because the idea was echoed in the cat's mind, he thought he had willed me to move and didn't mind. Thanks to the overdose of venom, it was the deepest connection I had ever achieved.

From above, I heard Duncan whispering. His voice was audible through the punta's ears, but his words were a confusing slur of uncomfortable sound. I willed the punta to look up, and my control bobbled when I saw Duncan through the punta's more sensitive eyes. I gave the punta an emotion of fear-for-another to label the look upon his long face.

The punta's thoughts went confused, not understanding how one could be afraid for someone other than oneself. Uncertainty rumbled through him, and I washed the feeling of caring for young and one's mate into it, and he relaxed. A faint rumble rose. His claws were again moving in and out, but he was purring in the memory of a sunlit den and the smell of young fur. The stagnant air of the pit seemed warm from the sun and heated rock.

Seeing myself through the punta's eyes, I willed myself to

take a step forward. If I could prove that the punta wouldn't harm me, they'd let me out. *Wouldn't they?*

It was an odd sensation—a feeling of disconnection, of unbalance, a taste of confusion on the back of my throat. I was so deep into the punta's thoughts that I couldn't feel the earth under my feet. Struggling for balance, I felt my claws dig into the sand as I took another, then another step.

A soft murmur of men's voices broke over us. Slowly the awestruck sound rose higher until it died away to leave only frightened whispers. The punta didn't like this any better than the shouts, and I nudged the memory of waves on the sand into their place, calming him.

The punta's purr became louder and the men's voices more intent. He didn't mind when the tall, noisy animal coming toward him raised her arm and reached for him since he thought it had been his idea she should. It would feel good if she touched him, her soft, dull claws raking through his fur. Not as good as a mate's tongue across the underside of his jaw, but good.

His thoughts and mine mixed freely, me consciously nudging his and losing myself further the deeper I sank. I couldn't feel my shoulders ease, but I saw them through his eyes. I never felt my eyes slip shut, but the confusing mix eased into one vision of grays and yellows.

Carefully, almost having forgotten what I was trying to do, I suggested that the punta would like the animal that smelled of smoke to touch his head. I waited, forcing my arm to remain still. Again, I sent the thought, and a hint of annoyance went through him. *Why hasn't she sent her nails against my skin?*

Watching through his eyes, I sent my hand out. It was shaking, and it surprised me how brown it was. My fingers were long and weak-looking, useless in their bendability. The men above me were utterly silent. It was as if the world were holding its breath.

My fingers touched him, and a collective breath rose from the top of the pit. His fur was softer than water, warmer than sunlight. I dug my fingers through it, making him flick his ear. He willed me to scratch his chin, and my other arm rose to take his massive jaw between my hands.

He had willed it, not me. It had been his thought, not mine.

A frightened sound settled over us from the top of the pit, indecipherable to me now as we were connected so closely.

He had willed it, rose the thought in me again. He had willed it. That wasn't right. It had been him leading me, not the other way around. That wasn't . . . right.

He had willed it, came my thought once more, even as I sent my nails to rake the underside of his chin, my fingers brushing huge canines longer than my hand. My eyes opened, and in the confusing double sight, I could see the grooves where venom would run, etching his teeth.

The punta stopped purring. His ears flicked back, hearing the rising tide of men's voices, swelling in their fear. My hand kept moving, though I willed it to stop. Fear slid through me; I couldn't move away. I wasn't in control any longer. I was the bound. I was the charmed.

Panic bubbled through me, washing away the contentment I had been basking in. I felt the ribbon of connection start to fray, shredded by fear.

"She's bewitched it!" came a voice, and the punta's terror of having understood the spoken words reverberated between us.

My muscles spasmed, and I fell, as control over my body returned. Pain, like molten metal, ran through me. I cried out and the cat screamed with me. Then he attacked.

His canines sank into my shoulder. Fire itself could hurt no more. Venom poured into me. I stiffened, my mouth opening in a silent scream. My eyes bulged, and my throat closed lest I cry my last breath out in the agony of existence. The cat screamed with me. We no longer saw through each other's eyes, but he felt my pain, and I reeled under his confusion. The link wasn't broken, it had only been knocked into a state of confusion.

"Tess!" Duncan exclaimed, and the punta screamed again, understanding everything.

The punta wanted out. He wanted the peace I had given him, now frenzied by the memory I had returned to him that he had all but forgotten. A memory of clean air, wide spaces, and silence but for the wind.

His need to be free of the pit hammered at me, joining my own desire and rebounding into him threefold. I reeled, though I was curled up on the sand, seizing at the venom in me. It was ice and fire. It set my skin to tingle. I could feel every grain of sand abrading my cheek. I could smell the salt from my tears as my body convulsed. My heart raced into a steady thrum, and my blood was a current of power to burn my brain. I was going to die.

The punta, who had never considered what death was, screamed to the uncaring moon. The thought that the sun would never rise for him again had never occurred to him. The realization of death is a terrible thing for an animal to learn. Delving into my mind to try to understand, the punta learned from me the way of his coming death—alone and miserable at the bottom of the pit to be skinned and shown off.

His despair raged through me, so thick and choking that I couldn't breathe even if I had been able to stop convulsing enough to make my lungs work. He hadn't known of death. From me, he saw the end of his existence and understood.

I couldn't bear the thought that we both die. *Perhaps,* I thought, as my mind started to slow and my thoughts became disconnected. Perhaps I could find some grace in my death if I could save him. To pass from the earth knowing I had freed him might put my soul to rest.

As I shook and suffocated, unable to breathe, I wedged into his pain-racked, disjointed thoughts the image of him using my curled up, shifting body as a springboard. It was only a foot higher off the ground, but it might be enough. I showed him a vision of him springing from me at the men he hated, his big paws digging into the top of the hole, his haunches raking the side of the pit until he pulled himself up. I saw him in my thoughts scattering the men like mice, of him running from the torches and noise. And I saw him swimming, with his wonderfully webbed toes, to the setting sun, never stopping until he found the coast and the solitude of the mountains.

And the punta believed. It had been fear of what lay outside the pit that had kept him from trying before. Now, with my vision and understanding, he was willing to brave it.

A groan of pain slipped past my clenched teeth as the weight of him landed upon me and forced the air from my lungs. Then his weight was gone and my lungs rebounded, filling my chest with life-giving air though my muscles were clenched with an immovable strength. My mind cleared in the influx of new air long enough to hear the screaming of men and recognize the sudden absence of the punta's thoughts in my own. Distance had severed what I hadn't been able to. Then the blackness overwhelmed even that, and I slipped into a painless nothing.

My last thought was that I hoped I managed to leave a memory of me within the punta so he wouldn't be alone when he thought of death again.

nine

✤

It was emotion that returned to me first. Loss and heartache, a fury born of helplessness and lack of choice. The chaotic slurry was confusing. It didn't fit with what I remembered last. I knew the feelings were mine, and I would have tried to figure the incongruity out but that a new sensation was edging into comprehensibility.

The sound of wind and water became clear, and the choppy movement of a small boat in rough water. It was then I realized it was a dream, but like no dream I'd had before. I was conscious, my mind weighing the sensations and visions against logic and understanding rather than me simply accepting the more nebulous dream-state.

With that, it was as if a fog lifted from me, and the chaotic sensations swirled into something recognizable. I was a mere foot above angry waves on a raft made from barrels and torn sailcloth, and what looked like a door? My feelings of anger and stymied desires rose high, and I tasted the emotions as though they were someone else's. The wind streamed my hair out before me to make it hard to see, but I wasn't cold.

My hands were bound with black silk, and Jeck, the captain of the Misdev guards, was sitting cross-legged before me, tired and uncaring while the sun went down in the windy, cloudless evening of purple and gold. His pant legs were rolled to his knees, and his bare feet had fallen through a crack to rest in the water below. He watched me with dark, serious eyes as we bobbed. My angry emotions stemmed from him, which wasn't surprising since I seemed to be his prisoner.

Stingrays rose and sank about us, seeming to fly just under the surface. One flipped out of the water entirely, making an ungainly splash. I reached to wipe the salt water away with my shoulder, and the wind died.

The dream changed.

The rocking of the raft turned to the swaying of a horse. I was sitting before Jeck, my palms red and swollen. His black-uniformed arm was wrapped about me, imprisoning me, keeping me from running away. The salt water on my face had become tears leaking out in a steady stream. Feelings of heartache, betrayal, and bitterness had replaced my anger. Again I was Jeck's captive, but this time my anger had sunk to self-recrimination. I hated the pity coursing through me. Jeck was silent, but I could sense the tension of unhappiness and words unsaid in him. The horse under us stumbled. I clutched at his arm to keep from falling off, and the cold forest we rode through vanished.

Again the motion of a boat challenged my balance, but this time it was the long, slow swells of a ship at sea. For the first time, I felt comfortable with the motion, standing with my feet spread wide and holding on to nothing as I held a hand above my eyes and squinted at the horizon, painfully bright with sunrise. The wind pushed me, and impatience was a goad. It was my fault. I should have known better. Kavenlow would rightly think I was an incompetent fool.

I smelled burned wood and resin over the stink of men and strong tea. A cup was in my free hand, and my face went cold as I stared at it. It wasn't my hand. The fingers were too muscular, and the knuckles were too big, with a fine tracing of dark hair. The deck was farther away than it ought to be; I was too tall. Unfamiliar boots, terribly large, were on my feet. I was dressed in expensive black leather and linen: a Misdev uniform.

"Which tack do you think the bastards took, Captain?" a familiar voice asked, and my pulse raced. It was Captain Borlett, his gravelly voice tight in anger. I didn't look at him, afraid of what I'd see. I pointed to where the pirate's island lay, and panic slid through me as I recognized Jeck's more elaborate uniform upon my arm that wasn't mine. *Am I dead? Am I a ghost sent to guide Jeck to find us so my soul could rest?*

By all that is holy! I felt in my thoughts, the scent of Jeck's leather jerkin cascading through me. *Tess? You're alive?*

I jerked upon hearing my name in my thoughts said by someone else. *I was in Jeck. Heaven help me, I was in Jeck's mind!*

Jeck spasmed, spilling his drink. He pressed it into Captain Borlett's hands and staggered to the aft hatch. I felt the smooth wood against Jeck's hand, and the blackness under the deck blinded my sun-struck eyes.

A sudden, real pain shocked me from my dream. I clenched, hearing a thin groan of agony. My heart raced, and my muscles cramped with a mind-numbing agony.

"No, Tess," Duncan's voice intruded, real and insistent, full of a sympathetic regret. "You're alive," he whispered. "I'm sorry. I know it hurts, but I have to loosen your bandage again— just for a moment—or you might lose your arm."

It had been the overwhelming pain that pulled me from my dream. I reached for the nothing of unconsciousness, finding it taken from me. Hearing my breath rasping and ugly, I opened my eyes to find Duncan kneeling beside me.

I was in a hut, the light dim and the air stale. His hands were pressed against a bandage atop my shoulder where the cat had bitten me. I tried, but I couldn't speak. The pain from my shoulder took everything from me. His eyes pinched in apology, Duncan loosened his grip. My blood became fire. I managed a gasping moan, my eyes closing in misery, and I shook.

"I'm sorry, Tess . . ." he whispered, as my body started to jerk. I couldn't feel my arm or fingers. I instinctively fell into the breathing pattern Kavenlow taught me when I had been building up my resistance to the venom so many years ago. It made no difference. The agony was too much and lasted too long for my mind to endure. I was going to pass out.

I fixed my blurring gaze to Duncan, wanting to tell him I was sorry for not trusting him. I wanted my last sight—should I not wake up—to be of him. It was with an overwhelming feeling of relief and a tinge of guilt that the blackness overtook me, and the pain vanished.

Between one struggling breath and the next, I was back in a dream, my mind seizing the release from pain though I knew it lurked nearby, waiting to claim me. I was on a horse again, back in the same woods, the icy cold bite of melted snow replacing the stink of my sweat and fear of dying. The slow thuds of hoofbeats were soothing, like the pace my heart should be. The track was soft and damp, giving easily under the animal's pace. It came as no surprise that it was Jy I rode.

This time my cheeks were dry and my hands unburned. But Jeck was still behind me, giving me the impression of a wall with his heavy muscles hardened by long practice with a sword and the quiet demeanor that hid his intelligence.

Anything was better than the agony of my reality, so I eased back into his warmth. *It is only a dream,* I told myself and, allowing myself a small fantasy, breathed deeply, taking in the delicious scent of horse and leather. I was hurt and in pain; I would take my comfort where I could. And there was little that could instill more security than a pair of masculine arms about oneself, even if it was a dream. The memory of his backhanded compliment over dinner intruded, setting my thoughts to a softer bent. Jeck's front was warm, and I molded myself to him further, feeling his grip about me gentle.

Shoulders easing, I paid more attention to the thick woods than Jeck's arm wrapped comfortably about me. It was early, just past sunrise, cold and smelling of rain recently fallen. I was mildly curious to realize I was sitting far up upon Jy's withers, my feet politely on one side of him—I usually rode like a man. There was no saddle, making everything unreasonably difficult. The scent and creak of well-oiled leather was comforting, even if it stemmed from Jeck and not Duncan.

My thoughts flashed back to my cheat, the worry and fear in his eyes as he loosened my bandage and sent pain through me to save my life. I wanted to be angry with him since it had been his idea to put me in the pit with the punta, but he couldn't have known what it was, and he had seen me do amazing things in the past. And he had looked so worried as he tended me. The heartache that had filled me the first time I rode through this dream woods seemed to swell, pushing all else out. "I should have told you," I whispered. "I'm sorry. If I could have done anything different, I would have told you."

"Told me what?" Jeck said, his masculine voice echoing up through me where my back met his chest.

Surprised he had spoken, I twisted. The keen awareness of his eyes from under his parade hat decked with black feathers jerked me straight. His presence in my dream was as eerily aware and comprehending as mine. I would have fallen off Jy if the man hadn't tightened his grip on me. Suddenly, the warmth and comfort from him became a lie.

"Let go!" I shouted, squirming to get down, though it was my horse.

He pressed his lips, hiding them behind his neatly trimmed, jet-black beard and mustache. Annoyance flickered in his brown eyes. Muscles bunched in his shoulders, and he bodily lifted me and set me back atop Jy. The horse nickered, shying.

Undeterred, I swung the flat of my hand at him. He caught it, gripping my wrist where the ropes had burned them and sending new tendrils of dream-pain up my arm.

"Stop it," he said calmly, bringing to mind the first time we had shared a horse. He had swooped down out of nowhere and abducted me, riding off with me across his horse's shoulders.

"Then get off my horse!" I demanded, pulse fast.

"I can't," he said, eyes narrowing. "Believe me, if I could, I would."

The surprise of that stopped me cold. "You can't?" I asked, and he released my wrist.

"This is your prophetic dream, not mine—I think. It would be better to play it out and try to learn something rather than to give in to your natural tendencies to hit me and run away."

"I wouldn't run away," I said while I rubbed my wrists, though I probably would have. I didn't trust him, and he knew it.

Jeck said nothing, not even a sigh, and I shifted atop my horse to try to find a more comfortable position. Immediately I slid back into Jeck as his hands were no longer around me. We walked through a patch of early-morning sun that had found its way through the canopy, and I watched the glimmer of light upon his quiet face, reading nothing but a tired worry.

"Prophetic dream?" I asked. "Is that why everything is so real?"

"What the hell is Kavenlow teaching you? How to crochet doilies?" he muttered.

It was condescending, prompting a quick, "He said I shouldn't trust prophetic dreams. That they could be manipulated by your unconscious to give you false truths. What the chu pits are you doing in my dream, anyway?" It was rougher than I had intended, but I let the emotion stand without any softening. I was thoroughly embarrassed. I had been snuggled up to him as if I enjoyed it. Well, I had, but that wasn't the point. He was a rival player. Not only was it inappropriate, but it could get me killed.

Jeck searched the underside of the canopy with his eyes, reaching to keep his elaborate dress hat atop his head. I knew he hated the black-and-gold monstrosity with the drooping feathers across his back even as he wore it without fail to official functions. "I have no idea why I'm here," he finally said, not meeting my eyes. "But he's right. Unless you know what you're doing, a prophetic dream will do more harm than good. It's possible to make some use of them if you handle them properly."

"How do you handle them?" I asked, thinking it was only a boast.

"Are you my apprentice?" he shot back.

Embarrassment turned to an old anger. "Never mind." Peeved, I stared ahead, slipping backwards into him inch by inch as Jy plodded forward. I'd ask Kavenlow. If I survived. But if this was a prophetic dream, than it seemed likely I'd live past my punta bite. Somehow.

Jeck was silent, then slowly offered, "The skill lies in interacting as little as possible. Behave as if you're an observer, not part of it. Letting things happen and doing what feels right, even if it's something you normally wouldn't do. You can't partake of the future properly with only the memories of today."

I didn't understand, and I wondered if he was being nebulous with the intent to make me feel stupid. Hearing my silence, he added, "What I mean is we started this with my arm about your waist, holding you. If you won't hit me, I'll put my hand back, and we'll be closer to the true future than we are now."

My eyes narrowed, but it was hard to stay on Jy without a proper saddle, so I nodded. The memory of how I had curved my body to fit his rose high, and I recalled the sensation of protection I had felt. *And it had all been in my mind,* I thought.

His arm went about me hesitantly, with an imprisoning strength equal to that when he had abducted me. I looked at his hand, its tanned length holding me firmly. There was a flash of rightness, then it faded. "Not so tight," I whispered, only some of my nervousness due to the fact that I was starting to understand what he meant. The rest stemmed from his holding me at all.

"I thought so, too," he breathed, and his fingers loosened. The lighter grip imparted an uncomfortable feeling of intimacy. Even worse was that I could feel the rightness of it, almost like bolts sliding into place. I knew if I leaned back into him, setting my head against his cheek, that it would feel even more right, but I wasn't going to do it.

Instead, I handed Jeck the reins though I didn't want to. "Yes," he said softly, the one arm of his clean uniform reaching past me. "That's better."

"What else?" I asked softly so he wouldn't hear my voice tremble. I felt sick, my emotions conflicting horribly as I was experiencing both my real feelings of unease and fear and my dream emotions of a bitter anger, betrayal, and recrimination. I wondered if Jeck was suffering through the same thing.

"I don't know," he answered. "We won't get the conversation right, but this?" He took a slow breath, his chest pressing into me for an instant before he pulled back. "This will happen."

He sounded as unhappy as I felt, and I was glad the brief flash of the raft with my hands bound before me had been wholly my experience and not his as well. As least I thought it was only my vision; the Jeck aboard the raft lacked the awareness that this one had. But the voice in my head aboard the *Sandpiper* had been his.

"The dream aboard the *Sandpiper*?" I prompted hesitantly.

"That wasn't a dream," he said, tension lacing his deep voice. "That is now."

"But it's not possible to share thoughts," I stammered, wondering if my frequent use of him as a subject to follow emotions had sensitized me to him more than was prudent.

I turned to face him, but he wouldn't look up from the leaves, the muscles of his square jaw tightening and relaxing as his thoughts shifted. "No, it isn't," he finally said.

"We're sharing them now," I protested.

Jeck's eyes flicked to mine and away. "As soon as I realized what was going on, I went belowdecks and dosed myself to my limit on venom," he said, his voice soft and carrying a new, unfamiliar vulnerability and reluctance. "Just how much venom did you give yourself trying to find me? You're a fool. You know that, don't you?"

Now it was my turn to look away, though I thought I heard a sliver of astonished admiration in his words. "I wasn't trying to find you," I said, barely above a whisper. "The pirates threw me into a pit with a punta. It bit me before I got it out."

Jeck's breath audibly caught, and his grip about me tensed.

"I think I'm dying," I said in a small voice. "I don't know why I'm still alive, except that Duncan has wrapped my shoulder and is slowly loosening it to release the venom in doses that I might survive."

The clop of Jy's hooves grew hard for a moment as we passed over a rockslide, then became soft again. "That's not enough alone to save you," Jeck said, his voice flat. "You were bitten in your shoulder?"

Fear stabbed through me, and my stomach churned. *I am alive,* I thought. *I am still alive.* "It scratched me, too." I reached up to it, surprised to find a small bandage and dull ache under my dress. Surprised, I fixed upon his eyes.

"It looks like you survived," he said, his face showing no emotion. "Let me see it. I want to know how long it's been healing."

"No," I said, afraid. I didn't want Jeck to know when he would capture me, ending the game my teacher had started. *I am alive. I will survive. The punta didn't kill me.*

Jeck shook the reins harshly. With no warning, he reached out and yanked my dress from my shoulder.

Gasping, I awkwardly backhanded him. The flat of my hand met his cheek, shocking through me, but even as I hit him, the cold spring air of the coast touched upon my new skin as he yanked the bandage aside. Glancing at my shoulder, he pulled the wrap back up to hide it.

Heart pounding, I sat on my horse, furious, as his hand gripped my waist again. "You touch me again, and I swear, I'll dart you in your sleep!" I shouted, incensed. There was a faint reddening beside his eye where my hand had hit him.

"I'd guess two weeks of unaided healing," he said calmly. Taking his hat off, he threw it into the scrub. "This is useless," he said. "With both of us aware and interacting, there's nothing left I can trust but that you and I end up on a horse together. I can't even pull any emotions from it anymore."

"Well, isn't that a shame," I mocked, still stinging from him having yanked my dress off my shoulder. "The big strong captain unable to steal anything from *my* prophetic dream."

Irritation creased his otherwise smooth brow. "I don't know why I care," he said. "Just shut up and hold still."

Breath catching, I shied away as he forced Jy's reins into my grip and reached for my shoulder. He stopped at my warning look and exhaled loudly. "I'm not going to hurt you," he said. "Pressure bandages aren't enough to survive a punta bite. If I don't do something, you'll be dead in two days. Or would you rather be dead than let me help you?"

A wash of fear pushed out my anger. Kavenlow had told me surviving a punta bite was impossible. Perhaps between Jeck's ability to heal and Duncan's pressure bandage, I could manage it. I didn't want to die. And the memory of the agony waiting for me when I woke up burned out much of my pride. If Jeck wanted to kill me, all he would have to do was nothing. I would have to trust that he would help.

Eyes fixed to his, I nodded, terribly unsure.

With a grunt of what sounded like surprise, Jeck gently placed his sun-browned hands to either side of my bare shoulder. I stiffened, feeling his masculine strength as he pressed until the soft throb turned to pain. My breath came in, shaking, and he eased up, his eye twitching.

Under me, Jy plodded forward, the thumps of his hooves jarring. Jeck exhaled, his gaze going vacant, as if slipping deeper within himself in intense thought. I tensed as he relaxed, hoping I might be able to steal from him the knowledge of how he healed with his hands since he wouldn't teach me, preferring to keep that particular carrot possibly to entice me from Kavenlow at some future date.

As my pulse hammered in expectation, a warm tingle replaced the ache of the bite. My shoulders slumped, and my eyelids drooped. Like warm water, it pulsed in a slow rhythm through me, and I wasn't surprised to find my breathing had matched Jeck's. It was like . . . being wrapped in a fire-warmed blanket, and I ignored the tiny thought of possible betrayal and just let it happen. It was comforting, and I needed comfort—even if it was a lie.

"My God," he whispered, and my eyes flew open, the peace he had instilled flicking to nothing. Fear slid through me when I caught a sliver of panic in his expression before he steeled it back to nothing. "There's so much," he added, his brown eyes unable to hide his shock.

I forced myself to be still under his hands, though a faint itch demanded I move. "Venom?" I guessed. Warmth was still coming from his hands, and I was reluctant to move. I could feel it spreading through me, touching on my scratched arm before dissolving into a general feeling of well-being.

"Even your residual levels are dangerously high," he answered, his voice slurred slightly. "I can't take it from you, but by speeding up the healing, I can wall it off in the tissues so it won't kill you. It's going to act like your thief's bandage. I'm sorry, but it's the best I can do."

His eyes met mine. Like a fog lifting from the harbor, his gaze cleared. His hands dropped from my shoulder. Still, my body tingled from his touch. Under it was the promise of the coming return of pain, but for now, it was gone.

"Thank you," I whispered, somehow even more frightened. *Why had he done it?* Kavenlow couldn't fault him for my dying from a punta bite. He was free and clear, and my death would further Jeck's game considerably since Kavenlow would be forced to divide his attention between the game and bringing up a new apprentice.

Jeck wouldn't look at me, taking the reins back from my slack fingers. "That you survived this long is a miracle," he muttered. I didn't think he had heard me, so deep in thought was he. "I don't know what that much venom is going to do to you."

"You saved my life," I breathed, my eyes going blurry as I refused to cry. "Thank you," I repeated, determined that he acknowledge my gratitude. My shoulder felt cold with his palms' absence, and I reached to touch it. The tingling was slipping into memory, leaving a faint, dull ache. It was the reality of my hurt shoulder slipping into our dream.

Seeming startled, Jeck met my eyes and looked away. "Don't thank me until you've talked to your teacher," he said cryptically.

I had slid back into him, and he was very close. My hand dropped, and I went frightened at his suddenly closed posture. "What is it?" I demanded. "What did you see?"

Jeck shook Jy's reins, but the horse never shifted his pace. "Your residual levels are too high," he said softly. "You can't play the game anymore."

My eyes widened. The breath in me turned to ash, and I found I couldn't breathe. The residual levels of toxin in a player rose slowly with time and repeated use of venom. Those same levels fell even slower when a player avoided using the toxin at all. It was the residual toxin that a player drew upon to perform magic unless he or she dosed up on venom to give his or her skills a temporary boost, as Jeck had done to join me in my dream.

But if my residual levels were too high, forced into an elevated state by the punta bite, then I was just as vulnerable to a rival player's dart as a commoner. One dart could kill me. I couldn't . . . Kavenlow wouldn't let me play the game.

The reality of my situation hit me like a sudden rain, drenching, to leave me shaking in a frightened anger. That's why he had done it. He had saved my life, but in the doing, made me useless for the game. "You did this on purpose!" I shouted. "Is that why you helped me? You knew I couldn't play the game if my residual levels were too high!"

"Don't blame this on me," Jeck said, red-faced and stiff as he yelled back at me in a voice barely above a whisper. "I'm not the one who threw you into a pit with a punta. I just saved your life, princess. That your residual levels are elevated is not my problem."

I could feel the heat of anger coming from him, but that paled in importance as I sat on Jy watching my life fall apart even as I regained it. If I couldn't play the game, what was left to me? *Kavenlow,* I thought, my heart clenching. I couldn't be his apprentice if I couldn't handle toxin.

Fear took me then, real and debilitating. He would have to abandon me. He needed someone to succeed him in his game, and if one dart would kill me, I was worth less than nothing. All the pain and sacrifices would mean nothing. Jeck might as well have let me die.

I swallowed hard, not wanting him to know how scared I was. "Residual levels drop," I whispered, knowing my eyes were panic-stricken when I met Jeck's, and he jerked his attention away. And by the tightening of his lips, I knew the more experienced player thought they'd never drop soon enough for me ever to take up the game again.

"Of course they do," he said, but he wouldn't bring his gaze to me. "It will just take time. What I didn't trap in your healing tissues has already started to work itself out, but your teacher will need to evaluate your new level of residual toxin very carefully."

How am I going to tell Kavenlow? "How long do you think it will take?" I said, gaze blurring on the passing vegetation, bright with the morning sun.

Jeck was silent, the jostling of the horse shifting me back into him. "Several years, I'd guess," he lied. I could hear it in his voice, feel it in his emotions I was picking up whether I wanted to or not.

"A year or two," I breathed, knowing a decade or two was more likely. God save me, I was going to lose everything I'd worked my life for.

My breathing went ragged, and I gritted my teeth, refusing to cry. He was wrong. There was no way to survive a punta bite, so I must have gotten less venom than he said. My levels would drop sooner than he thought. Slowly I straightened, taking a deep breath and looking ahead down the sun-dappled path. Jeck took in my new posture and sighed heavily.

"How long is this dream going to last?" I said, cursing the quaver that remained in my voice. *He isn't that much older than I. How can he know how much venom I had?*

"I don't know." He shook Jy's reins as the animal tried to snag a quick bite of thin grass by the edge of the path.

The memory of feeling his arms securely about me, comforting but not binding, rose high, and I cursed myself for wanting to feel them again. I recognized the desire for what it was—a desperate reach for something safe when my world was falling apart. Duncan would have held me the same way, had I let him. *But Duncan isn't here,* my thoughts prompted.

I shivered, refusing to slip back into his warmth. Jy plodded forward into the darkening forest, and Jeck didn't put his hands back about me.

It was going to be a long night until I woke up.

Ten

❖

"*You just put down what I said,*" Captain Rylan demanded, stirring me from my restless, pained sleep. I left unconsciousness reluctantly. It was my only escape from the throbbing agony my right arm had become. I couldn't feel my shoulder, but my uninjured arm and my entire right side were pulsating waves of fire. Jeck had hastened my healing, and I couldn't imagine what it would feel like if he hadn't. *I am alive.*

"If I scribe what you say, he won't believe it's me," Contessa snapped. "Your syntax is that of a gutter worm."

"You sorry little wench," he growled. I heard a jingle of bells followed by a feminine gasp. I would have sat up if I could have moved. I wasn't even sure if what I was hearing was another dream or my nightmarish reality.

"Go ahead," Contessa said belligerently, and I managed to crack an eyelid. Squinting, I saw a rumpled blanket, and beyond that, the sand bright with sun. By the sound of it, Contessa was behind me somewhere, and I could clearly imagine the fire in her eyes and the clench of her jaw that reminded me so much of our mother. "Hit me," she threatened, "and you won't get your letter until tomorrow after I stop crying."

It was obvious her temper had put her far beyond tears, but her threat was real enough. She had already proven she could fall into hysterics—whether real or contrived—and stay there for hours. For the first time, I appreciated how her fishwife temperament gave her strength. *Alex,* I thought, *must be getting better.*

I shifted my head, enduring the slivers of pain in my neck to gain an inch-high view of the compound. I was lying in the open, a wool blanket over me and the dappled sun making shifting patterns on the shadow-cold sand. It was late afternoon I'd guess, and the seabirds were quiet. To roll over and see Contessa was beyond me. I hadn't known it was possible to hurt this badly and still be alive. At least when Kavenlow had been building my resistance to the toxin, I'd only suffered pinpricks, not a mauling.

Captain Rylan made a rude grunt. I heard the rustle of silk, and I imagined he had let go of her and moved away. "You just write that I want a wagon of coin and spice. And free passage for it and my man to outside the city. I don't care how you say it. Anything happens to my man, and I'll send your heads back to your Chancellor and Admiral."

My stomach was a hollow ache of hunger and my lips were cracked. There was a shallow bowl of water nearby, and the faint movement of tiny flies about the rim attracted me. Several were floating on the surface, their wings acting like little sails as they struggled to break from the water. Apparently surviving the punta had granted me a measure of respect. The pirates wouldn't let me die of dehydration.

My tongue scraped the inside of my mouth. I wanted that water, flies and all. My good arm was pinned between me and the sand. To shift onto my stomach was too much to ask.

Holding my breath against the expected pain, I tentatively tried to move the fingers of my right hand. The dull throbs of pain burst into shimmering sparkles—and they shifted. I couldn't feel my fingers against the rough wool, but tears of relief pricked my eyes; my arm wasn't paralyzed. Slowly I let my held breath out, the hurt clenching my stomach until I felt nauseous.

I wanted to reach up and touch my shoulder, but now even the slight movement of my breathing made things worse. Dull throbs ran down my arm and side. *I am alive,* I thought. I had been bitten by a punta and survived. Through Duncan's pressure bandage to wall off the poison and Jeck doing the same by speeding my healing, I lived. My residual toxin levels would eventually drop, and Kavenlow wouldn't abandon me in the time between then and now.

I lay on the sand in the shade with the chill wind off the water gusting over me, trying to keep my breathing slow and shallow as I listened to Contessa's quill scratching. Slowly, the nausea eased, and my shoulders relaxed. I stared at the bowl past the lank strands of my hair, wanting it more than I had wanted anything in my life.

"Here," she said belligerently. "And mind you don't smear the ink."

"My God," he swore, boot bell's chiming. "You're a pushy dock-chull of a woman."

"And you're a worthless gutter-down, not even worth calling a man." It was loud, and I heard a stirring from somewhere behind me. I recognized Alex's breath quickening as he woke.

"Read it to me," Captain Rylan demanded.

"May I skip the preliminaries?" she asked, her voice softer, but still tart. There was a hesitation, then she said, "My Respected Chancellor Kavenlow. Alex, Tess, and I have been taken by"—she paused—"men intent on ransom. They would ask that you allow their representative safe and unhindered passage in and out of the city. Give him as much free coin and spice as will fill a wagon of his choice and do not molest him in any way. When he reaches the safety of his comrades, Alex, Tess, and I will be released. If you do not do this, he will send our heads to you."

My breath caught at that. I was to be freed? But my brief hope vanished when Captain Rylan said, "Cross off her name. She's mine."

"I thought she was Duncan's," Contessa said. "He bet his take she would survive."

"She hasn't survived yet." His voice was low with a dark promise. "Cross her off."

I heard the scratch of a quill. "There now," he mocked. "You can be properly obedient."

To Contessa's credit, she stayed silent, though I could almost see her narrow chin trembling in anger.

"You," Captain Rylan said loudly, and a pang of fear went through me. The sound of jingling bells grew loud as he approached. He was talking to me. "Wake up."

"Leave my sister alone!" Contessa cried, and I heard Alex sit up and murmur for her to be still and that she couldn't help me by antagonizing him.

"One more word outta your mouth," the captain said calmly, "and I'll have Mr. Smitty tie you so you can't reach either of them."

"Captain Rylan!" came Duncan's distant call, followed by the sound of his steps in the sand. I kept my eyes shut, praying the captain would go away. I felt as if the pain would break me apart if he touched me.

"She isn't yours yet!" Captain Rylan retorted loudly. "That poison could still drop her."

"It will if you keep moving her," Duncan said, his voice thick with a cautious anger tempered with respect. "This is the first natural sleep she's found. I won her. She's mine."

The hesitation had been obvious, but Captain Rylan took less offense than I'd have expected, sighing with a tired patience rather than cuffing Duncan for the insolence. "Duncan?" he said, his tone fatherly. "I'm saving you from yourself, boy. She's a woman, and there hasn't been a woman born yet that was worth more than a tumble in bed."

"Tess isn't like that," Duncan retorted, and I felt a wash of gratitude. "She's smart. Her eyes are sharp, and she isn't afraid to do what's necessary. The things I've seen her do are amazing. You saw her in that pit. Just imagine—"

"I know her kind," the captain interrupted. "She won't be swayed from her kin, boy, for love or money or respect. Start thinking with your head instead of your third leg. This isn't going to work no matter how bad you want it. Soon as I find a way to get rid of her without setting Mr. Smitty and his men off on a superstitious fit, she goes. Surviving a bite that killed a drunken man does not give her power to curse them. Damn fool sea rats."

"Captain . . ."

"Wake up!" This last was directed at me, and I couldn't stop my groan when a jingling, booted foot nudged the small of my back. "I've got something I want you to read."

"Please stop," I whispered, my eyes shut and breathing shallow through the pain.

"Get her up," Captain Rylan growled.

The sand before me shifted, and I opened my eyes. Duncan

was kneeling before me. "Sorry, Tess," he said, his eyes pinched. "Sit up. I'll get you some water."

It was the carrot of water that solidified my will. With Duncan's help, I managed to rise. He shifted my legs for me as I was too weak, and he moved my arm like it was a dead thing, setting it in my lap. I gritted my teeth and focused on the swaying fronds until the fire and needles subsided. It left a steady burning sensation through my entire right side.

Duncan watched my eyes carefully as I panted through the last of the pain, his expression worried. Seeing I was upright and had my balance, he extended the bowl.

I grasped it, sucking in the water with a hungry sound. It was warm and tepid, tasting of husks. I didn't care.

"That's enough," Captain Rylan said, and I caught sight of his legs to my right. His shadow fell over me, and I ran my gaze up his worn finery while I drank, thinking it looked ridiculous out here on the sand.

Duncan tried to take the bowl, and my eyes went to his over the edge of it. I wouldn't let go, and Duncan whispered, "Give it to me, or he'll likely kick it out of my hands."

Reluctantly, I loosened my grip, my eyes never leaving the bowl as Duncan set it aside out of Captain Rylan's reach. My cracked lips stung, and I licked them.

"Read this," the short man demanded, Contessa's letter extended.

My left hand shook uncontrollably as I took it from his soft, many-ringed hand. I glanced past him to Contessa. She was sitting upright with Alex, and I tried to smile at her, finding myself unable to do anything but simply breathe. The weight of my body seemed to press into me, making just working my lungs seem like a chore. Contessa's eyes were wide and haunted, her lips parted and her face ashen. *I must look like a beaten dog in the gutter,* I thought.

Alex rested in her arms, propped up and seeming as weak as a kitten, pale and drawn. But his eyes were clear, and his lips behind his new beard were pressed tightly. The fever was gone. He would live. Captain Rylan moved to block my view. "Aloud?" he prompted.

I focused on the paper, reading Contessa's careful script very quickly. It told Kavenlow that we were likely to be a day's sail north or south of the capital in a few days' time, and that he should take all action to retrieve us. She and Alex had decided that under no circumstances should the ransom be paid since it would only lead to more attempts to capture them in the future. She asked that if the worst happened, that the king of Misdev be told that the true worth of the Misdev blood showed itself, and that Alex was brought down by overwhelming numbers and mortal weakness, not that of spirit, and that she was proud to have died beside such a noble man of such a high swordsmanship. At the bottom, the word *together* had been crossed off.

"Read it!" Captain Rylan prompted, his foot in my ribs making me jump. A blanket of pain dimmed my vision, and I wavered where I sat.

"It says we have been taken for ransom," I said, shocked at how raspy my voice was. "It says to give a wagon of coin and spice to your man, and that if they molest him in any way, you will send our heads back to them." I looked up, squinting. "Why is my name crossed off?"

"Because you aren't going back," he said. "You belong to Duncan." His even gaze went to Duncan, not a shade of his lie showing. "Take it up with him."

He bent at the waist to snatch the letter from me, and I entertained a brief thought of how easy it would be to break his nose with the heel of my hand—if I could move. My chin dropped to my chest, and I concentrated on breathing. Even with my gaze down, I could see the confident, cocksure jingling walk as Captain Rylan went to the central cooking fire, yelling for Mr. Smitty all the way.

Duncan dropped down beside me. I looked first at him, then past him to Contessa and Alex. I gave her what I hoped was an encouraging smile. She had been shackled and couldn't reach me. "Water?" I asked. My throat felt raw, and I held my breath so I wouldn't cough and accidentally kill myself.

I held the bowl with my one good hand, his fingers over mine to steady it as I was shaking again. It seemed terribly heavy, and after the first few gulps I watched his eyes. They were fixed tight on what he was doing, tired and worried. Guilt joined my pain. He was a good man. Keeping the reality of the game from him was an insult. I gently pushed on the bowl, and Duncan lowered it.

"Tess, you're going to be all right," he said, his smile tinged with an overwhelming relief.

"Duncan," I started. "If I don't make it—"

"Shhhh," he whispered. "None of that." He scooted closer, a sly glint coming into his gaze. "You're mine, now, and you have to do what I say. I won you fairly."

I almost laughed, catching it when the fingers of pain worsened. Black spots danced before my eyes, and I quickly sobered. He reached for my bandage, and I drew back, frightened.

"Let me check it, Tess," he insisted, brow pinched. "No infection so far. It's a miracle."

"That's nothing compared to surviving at all," I said, feeling a rush of gratitude. "Thank you. What you did probably saved my life."

He shrugged, his long face looking embarrassed. "I just remembered what you tried to do when I pricked my finger on one of your darts."

"You remember?" I questioned, thinking Kavenlow wasn't as good at manipulating memories as he thought he was.

"I almost died." His brown eyes were very intent upon my shoulder as he loosened the knots holding my dress closed and picked carefully at the bandage's tie. "You think it's easy to forget something like that?"

"No," I whispered, thankful he hadn't. "But how did you know it was the same poison?"

He flicked his gaze to mine, squinting from the sun. "I didn't until just now."

My stomach hurt, growing worse at the jolt of pain when he tugged too hard. "Leave it," I finally said. "If you keep pulling on it, I'm going to lose the water I just drank."

"Sorry." His hands fell away, and my eyes met his in the new silence. "Do you think you can keep down some soup?" he coaxed. "You haven't eaten in days, but I can get food and water for you . . . now that the crew thinks you've got some spiritual connection to animals."

I haven't eaten in days? How long have I been out? I thought, but the compassion in his voice caught at me. It must have been hard for him knowing I was below the deck and unable even to slip me a crust. And even worse when he had been unable to do anything when they shoved me into that pit. "I heard what Captain Rylan said—before I woke up," I said, softly. "He's going to kill me the first chance he gets. Don't lie to me, Duncan. I can't bear it."

His hands found mine, gently cupping them and holding them unmoving. There was a twinge from my injured shoulder, but I bore it, not wanting to tell him it hurt. Duncan looked at my dirty, tar-smeared, small hands in his, his thumb gently moving against mine. "I won't let him," he whispered. "And in the meantime, you'll get food and water. You'll get stronger, then we'll escape." His eyes rose to mine. "We all will."

I couldn't bring myself to argue with him, though it was likely we would all die before the sun rose twice. Pushing my despair away, I looked past him to Contessa coaxing Alex to sit up. They might make it, but my survival was going to be a lot harder.

While I concentrated on my breathing, I watched Contessa help Alex. The new tenderness between them was obvious and struck me to the quick. As a royal, I had grown up with the concrete understanding that I would probably have a loveless marriage, the needs of the realm coming long before mine. My brief elation in finding out I was free to search out love as I could find it had been voluntarily crushed under my own heel when I accepted Kavenlow's apprenticeship. Secretly this time, the needs of the game had superseded my own.

Seeing Contessa shift the palm fronds so that Alex's healing shoulder—and only his healing shoulder—would be in the sun, I vowed she, at least, would have the chance at happiness. I couldn't risk Duncan's life by asking him to stay with me. He'd become a target for an assassin's dart, a tool with which to manipulate me. I knew that I would risk Costenopolie to keep him safe, and as a player, I couldn't allow such ties of love.

"Duncan?" I said softly so my voice wouldn't crack. I felt the tears start to well, and I reached with my good hand to wipe them away, hating them even as they appeared. It wasn't fair. To remain silent as to why I continually said no felt like such a betrayal, but if I told him, I knew he would risk the danger and stay with me, bringing about both our downfalls.

"Oh, Tess," he whispered, the sand moving in a soft hush as he scooted closer. He gently set my deadened right hand in my lap and cautiously leaned until his shoulder rested against my good side, blocking the wind. "Don't cry," he said, making it worse. "We'll be all right."

"That's not what I'm crying for," I said, becoming more miserable when his arm went carefully around my waist. I wanted to give in, to sob uncontrollably into his shoulder, to tell him I was angry at the decision I had made, to tell him why I had made it and ask for his forgiveness for choosing an empire over him. He was the only person I felt wouldn't think me weak or foolish for breaking down, and I still couldn't bring myself to do it. If he stayed with me, either he would die from a rival's dart or I would sacrifice my kingdom to save his life. And the game meant more to me than life itself.

"You don't understand," I said, my words muffled. "If I don't make it—"

"No," he interrupted. "Don't talk like that. You will. You retook an entire palace. You can do this."

Sniffing, I pulled my head from his shoulder. "I had help," I said. "Remember?"

"I opened a few locks, and I was the one that got them shackled to me."

"If I don't make it," I interrupted, "will you see them safely returned to Kavenlow?"

"Don't," he protested, the fear a thin wisp in the back of his eyes. "Kavenlow will pay the ransom, and you will all go back. I won't let anything happen to you. I . . ." He hesitated, and my breath caught. I could see the words of love in his pinched and worried eyes, and I didn't think I could survive hearing him say them.

"Duncan, no." I rushed to block his words. "Don't say it." Fingers trembling, I reached to stop his words with my fingertips. His eyes closed, and his hand came up to take mine away.

"But I want to," he whispered, his brown eyes fixed on mine.

The wind tugged at his overly long bangs, and I felt the tears start up again. "I can't hear it," I said, pulling my gaze from his. "Not now. I can't bear it. You mean too much to me."

"But . . ." He took a hesitant breath, leaning closer to block the wind and brushing the tears from my cheek. Wonder shone in his eyes, bright in the sun. "I thought you didn't like me. I thought you thought I was beneath you. That that's why you always said no."

"You thought I believed you were beneath me?" I said, a hiccuping sob breaking free and sending a flash of pain through me. "I'm the one who was bought in the gutter. You, at least, have a name that's yours, not given to you out of . . . convenience."

Relief seemed to pour from him. "Tess," he breathed, his featherlight grip around me a mix of protectiveness and gentleness that made me feel all the worse. "You silly, silly girl. I'd give you my name. I said I never would give it to anyone, but I'd give it to you. If you'd have me."

I closed my eyes in misery. "Stop . . ." I whispered, hardly audible as my heart broke. "I can't, Duncan."

His arms about mine didn't move. I could smell the sea on him, and sand. "Why?"

My eyes went to Contessa. "No," he said as he followed my gaze. "You can't blame this on your sister anymore. Alex is going to live. Look at them. She'll be fine. He can help her become a proper queen. And I won't let Captain Rylan hurt you, so don't tell me it's because you don't think you're going to survive."

"Contessa didn't write what I told Captain Rylan," I said, grasping at anything to avoid telling him the truth. "She told Kavenlow not to pay the ransoms and that we would be within a day's sail of the capital in a few days. He's going to try to retake us under her orders, and he'll do it, even knowing we might all die in the process."

The tension in his arms shifted, then relaxed. "You clever, clever woman," he whispered, tilting his head so his lips brushed my ear. "That's why I love you, Tess."

"Duncan . . ."

"Not a word," he said, gently turning my chin to him with a sun-browned finger. There was sand on it, and the grit rubbed against me, making my venom-sensitive skin hurt. "I'm going to kiss you, and there's not a thing, legally or otherwise, you can do to stop me."

"Duncan . . ." I protested, but it would hurt too much to try to stop him, and in all honesty, I didn't want to.

His hand brushed the hair from my face. Cupping my chin,

he leaned forward until the wind was gone. Soft, and with a tenderness born from his fear of hurting me, he met my lips with his own. The warmth of the sun was replaced by the heat of his touch, almost not there. It was that very hesitancy that struck a chord within me. *Oh God. I think he loves me.*

Knowing it was a mistake, I leaned forward, prolonging it. Nothing else mattered right then. Nothing. My eyes closed, and my good hand rose to find the back of his neck. Duncan seemed to hesitate, then accepted it, his kiss turning deeper and more dangerous. Mind whirling, my thoughts jumped to our first kiss aboard the *Sandpiper* last fall. My desire rose twofold, building upon old emotions kept in check too long and for reasons the heart couldn't understand. My pulse quickened, and my entire right side seemed to tingle from the increased circulation.

A small sound escaped me, and he pulled away with a shocking suddenness. My eyes flashed open, finding his wide with worry.

"Did I hurt you?" he asked breathlessly, eyes pinched.

"Only my heart," I whispered. *Why did I do this to myself? To him?*

His eyes were deep with emotion as he tilted his head and leaned forward again.

"Duncan!" came Captain Rylan's shout, jerking him to a halt. "Get your no-account arse over here and away from that woman!"

Our eyes never left each other as Duncan ignored him, coming close to give me a fleeting, last kiss. My heart pounded, and I felt weak from the toxin coursing through me. "I'll be back with something to eat," he said as he rose and brushed the sand from his pants. Head down and steps slow, he went to the community fire. I was left sitting on the sand, my thoughts confused and conflicted.

Miserable, I shifted position, my breath catching as all my hurts, forgotten in the passion of the moment, reminded me of their existence. Behind me, I could feel Contessa watching, wanting to help but utterly unable.

Giving in, I silently wept, my face to the unseen ocean so no one would see me cry.

Eleven

❖

"Contessa?" Alex whispered, his low voice soaked up by the chill darkness of the night.

"Yes?"

Her response was equally soft, almost inaudible over the wind in the palms brushing the swelling moon. I snuggled deeper under the blanket the mystery of surviving the punta had granted me. The pirates had fed me well today, too, now that I was going to survive the cat when poor Gilly hadn't. I'd like to say that it had been common decency that prompted the show of humanity, but it was fear. If I died under their care, the superstitious crew believed my soul would haunt them forever. They would have to find a way to kill me that wouldn't give my soul a clear way to hunt them down. And I was going to hoard that card as long as I could.

I heard the sand shift, and I cracked my eyes. A dark patch of night moved. It was Alex propped up on his elbow. Beyond him was the community fire, a few crewmen yet sitting around it. We weren't being watched very closely, much of that due to my sorry state.

"I never thanked you for tending me," Alex said, his voice clear in the night-silenced air.

"Shhhh," she soothed. The gray lump that was my sister

never moved, deep within the windbreak they had put up earlier. It had been the first time I'd seen them do anything together without arguing about it. "I'm glad you're better," she
said. "As your wife, it's my place to see to your comfort."

"No, it isn't," he protested. "And a queen shouldn't be tending the sick."

Her shadow shifted. "I helped the nuns heal the sick. I gave
no thought to it. You shouldn't either."

"Thank you, anyway."

I closed my eyes, wishing I had put my bedroll farther
away. Captain Rylan had allowed me to move closer to Contessa so she could tend my wounds instead of Duncan, and
today had been an awful mix of satisfaction and envy as I
watched Alex and Contessa interact in close quarters, their
cautious hesitancy turning to a timid closeness.

We were all shackled like errant goats since I was again
mobile—though my movements were frustratingly pained and
slow. Alex, though, was showing vast improvements. He had
spent some of his day making slow and careful poses, bran-
dishing a lengthy piece of driftwood as if it were his absent
sword as he gently stretched idle muscles. A few pirates had
watched, laughing and mocking him until Mr. Smitty took the
stick away, sullen and bad-tempered.

I'd found Alex to be a good man despite his Misdev
heritage—proud but not overbearing, with the wisdom to know
when to hold his tongue and when to speak, down-to-earth
and a realist, never complaining about the poor conditions and
food though I knew he had never been deprived of anything in
his life. Much as I wanted Contessa to remain true to her heart,
I was finding myself thinking she would be a fool to toss aside
his offer of a real marriage.

My eyes flashed open when a soft shift of sand reached my
ears. I expected a drunken sailor to come torment us at any moment. But it was only Alex, sitting up. "Contessa?" He seemed
unusually awake, almost eerily so.

"Yes?"

"When I was in fever . . . did I say anything?"

"No, love," she whispered. "You didn't."

My brow rose as much for the lie as the word *love*, and I
wondered what had shifted in her thoughts. The slim line of

her arm broke the plane of her body, and she pulled him down. "Go to sleep."

"Sleep is all I've done for the last four days," he said, an unusual petulance entering his voice. "I'm tired of sleeping."

"Lie still and keep me warm then. It's cold."

It wasn't, the southern current keeping the island warmer than one would expect, and I kept my eyes open while my thoughts whirled at what it might mean.

"You're too good to me," he breathed, and his shadow settled beside her.

"You deserve better," came her hesitant answer. I closed my eyes then, as he leaned closer as if for a kiss. Or perhaps it was to whisper something more private in her ear. Either way, I didn't want to watch.

I must have fallen asleep, for the next time the sand shifted to pull my eyes open and make my body tense, the light from the community fire was only coals. Nothing moved, and I lay still. My bitten shoulder started to itch, and I ignored it, listening for whatever had woken me. If we were going to be accosted, it would happen in the small hours of the night. The moon had shifted, being almost straight up and lighting the clearing in a dappled silver.

Faint in the distance, I could hear the waves on the beach. My pulse stayed fast, though the night seemed safe. The dull ache in my punta bite worsened, and I maneuvered my left hand up to rub it gently, the motion hidden by my blanket. Overhead came a whisper of wind in the fronds, and a scattering of seeds fell with the sound of pattering rain. My breath eased out of me as I decided that's what had woken me.

Stomach unclenching, I eased myself upright in painful stages, breathing through the lingering pain that pulsed in time with my heart. It left trails of fire down my side to my toes. The soft ache, punctuated by surprising jolts of hurt, seemed easy to bear.

Not liking how weak I had become, I rubbed harder at my shoulder, wedging past the rude lacing Contessa had used temporarily to stitch up the rag my sleeve had become. Driven by the itchy pull, I dared to run a careful finger under the bandage. It felt far better than it should for having been bitten only two days ago, or had it been three? My shoulder itself was mostly numb, the ache having spread down my side and into my hip. My fingers, too, had regained most of their movement, if not all their feeling. The most I had been incapacitated by toxin when Kavenlow had been building my tolerance had been a day, and that had only been a mild ache. I could only hope that tomorrow would be better.

Holding my breath, I dug a finger deeper under the bandage, feeling the soft ache start to feel good. With a sudden decision, I undid the loose stitching and completely exposed the bandage. I wanted it off.

Like an animal in a trap, the need to be free of it became all-consuming. I tugged and yanked, picking at it with my fingers of my good hand, ignoring my clenching stomach and the slight nausea. The sharp jabs of hurt only urged me on until, with a moan of relief, I got it off.

I dropped the bandage to the sand and immediately rubbed the scabs with a gentle finger, trying to soothe the itch. Flakes of dried blood came away under the soft pressure, and I slowed, exploring the healing gashes with a careful touch. It hurt under my gentle prodding, but it was a good hurt: the hurt of a healing wound.

I hadn't let Duncan look at it since regaining consciousness, and Contessa hadn't said a word when she had tended it before sunset, washing it and binding it up with pursed lips and a confused expression. It didn't surprise me that, when I twisted to look, I found the two upper tears made by the punta's canines and the one lower gash were almost healed over with wide slashes of tender, pink skin.

It left me with a funny feeling. The bite looked good—over a week's healing, I'd guess, in two or three days. I didn't understand how Jeck made his magic work through a dream, even if we had both been dangerously overdosed on toxin at the time. And knowing he could have killed me just as easily as healed me only left me more concerned.

The flesh running to my elbow and waist was slightly numb and swollen yet from the poison. I went worried upon recalling what Jeck had said about the venom fixing itself into the healing tissue instead of working itself out as it usually did. Resigned that there was nothing I could do about it, I tugged the cord holding my dress together tight. The bandage lay beside me, and thinking it ugly, I scratched out a shallow hole and buried it.

I felt the strain from the effort of doing just that, and disgusted with how weak I was, I sat in the dappled moonlight, sleep gone and feeling restless. The sand was cold upon my left hand; the sand upon my right hand I couldn't feel but for a faint whisper of movement. I stifled a surge of pity, telling myself I was a fool.

My gaze drifted to where Contessa and Alex lay, and I froze in a sudden wash of fear. Alex was there, but Contessa was gone.

Pulse hammering, I looked to the fire and the pirates, then the silent huts. *Had someone taken her without my knowing? How could I not have heard?* I thought, my mouth opening to call Alex.

But then a movement at the edge of our tether's reach caught my attention, and my held breath escaped me. It was Contessa, her knees drawn up to her chin as she sat in the shelter of a water-smoothed root that had washed ashore long ago, sitting to look toward the unseen ocean.

She was fine—as much as any of us were—and, feeling foolish, I decided she looked too melancholy to leave alone. Carefully I got first to my knees, then my feet. Right leg slow and lethargic, I adjusted my blanket about my shoulders and crossed the sand. My tether dragged behind me, and I hated it.

Contessa jumped as the sound of my approach reached her. "Oh, it's you," she said, giving me a weak smile as she wiped a hand under an eye. The thin moonlight that made it under the trees made shadows on her face, but I could see where tears had left a soft shine.

"Sorry," I said, hunched and holding my blanket tight with my good hand. "Didn't mean to startle you."

She made a very unqueenlike face and scooted sideways. "Here. Sit. It's warmer with your back against something. Just watch out for the clams. They're sharp.

I squinted, seeing where mussels, not clams, had attached themselves when the root had been submerged. Feeling old and pained, I cautiously lowered myself to sit beside her. She was right. It was warmer. With a sudden thought, I took the rope about my ankle and started rubbing it against the remnant of a sharp shell.

Contessa saw what I was doing. Saying nothing, she sniffed loudly and pushed her hair back behind an ear. I had tried to braid it for her today with one hand, finally giving up when she told me to stop. "I don't know what to do anymore," she said softly. "Everything was so much easier when I was a foundling at the nunnery."

I stifled a bark of rude laughter. Life had been easier for me when I was the crown princess, innocent and unaware of my true potential. "Alex?" I guessed.

She nodded. "He's like no man I've ever met. So neat and tidy."

My hair swung into my eyes in time with my sawing. *Tidy? She thinks he's tidy?*

"He shaves every day that he can," she continued, but her eyes going everywhere but to mine told me she wasn't saying what she wanted. "And he's always concerned about me."

"He teases you," I prompted, digging. "You hate that."

"No," she breathed. "I don't." She was silent, bringing her gaze back to me. "I like him, Tess. And that's wrong. I love Thadd, but I don't want to hurt Alex. He's too good a man."

The last was a faint whisper of guilt. I didn't look up, busy with the rope. I knew there would be more.

"And he gave up everything," she said, her tone bordering on that of justification. "Everything so I wouldn't grow to hate him and his Rosie."

The first strand of the rope parted. I cut my finger, and took a moment to stick it in my mouth.

"It's not fair," Contessa all but whined.

"No, it isn't," I said, unable to keep silent anymore. "It would be easier if he was ugly and fat and beat you to leave bruises where no one could see. No one would fault you if you should find your own happiness among your court then."

"But Alex is so . . ." Contessa said. "He's so . . ."

"He's a Misdev prince," I finished for her, resuming my work. "Sound of body and reason. Courtly and kind. Able to make you laugh and willing to die for your safety, with nothing promised from you in return. God save you, Contessa. You couldn't ask for a more fortunate match. I know you love Thadd, but you have to face this."

Contessa turned to me, looking like a younger version of our mother. The shadows hid the hunger and fear, making her beautiful. "I don't know what to do," she admitted. "I promised Thadd—"

"I can't tell you what to do," I interrupted. "I don't know either. But our parents loved each other, and it made them stronger."

"They knew they would wed strangers," she said bitterly. "They didn't make ties to anyone else. I did. I can't just leave Thadd because—something better came about."

"That's not fair," I said shortly, tired of her whining. "And Father . . ." I took a slow breath, asking Father to forgive me for the coming falsehood. "Father did."

Her eyes went wide in the faint light.

I nodded, unable to hold her gaze. "Father had a courtesan he loved very much," I lied. "No one talks about her, and everyone denies she ever existed. Mother was said to have been very polite, though it must have torn her inside. Father grew to like Mother, finally seeing the pain he was inflicting on her, and because of it, he finally asked his mistress to leave."

I sawed at my bindings, not knowing if the sudden slickness was sweat or blood. "It must have been one of the hardest things he ever had to do," I said softly. "He offered to put her up in a fine house with servants, but she simply left one night, and he let her go, never searching her out. I think it was the sole best thing he ever did to ensure the safety of the realm."

"How?" Contessa asked, and I could hear the pain in her voice for her understanding of what I was telling her to do.

I glanced up, then back down to the rope. I was almost through it.

"When she left, Mother's wounded pride healed. Their love deepened, and their trust in each other grew absolute. There was no way for a manipulative, power-hungry lord to drive a wedge between them, splitting the throne and making political upheaval possible."

"Oh," she whispered, reaching up to touch her lips. "I never realized."

Satisfied, I nodded. "The palace was sound, and the populace felt secure. Happy people don't listen to dissidents intent on revolt."

"I can't ask Thadd to leave," she blurted.

"And I can't tell you what to do," I replied. "No one expects you to like all the choices you make."

"But you were the crown princess, once," she said. "Didn't you ever find the needs of the kingdom crosswind to your desires? What did you do? How did you decide?"

I sighed, taking a moment to shake my left hand out before continuing to work on the rope. "I didn't allow myself to have desires," I whispered, thinking that admitting that aloud was probably the lowest point of my existence.

Her chin dropped, and she sniffed once. "You can't say that. I saw you kiss Duncan," she said, and my face warmed.

The rope snapped under my efforts, and I jerked forward, my knuckles hitting the sand. Contessa moved her tiny feet so I could reach her tether. Somewhere between reaching the island and now, they had taken her boots. Silently, and without comment, I started working on her bindings, being very careful not to hit her pale skin. If we could get Alex free, we might sneak out and find a place to hide. What I'd do then, I'd worry about later.

Contessa pulled her blanket tighter about her shoulders. "Please don't be angry with me. But, Tess, I don't trust Duncan."

My fingers were cramping, and I stopped, looking up to see her miserable for her admission. "You don't trust him?" I said, my back starting to hurt high up my shoulder. "After all he did for us? Is doing right now? I'm alive because of him." *And Jeck, but no need to bring that up.*

She curled her lips in on themselves, her eyes on the moon. "I know you like him, and I think he likes you, too, but . . ."

With a huff, I returned to her rope, watching the strands start to part. "But what? Is it his thief mark?" I asked. "I told you he got it by mistake. A so-called friend tricked him into taking the blame for his thievery. The man was a god to him, and he felt he owed him his life. Duncan is a good man under the street dust."

Her tether parted, and I heaved a sigh of relief. Her hand went down to rub her ankle. "You're right," she said. "Never mind."

I sat on the sand, my pulse fast from just that little exertion. She had said never mind, but that's not what she wanted to say, and I didn't need magic to see it. "Is it because he lived on the streets?" I asked belligerently. "Because that's where I would be if it wasn't for Kavenlow."

Contessa's face pinched in the moonlight, and she hunched into herself. "I'm sorry. I shouldn't have brought it up. I've been watching him, and yes, he cares for you. He almost spends as much money on you as he does himself, which is saying a lot for him. It is obvious that he thinks highly of you and doesn't want anything to hurt you. It's just . . ."

I rubbed my ankles, glad to be free. I wanted to leave, but I had to catch my breath first. Silently I waited.

Her held breath slipped from her. "When you were bitten," she said reluctantly, "he was the first one into the pit. He saved your life, but Tess, it was almost as if you were a thing to him. Something that he wanted to put on his shelf that would ensure his future. He fought hard to keep the crew from leaving you down there and filling up the hole, but it was greed in his voice, not love."

I watched her worried, pained eyes—and listened, weighing her hard-to-spot but substantial savvy with people against the touch of his fingers on me and the shared pain in his voice when he caused me pain to save my life. "He's been hungry most of his life," I said hesitantly. "Maybe that's the only way he can convey his need for someone," I said, and she dropped her eyes, adjusting her dress about her bent knees.

"We should get Alex free and find somewhere to hide until the palace finds us," I said, awkwardly getting to my feet. I dropped the ends of her rope in the sand beside her, then reached down with my good left hand and pulled her up. The food I had eaten today gave me a new strength, and the freedom beckoning beyond the dark vegetation was better than any tonic.

Contessa brushed the sand from herself and glanced at the distant coals of the community fire. A shuffling in the brush beside us brought a small gasp from her. Pulse hammering, I spun, my hand going over her mouth.

"Or," came Jeck's voice out of the black, "you could row out to the *Sandpiper* and be gone entirely."

Twelve

❖

"*Jeck!*" I exclaimed in a muffled oath, wondering how long he had been listening. "How did you find us?" I stammered before remembering I had slipped into his mind during my overdose of venom and pointed the way.

My left hand dropped from Contessa's mouth. An uncomfortable flash of emotions ran through me at the sight of his tall shadow lurking at the edges of the underbrush: embarrassment for my sorry state and that I needed rescuing, fear that I looked weak and that Jeck would take advantage of it, and worry that he was a better player than I and that I would ruin my master's game beyond repair. And over it all was the knowledge that he had saved my life.

I didn't like any of the things I was feeling, but I was glad to see him nonetheless. The *Sandpiper* was nearby. Freedom.

He made the smallest of motions with his head. "This way. And keep it quiet. You make more noise than three children with candy."

Contessa stiffened. "Captain, you forget your place. Don't talk to my sister like that."

Jeck made a little start. I could see it as the moonlight glinted on the brim of his hat. "My apologies to Your Majesty and her lady," he amended, so sincere that I almost missed the faint sarcasm he hid in his slight bow. "If you would *please* come with me with all due haste and stealth into the shadows so I may cut your tethers?"

Contessa made a short harrumph as she gathered her filthy skirts and headed after him, awkward because of the sand. "Tess already cut our bonds, Captain. We're not so helpless."

"Contessa?" I whispered, lurching to follow her. "It's generally customary that the rescued not harass the rescuer but swallows any insults in the spirit of the moment."

Her narrow face went worried in the moonlight. "Oh . . ."

The soft glint of steel showed as Jeck put his knife away. "You're free? Why the devil are you still sitting here?"

"Alex," Contessa breathed, her head turning to their shelter. "We need to cut Alex free."

A bump leaning against a tree moved. "Here, Contessa," Alex said out of the dark, and Contessa hiked her skirts up and pushed past Jeck. The relief in her was obvious when she stopped before him, the white of her dress tumbling as she ran her hands over him to make sure his exertions hadn't pulled any mending tears.

Following, I tripped on a root and staggered. I reached for a tree, skinning my palm. Pain raced down my right leg, reverberating back up to my shoulder. I panted through the hurt and said nothing. Jeck paused and looked back. "I'm fine," I said. "Do you have Duncan?"

"Your thief? No. He's one of them."

Contessa turned, the white shadow of her dress giving away her position. "He's only pretending so he would be in a better position to get us free."

My lips parted. She had just told me she didn't trust him. Her eyes in the moonlight flicked to mine, and she shrugged. As I held a tree for balance and waited for the pain to lessen, Jeck pressed into motion. "What about Duncan?" I said, my voice bordering on the unsafe.

The captain of the Misdev guards came to a respectful halt before Alex, and the prince took Contessa's arm. "If you would, sir, please assist Queen Contessa to that tree? I'll be with you directly and show you the way to the boat."

Alex nodded. "This way, Contessa," he murmured. "Watch

the roots. Here, let me help you with your dress; you've snagged it."

She glanced back at me once for reassurance, then went with Alex, her mouth shut and her arm supporting him rather than the other way around.

Jeck waited until I hobbled the few steps between us. "You softened her to him?" he said, his low voice almost unheard. "I'm doubly impressed."

For a moment, I could do nothing but stare, my mouth hanging open. *A second compliment?* Then I shook myself. "Duncan is coming with us."

The shadow of his head shifted back and forth. "No. I'm here for them only."

I looked past him to the white shimmer of Contessa, the only giveaway that they were nearby. "We aren't leaving him behind."

Jeck scoffed deep in his throat. "I'm not going to tiptoe through an enemy camp to find a thief."

"You chull!" I exclaimed softly, my cheeks warming. "He isn't a thief. He's a cheat, and he helped keep us alive by pretending to join them. I'd be dead if it weren't for him."

"I'd be willing to wager it was his idea to put you with that punta."

His voice had a hint of challenge, and my breath caught as I fumbled for words, finally saying, "He didn't know what it was. And he kept them from burying me alive after it bit me."

Jeck's lips pressed together as if I had confirmed something he already knew, making me even more angry. "I'm not going back for him," he said.

"You and your damned game," I whispered, heart pounding and very aware of the royals just out of earshot. "Don't you think of anything or anyone else? Ever? Is that all you live for?" My knees shook from my weakened state, but I wouldn't back down.

"The game is why I'm still alive—apprentice. And you have no right to talk. Do you think I don't know you're going to lie to your master about the extent of your damage so you can stay in the game, risking your life to continue it?"

My heart pounded that he could see through me so easily.

He didn't move, but somehow he changed, becoming threatening as his bangs shifted about his eyes. He wasn't much older than me, but he was nearly twice my weight and held twice the wisdom of venom that I had.

Tucking my hair behind my ear, I took a step back, frightened. "Give me your knife," I demanded. "I'll get him if you think rescuing him is beyond you."

It wasn't an insult, but it was close. "No."

"You can't tell me what I can and can't do, Captain," I said, frustration mixing with my worry for Duncan. *What would they do to him if they found us gone?*

"I don't care what you do," Jeck said. "But I'm not giving you a knife. If they catch you with it, they'll know someone else is on the island and come looking that much sooner."

"Don't send me in there unprotected!" I said harshly.

Jeck glanced over his shoulder to the white shadow of Contessa's dress. "I'm not sending you anywhere. You want your cheat? Go. I'm not your master to tell you you're being a stupid woman, thinking with your heart instead of your head. I saved your life once because it would have been a foolish waste and it didn't cost me anything. But this?" His dark eyes narrowed, barely visible in the moonlight. "I'm not helping you in this. Our games mesh. They're not the same."

"Common decency," I insisted, embarrassed to be arguing with him after the reminder that he saved my life, "not foolishness. And I'm not asking for your help. I'll get him by myself and catch up with you. Where's the dinghy?"

Jeck paused in thought. Slowly he rocked back. "I won't wait. If you're dead set on this, go to the west side of the island. The *Sandpiper* will be off the beach in about ten minutes."

"Fine." My breath was fast and shallow. I had told him I didn't need his help, and here I was, unable to stand up without pain. "Could you at least give me a dart? They already found them on me so they won't think anything of it."

He shook his head. "You aren't my apprentice, and you shouldn't even ask me for it. And if you were my apprentice, I wouldn't. You should be dead from the toxin as you stand there. One more might tip you over the edge."

He turned to leave, and I reached out, grasping his uniform's coat sleeve and stopping him dead in his tracks. Jeck turned. He looked at my hand on his arm, and I pulled it away, wanting to hide it and feeling as if I'd made a mistake. "Jeck," I pleaded, thinking of Duncan, "you can't just leave him here. They'll kill him when they find us gone."

"You want him? You get him," was all he said, then pushed himself into motion. His steps were soundless, and he vanished so quickly into the dark vegetation that I wondered if he was using his magic to stay unseen. There was a glimmer of gold on his coat sleeve when he pointed the way to Alex, and the swirl of white as Contessa turned.

"Tess?" she called softly, worry heavy in her voice, and I waved at her.

"Go with Captain Jeck," I whispered. "I'm getting Duncan."

"But you're not well," she protested. "Captain Jeck? You get him. Tess can escort us to the boat."

I glanced at Jeck thinking that she was exactly right, then grabbed my filthy skirts and slogged forward. "You and Alex are more important," I said as I came even with them, and Jeck's face went impassive. "He'll see to your safety." *As long as it fits in with his game,* I added bitterly in my thoughts.

"Come on, Contessa," Alex urged. "Every moment counts."

Contessa hesitated, her breath held as she balanced. I'd seen that look on her before. It was the same one she wore when Thadd begged her to leave me to face Alex's brother alone, buying them time to shinny down a rope from my old rooms and escape. She had left that time, but I knew she had never forgiven herself.

"Please, Contessa," I whispered, and she dropped her head.

"Don't be long," she said. Clearly upset, she turned and helped Alex down the narrow path. I watched them, both relieved and afraid. I could do this alone. I didn't need Jeck's help.

Jeck's dark eyes watched me for a long moment. He took a breath as if to say something, then spun to follow Alex and Contessa. The white of her dress blended into the moonlight, then they were gone.

I steadied myself with a slow breath and headed to the camp, finding myself reaching for my nonexistent dart and topknot. My hair, I realized, was all over the place. Contessa had tried to comb through it today, but I had made her stop as every snarl she found sent waves of hurt to my toes. I had to be a sight, stumbling through the brush with my curls about my ears, my dress ripped and torn, and no shoes. I hadn't seen anything but drinking water for days.

I am concerned about how I look? I thought, as my toes curled into the cold, grass-rimmed expanse of sand at the edge of the clearing. Pulse pounding, I scanned the unmoving bumps. To walk among them searching for Duncan to seem more frightening than being pushed into the pit with the punta. My head turned to where I had last seen Contessa and Alex. *Maybe Jeck was right.*

Swallowing, I turned to the camp with stinking bodies of men sprawled everywhere. The collective breathing and soft sounds of sleep gave the impression of a living beast. I had walked the halls of the palace unnoticed using my venom-induced skills. I could do the same here.

Closing my eyes, I forced my hand from my shoulder and took three slow breaths. To remain unseen was very different from sensing emotions from animals, and because of how Kavenlow had taught me this skill—disguising it as countless games of hide-and-seek—it was very nebulous and I was never sure it was working when I tried to do it intentionally. But Kavenlow said that was the nature of the magic and to trust in myself.

Settled, I reached my thoughts out to touch my magic.

My breath hissed in. Dizziness came from everywhere and nowhere at all. Gasping, I dropped to my knees. My eyes were wide but unseeing as I fought to keep from passing out. I fell forward, one hand on my shoulder, the other clutching at the cold sand.

"God help me," I panted. Holding my shoulder, I hunched into a kneeling huddle, the tingles of pain my fingers made pressing into healing flesh breaking through the numbness. Slowly the black rim edging my sight faded to leave me shaken. *What, by the Heavens, happened?* Trembling, I looked past my hair to the sleeping men. They hadn't heard me.

It's the bite, I decided, recognizing the sensations of an overdose of venom. Toxin was spilling into my veins, coming from my healing wound. It coursed through me as if I had been bitten an hour ago, not two days. It wasn't my residual levels I was drawing on, it was fresh venom.

A wash of anxiety took me as I knelt in the shadows, a worry that had nothing to do with the men surrounding me. Jeck had said he fixed the toxin in my tissues as he healed my wound, preventing an overdose of venom from killing me. Apparently it wasn't fixed permanently, but subject to being pulled out when I tried to work my magic, sort of like loosening the bandage.

One hand on my shoulder, the other on a tree so I wouldn't fall over, I waited for my body to absorb the venom. My knees shook, and my fingers tingled. I swallowed, trying to find enough spit. *It's just working its way out,* I thought.

Nothing had changed. It might take a little longer to get rid of it, but then everything would be as it was before. Kavenlow would be peeved, but he would wait while the punta venom worked its way out of my tissues. And time would cleanse the excessive residual toxin from me, bringing my levels back to a level where I could safely be a player.

Just a matter of time, I thought, my heart pounding when I pulled myself up from the sand. I could do this without magic.

Feeling ill and weak, I scanned the drunken, sleeping men. Duncan was likely to be on the outskirts as the newest member and not well liked. *It's his own fault,* I thought while I edged around them, keeping to the shadows where I could. He won at cards and dice too often to make friends. It had been the same on the *Sandpiper.* He never seemed to fit in. Just like me.

Carefully, I edged to a bedroll set well back from the fire. As I had thought, it was Duncan, his long face slack in slumber. His stubble had grown into a decent beard, and it made him look older. I crouched beside him, taking in his brow pinched in a worried dream. *And he cares for me,* I thought as I found a stick to prod him awake. What did that mean to him?

Well out of arm's reach, I pushed on his knee. His breathing shifted only slightly as his eyes flashed open. Never moving, he stared up at the fronds over his head. Slowly his gaze rove over the night, though his head never did. His eyes fell upon me, and they widened. "Tess," his lips moved, but not a sound came from them.

Smiling, I put a finger to his mouth. My legs ached, and I slowly fell to kneel.

His gaze dropped to my ankle, reddened and showing a trickle of blood where I had nicked it. Easing himself up, his blanket fell to show he was sleeping in his clothes. A lump filled my throat when his hand fell upon my left shoulder and he pulled me closer.

"I knew you would find a way to escape," he whispered in my ear to send a wash of feeling through me. "You're the smartest woman I've met, Tess. God help me, how could I not love you?"

My throat closed, and I made my eyes wide, refusing to cry. Jeck thought I was foolish, and Duncan thought I was smart. Managing a smile, I rose, beckoning him to follow.

Duncan got to his feet, soundless over the wind in the tree-tops that failed to reach us below. His hand slipped into mine at the edge of the brush. It was warm and solid, and I unhesitatingly led him farther into the dark. "It gets better," I said as soon as it was prudent. "Captain Jeck is here. He's going to meet us with Alex and Contessa on the west beach."

There was the barest falter in his pace. "Captain Jeck?" he questioned. "How did he find us?"

"There were only so many islands to look," I said, feeling guilty for the lie. But my unease at how Jeck and I had melded thoughts—allowing me to point out the way through him— was even stronger. That both of us had been unusually high in our venom levels probably had everything to do with it. It still bothered me, though.

I tripped on an unseen root, and Duncan was there to keep me from falling. "Thanks," I whispered when the pain from the jolt eased, and I got a white-toothed smile in return. I wasn't afraid to show weakness before Duncan. I didn't have to prove my worth to him. He could see me fall and think nothing less of me.

"That way," I said, catching a glimpse of the moon. "We need to get to the westernmost beach. There's a boat, but I don't know how long Jeck will wait."

"You're going to do this, Tess," Duncan said, his voice still a whisper though no one could possibly hear. "I told him you would escape. I warned him."

"Captain Rylan?" I asked, fear joining my pain. "Why did you tell him I'd escape?"

Duncan grinned. "Two reasons. One, if I said you could, I wouldn't be blamed if you went missing. And two, I wagered one of my rings for his that you would. Shame I won't be around to collect on that."

I would have laughed if it wouldn't hurt so much.

A slurred, drunken cry rose up behind us, and my pulse leapt. "I thought we'd have more time," I said, my numbed right foot hurting as I stumbled.

Duncan tensed like a deer scenting the wind. His attention was behind us. "West beach?" he said softly. "Let's go."

He pushed ahead of me. Branches snapped and leaves tore. Ignoring the ache of my right side, I followed. I kept one hand on his back, ducking when branches whipped back where my head would have been. I didn't watch where I was going, trusting Duncan to force the way. My heart hammered, and I struggled to keep up. The venom pulled at me.

Behind us came the increasingly loud shouts of the crew. Duncan crashed ahead, leaving a trail anyone could follow, even in the dark. Fear of recapture struck me like a goad, sending me stumbling forward despite my trembling muscles. They would kill Duncan. If I was lucky, they would kill me.

My bare foot found a piece of coral, and I cried out, lurching to a halt against a tree. Duncan jerked to a stop, turning.

"I'm all right," I panted, my air coming in quick sounds as the venom leached out of my healed shoulder and into me. The surge of unfocused magic was pulled into existence by my rapid pulse and faster blood. I could do nothing with it; to use my magic would hurt even more.

I will not be taken, I thought grimly, as Duncan resumed pushing through the underbrush. I followed. There was no sound of close pursuit as of yet. A dim glow showed when I risked a glance behind. They had built the fire high, and torches were probably being lit. I could hear Captain Rylan's voice over them all, and Mr. Smitty bellowing out terse demands in a voice used to battling storms.

Duncan seemed to stumble and disappear. "Goat path," he said, when his head popped back through the underbrush. "Here."

My vision swam as I accepted his extended hand, and he helped me down to the thin trail. His grip was firm, and I took strength from it. Lungs heaving, I looked up the trail. The ground was soft, spongy, and cold under my feet. We would make it. We had to. Jeck was waiting. We would be safe if we could move fast enough.

"Go," I said, though the hurt rising up my leg was growing worse.

Still holding my hand, Duncan started to jog. I trailed behind, unable to watch where I was going. It was all I could do to breathe. The air was like fire in my lungs. I couldn't see, the moon making silver-and-black shadows where there should be none. My right leg had gone numb, and I couldn't feel anything but a dull pressure when my foot hit the ground. I thanked all that was holy Duncan was here, leading me.

I stumbled, having to consciously force my leg to keep moving. My vision blurred. The light on the ground suddenly brightened with moonlight, and I drew my head up as Duncan halted. Panting, I dropped his hand and pushed the hair from my eyes. We had found the beach, and my rasping intake of breath sounded loud against the faint surf.

The strip of white sand was narrow; the tide must be just past its full height. A soft hush of incoming waves was muted by the night. I scanned the shore for the *Sandpiper*'s rowboat, my face becoming cold when I didn't see it. Taking breath after grateful breath, I held a hand to my side and searched the horizon for the *Sandpiper*, not seeing it either. *Where were they?*

Duncan turned at the faint sound of the pirates growing loud in discovery, then soft.

"You said the west beach," he said, clearly afraid. "Where's the damn boat, Tess?"

"I don't know." This was the right beach. With the moonlight, it was almost as bright as noon. The *Sandpiper*, at least, ought to be visible.

"He's not here!" Duncan said, the anger heavy in his voice. "That damned captain of yours isn't here! He lied to you, Tess. He lied!"

Eyes on the horizon, I felt my hope turn to ash when a distant white shadow pulled itself from beyond the break of trees. It was the *Sandpiper* in full sail—headed away from us. "There she is," I whispered, and Duncan spun, waving his hat frantically.

I stood still and silent while my pulse slowed and my leg regained its feeling with the sensation of needles and pins. Jeck had said the boat would be off this beach in about ten minutes. It was about that now. I had assumed that meant I'd be able to get on her. Apparently not. Jeck hadn't lied. I had let him trick me.

It wasn't anger at Jeck that rushed through me, hot and potent. It was anger at myself. I was a fool. I was a weak, foolish-minded woman, and Jeck had taken advantage of it, using Duncan and me to lure the pirates away from not only the real point where the *Sandpiper*'s dinghy waited, but also by bringing them halfway across the island away from their boat and increasing the time it would take before they could mount a pursuit.

"Uh, Tess," Duncan said, his arm falling to his side. "They aren't stopping." He hesitated, his face turning sick and pale in the moonlight. "Um, I think they're already aboard. I think . . . they left us."

I couldn't bring myself to say anything. I was so stupid to have trusted Jeck.

A distant call spun me to the trees behind us. They were getting closer. If they found Duncan with me, standing on a beach with the hostages gone, they would know he wasn't really one of them and that he had been trying to escape. Jeck had sentenced us both.

Duncan took two steps to the water, then stopped. He looked like a trapped animal, his lips a thin line and his brow furrowed. I numbly watched his thumb rub his second finger. It was his tell that he was worried.

"They'll kill you," I whispered, trying to find a way to accept it.

Duncan glanced over my shoulder at the approaching noise. "Not if I can help it."

There was a new hardness to his voice that I'd never heard before. *No,* I thought. I'd heard it when he had been shackled under the guard quarters. He had picked every lock down there, freeing my guards so they could retake the palace. It was the tone he had when he found himself forced into a choice he didn't want to make.

"I'm really sorry about this, Tess," he said as he pulled me close.

I pressed into him, feeling his warmth as the wind cut off. I could smell the sea on him, mixing with sweat and sand. "It was my fault," I whispered, and he tucked a curl behind my ear. "If I had just gone with Jeck, you might have been safe. You could have slipped away at the next harbor and met us back at the palace."

He shook his head, an uncomfortable pinch to his eyes. "No, I mean for what I'm going to do."

I pulled back, staring up at him, not understanding.

"Tess," he fumbled. He glanced over my shoulder at the sound of approaching men. "The only way I'm going to survive this is if they think I took you out for a walk."

"A walk?" I said, bewildered.

He winced, not meeting my eyes. "Um, yeah. See, I won you—according to them—and if I wanted to take advantage of that and not have to share . . . uh . . . you, I would probably take you somewhere they wouldn't hear while I, um . . . took you."

Understanding flashed through me. "Oh!" I exclaimed, suddenly very much aware of his arms wrapped about me and how close we were standing.

His head bowed, and he put his forehead against mine. My brown curls mingled with his bangs in the gusts of wind. "I'm really, really sorry, Tess," he whispered. "You must believe me. I don't want to do this."

"Do what?" I asked stupidly.

He sighed. I felt it through every part of me. "This," he said.

In a sudden motion, he jerked my torn sleeve, tearing the temporary stitches out.

"Duncan!" I shrieked, pulling away only to be yanked back into him. The wind cut at me, and I panicked. He had torn my dress almost to my waist. I clutched the ends to me, having managed to wedge my bitten arm between him and me. It hurt, but I wouldn't move it for anything.

A distant call had gone up behind us. I had been heard. Pulse pounding, I stared at him.

"I'm sorry," he said again, whispering over the wind. "But if it doesn't look real, they won't believe me."

Fear, real and icy, slid through me. I didn't know what he was going to do anymore. "Duncan!" I cried, as he dropped to the sand, yanking me down on top of him.

I gasped as I fell, grunting in pain when I hit him. Every muscle twanged in hurt, taking my breath away. Helpless, I struggled to breathe, doing nothing when he slid me off him so that we were lying next to each other. He shifted, pinning my unhurt shoulder to the sand under a heavy hand and loomed over me, a frightening look in his eye.

"Duncan?" I said, trusting him but feeling sick to my stomach. He wouldn't. Even for show, he wouldn't. But in my weakened state, he could.

"You really should be struggling," he said, his eyes under his thick bangs unreadable.

I licked my lips, feeling his weight pressing into me lightly. "But I don't want to."

He leaned to me, the wind vanishing as he grew close. The faint scent of ale and leather filled my senses, and my eyes closed. A sound escaped me, seeming to meld me farther into him as his lips met mine. Salty from the wind, I tasted them, and his grip on my good shoulder clenched and relaxed.

My pulse pounded. I reached up with my uninjured hand, pulling him closer. My fingers twined in his hair at the nape of his neck. He pulled away with a surprised intake of air. My eyes opened and met his startled gaze. *I shouldn't be doing this,* I thought, not caring

"Come with me," he whispered. "Please, Tess. When this is over, promise you'll come with me? There's nothing to stop you now."

I couldn't answer. Knowing it was a mistake, I pulled him back to me.

He came willingly and with such a sudden fervor that I hesitated a bare moment before responding. *I should not be doing this,* came my thought again. *I should stop, and push him away. I should pull myself away from him and sit up. I should fight him so the pirates would believe his story.*

But all I could do was close my eyes at the unexpected want of desire rising in me.

The fingers of my right hand twitched, and, ignoring the hurt, I lightly curled my arm over his back, trying to pull him tight. His breath came in a quick sound, and his beard brushed against me as we kissed, softer than I would have expected. The weight of his hand met my waist, our skin touching where my dress had been torn. It wasn't the first time we had kissed, but every time we did, I lost a little more of my resolve.

An unwelcome, sudden commotion of light and noise broke upon us. I gasped as Duncan jerked away. I had forgotten.

Annoyance was real upon Duncan as he pushed himself up on one stiff arm and his knees. Scowling, he stared at the pirates ringing us, his anger clear in their flickering torches. I stared, wide-eyed, not knowing what to do. I clutched my dress closed about me the best I could, heart pounding.

"Git up," Mr. Smitty snapped, and I gasped when Duncan was yanked from beside me.

Ignoring my hurts, I scrambled up before any of them could touch me. I daren't look to the ocean, lest I give away that I knew the *Sandpiper* was in sight.

Duncan, though, was enough to distract anyone. "A pox on your souls!" he shouted, hunched and angry as he shook off the restraining hands on him. "She's mine. A man ought to be able to have what's his without you chull bait, river sludge, sheep puckies coming in to muck it up! She's mine! What the hell is wrong with you!"

Captain Rylan took in Duncan's anger and turned away. Mr. Smitty, though, rounded on him with enough fire to make the cheat stumble back a step.

"Where are they!" he bellowed, his face inches away from Duncan's suddenly startled eyes. "Where are the royals!"

Duncan blinked. "They were on their tethers when I cut her loose," he said, innocence thick and believable on him.

"Captain!" one of the crew shouted, pointing to the sea. "There they are!"

Everyone turned, and, peeping around them, I put a hand to my mouth as I saw the *Sandpiper*, her white sails full and round as she sailed from us, clear in the moonlight.

"Back to the ship!" Mr. Smitty shouted. "Back to the ship and on her. I want anchor struck afore I touch her decks. Go!"

All but Captain Rylan, Mr. Smitty, Duncan, and I scattered.

The men ran up the goat path, the light from their torches quickly vanishing to leave us in the glow of a single torch and the moon riding high and almost full.

"And you!" Mr. Smitty said, giving Duncan a push so he almost fell over. "I want you on the aft sail. You'll be bringing her up by yourself till I say different!"

"Aye, sir," Duncan said, the fire gone from his voice but not his eyes.

"Now, Mr. Smitty," Captain Rylan soothed. "Duncan couldn't have had anything to do with them escaping. He's just thinking with the wrong part of himself. If anything, he saved one of them for us."

"A whore I'd just as soon see dead!" the incensed man shouted, gesturing for Duncan to get moving. "And you're paying me to keep crew. You leave seeing to them to me!"

I held my dress closed as I stumbled to walk before them. For the first time in my life I felt shame for what I had done. No one had commented on me or my torn dress. I wasn't a woman any longer. I was a whore, a guttersnipe. I was the harlot that my mother had been and Kavenlow had bought me from. I was beneath notice and consideration.

My throat closed, and the warmth of tears pricked at my eyes as I weaved on my feet. Duncan caught my elbow, and pain tore through me. It was my bitten arm, and I almost passed out.

"Sorry, Tess," he said, as I staggered.

Duncan fell back when Mr. Smitty cuffed him. "Git your hands offa her!" he shouted, his voice rough and sounding like tearing cloth. "She looked eager enough to tumble with you, so she's well enough to walk on her own. Tie her to the foremast when you get her aboard," he added. "That's where whores belong. And she'll have a good view for when we take her queen back. I'm burning her boat to the waterline this time."

Thirteen

❖

I had watched the sun come up this morning while tied to the foremost mast. Mr. Smitty had tightened my ropes with a cruel severity, and my wrists stung from the repeated washes of waves that cascaded over the bow of *Kelly's Sapphire*. Salt water dripped from my curls and ran down my face, making me shiver in the gusts of cold wind. Mr. Smitty was turning the ship to intentionally hit the occasional wave wrong so that the water would come over the deck. Normally the crew would be complaining for the rough ride. Today, though, they stopped their work and cheered whenever an especially big wave hit me.

Adding to their delight was that Duncan had already been appointed to clean up the deck. Mr. Smitty had put him to work shortly after sunrise and the first wave hit me. Of course as soon as Duncan got the deck cleaned, a wave would crash over the stanchions and he'd have to start over. He was as wet as I was, and he wouldn't look at me, his neck red and his motions stiff with anger.

I was miserable, cold to my core and shivering. It was only an hour or so past sunrise, but I felt as if I had been tied to the mast forever. I didn't think I could get my cramped muscles to move even if I hadn't been tied.

My eyes had been fixed upon the sails of the *Sandpiper*

ever since we turned our bow to follow her, first by moonlight and now by sun. We were gaining very slowly, but I hoped that when the *Sandpiper* hit the stronger wind past the next string of islands, the longer boat would leap ahead. The capital was four easy days of sail ahead of us. They could make it in two hard days of sail, and perhaps as little as one and a half if they rode as if the hounds of hell were chasing in their foam path and the wind held.

We were now close enough that when the salt wasn't making my eyes tear, I could see figures moving about the deck. They had been throwing things overboard for the last hour, trying to lighten their weight so as to move faster, but the burned sails and limited rigging was slowing them where they once would have left us far behind. I fancied I could hear Captain Borlett shouting from time to time over the wind in my ears.

Captain Rylan was pacing from mast to mast in worry that we'd lose them despite the obvious inevitability of how this day was going to end, but Mr. Smitty and the crew had a confident, almost festive disposition.

"Captain Rylan!" the dour Mr. Smitty called, his voice carrying well. "I told you we'd catch them, and we will! You'll be walking a hole in my deck if you're not careful. Then poor Duncan will have to fix that, too."

I heard the well-dressed, bell-decked man's boots come to a halt close behind me. "I don't share your confidence, Mr. Smitty," Captain Rylan said, clearly peeved and impatient. "We should lighten our load as well."

"No need," Mr. Smitty said, and the men listening chuckled. "We'll be treating you to a fine bit of piracy afore the bloody boat gets halfway past that next island."

Looking bothered, Captain Rylan stomped past me to the bow, holding on to the railing through the waves as several of the crewmen laughed their agreement. The position of the sun shifted slightly, and the bouncing grew less. I relaxed a notch, knowing that as long as the captain stood there, no water would be coming over the deck to soak me.

From behind me came the soft sound of instruction being given, and soon Mr. Smitty padded up in his silent boots to Captain Rylan. "My boys," he said by way of greeting. "They set the markers as soon as we got here on the chance a merchant vessel came through early."

Captain Rylan grunted, the silver of his beard glinting in the sun when he turned to the shorter man. A wide grin came over his face, worrying me. "Where are they?" he asked, squinting as he looked forward.

Mr. Smitty pointed, and I followed Captain Rylan's gaze to a large stake jutting up out of the water to warn ships of a shallow spot. "I'll be damned," the captain swore. "How's the tide, Mr. Smitty?"

"Hanging as low as my dear mum's breasts," the man said with a cackle. "She might see the shallows, but in this light and with these waves, it won't do her any good. It's as fine a wrecking spot as we've ever had. She's a long vessel, and she'll never make the turn to get out. Not goin' as fast as she is. I don't care how much she threw over to lighten herself, she's going to ground."

I slumped into my ropes as I realized what was going to happen. The pirates had moved the shallow-water markers. A ship aground was easier to take than one moving.

"She's coming about!" came an excited call from the man hanging carelessly from a shroud high above the deck, and my eyes flew open. "Her sails are flapping! She's going, going . . . She's aground!" the man shouted. "She's aground and listing!"

A flurry of motion thundered as bare feet raced over the deck. Mr. Smitty looked like a wild man, his eyes glinting in anticipation. I sat helpless as he nodded once to Captain Rylan, and the two men walked past me to the wheel, their steps eager and fast. My heart sank. I was tied to the foremast and could do nothing but listen to the excited talk of how to best take my boat. Tar was being heated, and knots were being checked. The snick, snick, snick of metal being sharpened chilled me. I could do nothing. All my magical skills meant nothing.

We closed upon the floundering *Sandpiper* quickly, skimming over the shallower water with no hindrance. "Prepare grapples!" Mr. Smitty shouted, when we neared close enough to hear the shouts from the *Sandpiper*, and the men aboard her swarmed to the railing, ready to repel them. I searched the familiar faces, meeting them, seeing their resolve. Sailors with bared metal guarded the entrances to the lower decks. Captain

Jeck was among them. His face was empty, and he wouldn't look at me. My chest tightened in fear and shame that he had used me so easily.

"All hands to starboard hull!" Mr. Smitty bellowed, and I tugged at my bindings. "Not you, Duncan," he added harshly. "Get back here. You'll be my messenger boy."

Frantic with the need to be free, I squirmed and wiggled, trying to find enough slack to do something. My stiff muscles protested, and my shoulder throbbed. The best I could manage was to shift my position so I could see better. My sister was aboard that boat. I was responsible for her, and I'd lost her twice.

Panic started a slow burn in my belly. My pulse quickened at the sound of men shouting. I stiffened when the tingle of venom scoured through me. Frightened, I looked at Jeck, wondering if he had darted me over the closing distance for some reason. But though his face was grim and his muscles bunched in anticipation, he wasn't paying me any attention.

A wave of dizziness rose high through me, and my cold, sun- and water-soaked body began to tremble. I felt my face go ashen when I realized what was happening. I hadn't drawn on my magic, but the lingering venom in my healing tissues was being washed out by my increased blood flow. *God help me. Was this going to happen every time I was afraid?*

The sound of slapping water and the shouting of Captain Borlett drew my frightened gaze, and I breathed shallowly trying to fight off the vertigo. The shadow of the *Sandpiper*'s rigging fell over me, cold. "Hooks, away!" Mr. Smitty shouted. He was standing behind the wheel with an exuberant Captain Rylan and a sullen Duncan.

With a horrendous yell, the men with hooks flung them.

Pulling against my ties, I watched helplessly as Captain Borlett sent his men forward and they sawed at the ropes or tried to pry them loose.

"Haul us in!" Mr. Smitty shouted. Grunts rose as the ropes were tossed to the largest crew members waiting behind them, and muscles bulged and tensed.

"Board her! Take her!" Mr. Smitty screamed, and men swung from the stays, dropping to the deck like birds from an arrow. I watched, aghast when what looked like a hundred men swarmed aboard the *Sandpiper*. All were shouting and swinging their weapons. The two vessels slowly came together, meeting with a crack and groan that sent my heart into my throat.

Salt water burned my wrists, and they grew slick when I gave a cry and tore the skin. Spitting the hair from my mouth, I flung my head so I could see. "Jeck!" I cried when I found him. He stood taller then most, his black uniform a dark splash among the bare skin and colorful reds of the pirates. Again, I twisted, managing to gain my knees though my arms were bent cruelly backward and my legs ached so badly I had to hold my breath against the pain. He had to protect her. I didn't care if I lost my kingdom before I gained it. She was my sister.

My overwhelming need to get free died in slack amazement as I realized Jeck was killing the attacking crew with an eerie regularity. Sword swinging, he made the same four moves over and over again. Strike, parry, strike, strike—and the man was gasping his last atop the deck, and Jeck was stepping to the next.

Ringing him were men unmoving and spilling their blood or shuddering men dragging themselves away. Red made the deck shine under his feet. His bearded face was empty, his eyes lost under his black hair. I could see his jaw clench and release with every blow. The mindless numbness in his eyes and the savagery and strength of his motions were shocking in their contrasts.

I'd heard of men possessed by death before, but I'd never seen it. And that was what he looked like, one of death's minions standing atop my boat in his black-and-gold uniform, muscles moving untiringly as he fought with a silence that struck fear into those he fixed his eyes upon. I watched him strike another pirate with no care that the man had lived and breathed and would take no more joy in another day. The man fell, screaming his last breath out in pain and fear, and Jeck moved to the next.

Sickened, I hung my head. I would not say it was wrong. I would not say it was right. Stupid, stupid men who knew no other way to be, and so those who did had no choice but to respond in kind. My sister was helpless, and I knew I would do the same as Jeck if it would ensure her life.

But the sound of battle drew my head up as I hung in my

ropes and fought to keep conscious while the venom swirled in me. I watched through blurring vision the three men fight to protect a small forward hatch. Black spots swam before me as one fell. Captain Rylan shouted from the safety of his ship, and three more pirates hacked into the fray, headed for them.

I took three slow breaths, the muscles in my arms and legs starting to shake when I realized what was going on. Captain Rylan had just sent his best men to the hatch. *Contessa.*

Tension slammed into me, my racing pulse making venom burn in me like molten metal. "Jeck! The hatch!" I shrieked, when another Costenopolie sailor went down. The last quickly followed, overpowered by three pirates. "Jeck!" I cried, unheard over the shouting men and flapping sails.

He didn't hear. Sword swinging he cut down another, drawing a breath before he strode to the next.

My panicked gaze shot to the hatch. Two pirates stood before it, swords bared, but not fighting. They were belowdecks. The pirates had taken the lower deck!

I tried to stand, failing. Frustration scoured my veins, and I gave a mighty heave at my ropes. Pain raced up my arms and into my skull. I fell back to my knees, almost crying. I could do nothing. Jeck couldn't hear me.

"Jeck!" I cried again. The venom rose as fear and frustration made my heart pound.

Venom, I thought suddenly. If Jeck couldn't hear me, perhaps I could tell him in his thoughts. Fear for my sister brought my head up. My breath caught. I was balancing on the edge of unconsciousness already. If I tried to use my magic, I might pass out entirely or flood my body with so much toxin that I died. Searching my feelings, I decided I didn't care.

Frightened, I shut my eyes, trying to ignore the sounds of clattering canvas and the screams of men. I took three breaths, willing the venom into play. A feeling of disconnection made my head spin. I had to find Jeck's thoughts. I had to warn him they were below.

Vertigo came out of the darkness like a wave, smothering me. I gasped for air, unable to get enough. My hands cramped into a painful twist, and my head pounded as though someone were hammering on it. Tremors took me, the ropes binding me the only thing keeping me upright. I sent my thoughts out, searching for emotions not mine, wondering how I would find and separate Jeck from the swirling mass of fear and determination around me.

Mirror-bright thoughts of manta rays intruded, shocking me. I pushed them away, sensing their wonder and excitement at the new, curious things that had been sinking slowly and leading them here.

Panic took hold; I'd never find Jeck. I sank deeper into my search, hearing my breath go raspy and irregular as the venom started to affect my involuntary muscles. Suddenly, I fell into a frightening emptiness. I found myself willing myself not to think. There was no emotion for me but to finish a task I no longer knew the reason for. My muscles felt weary and heavy. They had begun to tremble, and I spared a thought that I must be getting old if I was feeling tremors after only this small exertion.

Faint in my thoughts was the barest whisper that something was wrong. This couldn't be right! But like a soap bubble bursting, it came to me.

I had found Jeck, his body weary and his mind shut down to all but one purpose. Our thoughts were mingling. He was feeling my body shaking under the overdose of toxin, and I was experiencing the empty emotion he coated himself with when he killed.

Jeck! I thought. *They've gained the lower decks! They're belowdecks!*

A new pain ripped through me. I gasped as my eyes flashed open. For an instant, I was on the deck of the *Sandpiper*, staring at my bright blood splattering the face of the frightened man before me. *She was in my head*, I thought, the notion not mine but Jeck's. *The chancellor's apprentice was in my head!*

Get out! I heard him demand. A fearsome cry of determination rumbled up from inside me, bursting out as Jeck shouted aloud. The two of us together sent his sword into the man before us with a strength born from his fear at what I had done.

Nausea bubbled up through me when I watched through Jeck the man's eyes bulge in a silent scream. He fell to his knees, his hands clutching Jeck's sword protruding from him. Then he fell to the deck, blood flowing as he tried to get away, his motions quickly losing strength as he drowned in his own blood.

Panting to keep from vomiting, I tore myself from Jeck's thoughts, finding myself kneeling and tied to the mast. Now I knew why Jeck emptied his mind when he fought. To watch himself do that would drive any man insane.

"Cease fighting!" I heard Alex cry out, his voice harsh in fear. "God save you, stop!"

Kneeling with my arms twisted behind me, I brought my head up. Tears blurred my vision. The shouting diminished to leave only the harsh clattering of the unattended sails. I tossed my head to see past my dripping curls, and my rasping breath grew steady. Tears slipped down my face unremarked upon. I had failed.

Contessa was on deck, a pirate's hairy arm about her neck and a short dagger digging into her side. Fear struck me like a slap. I'd seen a knife at my mother's neck once when Alex's brother had taken my kingdom through blood instead of marriage. And she had died in my arms, thinking he was bluffing.

Contessa was frightened, but her lips were pursed in that same defiance I had seen upon my mother before a soldier had slit her throat. Alex's sword was already in another's possession. His eyes were on Contessa, and his face was riven with failure. But it wasn't his failure, it was mine.

"Drop your sword, Captain!" Captain Rylan shouted from his wheel, his hands on his hips and his hat shading his face from the morning sun. "Your boat is aground and your prince and his queen are mine!"

"Do it," I whispered, knowing he couldn't hear me. "Jeck, drop your sword." The memory of my mother's death swirled up, choking me.

Jeck stood alone, surrounded by the carnage he had made, his stance wire-tight and unwilling to bend. One long tear in his uniform showed where a sword had reached him when my thoughts had distracted him. Past it, a shallow cut slowly oozed. The crewmen of the *Sandpiper* had already surrendered their weapons and were kneeling on the deck by the railing. Jeck was the only one left.

Never taking his eyes from Captain Rylan, Jeck tossed his sword into the air and caught it by the blade. His jaw clenched to make cords of muscle in his neck, he handed it to the man closest to him.

A cheer rose from the pirates. Contessa was pushed to the railing. A plank had been extended between the two vessels, and she was carried across, frightened and clutching at the man who held her. Alex was next, allowed to walk it with a sword pressing into his shoulder.

Contessa's eyes found me when her feet touched the deck. Her defiance washed away in panic. White-faced, they pushed her belowdecks right after Alex.

The surrendered crewmen were led across one by one. My spirits grew lower and tears closed my throat as Captain Borlett was dragged onto the pirates' ship, slung between two of his battered crew members. Blood seeped from him, making an ominous trail from his thigh to his foot. *Why?* I thought as I leaned forward into the ropes, uncaring that they burned into me. *What had it all been for?* It would have been better had Jeck never tried to free us.

My gaze went to him, now kneeling in the sun. His hands were bound behind him, and the surrounding men had nicked pieces of his skin to make his blood run. Jeck took it without comment, not recognizing the pain but for a steady tightening of the muscles in his shoulders. I felt sick. I had tried to make things better but only made them worse.

"What about him?" one of the men called, pointing his blood-smeared dagger at Jeck.

"Leave him," Mr. Smitty said. "A man like him won't leave his sovereign to become pirate. More likely he'd lie to remain free, then try to help his prince." He lifted his chin and ran a hand across it. "Isn't that right, Captain?" he called out.

Jeck raised his eyes from the horizon. "Yes, sir," he said softly, his resonant voice carrying over the slapping waves and thumping canvas. The captured Costenopolie soldiers were silent in their shame and fear.

"But bring me his boots afore you set the boat afire," Mr. Smitty said. Then he paused, turning to Captain Rylan. "That is, if you don't mind?"

The graying man snickered and moved his feet to make his belled boots ring. "Take the spoils of the battle, Mr. Smitty. I'm after the wealth of the war. And that tin of ointment he has in his things."

Mr. Smitty grinned. It was the first time I had seen such an expression on the short, dour man, and it didn't make him look anymore pleasant. "Get me his boots!" he demanded, and I watched, helpless, as they pushed Jeck down, cuffing him to stillness and taking his boots. His bare feet looked white in the sun, and odd, as he still wore his leather gloves.

The ship's boy scampered under the deck while Jeck clenched his jaw in frustration. A laughing cheer came from the pirates when the boy levered himself back onto the deck wearing Jeck's second coat. The black-and-gold fabric fell all the way to the planking, almost tripping him. Grinning wildly, the boy held up Jeck's stock of toxin in one hand, the player's second sword in the other. He scrambled back aboard the pirates' ship, running to Captain Rylan and getting his hair tousled fondly as the man tucked the tin into a wide pocket.

The last of my will to live turned to ash as they coated the decks and sails with oil. They were going to burn my boat—my beautiful, beautiful boat—with Jeck aboard it. My head slumped, and my hair swung to hide my vision. I couldn't bear to watch.

"The whore!" an excited voice called out, and I looked up. "Put her with him!"

My pulse swung back into full play, making my blood pound in my head and bound wrists. I scanned the deck, finding Duncan white-faced and standing with a paralyzed stillness. He looked from me to Captain Rylan, his mouth open but nothing coming out.

"Burn the whore!" the call went up and down the deck. "Her soul can't find us if it's been turned to smoke. Burn her!"

I held my breath as Duncan strode across the deck to the captain. The man in his faded clothes of past wealth pushed him away in disgust. "It's for your own good, boy," I heard over the calls to leave me on the deck of my burning boat. "She'll bring you down. Shut up, or I'll make you drop the torch."

Duncan persisted, his back to me as he gestured wildly. Captain Rylan scowled at Mr. Smitty, and the dour man barked an order. Two crewmen pulled Duncan from the captain and yanked him belowdecks.

"Tess!" I heard him shout as he disappeared. "Tess! I didn't mean this to happen. God help you. I didn't mean for this to happen!"

I clenched my jaw and tried to keep the air moving in and out of my lungs. I didn't protest when rough hands cut my bonds and pulled me to a stand. The pain in my arms and knees meant nothing. I hung in their grip when the pain of returning circulation brought a moan from me. Everything had been taken from me. I had lost. I had lost everything. And now I was going to lose my life.

The pirates were a slurry of color and noise. Faces came and went. Insults were layered upon me, each bending my head closer to the earth though I heard none of them. I went where they pushed me, numb and uncaring.

I felt the rocking of the ship cease and realized I was on the plank connecting the two. Self-preservation brought my head up. The smell of oil caught at my throat. A sheet of tossed oil slapped into me, and I stumbled, the sudden, shocking weight of it pulling me to the slippery deck of the *Sandpiper.*

Sprawled on the planking, I was suddenly aware I was covered in oil and my dress was all but falling off me. The pirates lined the railing, shouting and gesturing. My eyes fixed upon the one with the torch. He was waiting for the order, an ugly grin on him as he threatened to drop it early.

I scrambled up, and Mr. Smitty gave the call for the lines to be struck. I stumbled, my balance chancy with my hands bound behind me though the boat was still aground and unmoving. My legs were starting to work again, my knees protesting and aching.

"Here," Jeck said from behind me, and I spun. "Let me get your hands free."

My heart pounded as he took a knife gained from one of the downed men and sawed through my bonds. They fell away, and I swung at him.

"You chull!" I exclaimed as the watching men roared when Jeck easily caught my wrist. "How could you just leave me like that!"

I twisted, and Jeck pulled me closer until I was unmoving against his chest. "I never lied to you," he said, voice low and what looked like guilt in his eyes. "You made a bad assumption."

He was right, and realizing that the only way even to have

a chance at surviving would be to work together, I stopped fighting him. He felt it and let go. I fell back several steps, not knowing what would happen next.

"Captain Jeck!" came Captain Rylan's merry voice, and both our heads turned. He was atop the wheel deck with his hands on his hips and his hat shifted jauntily. "Don't worry about the whore's temper," the man said with a smirk. "The last man she went after like that, she rolled around in the sand with."

Jeck's breath came in a questioning sound, and the watching men hollered. One made kissing noises, hips gyrating suggestively, and I warmed. "Did you and your cheat—" Jeck started, his usually stoic face full of shock. If I didn't know better, I would think it bothered him.

"I had to find some reason to be on an abandoned beach with you sailing away," I snapped.

A whoosh of sound brought me spinning around. Heat slammed into me, warmer than the sun. The deck was on fire. My gaze went to the pirate ship. The torch was gone. It was on my deck. We were on fire. *God save me. I'm covered in oil.*

"Fill sails!" I heard Mr. Smitty shout. "All able men line up! I want a head count."

I stood blinking stupidly. They had set my boat on fire and were sailing away.

"Wake up, princess!" Jeck shouted, snapping me out of my stupor.

Tension slammed into me, and I reached for something to beat out the flames.

"No!" Jeck shouted, pressing a coil of rope into my hands. "She's going up. We can't stop her, and even if we could, it takes four men to raise a sail. Throw anything we can use overboard. And be careful!" he added, as I hunched into a fit of coughing when the black smoke took us. "You're covered in oil."

Jeck's hunched form vanished down the nearest hatch. A cask of water rolled out. I didn't know what else to do, so I pushed it to the railing, watching it almost sink as the flames grew closer and hotter.

"Jeck!" I shouted, as a wave of smoke rolled over me, turning the sunlight dim. "Hurry! It's getting hot!"

His head poked out, his bearded face wild as he took everything in and vanished. The end of one of Captain Borlett's old - square-rigged sails appeared. "Jeck! There's no time!" I cried.

"Just pull it out!" he bellowed from below. "Get it in the water!"

A crackling pulled my head up. I gasped when one of the stays snapped through. The mast creaked and groaned. "Jeck!" I shouted, my legs trembling as I gripped the sailcloth with my one good hand and tried to pull.

"Move over," he said from behind me, and I spun, surprised. He had come up the fore hatch. He roughly pushed me out of the way to reach around the wrapped wood and cloth. Muscles tightening, he pulled the heavy sail from the hatch. It was the smallest sail, but too much for most men. I took the end when it showed and probably was no help at all as I tried to carry the rope-bound bundle to the railing. It went over, and I looked at Jeck through the smoke, my arms shaking and my heart pounding as it slowly started to sink.

"You're next," he said, and he picked me up and dropped me over.

I barely had time to take a breath before I hit.

Water rushed in, cooling my fire-warmed skin. I bobbed to the surface, hacking and coughing, struggling to stay afloat with my tattered dress pulling me down. Jeck hit the water beside me, and I sputtered on the splash he kicked up. "What now?" I called, when he came up, water streaming from his beard.

He shook his head, sending beads of water flying in a shimmering spray. He glanced at the burning boat, then the nearby island. "Grab something and swim for shore," he said.

"Grab something and swim for shore," I muttered. "Now, why didn't I think of that?"

"And princess?" he said as he tied the wrapped square sail to a bobbing crate. "Don't ever go into my head again. Ever. Or so help me, I'll kill you myself."

"Don't worry," I whispered, remembering the mindless savagery that had filled me, an echo of Jeck's killing rage. "I won't."

Fourteen

❖

"Come here and pull this rope," Jeck said, jerking my attention up.

His voice was soft, preoccupied. If it had been anywhere near demanding, I wouldn't have moved. But as it was, I set my sewing aside on the sand and rose. Immediately, my eyes went beyond the surf to what was left of my boat, and I slumped. I'd been trying not to watch the *Sandpiper's* slow demise, but it was hard not to.

Most of the flames were gone since the rising tide had extinguished all but the highest. The tide had gone back out again, leaving the harsh black outlines of a broken boat and slumped canvas. The smoke had dwindled to a thin haze, and the ropes and a single half-charred sail dropped ash as she lay on her side and smoldered. What we had saved was pulled up past the high-tide mark in the sun. Jeck had gone out after the worst of the flames had subsided, bringing back rope, crates, and a second cask of water, which was slowly leaking.

My pace to join Jeck slowed, partially from the sand but mostly from my leg pulsing into a slow throb. The cold water had given me some relief, but my muscles had stiffened after sitting so long in the moving shade of the fronds.

Jeck had stretched the sail he had saved between the trees as

a canopy. Under it he was building a raft out of the conglomeration of planks, ropes, crates, empty ale barrels, and anything
else he thought he might be able to use. I frowned at the door
propped up and set aside to use as part of the deck, recognizing
it from the venom-induced dream. I knew where this was heading, but I wasn't going to tell *him* that.

Jeck was bare to the waist, having carefully hung his ruined
Misdev coat, black silk sash, and bloodstained, torn, white-
linen shirt up in the shade. The cuffs of his trousers were rolled
up in meticulous, even folds, coming to hang the same distance below his knees. Drying salt had stained the black wool
of his uniform's jacket, making ugly smears of uneven white
he couldn't brush out. I felt bad for him since he obviously
took pride in his appearance.

His bare feet shifting in the sand were big, ugly, and pale,
and he had flushed the time he caught me looking at them. The
deep cut he had received when I distracted him was red and
sore-looking, making him wince when he thought I wasn't
watching. Seawater had cleansed his smaller cuts and nicks
until they almost disappeared among the many old scars of his
profession.

The man was exhausted, and he still managed to look good.
It wasn't so much his appearance, though I'd be blind not to
notice how his muscles moved under his sun-darkened skin, or
how there was not an ounce of unneeded fat on him. No, it was
his confidence, his methodical pace of action leading to a pos-
itive end, his ease with himself, almost. He didn't need me to
tell him he was doing well or look to me for encouragement.
He didn't care what I thought, and that was an odd feeling for
me, one I found both irritating and intriguing.

Sweat shone on his wide shoulders in the lowering sun as
he dragged a tall beam to the block and pulley affair he had
rigged under a bending tree. Below was his makeshift raft. I
could feel his fatigue flow from him like a shadow as I stopped
beside him, the smell of his sweat not entirely unpleasant. Not
acknowledging me, he wrapped one end of the pulley's rope
around the top of the beam, tying it off. "Here," he said, handing me the tail end of the rope.

The rough rope scratching my fingers, I peered up at the
block and tackle he had rigged to hoist the heavy beam upright

so he could set it into place. A sigh sifted through me. It looked heavy, though the pulleys would lessen the work.

Jeck gave me an inquiring look and wiped a hand across his forehead. "Can you do it?"

Grimacing, I strengthened my grip, knowing my right hand was all but useless. I pulled, and with a sliding rattle, the rope ran through the pulleys and snugged up tight. I tightened my hold and pulled again. The end of the mast lifted. Jeck angled the lower end where he wanted it, so it would fall through the hole he had left in the raft if I managed to lift it high enough.

My shoulder started to hurt, and I turned to put my back against the rope, leaning into it so I could use my body weight to lift it higher. Salt from the rope burned into my palms, but the end rose another foot. Pulse quickening, I strained to raise it farther, feeling my body rebel.

"Let me help." Jeck gave a strong pull on the rope. The cord ran through the pulleys, and I staggered backwards. The mast hung at an awkward angle, one end right above the hole. "Got it?" he asked, eying me as he easily held the rope taut as if it were a kite string.

I snugged the rope over my backside and leaned back to use my weight instead of my muscle. He waited a moment after my nod to be sure, then gradually loosened his hold. The rope tightened against me, and I shifted my feet to counter its weight.

Jeck turned to the mast. "Good. Lower it slowly, and I'll tell you when to stop."

I inched my feet forward in the hot sand, and the mast eased into place.

"Hold it there," he said softly. Darting forward, he took a hammer and spikes, jamming wedges of wood between the makeshift mast and the edges of the hole.

Squinting from the bright light, I watched the sun shift across his bare shoulders as he swung the hammer with rapid, precise motions. Sweat trickled between his shoulder blades and across the whip marks he had gotten when I escaped last spring while under his guard. They were white, now, and well healed. I wondered how much had been due to the salve I had put on him and how much had been from my magic spontaneously trying to heal him while I did it. The curious warm tingling had never happened again, even when I had willed it with all my being. It was something Kavenlow couldn't teach me and Jeck wouldn't unless I became his apprentice.

It would never happen. I owed Kavenlow my life; Jeck had merely saved it.

"Almost . . ." Jeck muttered, dropping the hammer and reaching for one of the ropes he had previously tied around the top, settling them in grooves in the deck of the raft that he had laboriously chiseled out earlier. My balance shifted as he tugged, knotting three ropes upon one side, equally spaced along the length of the raft, and three upon the other. The rude stays looked shaky, but they would be better than nothing.

"Careful, now," he said, straightening. "Let it go."

The pulley clattered as the weight of the rope slid through and it swung free. I watched the mast. It held firm. Jeck leaned his weight into it, then more. Giving it a final shove and seeing it hold, he smiled for the first time all day. "Thank you," he said, and my lips parted at what he looked like smiling.

"You're welcome," I said, but he had turned away before he could have possibly heard me. His lips pressed together as he eyed the canopy, probably estimating how much of it he would have to cut to make a proper sail. I waited a moment, then returned to my spot in the shade. I didn't have anything to do and had been trying to mend my dress. It was likely going to be cold tonight, and I wanted it to be whole and dry if I could manage it.

I was in my underthings right now. Jeck either didn't know the white lightweight dress was really my underskirt and bodice—or he didn't care. I'd be willing to wager it was the latter.

Sitting back down under the trees, I tucked the braid I had made of my hair out of my way and finished sewing the torn side of my dress back together. My fingers felt thick and slow, but I refused to get depressed about it as I was lucky even to be alive. Taking a moment to stretch them in one of Duncan's finger warm-up exercises, I watched Jeck putter with the ropes.

I didn't know what to think about Jeck anymore. I'd found him to be very quiet, reserved, and single-minded to the point of being rude. I wasn't angry with him any longer since he seemed to know what he was doing better than I did. And he was a master player where I was a student—a student of a rival player, no less. I had no problem taking direction from someone I respected, and much as I hated to admit it, I was starting to respect Jeck for who he was and what he was capable of. *I* couldn't make a raft.

I dropped my attention to my stitching when Jeck poured salt water on the stays to tighten them. Finished, he straightened, stretched with a moan of exhaustion, and headed toward me and the shade. I said nothing as he sat, puffing from his exertions, but my pulse quickened.

Seeing him wipe the sweat from his brow pinched with weariness, I dipped a shell of water out of the cistern he had put me in charge of and offered it to him.

Jeck looked askance at me, still breathing hard. I could smell the sweat on him, and the ocean. "I've had my ration until the sun sets," he said, the words leaving him in a breathy sound.

"It's my ration," I said. "I'm not thirsty."

He wiped the back of his hand across his bearded chin and gazed at the *Sandpiper*. "Drink it. It's yours."

"I'm not thirsty," I repeated. "And you've been doing most of the work."

"Princess, don't try to soothe your conscience by giving me your water ration."

Affronted, I nevertheless kept my tone even. "My conscience is fine, Captain. It was your miscalculation that allowed them to catch my boat and burn her to the waterline, not mine. I'm not thirsty. You are. Take the damn water and drink it. We have two casks."

Face expressionless from behind his black beard and mustache, he took the shell from me. His hands were red from the sun, the knuckles starting to swell. He downed it in one gulp, handing me the shell back and looking out over the surf to the *Sandpiper* again. "Thank you."

I said nothing, feeling vindicated.

He was silent, then, "My miscalculation?" he asked, his tone mild and slightly amused.

I wasn't angry; I wasn't anything. "Yours."

Jeck didn't seem upset as he stretched his legs out with a soft moan of ache. His eyes flicked to me and away as I sat cross-legged and finished my sewing. He had an entire beach to sit on. Did he have to sit this close?

"I thought you were angry," he said. "For my tricking you about the beach."

Tying a knot in my thread, I bit the needle free and replaced it in the damp sewing kit Jeck had rescued from Contessa's things on his third trip back to the boat. "At the time I was so angry I could have tied my pillow in a knot," I said. "But in hindsight, it was a good idea."

My eyes met his, holding them. "I've been a decoy before. Next time, I'd prefer to be told my place in the game. I'd have led them on a merry chase for you if you'd been honest with me. Given you time to put more distance between you and any pursuit. Perhaps enough that you wouldn't have been caught in those shallows." *Idiot*, I added in my thoughts, but I didn't say it.

Jeck's impassivity trickled away into amazement. "You would have voluntarily stayed behind?" he said, his brown eyes wide.

Uncomfortable in that I didn't know for sure, I looked at my finished stitching. "She's my sister. She's my master's most important piece. And with the two of them safe, I was the pirates' only chance at gaining a ransom, so I would have been reasonably safe once they started to think again. Besides, I already know I'll survive—somehow." I didn't need to bring up the prophetic dream. I was sure Jeck's thoughts were turning the same direction.

"What about your cheat?" he asked, moving so the sand hid most of his feet. "Would you have left him behind knowing you weren't going to make it off the island?"

My fingers worked at the tie of the sewing kit, unable to manage a simple knot without fumbling as the memory returned of Duncan pressing into me and the feelings his kiss had stirred. My attention flicked to Jeck, then away.

Jeck pulled his knees back to him and started to unroll his trouser legs. "I left him behind. You called me a coward—"

"No, I didn't," I interrupted quickly.

"No," he said slowly. "I guess you didn't." He took a breath. "Princess, about your cheat . . ."

"Don't call me that." My pulse quickened, and I didn't

know why. He hadn't said more than three words to me all day, and now he was touching upon things that weren't his business.

"But you are," he prompted. "Technically."

"Technically, I'm a guttersnipe," I shot back, feeling my anger rise.

"No," he insisted. "They bought you a name."

He sounded almost jealous, and my lips pursed. "Your father gave you his." There was a difference. It was subtle, and I really didn't know what it meant.

Jeck sat up and reached for his shirt, hanging beside me. "Princess, about Duncan."

"Oh?" I mocked. "He has a name now?" I didn't want to talk about Duncan, and anger seemed to be my best defense.

Just as I'd hoped, Jeck's face closed. "Never mind," he muttered, jamming his arms into his sleeves and working the front laces. Shirt half-undone, he rocked to his knees and reached out for me.

"Hey!" I shouted, pulling back. "What the chu pits are you doing?" Surprised, I rolled to my knees out of his reach. My muscles protested at the quick motion, and my pulse hammered. *I'm in my underthings! Does the man have no sense of propriety?*

His dark eyes were empty. "I saw you hurt your shoulder while pulling the mast up. Let me see it. You may have torn something open."

My hand rose to hide my shoulder. All the wounds were closed, covered in new skin. It looked a week healed, not three days. I didn't want him to see it. I didn't want him to know how close we were to the time where that prophetic dream figured in. "It's fine," I said, voice shaking. Knowledge was power, and me knowing how far off that dream was and him not was all I had. And I didn't trust that empty look he was wearing.

"Let me see," he insisted, inching forward on his knees in the shade-cooled sand.

"No." I got up, sand shifting beneath me.

Irritation crossed his bearded face—emotion at last. "I'm not going to hurt you," he said, standing as well.

My breath came fast as I ran my eyes up his much bigger frame and felt my face go white. "Then you won't have a problem staying away from me. I'm going to check the tide pools for fish." Turning my back on him, I started to walk away, moving faster than my aching right leg was ready for.

Hard and fast, my heart pounded as I heard him start after me.

"Princess . . ."

"It's Tess," I said. A hand hit my left shoulder, and I spun. My hand was swinging for his face, and he caught it.

"Just let me see," he demanded, holding my left wrist. *Damn it, he's almost smiling.* "I want to know how long until we reach the mainland and find that horse in your dream."

"No . . ." I insisted, frightened. He was a master player. I was a student. Why was he making me defend myself?

My blood abruptly sang as he pressed his lips together and tugged me closer. I staggered as the venom from my bite surged, pulled from my healing tissues by my fear. My vision dimmed, and I sagged to my knees. Jeck followed me down, half-supporting me.

"Just let me see," he said grimly, reaching out.

"Jeck?" I said, my eyes suddenly unable to focus. An unreal feeling of disconnection reverberated through me. I felt like a plucked wire, tension singing through my bones and setting my hands to tingle. "Jeck?" I called again, louder, this time as a plea for help.

Something was happening. Panic clenched my heart, forcing it to beat faster. A bubble of force glowed in my belly, hot, angry, demanding to be used. Jeck's hand was gripping my upper arm, his fingers working at the tie of the bandage beneath my underdress.

"Jeck, let go," I panted softly, afraid if I raised my voice, the bubble would break. But my fear wiggled under it, forcing it higher, closer to the surface. "Jeck, let go!" I said, louder, and the anger swirled, creeping upward to send red tendrils into my head and squeezing.

"Jeck!" I shouted, unable to feel his grip any longer but knowing he was still there by the anger building in me. "Jeck! Let—*go!*"

The last word was a shout, the sound of it breaking the bubble of anger in me. It rolled through me, gathering up my will and taking it with it. Anger poured from me, burning as it went. I couldn't control it. It controlled me.

I watched as if from outside myself when my hands reached for Jeck, grasping his forearms as he held my shoulders. His black eyes widened when my fingers fastened about his muscular arms. "God, help me," he whispered as if he saw what was coming.

And then my anger hit him.

White-hot and ravenous, it spilled from me. The fear, the pain, the frustration I'd been holding in raged from me in a single instant. I heard myself screaming. It was too much, and a gray haze of denial slipped between me and my fury, protecting me. But Jeck got it all.

Crying out, Jeck jerked himself backwards, falling to the sand.

"Leave me alone!" I found myself shouting, standing over him. "I will not be pawed over! I am not a thing to be bought or sold. I am not a child or a dog that you know what's best for! *I* make my choices, and *you* will not force them on me! I said no, and *I mean no!*"

Shocked, I closed my mouth, my hand rising to cover it as I realized I was screaming. The anger was gone, spent. As hot and furious as it had been, it was gone, leaving me feeling cleansed. The hurt in my shoulder was absent for the first time since I had been bitten, and I stood upright and unpained. Jeck, though, wasn't moving, sprawled before me on the sand.

"Jeck?"

Worried, I looked at my hands. They were red, and the wind across them made them tingle. "Jeck?" I called again. *Oh God. I've killed him.*

"Jeck!" I dropped to my knees beside him, the jolt from the hard-packed sand reverberating up my spine. I reached to touch him, then snatched my hand back when he moved. My heart hammered, and I felt like I was going to pass out. The feeling of euphoria was gone, and the trauma of the last few days thundered back down on me.

"Did you catch it?" His voice was thready, a hand over his eyes as he faced the sky.

Relief shook me, and my fingers trembled. *He's alive.* "Catch what?" I said, lurching back when he rolled over to sit up, his head bowed over his bent knees. Sand caked him, and he brushed it from him, not looking at me.

"Your hands," he said breathing heavily. "Did you see what you did? Did you feel it?" He coughed, hunching as if his ribs hurt. "Please tell me you did." He took a shaky breath, dropping his forehead to his bent knees. "I don't want to do that again."

A sick feeling slipped through me, and my gaze flashed to my hands. "What did I do?" I whispered, frightened. I felt numb, disconnected. *What had I done?*

Jeck's brown eyes were pinched when he pulled his head up. "You tried to kill me. This morning, you nearly released a killing pulse when you tried to slap me." Still hunched, he wedged his legs under himself and lurched to his feet and stared into the vegetation. "You stopped yourself, not even conscious of where you were going. You're a half-tamed wolf, Tess, ready to bring down foe or friend alike until you learn to control this."

I couldn't seem to get enough air. A wash of cold went through me despite the sun. The waves hitting the beach sounded hollow, echoing in my ears. *What had I done?*

"I've been trying all day to get you angry enough to do it again," Jeck said, continuing to brush himself off. "So you could learn to recognize it and gain control of it before you kill someone you care about. But the more closed I got, the more you seemed to like it. I should have known all I needed to do was try to touch you."

My mouth was dry, and I couldn't swallow. "You taught me how to kill a person with my hands. . . ." Slowly the realization forced itself into my consciousness. *How dare he!*

He squinted at me, looking beaten and tired. "Yes, I did."

My anger started to rise, and my jaw clenched. "You taught me how to kill with my hands." The glow of anger started anew. I recognized it this time, and I willed it to grow. He nodded, and I whispered, "You dirty . . . filthy . . . dock bastard."

Jeck's head jerked up. Surprise flicked over him. "Now, wait a moment . . ."

"I am not your apprentice!" I shouted. The warmth trickled

upward, fanning my anger to a white-hot heat. It was happening again, but it was as if I was beside myself, watching.

"Princess . . ."

He was backing up, now, and I was following, feeling the venom surge as my pulse increased and my anger topped. "I will not owe you anything!" I said. "I didn't ask for this!" I flung my hands at him in accusation. My pulse pounded, and venom scoured unchecked to make my fingers tingle and my leg sluggish.

Jeck's eyes were riveted to my hands, but he wasn't afraid. "Princess—"

"Don't call me that! I didn't want to know how to kill with my hands! You knew that!"

"Tess." His hands were out in placation, moving but not touching me. I took a step forward, and he retreated, going ankle deep into the surf. "Tess!" he exclaimed, a hint of alarm in him. "It was Kavenlow. Kavenlow wanted you to know, not me!"

I rocked back in disbelief, reading the truth of it in his pained eyes. He stood barefoot in the surf with an old look of pain flitting in his dark eyes. My heart pounded, and I hesitated.

"You taught yourself," he said, his low voice soothing, seeming to go right to my core. "It was going to happen one way or the other. Listen to me," he pleaded when I turned away in confusion. "It was going to happen. You were going to learn this whether you wanted to or not. This way, you only hurt me, not accidentally killed the person you were arguing with."

And with that, my anger vanished in an icy wash. My lips parted, and my knees shook as the venom swirled, magic unfocused with nowhere to go. I felt it slowly seep into me, easing from my healing tissues into my veins to make me dizzy and nauseous.

"Like Duncan," he said, his eyes wise and knowing as I stood in shock, realizing what he had done in his past; the hurt in his eyes was too real. "Or even Kavenlow," he whispered, taking a step out of the surf. "Neither of them would have survived that. I could see it happening and prepare for it, protect myself. Anyone else would have died, Tess."

My throat closed, and I turned away, clenching my arms about myself. From behind me, I heard him step out of the gentle surf. "Killing a person with nothing more than your will leaves a bad enough scar," he said from right behind me. "But to kill someone you love by accident?" He took a ragged breath. "In an instant of easily forgotten anger?"

I clutched my hands about myself and turned to him. The ocean touched my heels—a cool caress that quickly retreated to leave me colder. Jeck stood before me with his trousers wet about his ankles and his white shirt still undone. The wind ruffled his black hair, and he looked far and distant from the upright, refined if somewhat rough, Misdev officer he was. He took in my understanding, obvious by my white face. *God help him. He killed someone he loved.*

Pressing his lips together, he dropped his gaze. "This was your master's choice, not mine. Be angry at him, not me."

Back hunched, he walked past me, leaving me frightened and confused. I hastened after him, the sand cold and firm under my feet. "Kavenlow?" I quavered.

Jeck never slowed. "That's why I was able to come on this trip," he said, still walking away. "He didn't want me here. He had everyone convinced I wasn't necessary for security. I bought his permission to enter his playing field with the understanding that if your skills grew to this point, that I would teach you how to control it properly." A rueful chuckle escaped him, and he stopped, hands on his hips, head cocked, and his back to me. "I didn't think you would reach this point for five to ten years more. He made a good deal, your master. We're even now."

He started to walk again. I followed. "Jeck," I said, fear heavy in me for what I had become—what we both were. "Who . . . did you kill when you learned how to do this?"

Wide shoulders tense, he hesitated. "A woman," he said, not turning. "It was an accident. I might have cared for her. I don't remember."

"Yes, you do," I whispered, the cool wind lifting a lank strand of my hair.

At that, he turned, his stance tired and his motions weary. "It's easier if you don't."

I swallowed, remembering what he had said about my hurting him instead of killing someone I loved in a moment of anger. I knew without asking that he had loved her, but making him admit it would have been cruel. And for that, I pitied him.

Jeck scanned the horizon behind me, his weary gaze lingering upon what was probably the wreck of my boat. "Soon as the tide shifts, we float the raft out on it." He met my eyes, frightening me with how empty they were. "Don't touch me again."

Without another word, he went to his raft, his steps slow and his back bowed. I was left standing alone, the wind from the sea tugging at me. *Don't touch me again,* I heard in my memory as he tried to brush the salt from his dried coat. *Don't touch me again.*

Fifteen

❖

The sun had gone down, and the wind coming off the sur-
rounding water was chill. Despite having spent most of the
day in the shade, my skin was warm to the touch and had the
rosy glow of a mild sunburn. Jeck was fine. Either his darker
skin was not bothered by the sun, or perhaps he was protected
by his ability to heal, an ability he wouldn't share with me lest
I figure out how to do it. I thought it disgusting that both
Kavenlow and Jeck apparently thought it necessary that I
should know how to kill with my magic, but neither thought it
important to be able to heal with it.

Jeck's raft floated, and if the wind had stayed with us, it
would have sailed. We had left our island on the outgoing tide
and a midnight breeze. But now the wind had died, and the
tide had slacked. We drifted in a silver world of moon and soft
waves, far from anything and at the mercy of the currents.

Jeck hadn't said a word since the square sail had grown
limp, the canvas and ropes hanging like dead things. He sat
cross-legged near the edge of the raft atop the flat panel of the
door, pensively watching the rays ghost beside us, occasionally
rising to within inches of breaking the surface, then sinking
again. The two casks of water were lashed to the mast beside
the small bundle of perishables he had managed to save from

the floundering *Sandpiper*. I eyed our food supply, hungry but not enough to argue with him that we should eat it now before the waves and sun spoiled it. I recognized the night as almost twin to my first venom-induced dream, and I vowed that it would not end with me tied and his prisoner. Warned was armed, and the future wasn't set.

I sat in the middle of the raft beside the tapped water barrel, the fingers of my good left hand wedged between the wood and the rope for stability. My forehead was pressed against the damp cask, and the fingers of my right hand trailed in the water through a large gap in the planking. The coolness of the water seemed to rise up my arm and soak into me to soothe my sunburned skin. I should have been sleeping, but my concern for Contessa and the memory of that venom dream kept me as awake and jittery as if it were noon.

"How long, do you think?" I said, then coughed, as I hadn't spoken since sundown.

Jeck met my eyes before sending his to the silver-marked horizon. "Longer if we don't get any wind," he muttered.

"How long?" I persisted, clearer this time. My lips were cracked, and salt stung them.

"I don't know the coast as well as I do Misdev's mountains."

I did, thanks to my afternoons spent in the solarium copying them. Maybe it hadn't been such a waste of time after all. "We're somewhere south of Yellow Tail," I said. "It might have been faster to have gone farther south to Dry Fort, and get horses there to ride to the capital." A growing sense of urgency tightened my stomach, and I forced the tension out of me, imagining it going into my fingers, then out into the water. Nearby, a ray kissed the surface. "I have to get to the capital before them. If Kavenlow believes Contessa's note, he'll be working with bad information. He might not pay the ransom. They'll kill them both. I know it."

"Kavenlow will manage it." Jeck bowed his head in what I thought might be embarrassment. The moonlight hid the grime and sweat, making him a shadow of black and white against the slow, flat swells. "It's going to put him in a hell-fire good position, no matter how it turns out. God help me, I never should have agreed to this."

My back stiffened. "I'm worried about my sister, not the fool game," I said, allowing a hint of anger to color my voice. My attention dropped to his black sash, tightened about his middle again. *He wouldn't tie me up for arguing with him, would he?*

He turned to me, shaking his head. "You really care for her, don't you? Why? She's a piece in your game. You've only known her for three months."

"She's my sister," I said, affronted.

His face went unreadable behind his beard in the dark. "Only by law. You shouldn't care for her. Someone will use it against you."

"You?" I asked belligerently.

He nodded, his dark eyes expressionless. "If I can. If I need to."

"Chull bait," I swore mildly, not having the impetus to dredge up anything more. "You are chull bait, Captain."

The soft sound of water lapping the edges of the raft seemed loud as he turned away. "Players don't have family. You should remember that you have no ties of blood to her."

"Yesterday you said they bought me a name, and I should use it."

He cocked his head so the light of the moon fell on him. "Don't confuse ties of law with ties of blood. She isn't really your sister."

"Kavenlow is like a father to me," I said, taking offense.

"That's his failing, and it's going to bring an end to his game someday."

"It makes him stronger," I asserted.

"Being moved by emotions is dangerous," he said, his voice mixing with the silky wave tops. "It leads you to take risky chances, ignore possibilities and deny uncomfortable realities."

I pulled my fingers from between the rope and the water cask, tucking a strand of lank hair behind my ear. "I disagree. It emboldens your spirit and keeps your mind open to possibilities that you might not consider. You're lacking, Captain, and you don't even know it."

He grunted and shifted his foot so that his bare heel touched the water. I couldn't help but feel we were connected somehow

through the water. Immediately, I pulled my fingers out and
dried them on my grimy dress. A manta ray jumped nearby,
and remembering having seen them in my dream, I vowed to
do nothing that would make him tie me up. But it had been
stormy in my dream, and after seeing the sun go down in a
faultless sky, I was fairly confident we would get nothing but
clear weather for days.

Jeck pulled his foot out of the water. It was very slow and
casual, but I could tell the rays were making him nervous.

"They eat shrimp and small clams," I said, dangling my
hand back in the water to prove I wasn't afraid. I felt restless,
and the dark water seemed to help.

"It's said they jump out of the water to capsize small boats,"
he said wryly.

Landlubber, I thought, shrugging. "Only if you have shrimp
with you."

He was looking at my submerged hand. Smug, I took it out
and replaced it with my foot, sinking it almost to my knee. I
had done it only to bother him, but it felt so good, I decided to
keep it there, even when a ray bumped my calf with its rough
and smooth skin.

"And how would they know if there're shrimp in the boat
unless they sank it first?" he asked, clearly uncomfortable.

A second ray jumped, bigger and closer, and the water
thrown up from its clumsy reentry sent splatters of seawater
across the raft. "That one knows. He'll tell the rest."

Jeck made a scoffing noise. "Bring your feet in, Princess.
There are things in the water that want to eat you."

So of course, I left it there, enjoying the slow current brush
against me with the softness of silk. I felt odd and disconnected
from the late hour and the unreal look of the moonlight. The
chill from the water was soothing. It was closer to sunrise than
sunset. "Don't call me that," I whispered, feeling the rise of
quiet anticipation in me. The sail was flat. It should be full. I'd
never beat them to the capital. Not going this slow.

"Faster," I breathed, pulling my foot from the water and
lurching to a stand. The raft hardly moved, heavy and low in the
water. The sluggish numbness of my leg and arm had eased, and
though I was still stiff, and my stamina was nowhere near where
it should be, I could function without pain if I was careful.

I stood with one hand on the mast for balance, sending my dripping bare foot up and down to test my limits. There was a definite improvement, but even so, I was concerned. The venom was still in me. I could feel it, hanging right below my awareness, silent and still. It wasn't leaving my body as it ought to, almost as if it was renewing itself. As if by fixing in my tissues, I had unintentionally given it a home and a way to make more of itself, much like the punta did.

Tension pulled through me, and my grip on the mast tightened. If that was true, I'd never be able to reduce my residual levels no matter how long I shunned using the poison. *Kavenlow. What would I tell him?*

"Do they often follow rafts like this?" Jeck asked, jerking me from my uncomfortable thoughts. "The rays," he prompted, seeing my confusion.

He hadn't moved, still sitting by the edge of the raft with his head bowed. Moonlight had turned his black hair to silver. Letting my foot touch the planking, I shook my head. "No." From my higher vantage point, I watched them escort us. They seemed to be waiting for something as they flew under the raft from side to side, seldom more than a foot below the surface. Their dark shadows looked like the waves come to life, flowing like a current.

A restless feeling rose in me like a mist: an impending something. I needed to be going faster. I gazed toward the unseen mainland, fidgeting.

"From Yellow Tail we can purchase horses," I said, but I knew from his slumped posture that he wasn't listening. "If the wind would pick up, we could make better time by water to the coast. They have a stable at Sharp Bend, too. They'll remember us and give us horses. We might reach the capital before the pirates—if the wind would pick up." I was babbling. The restiveness in me wouldn't let me keep my mouth shut. I had to be moving.

"The wind isn't going to strengthen," Jeck said to his ugly feet. The canvas slapped the mast and ropes as a slow swell rolled under us. "Sit down before you tip us over. Your master will take care of them." His head rose to show his eyes were pinched and worried. "We're out of this game," he said, the sound of confession in his voice.

"I'm not." I wanted him to be quiet so I could think. Wind. All we needed was wind. It irritated me to be dependent upon something so fickle.

I scanned the black horizon. The sun had gone down in pinks and blues. No wind likely tomorrow, either. I'd be stuck on this raft with Jeck for days. By the time I got off, there would be nothing I could do but mourn my sister. If I got off.

"Wind," I whispered, closing my eyes. I would give anything for it.

A distant splash pulled my eyes open. Bubbles showed where a huge ray had touched the surface. Three more swam just below. I put my second hand atop the mast and stood before the slack sail, feeling the lack of movement all the way to my feet. The mast was like a dead thing under my palm. Even a tree had movement.

"Wind," I breathed, a sudden thought striking through me. The punta had called a gust of wind to confuse his escape. I had felt it: the surge of power through our shared thoughts. "I can do that," I said softly.

"What?" It was flat and emotionless, just like Jeck pretended to be. He lied to himself if he claimed honor and the game moved him alone. He had loved once. That he hid all emotion now proved it.

"I can call the wind," I said.

He pulled his head up at that, and I shifted from foot to foot, feeling the rough boards upon the bottoms of my feet. A thrill of anticipation struck through me, seeming to set my fingers and toes to tingle.

A snort escaped him. "You can't call the wind. This isn't a child's bedside story. You're stuck here until time and the tide bring us in. Accept it. Think beyond it."

My lips pursed. "I am a guttersnipe who is slated to secretly rule a kingdom. I can kill with a touch, thanks to you. I can walk through a crowded room unnoticed and can call my horse to me upon command. My entire life is a child's bedside story. Don't tell me I can't call the wind."

I didn't know why I was trying to convince him. It wasn't as if he could forbid me from trying. "I saw how the punta called the wind," I said, and he turned away in scorn. "I was trying to charm him so he wouldn't bite me," I admitted, and Jeck swung his head back to me. "It almost worked, and it hurt both of us when he bit me. He called the wind to hide his escape when I told him how to get out of that pit. I saw how he did it. I can do it, too." A shiver raced through me, the night air cool through the tattered dress that I had washed in seawater and dried hanging from a palm frond on an empty beach while Jeck built his raft. I would tell no one that the punta had turned the tables and charmed me.

Jeck's eyes were black in the dim light. "You told him how to get out of the pit?" he questioned, and when I said nothing, he raised a placating hand. "Fine. Call the wind."

It was patronizing and all but dripped scorn. Suddenly unsure, I shifted from foot to foot. The stars were few and small, and Jeck's silhouette was sharp against the lowering moon as we rode the slow swells. "Well?" he mocked, and my jaw clenched.

"Stop watching me," I demanded.

My face burned when he laughed and turned away, bending his knees and resettling himself on his useless raft. "Call the wind," he muttered.

I stiffened. "Kavenlow would believe me."

"Kavenlow is a dreamer. See what he dreamed up with you?"

It was very close to an insult—not like Jeck at all—and I wondered if he was worried that I could actually do it or if he might be jealous of Kavenlow's love for me. The punta could do it; I could do it. I had to do it. For my sister. For Kavenlow's game that I'd fouled up yet again with my inexperience and naïveté.

Hand upon the mast to steady myself, I snuck a glance at Jeck. He sat as if he weren't there, his eyes on the horizon, his mind on other things. Taking a steadying breath, I closed my eyes, willing my magic to fill me.

The vertigo came quickly, as if it had been waiting. Fingers tingling, I tightened my grip on the mast and shifted my feet. My heart pounded, sending a second, higher surge of venom into me. It was as if the last four days of the toxin working its way out of me hadn't happened. I was simmering with it still. Blinking profusely to ward off the dizziness, I snuck a glance at

Jeck to be sure he wasn't watching, then closed my eyes again. I could do this.

The blackness of the night was replaced by the blackness of my mind. Thick and potent, I felt the force in me rise, waiting for direction. My heart pounded and my knees grew watery at the strength of it. I'd never had so much magic in me. The punta bite had shifted my balance far beyond safe levels. But it was easier to bear now that I wasn't so weak. Or maybe I was just getting used to it. *Kavenlow,* I thought in shame. *What am I going to tell him?*

The surging power tugged at me, and my heart leapt into my throat when it all but slipped my grip. My shoulder started to throb, and my right leg and arm went numb. My breath became shaky, and I worked to even it out before Jeck heard. With a shock, I realized I had fallen into a pattern of three breaths and a pause, just like the punta's. It seemed to help with the vertigo, and so I kept to it, trying to be unobtrusive as Jeck sat four feet away from me and sulked that his fine new raft was useless without wind.

As my blood hummed with the potential in me, my mind returned to the pit and the punta. The big cat had called from the upper sky a fast-moving blast of air, channeling it with his will to a path it wouldn't take on its own. I needed far more than a whirl-a-wind. I had to call a veritable storm to reach the coast quick enough to do any good, and storms were born not in the upper reaches of the sky but the deep ocean.

Softly, carefully, I sent out a questing thought, skimming it above the slow wave tops the texture of black silk, past the warm current that kept my kingdom free from the worst of winter's cold, past the rising and falling mountains of waves. I sent my thoughts past the curve of the earth to the deep ocean, where the rays don't go, out to where the wind gathers power from the waves, which steal it from the moon and the tides born from the spinning of the earth and sun.

I shivered as the warmth of noon enveloped me, coming from within. The glitter of the sun on bright wave tops sparkled behind my closed eyelids, burning my vision though the sun was down. I heard the lonely cry of the albatross. *Here,* I thought. *Here is where devil storms are made.* But around me was nothing but soft whispers of wind. There was no storm to control.

You are mine, I whispered to the soft zephyr of wind coming from a sun-heated wave top. *Wake. You will come to me.*

My soul found and tentatively gathered a stillpoint of heat. The gust rose and flitted from me, and I snatched it with my will, trying to hold it, trying to bring it to awareness. *Wake.*

The gust rounded on me, turning into a breeze in its anger to escape me. I expanded my reach, soothing it. *How dare I?* it seemed to question when I surrounded it with my strength, claiming it as my own.

My pulse leapt, and it grew, taking power from the waves under it and the hot sky above. The breeze rose to become a wind, tearing the tops of the glittering waves and pushing them away in its sullen temper. I felt myself stagger when venom spilled into my veins, strengthening my will. Renewed, I fastened upon the wind, demanding obedience. *You are mine*, I thought. *You're mine until I free you. Do what I say, and I'll free you.*

It roared at me, whipping about and thundering its defiance. It pressed the waves flat for an instant, then pulled them high. Violent and wild, it tore at my thoughts, screaming at me as it tried to shred my will to break free. It grew to a murderous size, roaring up into the blue sky, falling back to smash into my thoughts.

I held firm, demanding that it find me. With the strength of the punta coursing through me, I had it. It was mine. It couldn't escape. The power of the spinning earth and rising sun was mine. Not until it did my will would I let it go.

And it swirled into a sly obedience, settling into my thoughts with false platitudes of submission. Flattening out the waves, it raced to find me. Like a child with a lie, I could see its intent. It was going to kill me.

I gasped, snapping back to myself and finding my hand atop the mast. Jeck was standing before me, his coat open and his pant legs rolled back down. I didn't remember him getting up. "Tess?" he questioned, his wide shoulders hunched and his brown eyes concerned.

A zephyr sent a curl to dance about my face. A chill took me at the thought of what I had woken. "I found the wind," I whispered, knowing the zephyr was a vanguard of the storm I had called. It would follow the zephyr to me to fall upon us like lions.

"You what?"

"I found the wind." The mast under my hand started to hum. My face tightened in alarm, and seeing it, Jeck bent his head to mine in worry. The force running in the mast doubled, and my grip upon it seemed to go numb. A breeze shifted my hair, and the slack sail tugged at its ropes and went still.

"God help me," I whispered, looking up at the stars against the fluttering sail. "Listen." I put a hand higher atop the mast. The faint fear in me hesitated when the breeze whispered in my ear. It was coming. I could hear the zephyr that the storm had left in my mind—it would be the trail the storm would follow to find me.

A ray broke the surface in a soft splash. My eyes rose from the trail of bubbles to Jeck's. "It's coming." The feeling of satisfaction tightened about my heart, pulled by the strengthening wind billowing the sail to a soft fullness. I had to get higher. I had to be among it. Eyes on the sky, I gripped the mast and tried to stand atop the water casks.

"Tess!" Jeck took hold of my left arm and jerked me back down. "What are you doing?"

I stumbled, catching my balance easily. "Can't you feel it?" I said, elated. I had captured the wind. It couldn't hurt me. I was stronger than it.

"Feel what?" He stared at me as if I had gone insane, but the coming wind had set my soul to resonate like a wire, making my blood hum in time with the waves under my feet.

He was still gripping my wrist, and I tried to tug free, failing. "The wind," I said, having to think about the words before I said them. "Listen." I threw my head to the sky. "It's coming!"

His lips parted, and his eyes grew wider. "Tess? Are you all right?"

"Yes . . ." It was a soft hiss. It was coming. It pushed upon the water, and the waves tried to take its strength, but they couldn't stop it. It was coming!

My bangs fluttered about my eyes, and I closed them, smiling. "Let me go," I whispered, and his hand dropped.

A slow thrum lifted through me as I touched the mast, echoing between my palms and my feet, setting my soul to ring with the pulse of heaven and earth. The ocean was resounding with the waves building a hundred miles out, but here the water was still flat. The rays could feel it. They fed on the emotion, and I fed on theirs. My grip tightened on the mast. I had to be higher.

"Tess!"

Jeck yanked me backwards, and I would have fallen had he not caught me.

"Let go," I threatened softly, turning to find him holding my arm again.

"You can't climb the mast," he said, his eyes angry. "You'll break it."

"But it's coming." I twisted my arms until he let go. "I have to get higher."

"What's coming?"

"My wind."

His face went expressionless, glancing at the wind pushing against the water as if it was a bad thing, not good. "Oh God, Tess. You called the wind."

The sail snapped firm against the ropes. My head came up, and I tasted the air. The glory of its power swept me as the first strength touched my skin. In my mind, the sound of whispering grew, the zephyr in me drawing it home. A strong gust hit us, streaming my hair back and pulling the ropes until they creaked. The raft shuddered, and Jeck fell to a half crouch, swearing under his breath.

I couldn't help it. I sprang for the mast. I had to be in it. I had to be among it. I had called it, and it was mine!

"Tess!" A hand gripped my dress and pulled me down. A low wave sloshed over the raft, making a cool current over my feet that went colder.

"Let go," I snarled, as the air pushed against me, the thrum in my head promising it could free me if I listened hard enough. But he had my arm. His eyes were wide and full of fear. I remembered fear. I didn't have any. The wind was calling. There was nothing else.

"Let it go, Tess," he said. "You have to let it go. You called the wind—I don't know how—but you have to let it go. Let it go now, before it takes you!"

He was holding my shoulders, but my head was up, watching the moon. There were no clouds. The wind pulled through my hair and swelled the sail as it swelled in my soul. I had summoned it, and yet I was chained to the earth. I could feel the anger building in me, the anger that he dare try to keep me from joining the power I had summoned. It was mine. "Take your hands off me," I said softly. My lips pressed together and my pulse hammered. Venom made me warm, and my skin tingled where the wind touched it.

He shook his head. "Tess, this was a mistake. Players don't call the wind because they can't control it. Let it go." His voice was soothing, whipping my blood to a frenzy. "Let it go."

A wicked contriving filled me as I looked to the moonlit horizon, silver and jagged. The raft jostled, but I held my balance, pushed by the wind and the waves. I controlled the wind; the wind did not control me. I was stronger than it. It was mine. And after it did as I demanded, I was going to keep it. I was so strong, I didn't need to hold to my word.

A sudden anger filled me when I realized he was still gripping my arm. "Let—go."

He shook his head. "I won't." His grip tightened, imprisoning me. Hurting.

Fury, hot and potent, rushed from my middle to my hands. The wind responded, swirling about us, soaking us as waves ran freely over the raft. I reached for him, placing my hands atop his shoulders. His eyes widened as he saw his death in my eyes. Clean and pure, it flowed from me, filling him to break him from his soul. He would let go of me. I would be free of him!

A cry of victory tore from me, almost unheard over the wind thumping the canvas and the waves crashing to make my feet warm, then cold. The hands imprisoning me clenched in a spasm, then strengthened. "No," a ragged voice rasped, and my joy turned to affront. He wasn't dead. He was still here!

"Free me!" I shouted, the sound of the wind goading me. I could feel it, singing to me—whispering words not spoken since the birth of time.

"No," he said again, his brown eyes wide and his jaw clenched under his beard. I howled and screamed at him, and the wind howled and screamed with me. I bit and fought. I thrashed and wrestled. He wrapped his arms about me and pulled me to the mast. He bound me with his arms and imprisoned me with his body.

The waves crashed over us, soaking and streaming through my hair, and I shrieked my rage. The raft tilted and righted itself. He wouldn't let go! I couldn't kill him! He was stronger than I. But I was the wind, and nothing was stronger than that. The wind could kill him. The wind could break him. Then I could be free.

I pulled to the wind, calling it to me with promises I had no intent to fulfill. With a contriving strength, it surged from the depths of the ocean, pushing the waves higher, running before them like a coursing hound over hills, its existence turned to one purpose. It laughed at my promises of freedom, telling me I couldn't give something I didn't have and that I couldn't hold it. Soon it would be free—and it could take me with it.

Denying it, I demanded obedience. The wind rebelled. The raft under me bobbed, and the waves soaked me. I didn't care.

"Tess!" a voice cried, loud in my ear.

Confusion jerked me from the sky. It wasn't the wind in my thoughts. The wind was both promising and demanding freedom, laughing at me as if I were a child with a string to hold a stallion. No . . . it had been a dark voice shouting to be heard, shouting to force a way into my head. "Let me go!" I cried, unable to move as the voice said my name over and over. I hated it. I couldn't hear the wind with it talking at me.

"Tess," the voice rasped. "I'll let you go if you make the wind push us to land. To land, Tess. Make it push us to land."

It promised freedom. My heart leapt. With a snarling vengeance, I stretched out my will and yanked the wind to me. It fought, and I subdued it. I had called it; it would do as I said! I made the same deal with it as the black voice holding me had. I would free it if it did as I told it to. But I lied. I would never let it go.

My curses and shouts grew vengeful as the sail above me snapped into shape. The crack of it was like a goad. The wind screamed its defiance, and I met it with all my will. It would do as I said. Only then would I free it. I was its master.

The heady rush of dominance scoured me, turning my blood to liquid metal. Like sand through my fingers, it poured unhindered, filling me with warm, heavy power. Wild and passionate, the wind fought to be free, and I held it. I saw its every move before it made it. I slapped it into obedience, and it roared its frustrations, making the waves higher and the sail strain at the ropes. It was mine.

A soft whisper of words ran through my awareness. I hated it, hated the voice and the one to whom it belonged. Hated the arms that held me and forced my compliance. I took my anger out on the wind, layering my will upon it even as it made stinging whips of my hair and fiery drops of sea spray. If I took the black voice to land, it would let go of me. Then I would be free.

And the voice was afraid. It was afraid even as it refused to let me go.

I was afraid of nothing. I was the wind. I belonged to no one.

Sixteen

❖

Land was coming. I knew this. The first of my zephyrs had touched it, arching up like angels to heaven, racing over the top of my wind and falling back to tell me.

Land, the zephyr sang to me, my heart clenching in thrill. Soon I'd be free of the black voice that held me down, whispering promises of freedom after my task was done.

I told the zephyr that when I reached the land I would free it. But I lied. The wind was mine. I would never let it go.

The zephyr swelled into a frenzy at my renewed promise, and a surge of wind smashed into the already bulging sail. A cry tore from me at its ferocity. It was beautiful in its uncaring that it might capsize us. Water black from the as-yet-unrisen sun sloshed over the raft, soaking me. The voice and arms that had imprisoned me woke from his fitful slumber.

I chafed at his grip, and he frantically sent his fingers over the silken knots he had tied about us, keeping us against the mast after I had tried to wash us off the raft. The mast was humming with the power of wind and water. The thrum had burned in my blood all night.

The voice behind me sang, too, but his song paled beside the glorious ferocity of the wind pushing on my face in brutal gusts. I laughed, watching the swollen canvas slowly grow first white, then pink as the sun neared rising. The last of the stars were caught by the wildly shifting rigging, and they vanished from the bluing sky in shame.

But the land was coming. I'd soon be free of the black voice whispering in my ear of things I no longer cared for. But he had promised to let me go.

Stronger now, the first of the real wind touched upon the shore, sending a reverberation back to me, inciting a stronger force. My hair blew to hide my face, and the sail began to tear as it rebounded, and we raced ahead.

Soon. Soon we'd be free. The black voice had promised. And then the wind would be wholly mine to do with what I pleased. My existence was a rushing sound of wind and water, and the rays leapt around us, trying to become one with both worlds, the sea and the air.

Behind me, the black voice whispered. I hated him. I couldn't hear the wind properly with him intruding. I wanted to hear the wind alone, to lose myself, but he was always there, an unwelcome rise and fall that hung and buzzed.

Sunrise was a silent thunder of heat. Red and swollen, the sun rose—my sly companion, my agent provocateur. It was where the strength of my wind was born. Silent, steadily moving, heating and cooling the earth and water to give my wind its power. The black voice holding me shuddered. He was afraid. I could smell it.

And then I saw it. An unbroken line took shape from the haze of sun gold clouds. My salvation. My end. Land. It was close. Close enough to touch almost.

The shadow whispering in my ear must have seen it, too, for his words increased, maddening me in their calm insistence, telling me where to go, what to make the wind do. I would be free of it. I belonged to no one!

Like a harnessed stallion remembering its colthood free on the plains, I bent to his demands, running in the direction I was given. The wind shrieked in my ears, pulling me forward, demanding release. The waves ahead of us ran into the submerged land, rising when the wind refused to let them rest.

A new sound rushed to fill my ears. I struggled to stand, failing as the ropes hindered every motion but breathing. It was my wind in the trees lining the approaching shore, harsh in the yellow light.

They groaned and cracked against the power I controlled, and I sent my strength to smash against them. And my wind willingly responded.

A tide born from my wind surged and crashed among the trees. The man holding me pulled me closer. I fought him, even as the raft was flung into land. We rode the swell into the scrub, lurching to a spinning halt against a willow.

The water flowed out from under us in a wild swirl of cold and pressure. The world no longer moved, but the canvas snapped and tore in the wind. We were here. I would be free!

I told the wind to swirl, and it did. I told it to rise, and my breath was taken from me as it pulled the air from my very lungs. Leaves, water, and sand rose in wild release. I had done what he demanded. Now he would free me, and I would be the wind. "Let me go!" I demanded, the waves drenching us when the wind continued to whip them into sacrificing themselves upon the land. The sun turned everything gold, and the water glinted yellow. "Free me!"

"Tess." It was a shout into my ear, almost unheard over the waves and wind.

"Free me!" I demanded, telling the wind to wait, and it swirled impatiently, gusting into a temper to break the trees around us to shattered stumps. Noise beat upon us, but still I heard the voice's one word.

"No."

Shock struck through me. I knew what that meant. That word had meaning. It meant he had—He had *lied to me*!

"Release me!" I demanded, pulling, fighting. He didn't, his arms pressing against me with more insistence.

"Come back," he whispered, a warm breath on my neck when all else was cold. "Let it go, Tess. Let the wind go."

"It's mine!" I twisted, feeling the burn of ropes for the first time. "It does as I say! I called it to *me*!"

But he wouldn't let go.

Angry, I whipped my will against the waves and sent it up-ward. My will hit the ceiling of the sky and rebounded. Hell itself screamed down from the heavens, out of a clear sky came a heavy stone of wind. It slammed into us like a wall of water. It snapped the useless mast, its demise unheard in the agony of wind and waves.

But he tightened his grip, telling me to let it go, demanding I hold to my word. "Let it go," he said. "Let the wind go first, then I'll free you, Tess!"

"No!" I shouted, tears starting to mix with my defiance. I was beaten. He knew my name. I had a name. Reminding me of it gave him power. He was stronger than I. And I knew that voice. I knew him. Damn him, it was Jeck.

"Free the wind," he said. "It wants to be free. You promised to free it. Let it go."

"But it's mine!" I cried out, frantic that I might lose it all. "I called it."

"I won't let you go until you free it," he said. "I promise. I'll let you go. But you have to free the wind first. It's not yours. Let it go."

"What if you don't?" I whimpered, and the wind beat upon us. I had meant to free the wind, but it seduced me. How can you let go of so powerful a force without regret? I was weak. I had no will.

"I'll never force you against your will again, Tess," Jeck whispered, and I wept as I felt my awareness return, making me less. "I promise," he said. "Let the wind go. Do it for Kavenlow, for Duncan. You'll never see them again if you don't let it go."

Duncan? I thought, my wildly blowing hair sticking to my damp cheeks. The wind howled, sensing a weakening of will. It roared its approval, demanding release. Tears blurred my vision as I bowed my head. How could I let it go? I'd be nothing. I'd fall.

"Let it go, Tess," Jeck whispered. "I'll catch you."

I could do nothing. He had bested me physically with his ropes. He had bested my soul by reminding me of my humanity. He had bested my will, forcing my obedience when I would lie and betray. I—who had called the wind, who had chained it to my will—would be beaten by another.

Sobbing, I loosened my hold on the wind. It was only the barest lessening of wills, but the wind felt it.

Shrieking in victory, it laid the beach flat. It swirled and whipped me for my audacity of thinking I could keep it, then it broke from me.

I cried out in heartache as it raced away. I hung in my shackles of cord and Jeck's arms, gasping for air. The hurt was so deep, I couldn't breathe. The wind had taken a part of me in its revenge. Unseen claws had raked my soul as easily as it raked the tattered remnants of trees.

"Stay with me, Tess," Jeck said, his voice in my ear rough and frightened. "Don't follow it. Stay here. Stay here."

I wanted to follow. I wanted to break free of my ropes and run after it. But I couldn't. Even if my ropes were gone, I had lost the will. Sobbing, I slumped my head against the dead mast and wept.

"Stay with me," Jeck whispered, his grip easing when he felt my awareness return. The roar of the storm about me gentled, not remembering me and my demands anymore. Between one rasping breath and the next, it became a fickle breeze, playing with my hair. It no longer recalled tearing wave tops and breaking trees. But I did.

Even my hair stilled. A faint zephyr brushed my cheek, then was gone.

I was left behind, tied to a broken mast on a shattered raft flung thirty feet past the high-tide mark, sobbing while the sun continued its uncaring rise into the sky.

Seventeen

❖

The sun was warm on my cheek, even where my hair was sticking to it. It was warm on my shoulder, too; bare to the slight breeze where my dress wasn't plastered to me. My front was out of the wind, seeing as I was still tied to the mast with my arms wedged in front of me. And my back was warm because Jeck was sitting behind me, his attempts at undoing the knots binding us as yet unsuccessful. I was warm, yes. But I was more than a little concerned.

Jeck's arms were wrapped about the mast and me both as he struggled to undo everything by memory and feel. He'd been at it for longer than I thought he should be, growling for me to be still or silent every time I tried to help or offer suggestions. If the truth be told, I think he was starting to get worried, too, since his breath coming and going on the back of my neck had gotten faster and more strained. My thoughts shifted to Duncan, and my eye twitched.

"Um, Captain?" I said uneasily when a muttered curse slipped from him. The raft was perched about two feet off the ground, cradled cant wise in the remains of a willow.

"What?"

It was sharp and terse, and I changed my mind. "Nothing."

"My fingers are numb," he said, his voice low. "I'm working as best I can."

A sigh shifted from me, temporarily tightening my bonds as I breathed. Had I thought anything but that he wanted to get away from me as much as I wanted to be away from him, I would have elbowed him in the gut and tried to slap him. As it was, we were trussed up so well, I could hardly move anything but my head.

I put my left temple against the mast and waited, suffering occasional jabs of pain on my tender wrist when he tugged the ropes too hard. My eyes drifted over the chaos of the beach. The waves were still high, rolling in white and gold with the stored strength of my wind. It was just past low tide, but one would never know it from the storm surge pushing against the beach.

Broken branches and foam made a thick line as the tide slowly crept in. Farther down the beach trees still stood, their branches stripped of their spring leaves. But where we had landed, the trees had been reduced to shattered stumps.

"Did I really do all this?" I said softly. My throat hurt, and I didn't dare raise my voice.

Jeck didn't answer, his breath coming in a relieved sound. "Got one," he said, and I felt an inch more room between us. Then it was gone as he pressed closer to get a better reach on the knots that remained. He smelled like ocean and leather, not entirely unpleasant.

"Why did you fasten them so tight?" I complained, not liking that he had been tied to me all night, and liking even less that I didn't remember any of it but snatches.

"You were trying to kill me."

Shocked, my breath caught and held.

He grunted, and my back went cold when a second knot loosened, and he leaned away.

"With my magic?" I asked, aghast. "I . . . I'm sorry. I don't remember that."

"No. You didn't use your magic. You were very sly about it." He seemed to be in a much better mood now that he was making some progress, and an almost jovial tone had crept into his voice. "Mostly trying to push me off when I wasn't looking. I tied you to the mast when you kept trying to climb it. But when you began inciting the rays to capsize the boat, I tied myself behind you."

The muscles of his arms still about me hesitated, then flexed as he renewed his work. Water plinked from the cuffs of his Misdev coat. "By then, the water was coming over the raft fairly regularly, and my voice seemed to be the only thing keeping you halfway to what was real and what wasn't."

My gaze went unfocused. Someone had been singing, low and soft. I remembered hating it, wanting to forget everything so I could hear the wind speak in tongues long lost, but the voice wouldn't let me. Jeck had kept me sane. "I don't remember that," I lied, thinking it would do neither of us any good if he knew I remembered.

"I didn't think you would," he muttered.

He shifted back farther when another knot came loose. The motion tugged the cord about my salt- and sash-chaffed wrists, and I yelped. It hurt my throat, and I held my breath lest I start coughing. Jeck's fingers of his left hand came into view. Part of his sash still bound his wrists, but he had more room to work. His fingers were red and swollen, the nails torn almost to the quick. My gaze lifted to the bush I had been eying. As soon as I was free, I was heading to it and not looking back.

"I'm sorry," I said suddenly, thinking he must not think me much of a player if he had to tie me to a mast to keep from killing myself.

"For what?" Another knot came free, and he pulled his arm from around me, groaning.

"For trying to hurt you," I said softly.

"It wasn't you." His voice was soft and preoccupied as his breath brushed my ear. He pressed against me to reach the knots holding his right arm to the mast. His beard brushed my cheek, and I forced myself not to move lest he think it bothered me. "And like I said, it was nothing I couldn't counter easily. You weren't really trying." He chuckled, surprising me. "You were very much like the wind: fickle, capricious . . . sneaky."

A frown came over me, and I pulled away from the touch of his beard. "Sounds like you enjoyed it," I said sarcastically.

"Maybe I did."

That, I didn't like at all. The entire night was slipping from me like a dream to leave only a feeling of deep loss. I knew what it stemmed from. The melancholy emotion worsened when the wind gusted, bringing my head up and my pulse hammering. It had been mine, and I had lost it. Jeck had made me let it go. I knew it would have driven me insane—and I was grateful to him—but the loss remained.

"Finally." He sighed when the last knot holding him came free. Groaning, he rose to his knees and moved around to the front of the mast. His shadow fell over me, making him into a black silhouette. He looked exhausted as he sat cross-legged before me in his sodden uniform, the sun rising behind him and his hair and beard still wet from the surf that had thrown us thirty feet past the high-tide mark.

"Why does my throat hurt?" I asked, hoping he might fill in the widening gaps.

"You were shouting a lot.

I said nothing, half-embarrassed, half-frightened. "Was it bad?"

His lips pressed together, his beard and mustache all but hiding them. "Could've been." His attention flicked to the broken mast, and I studied his face, seeing both his strength of self and his concern for me in the depth of his eyes. I looked away when he turned back to me, feeling cold from more than the loss of his body heat and his shadow now on me. He was a master player, and I was an apprentice. God help me, I must look so stupid. "Thank you," I said.

"Stop saying that."

I looked up as his shadow shifted. "Why?" I asked bitterly, as he worked on the knots tied with his silk sash. "Can't I thank you for saving my life? Or are you so uncomfortable that you might have emotions that you can't accept—that you might have done something for someone that wasn't required for your fool game?"

His face taking on a dark cast, Jeck glanced pensively at me from under his lowered brow. "I didn't save your life out of any misplaced feeling of emotion. If you had died, the wind would have, too. And we were making good time."

My breath came in a huff. "So," I said, miffed. "You kept me alive solely because of the game?"

"Yes." It was short and emotionless, and looking at him picking the knots free with his swollen fingers, I almost believed him. But remembering his hidden grief for having killed a woman he loved wouldn't let me believe him completely.

"Then I guess you should be thanking me."

He said nothing, his head bowed to show me the top of it. His wavy hair was plastered to him with sweat and seawater. I must look awful. Knowing I was pushing my luck, I said, "You didn't have to convince me to release the wind. You could have let me stay lost."

"Then I would have been tied to a lunatic all morning," he said flatly.

That bothered me. I licked my cracked lips as the memory of the wind filled me once more. I'd never call it again. It was too easy to get lost. That I had even managed to call it this once had been a miracle. I never would have tried it if my sister's and Duncan's lives hadn't been in danger. "You're wrong, you know," I said suddenly.

"About what?"

He didn't look up, and I hesitated before saying, "That love makes you weak."

The faint pressure of his fingers on my numb hands paused, then resumed.

"I never would have tried calling the wind if I hadn't cared for my sister so much."

"Love didn't make you strong," he said, tugging so hard I bit my lip to keep from crying out. "It made you stupid."

A sharp pain broke through my determination to stay silent. "Stupid!" I yelped, and he flicked a glance at me. A long tail of black silk was in his hand, and I found I could scoot back an inch. "It wasn't stupid to call the wind. It got us here in time to do something."

"It was stupid," he repeated, his eyes pinched when he took a stick and tried to wedge it into a knot. "But that doesn't mean I won't capitalize upon it."

He dropped the twig and stood. "I'll be right back," he said, carefully sliding off the raft. His feet hit the sand and, moving as if pained, he headed for the nearby bushes.

"I'm not free yet!" I exclaimed, my eyes wide and my throat hurting.

"I said I'll be right back!" he shouted. Hobbling from stiff muscles, he made his slow way over the wreckage and out of sight. I glanced at my proposed bush, hoping he would hurry.

Grimacing, I tugged at my bindings. There was enough slack that the circulation was starting to return, and it hurt. My legs ached from holding one position too long, and my bare shoulder was starting to turn pink. "Get to the capital before Kavenlow acts on bad information," I whispered. "Pay the pirates to get them back, and when I'm sure they're safe, crush the chu slingers so no one will dare to try it again."

It sounded like a good plan to me. No more impossible than say, chaining the wind.

Closing my eyes, I leaned my head up against the mast—remembering. The faint brush of wind on my cheek lanced into a sudden, unexpected stab of longing. It hadn't been so bad when Jeck had been here—his quiet presence distracted me. But now, the wind called unhindered, whispering in the trees still standing at the end of the cove.

A cold feeling shook me as something deep inside me heard it and set to humming. A wave of expectation, a feeling that was not mine, rose inside me, surging in expectation in response to the wind in the broken trees.

My eyes flashed open, and my heart pounded. It wasn't gone. The wind remained inside me. It heard the wind in the trees and woke, swirling in my thoughts and demanding release. Fear bubbled up. I threw my head up to the sky, eyes wide. The whisper in me rose and swirled, inciting the wind in the trees to do the same.

No! I thought, clamping down on the heady rush of wild feeling that wasn't my own. Terrified, I smothered the rush of power even as the tingle of venom scoured through me. *I loosed it! I let it go! Why is it still here?* But the wind trapped in my soul tugged and pulled, whispering for me to free it, to let it go, to let it carry me to the heights of heaven and the depths of hell.

I sat and panted, struggling to contain it. The breeze tugged my hair, swirling it with a new force. The whisper in my head cried out to join it, but I shackled it with new bindings of rational thought and denial. I tensed against the ropes still binding me to the mast. *This will not happen. I won't let it!*

Jeck's low, murmuring voice cut through my confusion, and the wind's voice in my thoughts jumped as if frightened.

The breeze pushing on me died; the chaos in my thoughts faltered. I looked up, panicked at what had happened. Heart fast and stiff, I listened to the wind in the trees forget the whisper in my head, lose interest, and flit away.

Jeck's voice rose and fell. Shaken, I sat straighter when another voice joined his. It was high and carried an uncomfortable rasp to it. He had found someone.

His seawater-matted hair showed above the stripped branches and tall bracken, moving slowly as he listened. Turning a corner with an almost comical slowness, he appeared with a bent-over old woman. Jeck carried a woven basket with bits of cloth and flotsam in it. I guessed she had been salvaging the storm beach.

Her time-grayed dress billowed in the wind, cut high above her spindly ankles. Strips of cloth and ropes were tied to her waist, making it look as if she were wearing nothing but rags though there was a skirt under them all. She was barefoot, her toes as brown as her heavily creased cheeks. A straw hat with a wide brim was atop her gray hair. It was arranged in one long braid that went clear down to her waist. She had a tight grip on Jeck's arm as she talked, never looking up from the sand just before her slowly moving feet. Her fingers were gnarled and strong, and in all honesty, it didn't look like she needed the help despite her apparent age.

As if feeling my attention on her, she looked up. Her eyes were so blue, I could see them from where I sat. The wrinkles on her face fell into deep crevices as she smiled. "Oh, there she is!" she called out, her voice high but strong. "Tied to the mast, were ya? Caught out in it, eh? I don't wonder. It came up without even a twinge from my knees. That hasn't happened in twenty-eight years."

She cackled, and Jeck winced, meeting my eyes briefly as he was dragged along beside her since she had yet to relinquish her grip on him.

"Hello!" I called out, trying to move. "Do you have a knife, ma'am?"

She laughed again, ending with, "I do, sweetness. Water tighten your knots?"

I said nothing, smiling as she lurched to the raft. "Always have a knife with me," she said, showing bad teeth and fumbling about on her person amid the rags and ropes. More nimble than her looks would credit her, she levered herself up onto the tilting raft and slid closer. She smelled like cooking clams, and she called out in success when her fingers found a tattered red ribbon with a knife tied to it hanging from her hips. Gumming her teeth, she refused Jeck's soft offer of help and cut his silk sash from me herself. It parted with a quickness that spoke of a very sharp knife or very strong muscles. I would be willing to wager it was a little of both.

"Oh, thank you," I moaned, when a painful ache rose through my arms and I bent them for the first time in hours. Blinking in hurt, I scooted away from the mast. I made a motion to get up, changing my mind when my legs refused to work quite yet. So I sat and rubbed my arms between picking at the knots still about my wrists.

"You're welcome, sweetness." The old woman beamed from the shade of her wide-brimmed hat. "I've been tied to more than one mast in my day." She laughed. "That's how I caught my husband, bless his soul."

Embarrassed, I flexed my hands. "It was so I wouldn't wash over," I said in explanation, and Jeck set her basket on the raft and took a step back.

"Of course it was." She gave me an appraising look. "Not much to you, is there?"

Speechless, I blinked at her. I'd never been spoken to like that before.

She reached out a twiglike arm and gripped my forearm, pinching the muscle. "You might be good for somethin', though."

"I beg your pardon?" My face went blank in surprise. Behind her, Jeck was grinning at my expense. I scooted to the edge, unable to stop my groan of pain when my feet dangled over.

"Oh, you are in bad shape, girlie," she was saying. "Come up to my house. It's just a little ways over that dune there. I have some aching liniment to rub into you. You can take a cup of tea. Meet my son. He's a fine lad, now that he done lost his first wife."

Alarmed, I glanced over her shoulder at Jeck. "No, thank you," I quickly said, seeing where this was headed. "We have to be going."

"Nonsense," she babbled. "One cup of tea. Do you good to get all warm inside. And I get so lonely out here."

Jeck took her hand to help her down off the raft. "I think it's a good idea," he said, surprising me. "Perhaps we could impose upon your hospitality for a few days, even."

"What?" I stammered.

"Oh, capital. Just capital!" the old woman said, clapping her wrinkled brown hands together. "We can talk, and I can show you how to make starfish cookies. The secret is in the eggs. You need to use eggs from brown hens. Not the ones with white tail feathers. They have to be all brown, you see."

I started to panic. He had to be jesting. "Whatever for, *Captain*?" I said in worry.

"My!" the old woman exclaimed, a gnarled hand to her hat. "You're a captain? Your ship go down? Where's your crew? Small boat, was it? Just you and your missus?"

"He's not my husband," I said. Jeck leaned forward when I made motions to get off the raft, actually giving me support when my feet hit the sand. I wobbled for a moment, finding my balance. I looked at my proposed bush, then back to him. "Thank you," I murmured.

"I'll go to the capital," he said, "and send a horse for you."

A flash of tension went through me in understanding. He was going to leave me behind, that's what he was going to do. "I'm coming with you," I said quickly.

He pressed his lips together, hiding them behind his filthy beard and mustache. "I'll make better time without you."

"I'm the one who got us here in time to do anything," I protested, not caring what the old woman thought. "I'm not staying here."

The old woman squinted up at me from under her wide hat, taking my arm. "Oh, you'll like my son," she said. "No one catches fish like my boy. Fine, strong man. Takes care of his mother real well, he does."

Jeck pried her fingers off me, and when he led me a few steps away, the old woman started poking about under the raft. "You said you would be willing to sacrifice yourself and your game to ensure your sister's safety," he said, throwing my words back into my face. "Someone needs to get there as quickly as possible. You can't keep up."

"I'm fine," I said, feeling my knees start to shake from hunger and exhaustion. "I'm not going to stay here and wait to be picked up like some kind of weak . . . silly—"

"Princess?" he finished for me. Then his eyes went hard. "I won't slow down for you."

"So don't," I snapped. My throat hurt, and I put a hand to it.

Jeck glanced over my shoulder at the woman blathering to herself, her eyes on the dead things washing up. He shifted his weight from one foot to the next, raising a hand and letting it drop as if having decided something. "Tess," he said softly, "your punta bite is healed over, but it's getting worse."

My breath caught, and I stared at him. *How had he known?*

"It's making your magic unpredictable," he continued, striking fear in me. "You shouldn't have been able to harness the wind. No player can hold more than a slight breeze. You stirred a hurricane."

I said nothing, frightened he might guess I still held it in my thoughts. "It's the residual levels," I said softly. "They'll fall given enough time. I'm fine."

Jeck's stance went apologetic and pained. "Tess," he said, his voice so full of pity it struck me cold. "I'm sorry. You didn't call the wind with residual toxin, and that killing pulse yesterday was too strong for even your elevated levels. That was pure venom coursing through you. I could feel it." His eyes squinted as he gazed into the sky, avoiding my panicked expression. "Even if I failed to wall off the venom properly and it was seeping out, there should be less. There's not. There's more of it. I think the venom is replenishing itself, not dissipating."

My breath came fast as he said aloud what I had been afraid to think. As if in a dream, I watched him turn and start back to the raft. "Jeck . . ." I took several pained steps to catch up to him, my arms clasped about me from the chill. "Jeck, you're wrong. It's not replenishing itself. It's just taking a long time to work itself out. No one's been bit by a punta before and lived. It's going to take time. That's all. Just time."

Even I could hear the lie in my voice, and pity hung heavy in his brown eyes, watching me from under his hair. Coming to a halt beside the raft, he exhaled long and slow. "I'm sorry, Tess," he said, watching the woman shifting through the wreckage on the beach. "Kavenlow has to know. Stay here until he comes for you. I'll tell him. I'm the one who fixed the toxin in your tissues, whether it saved your life or not, and it's my responsibility."

"No!" I exclaimed softly, fear striking to the quick of my soul. "You don't even know for sure that's what's happening. You can't tell him! He'll make me leave the game!"

Jeck pressed his lips together, his expression full of pity, and I hated him. Hated that I was begging. Hated that I knew he was right. Panicked, I took his arm, gripping it until my fingers hurt. "Jeck," I said, not caring my voice had a tinge of pleading in it. "I can't be a player if I can't withstand even one dart. Every rival player out there will see it as an easy way to take Costenopolie, and you know it. You should have let me die on that raft if all you were going to do was take everything away from me."

"You already figured it out," he said, wonder in him. "You know it's replenishing itself, and you were going to risk your master's game and your life just to keep playing."

My mouth dropped, shocked. I hadn't even realized it myself until he said something, but he was right. I was going to try to keep this from Kavenlow. "Jeck," I pleaded, quashing my sudden guilt. "You owe me something. You did this to me!"

"I owe you nothing." He roughly rocked the water casks, frowning when he realized they had both leaked and were empty. "If I hadn't done something, you would have died."

"And now you're taking away everything that makes life worth living! This game is all I have left! It's all I've ever had."

He put his hands on his hips and looked at me, his beard looking wild and unkempt. "What about Duncan?"

I felt my face go ashen, and I took a step back, remembering Duncan asking me to take his name and be with him forever. "I . . . I gave up love for the game," I said, dying inside all over again. "I hold to that promise. Even now."

Thoughts unknown pulled his eyes into a scowl as he turned to the old woman, poking a stick at a jellyfish that had washed up. "Ma'am," he called out, and she looked up, smiling with her broken teeth. "Does anyone nearby have a horse?"

My shoulders eased. He wasn't going to leave without me. He wasn't going to tell Kavenlow. I could figure this out if I had some time to think.

"Horse?" she rasped, leaving the stick in the blob of flesh and hobbling our way. "No. Not enough to feed a horse. Ponies, though. Sharp Bend is north of here about a day's walk. They'd have horses. Nothing here but birds and fish, and those cursed crabs. Keep eating my bait off my lines if I don't watch 'em quick."

North was the wrong direction, but at least we knew where we were. My eyes met Jeck's, and I felt ill. Two days of hard foot travel.

Breaking his stare at me, Jeck swung himself onto the raft, the grace starting to come back to his movement as his muscles loosened. "Can I borrow your knife, ma'am?" he asked, his hand out. She hesitated for a mistrustful instant before untying it from its red ribbon and handing it to him. He nodded his thanks, and, still not having looked her in the eye, he cut the sail down. I watched in confusion while he ripped two narrow lengths from it. My head bobbed in understanding when he used them to wrap his feet.

I tugged my dress back up over my shoulder, waiting for him to tear two more lengths for me, but instead, he tucked the knife in his waistband and began rummaging amid what was still tied to the raft. As the old woman talked about last night's storm, he made a pile in the center of the downed sail. I shifted from foot to foot, wanting to excuse myself and have a moment of privacy behind that bush, but all my pressing needs were forgotten when Jeck bundled the canvas up, turned, jumped off the raft, and walked away with it slung over his shoulder. No good-bye, no nothing. He had everything of value. All that was left was his ripped sash tied to the mast.

"Hey!" I exclaimed, taking an achy step after him. "You still have her knife!"

He didn't stop, but his neck stiffened, and his pace became stilted.

The old woman pinched my elbow, hissing in my ear, "Let him have it. It's not worth getting beat over."

Face warming, I lurched into motion, the sticks and shells in the sand sharp on my left foot, dull on my right. My muscles protested, but I was too angry to listen. The wind snuggled in my head behind my ear swirled to life, whispering. "Give her back her knife!" I exclaimed, then wished I hadn't, as my throat felt like it was burning. *What had I done? Screamed all night?*

"She said I could borrow it." He never slowed. His broad back was hunched. He knew he was doing wrong.

"She didn't mean forever. Give it back." I caught up with him with long, hurting strides. The old woman had turned her back on us, her posture telling me she was afraid to interfere. I grabbed his arm, and he yanked me off-balance when he pulled out of my grip.

"Don't touch me," he said, his voice threatening as he turned.

I stared at him, surprised. "Then give her the knife back," I said, suddenly unsure.

"No."

Anger sifted through me. He was bigger and stronger than I was, and he was going to use it to keep her knife, the chu slinger. "It might be all she has," I all but hissed. "Give it back."

"Or what?"

It was so childish, I could have just screamed. *The son of a dock whore*, I thought, as he turned his back on me and walked away. A heady, hot feeling rose unbidden from my belly and swirled in my head. The wind in my thoughts tugged at the bindings I had shackled it with. It flooded me with the memory of mindless power. My anger at Jeck gave it a clear, undeniable direction. Panic shocked through me as a killing force rose unbidden to my hands.

No! I thought, jerking my hands from Jeck before it flowed from me to him unchecked.

My hands exploded into hurt, and I gasped. I hunched into myself, clenching my hands until my nails bit my palms. The growing force came on me with the sensation of embers rolling under my skin. I stood in agony, unmoving and with my head down as I rode it out and my anger vanished in a wash of fear.

The wind in my head saw its chance to escape. It rose from a zephyr to a breeze to a storm in a heartbeat, swirling through my thoughts, heard and felt only by me.

My hands still resonating with death, I yanked the wind back, shackling it, pushing it down, making it behave. It beat at me, and I panted, forcing myself not to listen as it promised in words I didn't understand that it would teach me to fly. *God help me. I am breaking apart.*

Jeck jerked to a halt and turned. "What?" he said flatly, seeing me suddenly afraid. From the annoyed look on his face, I guessed he didn't know I had not only almost killed him but had also nearly gone insane in the span of two heartbeats.

"Keep it," I whispered, swallowing hard. It had almost gotten free. The wind had tricked me, and I'd almost killed Jeck over a stupid knife.

He glanced at me from head to foot, hoisted everything of value from the raft higher upon his shoulder, and walked away. I could tell his thoughts were already miles ahead of him at the capital. "I'm telling your master, Princess," he said, not looking back. "You aren't safe, and he needs to face up to his mistakes."

"Princess!" the old woman called out, looking up from tugging at the empty water barrel.

"That's just what he calls me," I said, standing in the sun with my arms clenched about me, colder than the deepest winter. But the woman wasn't listening, now talking to the dead rays that had washed up on the beach around us.

Eighteen

❖

The number of times I had been alone in my life, really alone, I could count on one hand and still have fingers left over. Always there had been Kavenlow, or my best friend, Heather, or any number of people. In the palace, guards were within shouting distance even if I had the illusion of being alone. Beyond the palace walls, Kavenlow was with me. The only time I had ever truly been alone was last year when I'd been traveling through a springtime woods fleeing a palace takeover and trying to find Kavenlow. And even then, Duncan had been with me most of the time.

And here I was, running through a cold woods trying to reach Kavenlow again.

The wind gusted, somehow finding its way under the trees to play with my lank curls. Its sly presence had set up a steady whisper in me, settling in for good within the spot it had made in my mind. A soft litany of longing had begun, the memory of wild abandonment swelling, hurting my spirit and mocking me.

"Go away," I breathed, trying to watch my footing in the growing dusk under the trees. I had been able to ignore the wind most of the day when the spring-happy birds and dappled sunlight distracted me. But now that it was getting dark, I heard it more clearly.

My right leg was going numb again, and I hadn't felt my right arm since the sun went down and the nearly full moon rose. Like a dead thing, my arm had hung until I tied it close to me under the cloak the old woman had given me. She had also given me a cloth-wrapped packet of food, tying it to my waist by a strip of red fabric. A white shawl of the most detailed weave I had ever seen graced my shoulders under her cloak. The shawl had been her wedding present from her husband's family, and she had given it to me freely after only a moment's hesitation, claiming she had been wanting to give it to her daughter-in-law but that the woman never came to see her anymore since leaving her son.

The truth of it was her son lay in a well-tended grave twenty steps from the house, his wife and baby's grave right beside it.

The woman lived utterly alone, her mild insanity protecting her from the more severe madness of isolation. Her second-best knife hung from my waist from a braided cord, and she had given me the boots her son's wife had once worn. I had refused to take any of her blankets though she gummed her bad teeth and scowled at me. But that had been most of the day ago, and the woman's voice was lost to me now, scattered among my memories by the wind's insistent whispers.

The natural breeze came in the trees again—and the zephyr in my head sang out in its melancholy, answering it.

I was so tired. It was getting harder to keep my feet moving and my thoughts from lingering on what the wind promised. I had to keep up with Jeck. If I didn't, he would tell Kavenlow about the punta bite and how dangerously out of control my magic was and that my bite was replenishing the venom every time I drew on it.

Kavenlow, I thought in indecision as I forced myself to keep moving. If my levels didn't drop, I couldn't be a player. Punta venom was the weapon of choice for a player. One dart from a rival and not only would I lose whatever game I was playing, but I'd be dead. But what could I be if I wasn't a player? I knew the secret of the players' existence, but I couldn't play the game. Not a player, not a piece: I would be little more than a target to be used against Kavenlow.

"I could leave with Duncan," I whispered, not finding as much joy in the thought as I should. It wasn't that I didn't care for him. Even now, my face warmed with the memory of lying on the sand under him, the bliss of his kiss and how I had felt about it. I knew he could make me happy, but I didn't think that was the problem anymore. The real threat of being removed from the game had brought into clear focus the realization that I needed more.

Duncan could make me happy. Together we could travel where we pleased like nomads, secure in his world-savvy and my abilities to earn a coin with my reading and writing skills. And while a part of me longed for the simplistic adventure of it, I knew it wouldn't be enough, and eventually I'd grow to hate Duncan for making me choose him over the life that had been promised me. Seeing to my security was too easy—I had been trained to see to the security of an entire kingdom, and without that challenge, I would wither, one day at a time.

I had been trained from birth to succeed Kavenlow. To rule, even by stealth, was what I was good at and what I enjoyed. But to do it, I would repeatedly run the risk of losing Kavenlow's game, kingdom, and probably my life. And Jeck knew it. It would give the rival player a foolproof piece of blackmail. There was no choice to make that I liked. There was nothing I could do to find peace. My options were as dark as the footpath I now stumbled upon, my head lowered to avoid the low-hanging branches, much as I avoided making any decision to delay the coming heartache.

Perhaps, I thought as I reached out with my good hand to fend off a briar, *I would die on the way to the palace and wouldn't have to decide.* Jeck would try to kill me anyway, as soon as it suited his game. He told me he would. Kavenlow's fondness for me put my teacher in a precarious position. And Jeck wouldn't hesitate to use it or my new vulnerability to venom. I was lucky he didn't have any, his stash stolen by Captain Rylan before he sank my boat.

My descending foot landed upon what was probably an acorn. Pain raced up my right leg through my borrowed boots, shocking it from its numbness. I stumbled, falling to my knees. My left arm wasn't enough to break my fall, and I went farther to hit the ground hard. All my body cried out in hurt, making my head throb.

I was so cold, so alone. I hurt all over. Holding my breath, I pushed myself up off the ground in painful stages, forcing my right arm to help. Hurt, I stared up at the branches making a more certain dark against the night. "You will not beat me," I said to the pain, fatigue, and the wind in my head. "You won't!"

Let me go, the zephyr whispered. Venom trickled into my veins, and my arm went tingly.

"Be still," I said aloud, but the toxin had been loosed, and my focus blurred.

Would have, should have, it sighed, inciting the wind in the trees to quicken. *Let me out to play.*

"No." My throat hurt, and I squinted to see my feet in the gathering dusk since the rising moon couldn't light the path under the trees. Shivering, I stumbled, lurching to catch my balance.

Let me play, the wind in my head said, and the sighing of the trees seemed to echo it, growing as it fed upon both my weakness and rising venom.

"If I let you out," I muttered, talking to myself, "you'll kill me."

If you don't let me out, I'll drive you insane, it said, the soughing of it sending a shudder through me.

"Stop it!" I shouted, hearing it come out as a harsh croak. I tottered into a faster pace to try to outdistance it. "Leave me alone!"

A soft rattle of last year's leaves brought my head up from the dark path. A fire glowed in the near distance. "Tess?" came a familiar hail, and my heart seemed to stop.

Jeck? My pace faltered, and I stood, hunched and squinting to find him sitting beside a small fire just off the path. His eyes were wide in the firelight, and he pulled himself straight, clearly trying to hide his surprise and find the mystique of a Misdev captain that he had lost somewhere between my boat burning to the waterline and his stealing the old woman's knife.

He had a fire. That was all that mattered: not my pride, not my self-respect, nothing. I lurched forward, up the small rill and off the trail. I fell to my knees right before the flames and held my hands so close they nearly burned. Sudden shivers shook me, absent until I stopped moving.

Jeck said nothing, a shadow at the edge of my awareness. My throat went tight, and I refused to cry. I wouldn't cry in front of him, even if this was the most miserable in mind and body that I had ever been. I was so cold and hungry, and the wind had made even my thoughts painful.

Jeck put another stick on the fire, and I looked at him, the first hints of warmth stirring me back to a wary distrust. I didn't see the woman's stolen knife, but the sail was about him like a blanket. The bottoms of his makeshift shoes were black from dirt, and I saw him look at my sturdy boots. "Where did you get the cloak?" he asked.

"Where do you think?" I grated, pulling one hand away from the fire to clutch it protectively about me. "It's mine!" I exclaimed, suddenly fearful. "Touch me, and I swear I'll hurt you. I will. *I can hurt you now!*"

His face was empty of emotion, but he didn't move, so I inched closer to the flames. "She *gave* it to me," I said, hoping he would start talking. The wind in my ear hadn't liked Jeck's voice and had gone to hide in my memories. "Her name is Penelope. She gave me water, too. I'll give you some if you talk to me."

Surprise flashed over his bearded face, making the powerful man hunched under the sailcloth blanket look even more vulnerable. "Talk . . . to you?" he questioned, the new firelight making flickering shadows on him.

Shamed, and not wanting to admit I found comfort in his voice, I looked into the fire.

He said nothing as I rearranged myself into a more comfortable position, pushing away the sticks and leaves to find the damp earth. Sitting on damp ground would probably leave me with a cold, but it wasn't as if I had anything better to sit on. I felt as if I might break if I moved too fast. I knew Jeck had food as I had watched him take it all, but the water barrel had leaked. I had walked the same path he had today, and there had been no water. He was probably parched.

His gaze was intent as I splashed a miserly amount of water into a deep, pink and pearl shell Penelope had hung from my waist. Untying it from me, I set it at arm's length. Jeck waited until I leaned back before he scooted closer for it.

Jeck moved with what I thought was a forced casualness, taking it up and draining it in one gulp. It hadn't been nearly enough, and I jealously tucked the flask in closer. If he came near me, I swore, I'd hurt him. But Jeck stayed where he was, silent while I unpacked the biscuits and strong goat cheese the woman had given me.

My fingers were cold, and I watched them to be sure they were doing what I wanted. With the returning warmth came pain, willingly suffered. The biscuits had been crushed, and it was only the thick, strong goat butter she had slathered them with that kept them together. Tears pricked at my eyes. She had been so kind, and I had given her nothing in return.

Jeck moved, and my head came up.

"Stay away from me," I growled, remembering his scorn when he refused to give her knife back. He had saved my life, but he had taken it away in the process. I didn't know if that made us any more rivals than we were before or not. But I didn't want him touching me.

His eyes dropped to the wickedly sharp filleting knife dangling from a red cord about my waist. "I wasn't going to touch you."

His eyes said different. Watching him, I jammed a bite of biscuit in my mouth and wiped my lips. "I know you aren't," I threatened.

Jeck's attention went to the water flask. "I'll sing you to hell and back in a basket if you give me that water."

My hand dropped to the ceramic flask she had tied about my waist. *Thirsty?* I silently mocked, but knew better than to say it aloud. "I'll give you half. When I'm done with it," I added, and he nodded, his eyes going to the fire and his posture easing. I hadn't even realized he was poised to move until he slumped. A shudder rippled through me. If I had said no, he would have risked death to try to take it from me. As it was, he would humor me to get half without risk.

I breathed easier when he settled himself back to the earth. He rearranged the fire and left the stick to burn, and I watched him in mistrust, reminded of the first time we had shared a fire in the woods. I had been shackled to a tree without my boots. He had stolen everything from me. Of course in the morning, it was me stealing his horse and everything on it.

"I heard you shouting," he said, then licked his dry lips when I took another drink.

My jaw gritted, then relaxed. If I didn't tell him why, he

would invent something worse. And he knew most of it anyway. "I was talking to the wind," I said, picking up a crumb on my knee and eating it. "It was getting annoying."

He grunted in surprise, and my shoulders eased in the familiar sound of it. "You didn't let it go," he accused.

"I tried," I said breathily, feeling the weight of the entire day fall on me. "I thought I did, but it's still there, in my head, talking to me, telling me to let it go."

"So let it go."

This wasn't what I had wanted to talk about. I pulled my gaze up, and his eyes widened, making me wonder just how bad I looked. "If I free it, it will kill me."

"If you don't, it will do the same thing," he said, his gaze unblinking on mine.

I took a bite of my last biscuit, pretending I didn't care and wondering how he had guessed it. "Probably." I could feel it simmering in my head. It would be whispering to me if Jeck's voice hadn't frightened it into silence.

My shoulder throbbed, and I massaged the healed tears with my free hand. Though it was no longer the debilitating pain of four days ago, my bite hurt. It ached, the pain mixing with the wind in my head. Venom had given me the strength to chain the wind to my will, the punta had given me the wisdom to call it, and my pride had given me the way to destroy myself.

"Would you like me to warm your shoulder?" he asked, holding up a strong, salt-reddened hand. "It probably won't do much for healing it anymore, but it will feel better."

I stared at him in disbelief. *He thinks I would let him touch me?* "I think you've already done enough damage, don't you?" I said caustically, and picked up my wedge of cheese. "You just want to see how close we are to that dream," I said hotly, thinking I hadn't been able to stop the first one despite my efforts. I estimated my shoulder had about a week more of natural healing to look as it did in that punta dream, and I wasn't about to hasten it along with a little extra magic from his hands. "I've seen that dream," I added, "and I won't let it happen."

"Probably," he admitted with a calm certainty, a hand running across his bearded chin. "Not if you're working against it. But I can't make anything worse, and if you're right that it's only old venom working itself out, then it can only help. You might even figure out how to use your hands to heal. You're very clever that way."

I sneered, my royal upbringing falling away to let my disgust show. His flattery fell on deaf ears. He knew it wasn't old venom working itself out; it was fresh and potent, robbing me of my future. "No." Appetite gone, I ate the cheese, not tasting it. What did it matter anymore?

Jeck bent his knees to sit cross-legged with the canvas sail draped over him. I glanced up, becoming sullen when I realized he had slipped a hand under his bloodstained shirt and was holding his hand to his side, right where he had been cut. His gaze took on a distant look, and his shoulders slumped. It was obvious he was using his magic to speed its healing and make it feel better.

My jaw clenched as I remembered the sensation of his hands on me, magic flowing from them to heal me from within. He could ease the numbness from me, melting the aches into a slurry of warmth and comfort. Better than a hot soak in water. Better than a fire on a winter night. Better than . . . anything.

His eyebrows rose when he saw me eying his hands, and I forced my gaze away, stifling a surge of jealousy. He would teach me to kill, but not heal. What a dung flop. "It must bother you I know how close we are to that dream and you don't," I said, satisfied when his eye twitched. He couldn't force his will on me anymore, treating me like a dog or whore. He had to ask, to treat me with the respect I deserved. I wasn't going to show him my shoulder, and he couldn't touch me without running the risk I might try to kill him with my hands.

"What is a pain-free night worth to you?" he said. His face shadowed by the come-and-go light from the fire, he took his hand from his side.

Shivering and miserable, I tucked a curl behind my ear and looked away. The lure of comfort wasn't enough to let him put his hands on me. But there was one thing I wanted from him. Pain couldn't move me, but shame could, and to avoid that, I would sell a look at my shoulder. My pulse quickened, and before I could change my mind, I blurted, "I'll let you heal my shoulder if you don't tell Kavenlow." Then I flushed and added,

•

"If you don't tell him of my punta bite and that I called the wind or that my residual toxin levels are high."

He seemed to freeze, his brown eyes fixed on me in disbelief. "You want a dose of healing and my silence for a peek at your shoulder? You overestimate your charms, Princess."

My face warmed even more. I felt like a dock whore, teasing with a flash of skin to get something I wanted. "You want a good look at my shoulder to estimate the time to the vision? This is the only way you're going to get it." Pulse quickening, I licked the strong taste of cheese off my fingers, finding the flavor of dirt underneath.

Jeck shifted his weight slightly, looking embarrassed, if I thought he could manage that particular emotion. "What makes you think once I get a look at it, I'll make good on my offer?"

I haven't really thought about that. "I guess I'll have to trust you."

His lips pursed, and he moved to put another stick on the fire, stirring it up before leaving it to burn. I watched him, edging closer to the flush of heat he had created. "Do you?" he asked, and I thought his voice carried an odd, questioning hesitancy under the surface scorn.

Pulling my cloak tighter, I soaked in the heat, shivering. My thoughts went back to his decisive action when we found ourselves on a burning boat, and the way he pulled me the last few feet to shore when my muscles started shaking, exhausted from dragging my waterlogged dress. I remembered the pain reflected in his face later that day, when he admitted he had accidentally killed a woman he had loved. I thought of his tight words and downright meanness when he walked away from the raft and left me with Penelope.

"No," I said. "But it's not going to cost you anything to heal my shoulder, so I think you will. I can't be a player anymore; you have nothing to lose and everything to gain if I fall asleep faster. You won't have to talk to me for so long."

He grunted and drew back slightly. "I don't have to talk to you at all."

Miserable, I stared at the fire, finding a spot of gold where there ought to be shadows, a bubble of trapped heat under a leaning log. It burned brightly in the protected space, but it would dissipate to commonality if out in the open. I didn't want to admit that Jeck's voice was keeping the voice of the wind in my head at bay, giving me the strength to fight it off. "Do you want to see it or not?" I asked, angry with myself.

I could almost see him thinking when I brought my gaze up. His lips were pressed tight so that his mustache and beard all but hid them. My breath caught when he placed his palms against the ground to rise. I put out a hand in warning, not wanting him to come to me, and he exhaled in a long sigh, falling back to the earth. "Fine," he muttered. "You come over here."

Suddenly I was a lot more nervous. I collected myself, feeling my legs ache as I stood, not realizing until now how intimate it was going to feel to cross those few steps and voluntarily put myself so close to him. We'd been closer when tied to the raft, but that had been against my will and necessary. This wasn't. Seeing me shifting awkwardly from foot to foot, Jeck arched his eyebrows in amusement.

That did it, and, gathering my resolve, I untied my knife from its string. Leaving it with the water, I moved slowly around the fire, settling where he pointed, beside and a little in front of him. The ground was damp, and before I turned my back on him, I saw him eying my abandoned water flask. I almost changed my mind, but deciding I was more curious if he would steal the water from me or hold to his word, I settled myself.

His bulk rose behind me, instilling me with an odd feeling of both protection and vulnerability. He was like a horse, all sweaty warmth and size. *Maybe if I think of him as a big sweaty animal, it might help*, I thought, then quickly dismissed the idea when it only made things worse.

From behind me, Jeck cleared his throat impatiently, and I shrugged both my shawl and my cloak from me. They puddled about my waist, and I felt like I had taken off all my clothes. I couldn't stop my shiver in the new chill. He leaned past me to build up the fire further, and I found myself at a wary stiffness, listening to him exhale when he reached, and inhale when he straightened.

"You first," I said, when he settled himself. "You can warm my shoulder through my dress, and when you're done, I'll show you my shoulder."

Jeck sighed. "Princess . . . Healing doesn't work through

clothing. I have to touch you. But if you want to forget the entire thing . . ."

"No," I said quickly, then felt myself warm. "Don't watch me."

He almost laughed, catching it and turning it into a cough. I turned where I sat, my brow furrowed. I didn't want him watching me loosen the rude lacing holding my dress together at my shoulder. Seeing my peeved expression, his face suddenly went empty of emotion.

"My apologies," he said, apparently realizing he was coming across as a voyeur.

I remained twisted at the waist, fingers fumbling as I undid the lacing and bared my shoulder, awkward since I wouldn't look from his eyes to see what I was doing. My pulse was rapid and my stomach uneasy. I felt like a seed-fluff-headed fool girl, letting him get to me. He was a rival player, and I had a right to be nervous.

I let my hands fall to my lap, and he turned from the dark. A small part of me eased when his gaze went to my eyes, not my shoulder, bare to the night and making me feel more exposed than I really was. God help me, he was only going to case my pain, not kiss me. It would only be his hands on my shoulder, not his lips. *Only his hands, sending a wonderful warmth through me, touching me more intimately than anyone else ever had.* Maybe I trusted him more than Duncan? *Maybe I'm simply foolish.*

He reached out, and I stiffened. "Promise," I said. "On your word as a player."

Instead of laughing at my worry or getting smug that he could use me if he wanted, he surprised me by nodding. "I won't tell your master you were bitten by a punta and what it did to your toxin levels, provided you promise me to tell him yourself."

Reassured, I let my body untwist, feeling my neck ease and my chest loosen. "All right," I said, not sure if I was lying to him.

I couldn't help but jump when he touched me, even though I had heard the sliding of his salt-stained coat against itself and knew it was coming. "Sorry," he muttered, making me wonder why he apologized, unless he thought he had hurt me.

That went along with the lightness of his touch, which was more disturbing than a firm grip. My pulse was fast, and I keenly felt the roughness of his fingers, damaged by salt as he first traced the new lines of flesh.

"How does it look?" I whispered, trying to find a more comfortable position.

I heard him pull away, and his moving fingers vanished. "It looks fine. No infection."

My head moved in acknowledgment. I wasn't surprised. It hadn't been warm to the touch all day. "No. I mean, how close are we?"

He was silent, and I heard in it his pondering of what he should tell me. "A week," he finally said, and I found myself exhaling.

"That's what I thought, too," I said, then jerked when his hands came back. Firmer, and a great deal warmer, he pressed my shoulder gently between his palms. A sigh slipped from me, and I didn't care that he could hear my relief and that it sounded like a sigh of pleasure. I didn't care at all. It felt that good.

A pulse of heat sifted through my sore muscles like water through sand, seeping deeper, unknotting the pain. I slumped only to jerk upright when I realized I was almost falling over. My stomach eased, and a tension I hadn't even realized I had been holding vanished. He couldn't see my face, so I let my eyes close.

Immediately his presence became shockingly more substantial: the sound of his breathing slow and sedate, the scent of his sweat and wool coat, the radiant heat on my back from his body behind me. I tried to remind myself that I was out in the woods, miles from rescue, vulnerable, that he was lulling me and that I should be more alert and wary for betrayal. But I couldn't find the strength for it.

It was the wind in the trees that snapped me awake, and Jeck must have felt it as his palms pressing into me shifted. It was then I realized that the zephyr in my head had gone completely silent in the short span that we had been talking. But now it was back, an unwelcome companion gibbering and trying to get me to listen to it.

"Please talk to me," I whispered to Jeck, desperate to get the wind to stop.

"Why?" he asked, clearly surprised.

I bowed my head, trying to decide if I should tell him his silence made me uncomfortable because I felt his hands on me more strongly, or if I should admit his voice drove away the wind in my head. The first made me sound like a silly woman and the second as if I was insane. I'd rather him think I was insane. Licking my lips, I said, "It helps keep the wind out of my head."

"Talking?" he questioned, not knowing that just that little bit had sent the zephyr into pathetic whines that held the promise of a quick departure.

I nodded, unable to stop my intake of dismay when he moved his hands. But he was only shifting his grip, and my shoulders eased back down. The heat returned, but he didn't say anything, so I listened to my breathing and said, "Thank you for not telling Kavenlow."

"Don't thank me yet," he said, and a trickle of tension started filtering back in. *Was he changing the deal?* "I think you'd rather lie to him yourself than risk him telling you that you can't be his apprentice anymore," he finished, and I pulled away, alarmed.

"That's not true," I countered, as his hands fell from me. Frightened, I scooted back even more, forcing my breath to stay even lest he realize he might be right. Holding my dress closed with one hand, and drawing my shawl and cloak up around my shoulders with the other, I moved back another two feet, then stumbled to stand. "You promised you wouldn't say anything."

"If you don't tell him, I will."

He looked up at me from where he sat, an obvious empty spot where I had been. Helpless, I turned away and went to my side of the fire, thinking it was colder than it had been when I had left it only a moment ago. There was nothing I could threaten him with to make him keep his mouth shut if he wanted to go back on his word. *Damn him, why had I trusted him?*

Unable to look at him, I sank back to the earth. My shoulder felt cold, the lingering warmth from his hands existing only in the deeper tissues. Across from me, Jeck rearranged himself, erasing every hint that I had been there. Frustrated, my thoughts whirled. I wanted to stay Kavenlow's apprentice. But if I couldn't, I didn't know if I could take a half life with

Duncan. "Please," I asked. "Don't tell him. I promise I'll leave with Duncan as soon as I know my sister is safe. You've already destroyed my future. At least give me the time to end this with dignity. He doesn't need to know if I just leave."

Jeck met my gaze across the fire, his angry expression that I might have lied to him easing. "You'd leave Kavenlow for Duncan?" he questioned. "You'd abandon the game and never tell Kavenlow why?"

Depressed, I reached for a stick and pushed on a burning chunk of wood. Sniffing loudly, I wiped my cold nose, feeling my back go cold. I didn't care anymore if he saw me cry, but there was nothing left. Slowly I nodded.

"I won't tell him providing you leave," he said. "But if you take too long, or I think you're going to hurt my game, I'll tell him sooner."

My eyes flicked to his. It was the most I'd get from him. "Thank you," I said, not understanding his change of heart. Perhaps there was a thread of humanity in him after all.

Jeck settled himself deeper onto the earth, looking as cold and uncomfortable as I was. It was a new look for him, and I wondered why he had dropped his stiff persona of stoic endurance. It made him look almost human. "I'm thinking we will find the capital tomorrow evening," he said, turning to a more benign topic. My eyes followed his to my water flask, and I took a swallow of it, trying to drain enough of it so I could give the rest to him and call our bargaining done. It was still tepid from lying next to me all day, and tasted flat.

"Late morning," I said softly as I wiped my fingers dry, dismayed when I made a clean spot and realized how dirty I was.

His eyebrows arched in disbelief, making deep shadows on his firelit face. "How would you know?" His eyes lingered on the flask. "You were out of your mind the entire night."

I pulled my cloak tighter, tired. Was he trying to irritate me so I'd give him the water just to get him to be quiet? It was working. "We could have rafted right into the capital," I said. "Why did you keep forcing me to angle south?"

"I didn't know the size of your storm," he said, his brow furrowing. "Can you imagine the damage you would have done to the ships at anchor and the dockside buildings had you blown in like that? Besides, if the pirates were ahead of us, it would have done them just as much good as us. This way, we have a chance to get there before them, not after."

We? I thought, deciding not to point his word choice out. But he was right. I would have destroyed everything three streets up from the docks. A day out was an acceptable compromise. I moved my shoulder experimentally, feeling it shift without pain.

"Early morning?" he questioned.

I nodded, hesitated, closed my eyes, breathed deeply. I had made out the better of this deal. "I can smell the filth in the streets," I said, my eyes flashing open at his snort of disbelief.

"I can't," he scoffed.

"You don't have the wind whispering in your ear, either." I was done with him. The wind was gone from my head, banished by his voice. I had wormed a promise from him that he would not tell Kavenlow how I got it there to begin with. Picking up the water flask, I jiggled it to get his attention, then tossed it across the fire to him. It was awkward since I used my left hand instead of my right, but he caught it.

Not even taking a sip, he lay down right where he was and tugged the canvas cloth tighter about him. His chin tucked to his chest, he pretended to fall asleep. I waited until his breathing grew deep and slow before I quietly found my own rest, shivering and cold beside the fire. I found myself thinking that if Jy were here instead of Jeck, I could snuggle up to my horse and at least be warm. Horses were better than men—for lots of reasons.

They at least listened when you talked, I mused as I watched Jeck pretend to be asleep. They took direction easily. They could carry lots of stuff and never complained about it. You always knew what they were thinking just by looking at them. They smelled good even when they were dirty, and when you were done riding them, all you had to do was give them a good brush and a dinner of oats, and they figured they got the better end of the deal. They were big and strong, and you could curl up against their warmth without them thinking you wanted more. *Horses,* I thought, shivering as I drifted into sleep, *are definitely better than men.* Why couldn't Jeck be more like a horse?

I woke only once, the remembered nightmare of being alone and betrayed jerking me awake. I started upright, my cloak clutched about me and the steam of my breath showing in the faint coals that remained of the fire. Heart pounding, I took in the moon hanging over the opposite horizon. Embarrassment filled me. It had been my own voice that had woken me: a harsh croak of a cry that seemed to still echo in the utter silence of the spring woods at night. Not even the wind dared break it.

Breath fast, I looked across the ash-dusted coals to Jeck. His dark eyes met mine as he lay on the ground under his ragged sailcloth, his gaze questioning. Clearly I had woken him. Not getting up, he stretched to reach what was left of the wood and toss it on the fire. Sparks flew up like memories, to die in the blackness of time. A small flame licked the new branch, and it began to burn.

Feeling cold and achy, I lay back down and closed my eyes, praying the dream wouldn't return. The feeling of loss still haunted me. It wasn't the loss of the wind, already grown familiar like an old pain. It was a new loss, still as sharp and bright as new metal. A loss of the heart, and it shocked me in its depth.

Duncan, I thought. Perhaps I should leave everything. Run away with Duncan and become a wandering vagrant. But even as I thought it, the feeling of loss swelled deeper. It seemed the demise of the game meant more.

"Jeck?" I opened my eyes to find him still watching me. "How close is my shoulder to the punta vision? Now that you healed it again?"

His jaw clenched, then released. "Two days. Are you okay?"

I nodded, not wanting to go into the details of why I had woken. Two days. Had I changed the future, or followed it? Tugging my cloak closer, I decided it didn't matter. My thoughts full and confusing, I fell back asleep. I woke later from the cold to find the sun up, the fire out, and Jeck gone. My knife had gone with him, but I was too weary even to curse him.

Horses didn't steal your stuff when they ran away.

Nineteen

✤

It didn't take me long to start out after Jeck. I had nothing to pack and was wearing everything I owned. The fire was out, and the biscuit I had saved from last night took all of a moment to choke down. My feet were cold and clammy in my gifted boots, and I thanked Penelope again for her selfless generosity. Thoughts on warm baths, hot fires, and how good it would feel to sign Jeck's execution papers, I pushed myself into motion.

"He stole my knife," I muttered, ignoring the whisper of wind calling to me from the tops of the trees. "He stole my knife right off me and left without waking me."

It didn't matter that I'd been pushed to my physical limits and had been sleeping the sleep of the dead. It didn't matter that he was a master player and had probably used his skills to keep me sleeping while he cut the knife from the ribbon about my waist. It infuriated me that his offer to heal my shoulder had probably only been to help ensure that I had a peaceful night sleep that I wouldn't want to wake from. He had taken my knife and left me behind.

Duncan had stolen from me before, but it had always been in fun, and he always gave whatever it was back, usually before I knew it was missing. *But Jeck . . .* I thought as my steps grew fierce and jarred me from my heels to my skull. Jeck had taken it in malice. To prove he could. To make me do without. And he had left me behind again. Intentionally.

The wind soughed louder, inciting the power behind my ears to a simmering chatter. First the wind came in the trees, then the voice in my head answered gleefully until they were singing an insane, distracting duet. The spirit trapped within me had ceased asking for freedom, instead now babbling with an irritating anticipation like a child eager for a favorite sweet.

I closed my eyes, then opened them when my balance left me and I stumbled. Pain jolted through me when I took a huge step to catch myself. I gritted my teeth and cursed Jeck as if it had been his fault. But if I were honest with myself, I would admit it wasn't the knife that bothered me. It was that he might get to Kavenlow before I could, deciding it would further his game to tell my teacher what had happened.

Horses are better than men, I thought as I stomped after him. You could tell them your most fearful secrets, and the worst they would do was snuff in your ear, not run away and tell your master. If Kavenlow found out, he would have no choice but to sever our teacher/student arrangement. I'd have to leave the game, shamed and lacking instead of lying that I chose to leave with Duncan and just . . . walking away.

Heartache came from nowhere, closely followed by panic when I stumbled into a faster pace. I couldn't leave the game. It was all I lived for. Duncan had made it very plain he would welcome me into his life, but to leave Kavenlow voluntarily was too painful to consider, even now when the game was falling apart around me. It was what my path had been bent to even before I had known of it, born with a natural resistance to the venom and trained from adolescence to use it. I wanted to be a player, even if it meant my death. I wanted a life with love as well, but to get it only because the first was out of reach seemed like a small consolation. I wanted both. I wanted both, curse me to hell and back.

The wind bubbled and simmered in my head, inciting the wind in the trees to swell. *I want to be a player,* I thought, the frustration rising in me. *I want to be loved.* And it looked like I was going to have neither since Duncan was with the pirates, having only his wits to keep his soul and body together.

Head down, I pushed after Jeck, clutching my cloak closed

about my neck with my good left hand as the wind sang to me. Worry and anger made my blood pound in my ears. My skin tingled, and my shoulder ached when the wind in the trees called to the wind in my head.

I had promised Kavenlow I would hold to his insistence of no ties that could not be broken easily, and though I had tried, I had failed with Duncan. *And see what happened?* I thought bitterly as I slogged down the path. Jeck was right. Love made you weak.

The wind whipped my filthy dress. The red ribbon that hung empty from my waist flung upward to slap my face. I stomped forward, the hurt rising through my body. "And he took my knife!" I muttered harshly, wanting to shove it deep into him.

A sudden gust mirrored my emotions, punching down through the trees. It hit me hard enough to send me stumbling back, eyes wide. The branches and leaves whipped upward to fly against my face. The howl swirling about me rose to a scream.

Staggering, I fell to my knees. Frightened, I cowered, hunching into myself and covering my head when torn leaves beat at me and the sky howled. From inside me, the tingle of venom surged, unrecognized until now. My lips parted when I realized the wind was coming from me. My faster pulse and anger had pulled venom from my poison-soaked tissues, and the wind in my head had used it to strengthen itself without me even knowing.

Cold struck through me and I hunched into myself against the power that still whipped at the trees. I had gotten angry, and the zephyr in my head had drawn the skies to fall upon me. Jeck was right. I was a danger to everyone.

Dirt and bits of bark made pinpricks when I pulled my head up. I squinted at the wildly tossing branches. *Silence!* I demanded, my heart pounding when the wind in my head bubbled and chattered in glee, glad to have found a playmate. *You will be still!*

It didn't hear, intent on calling down another gust of wind. My breath was pulled from me as an incoming blast hit the ground and ricocheted down the path. I cowered, ducking my head. Fear rode high, and I forced my lungs to work. *You will be still!* I demanded again, stronger this time as I wrapped my will about the hot ember of dark merriment inside me that willfully ignored me.

Feeling my bonds fall upon it again, it reared in an affronted passion, tugging once in complaint before it fell back to a soft, anticipatory, sullen grumble. The wind beating upon my shoulders gave one last push and died. A final soughing in the leaves, and all was still. The tingle of venom was a pulse of hurt in my shoulder and leg, vanishing to a dull ache.

I was left kneeling on the path with my arms wrapped about me and my heart pounding. *It almost took me over,* I thought, afraid to get up. I wasn't safe anymore, for me or anyone else. I had gotten angry and nearly let the wind take control.

Stomach churning, I slowly unkinked the grip I had on myself. My head hurt, and I could feel the palm of my right hand tingling.

I took a slow breath, eying the trees shifting in a natural breeze, the morning sun bright on the spring green leaves. *Never again,* I vowed. I couldn't slip again, or Kavenlow would realize how dangerous I was. I had to be very, very calm. I had to be very proper. I had to be silent and demure. I'd never make it.

But my worry turned closer to home when a small breeze spun about me as if looking for its playmate in my head, bringing me the familiar scent of leather and horse. Jeck. Just ahead. I hoped he had been out of hearing.

Muscles stiff as if I had been unmoving for hours, not moments, I started forward. My limbs felt weak and spindly, still trying to purge the recent venom from me, and the chalky taste of spent poison was thick on my tongue. I felt numb inside as I stumbled down the path to the faint brightening ahead. Jeck had saved my life, but I was too tired to hate him for it.

I slowed when the path opened up and the forest ended in an abrupt drop that stretched for miles either way. Below was an infertile field where the city's few horses and ponies found pasture. Beyond that was the smoke-wreathed capital, with its walls and towers, haze and stink. It had never looked so good with the strong morning sun glancing on the fog to impart a golden glow. Carts, ponies, and people made small from the distance crowded the gate. Some were going in, some were going out. None were taking the rough goat path up to here. And overlooking it all with his back to me was Jeck.

The weary man was standing beside a thick oak whose roots went right over the edge. My thoughts went back to his hands on my shoulder last night, giving me peace in my body with his hands and his magic, and peace in my mind with his voice. I clutched my cloak closer about me, suddenly nervous. I didn't want him to know what it had meant to me, finding comfort from him, even if I had to buy it with a peek at my shoulder and the future.

He looked cold, hunched under the sailcloth cloak he had made and rags on his feet. His breath steamed, and he had an uncomfortable-looking stance, awkward and very uncaptain-like though his shoulders were just as broad, and he stood just as tall. I hesitated to move as I took him in. He seemed afraid to go down among the people.

His head came up and he stiffened. And though he didn't turn, I knew he had realized I was standing behind him. "I should have knocked you on the head," he said softly.

I shuffled forward, halting on the path beside him and looking down at the oblivious city. In the harbor was the pirate ship. We hadn't beaten them here, but they had yet to leave. We were in time.

My shoulders slumped, and, looking askance at him, I realized I could feel the warmth from him, though we were a good arm's length apart. "Why did you wait for me?" I asked.

He took a slow breath. "The wind came up when you awoke. I knew you wouldn't be far behind. And after seeing that . . ." He pointed with his chin down to the milling people. "I would rather have you with me under the guise of bringing you safely home then to tell them you were an hour behind me, angry and hell-bent on killing me because I stole your knife."

I jerked back a step when he reached behind his cloak and pulled the blade out. Silent at my reaction, he extended it to me hilt first. Heart pounding, I snatched it, retying it on the red ribbon though I thought it an appalling place to keep it since it wouldn't take much for me to fall and cut myself on it. Penelope hadn't seemed to have a problem with it, but she probably didn't slip as often as I did. My gaze went to the mass of morning traffic below us as my fingers tied the knot by rote.

There were a lot of people. "Better part of valor?" I questioned bitingly.

Not looking at me, he pushed from the oak and headed down the steep trail to the gate. "I should have knocked you silly and left you there for them to find."

"I'm already insane," I whispered, and fell into place behind him. But his voice had driven the chattering wind in my head to a soft complaint, and I was grateful for his presence.

I had to concentrate to keep my footing while descending the rocky scree, and I lost sight of everything else until we reached the bottom. It was only when my feet were again on level ground that I realized how worried Jeck was, and I watched him carefully as he adjusted his makeshift cloak to hide his Misdev uniform before joining the mass of people before the gate. I was getting better at reading him. Though he didn't say anything, I thought he disliked the crush of humanity in which I took comfort in.

The chattering insanity of the wind in my head was all but drowned out by their combined noise. Being surrounded by the swirling mass of people was the best I'd felt since seeing the *Sandpiper* flounder on the reef at Midway Island and realized I had made a life-changing mistake. Chin coming up, I pushed ahead of Jeck. I was home.

"Stay behind me," I muttered, dodging a cart loaded with deadwood.

"The hell I will," he said, sounding affronted.

I jerked to a stop, not caring that people streamed about us to gain entry. I had endured enough of him. "You will mind your tongue, Captain," I said, loud enough so that the surrounding people could hear. From my peripheral sight, I could see them gossiping, starting to point. Despite my ragtag appearance, I was being recognized. Good.

Jeck must have realized it, too, since he pinched my elbow and all but hissed at me, "What are you doing? You'll start a panic if you're forced to explain why we're here, looking like this and without the royal couple."

Meeting his gaze with a satisfied calm, I raised my eyebrows mockingly. "We are out of the wilds, Captain," I said. "You're a Misdev officer who lost your prince and allowed brigands to retake my sister and burn my boat to her waterline. I am the sister of the reigning queen, and if she and Alex die, I succeed them. Half the people out here saw her reaffirm my title."

Jeck's brow furrowed, and he leaned closer so the surrounding people couldn't hear. "You're a player's apprentice. If you take the throne, every player will fall upon you, drag you to ground, crush your master's playing field, and squabble over the scraps like dogs on a downed cat."

I pried his fingers off me. "They don't know that."

My attention lifted when the swelling of questions rose around us and the inevitable, "Princess Tess?" was called out. More heads turned, and the milling people bent on gaining the capital hesitated, swirling to a stop about us a deferential four feet back. "Princess Tess?" it came again, worried and frightened.

I scanned the faces, my gaze alighting on a man standing atop the bench of a wagon.

"Look!" he called out, pointing when he saw me see him. "It *is* her. It's the princess!"

A worried murmur rose like birds from a beach. Jeck possessively took my elbow, and I let him, thinking it gave him strength. Smiling, I met the eyes that turned to us. Concern outweighed curiosity on all of them, and calls of "Where is the queen?" and "What happened?" and even a few, "Who hurt you?"

I tried to be reassuring as I raised my hand for silence, but the noise of the crowd swelled, becoming dangerous. From the gatehouse, the guards stood tall and watched from atop the observation platform. Jeck pressed close lest we become separated.

A woman pushed forward, putting a blanket over my shoulders. The smell of horse rose from it, warm and reassuring. I met her eyes, fixing her flushed, eager countenance into my memory forever. I could tell she thought it a rude gift, but I was so cold, it felt like the finest wool. My smile went grateful. I touched her hand and gave it a squeeze of thanks.

Almost as if it were a signal, the rabble pressed inward. Jeck stiffened. Questions rose and fell, unanswerable. A man elbowed his way to me, smiling to show he lacked a tooth as he fostered upon me a pair of mittens, thick and ungainly. Tears pricked my eyes when my stiff, aching fingers slipped into them and found them still warm from his body. I gave him a heartfelt expression of thanks. He bobbed his head in embarrassment and was swallowed up by the crowd. He dropped back willingly, having done what he intended.

"Please," I said, though I was sure no one heard me over the noise. "I need to get to the gate. I'll tell you all what happened, but I need to get to the gate!"

"The gate!" a man large enough to be a blacksmith bellowed, and I winced. "Princess Tess wants to talk to us from the gate. Make a way! Make a way!"

The call went out like a rippled wave, but no one could move until the outside people shifted first. Slowly a path opened, and I looked behind me to be sure Jeck was keeping up when his grip was torn from my elbow. His face was empty of all but a stoic nothing that I now knew was how he hid worry.

"Stay close," I said to him. "My people have long memories from the last Misdev war, and trust comes slow to fishermen if it comes at all."

He stumbled as he was jostled from behind. "I'll try to keep up," he grumbled.

More shouts for news came as the space opened wider before us. Smiling with a lifetime of protocol, I made my steps slow to the guardhouse, feeling stronger with each foot.

"Telling them is a mistake," Jeck cautioned as we neared the gate.

"My game, not yours," I said softly, sure he could hear me over the surrounding babble beating on us. I smiled at a frightened young woman patting a fussy baby at her shoulder, trying to tell her with my eyes that her child would grow up to be a fisherman, not a soldier.

"Your master's game," he corrected, and I glanced to see his brown eyes were pinched from behind his salt-stained hair. "You don't even know if he acted upon your queen's note."

We passed into the capital, and the guard at the gate held a hand to me to help me up the ladder to the raised observation platform atop the wall. He was young, not old. Kavenlow had gotten Contessa's note and emptied the guards' quarters. My soldiers were probably scattered from here to the borders of the realm in search, leaving the area about the capital free of close scrutiny.

I said nothing to Jeck, my eyes lingering on the sentry who pulled me up the ladder. He looked frightened, and I gave him a calming smile. Jeck was quick behind me, and from the top of the wall, I looked down into the city. People had gathered there as well, alerted to my presence by those who had gone in before us. My gaze rose to the palace, safe on its hill. Word would reach them soon whether I intended it or not.

"Did you dispatch someone to the palace yet?" I asked the young guard.

He paled. "No, Your Highness," he stammered. "I . . . I didn't."

"Good," I said, putting my mittened hand on his shoulder to reassure him. "Do so now. Tell the chancellor I'm with Captain Jeck and will join him after I speak to the city. Have the runner talk only to the chancellor himself, and only where others can't hear."

My hand dropped to the knife dangling from my waist from its bloodred cord. I awkwardly cut a curl from the nape of my neck and handed it to him. "Use this as a token to get past the sentries." The pirates had taken my rings; my hair would do.

"Yes, ma'am—I mean, Your Highness," the young guard stammered, gesturing to another sentry as young as he.

I started when Jeck leaned over my shoulder and muttered, "Young whelp. He wouldn't last three weeks in my king's army."

My brow furrowed in anger. The wind tugged at my hair, and I squelched it. "We don't normally put new officers in charge of the gates, Captain," I said tartly. "He's green, yes, but he's handling the situation well. No one is being crushed. No one is fighting. Everyone is calm."

The runner went out, a way parting for him until he got past the worst of the crowd and could start a faster pace. Jeck leaned closer yet, and I refused to shrink back. "That wouldn't have anything to do with those soothing thoughts you're putting out, now would it?" he asked, his whiskers tickling my ear.

Shocked, I spun, almost hitting him in my haste and only now recognizing the warm tingle coursing through me as my magic.

Jeck's smirk of satisfaction vanished as he saw my sudden

fear. "Damn," he swore softly. "You didn't even know you were doing it."

"No," I whispered when the young guard started shouting for everyone to be quiet. I placed my hands atop the railing, my mind going to the woman who gave me her blanket. I had sent her an encouraging thought of calm expectation. And the man who gave me his mittens . . . My gaze fell on them, seeing again their unadorned but sturdy construction. I had wished him to be calm and watchful, too. And the girl with the baby. She had looked so worried until I had smiled at her, and the old woman who touched my shoulder. It had given me so much strength, I was sure I had given her back tenfold the reassurance she had given me.

Even now I felt their whispers of emotion in me as they spoke to their neighbors, calming them, crushing the rumors before they started. And those they spoke to did the same to those beside them. The ripples of calm were passing through the crowd almost visibly, stilling them, turning their questions into a patient waiting.

I looked behind me to the people inside the city, talking with their faces turned up to me. My magic had filtered inside, rising through the streets like a slow fog. *God help me,* I thought. What if I had given them fear instead? How could I wield this much power safely?

The breeze in my head recognized my fear. It seized my distraction and called the wind to play. A gust flowed from the distant woods, visibly pushing the winter-worn grass tops to me. It raced over the crowd, inciting cries of dismay as hats were blown off. My hair streamed behind me, and I wildly bound the voice inside my head to be still.

Jeck took my elbow, and I suffered his touch, too shaken to resist. "Careful, Princess," he said softly. "Only happy thoughts. Lie to them."

The wind had died, but the soft sound of the crowd had swelled to replace it. My mind went to Contessa, probably bound and gagged on a dirt floor somewhere. She wouldn't be on the boat in the harbor but somewhere else, secreted away. I hoped Duncan was still free, waiting to move when he could be most effective. He was my best hope to get her back alive.

Steadying myself, I raised my hand. An uneasy silence

rippled out, first outside the gates, then in. I smiled thinly, then made it real. "There was a squall three days' sail from here," I said softly but clearly, and a faint murmur of voices carried it back to the last person. "The *Sandpiper* floundered. Queen Contessa and Prince Alex were moved to an adjacent merchant vessel. Captain Jeck and I remained aboard, trying to save her when she took fire from a fallen lamp and ran aground upon the shoals. She went down." It was a mix of lies and truth as two events were merged into one, and I felt not a twinge of guilt as my intent was pure.

"What of the captain?" someone called from the front.

I closed my eyes, and twin cold trails started down. My vision was blurry when I opened my eyes again, and I let them see my grief. They had been born beside the sea, and it was proper to show mourning to those lost to it. "I believe he perished trying to save his vessel," I said. "As did many of his crew."

A wailing of women rose, quickly muffled. I knew it would start again as soon as they heard it all.

"Princess," Jeck warned, pressing close and threatening. "Be careful."

"They are *my* people," I said, angry not at him but at how cruel fate could be. "I won't lie to them. I don't need to."

Questions of "What happened?" and "Where are they now?" were being put forth by worried, calm people pressing forward, their faces upraised in concern. No one asked about Duncan. Didn't they know how much he meant to me? Didn't they know he was risking his life to help keep their queen and prince alive?

"I'm not sure," I said, forcing my bitter thoughts down. "I need to get to the palace quickly. She may have written, and I'm as worried as you. I have traveled myself into exhaustion to reach the palace and get word of them." A hardness came into my voice, stilling them like a bell. "But my sister is as brave and resourceful as her mother, and Prince Alex is as honorable as my father. My sister will be returned to us unharmed, or I will hound those who dared touch her and my vengeance will tear the souls from their bodies and cast them into hell."

And with that, they knew she was taken.

The crowd went silent. Jeck's quick intake of breath for what they would now do was clear in my ear. His eyes went to the pirate ship in the capital harbor, and he shifted back a step. I was sure he thought they would whip themselves into a rage of vengeance and hatred. But they didn't. He watched in obvious wonder when they turned to their neighbors, voices soft and intent.

I had given them the truth—and they knew it—but first, I gave them a lie to cover their fear with. They would wait with me, ready to act when I asked them to, knowing I wouldn't keep the truth from them. Ever. And they trusted me to tell them the best time to act and how.

"You made a mistake," Jeck said, looking from face to face as if he didn't yet believe or understand. "They'll attack the ship in the harbor looking for them. Telling them the truth, even couched in a comforting story, is foolish. You've just lost your master's game, and probably your life."

My face went stiff in anger. "I may have lost my master's game, Captain, but not from telling my people the truth. Look again," I said, when the young guard fluttered away to fetch horses. "I have gained a thousand ears and eyes. They trust me, and they'll wait, knowing I'll call on them if there's anything they can do. I was honest with them and didn't treat them as children who must be protected from the harsh truth. I gave them dignity, though it was bound with pain. Because of that, they won't act against anyone on that boat, but they will tell me every single move they make down to how many men are relieving themselves every morning off the railing."

Clearly not convinced, Jeck followed me down the steps with a frustrated, angry look on his face. The people around us kept a deferential four feet back, and I walked alone surrounded by hundreds. "It was that same trust that allowed me to steal the palace out from under you last spring," I continued softly. "Open your eyes. Trust moves souls more surely than fear."

The clatter of hooves drew both our attentions. A second gate guard was awkwardly checking and rechecking the saddles of his stationed mounts. He seemed flustered that there was no sidesaddle. But an eager man had come close with two of his own horses, mismatched in their springtime shedding, patchy and ugly.

"We'll borrow these, officer," I told the young guard. "Keep yours for an emergency."

The common man broke into a wide grin, proud as he held the reins of the shaggy gray I lurched onto with Jeck's help. I laid my hand atop the stableman's and smiled. "Thank you," I said softly. "They will be waiting for you at the palace stables," and he stepped back, red and flushed.

Jeck's lips were pressed into a thin line as he reined in his taller animal, now prancing with excitement. A way opened up before us, and we started when Jeck shouted at his mount.

An unexpected pang of fear resonated through me as we left the crowd at a pace that was heartbreakingly fast after the days of slogging on foot. My thoughts spun to my sister, the pirates, Duncan's precarious position, and finally back to what I was going to tell Kavenlow.

As we raced upward through the busy streets, I looked at my borrowed boots to either side of the dirty animal I was on. My dress was torn and salt-stained. My hair was wild and had sticks and leaves in it. It hadn't seen a comb or water for days. I was wearing borrowed mittens and boots, hungry, cold, and heartsick. Jeck rode silently beside me, his expression giving no clue as to where his thoughts were.

If this is to be my last game, I vowed silently, *I will, by God, win it.*

Twenty

❖

The ceilings of the palace were lower than I remembered, and the walls tighter. After three weeks on a boat smaller than the palace's main kitchen, one might think that they would seem spacious. But the time spent outside and the vistas that stretched to the horizon made the once-comfortable walls seem almost claustrophobic.

I put a hand to my cheek as I walked the familiar halls, feeling the false warmth from the motionless air. Heather was half a step behind me, the well-rounded young woman fussing as she alternately scolded me about the state of my dress and wailed that I had ruined my hair again. Jeck followed right after her, a false-deferential two steps back, quick on my heels. Resh, the captain of my sister's guards, was beside me, meeting my rapid pace step for step.

Shortly after passing the palace's front gate, a young boy in Misdev colors had brought Jeck a new coat, a sword and belt, a worn but clean pair of boots, and an overdone black hat with feathers that draped down over the back of his neck. The hat was in Jeck's crushing grip. It was a Misdev officer's hat, and I knew Jeck hated the gaudy thing.

The fresh clothes and dirty exterior made him a heady mix

of rough and wild, clean and polished. Heather had been eying him between her fusses at me, the poor woman still not having wed, despite my assurances she wouldn't forfeit her place beside me should she lose her unwed status before me. I knew for a fact she hadn't been a maiden for almost five years; having lived vicariously through her for so long, I didn't know if I could separate her fact from her fantasy.

I glanced at her, and my longtime friend and official handmaiden took a breathless half run to come even with me. She was the only woman in the palace who had the impunity to scold me, and she never missed an opportunity. "Look at your hands!" she exclaimed, seemingly oblivious to the real problem of Contessa's capture.

"What about my hands?" I said, yanking them from her and halting. Jeck stopped, almost running me down. Fear took me. She could tell. She could tell I could use my magic to kill with my hands.

Heather stared at me. Her eyes went wide as if worried she had done something wrong. "Nothing!" she said, mystified. "They're so brown. That's all."

Relieved, I pushed back into motion, ignoring Captain Resh's soft murmur at my elbow. They were brown. That was all. Despite her surface impression, Heather was quick and intelligent, and it wouldn't have surprised me if she *had* seen a difference in my hands other than their color. Her apparent flightiness was an act helped out by her curvaceous figure and deep blue eyes, and she used it to her advantage to all who were ignorant of it.

"And your hair!" she wailed, as we passed through the front entryway, heads turning and gossip rising like a boat's wake behind us. "Lord love a duck, where have you been sleeping? The dirt?"

"Yes," I said shortly, and she put a delicate white hand to her mouth. Captain Resh was trying to get my attention, and I came to a stop in the main receiving room. You could get to anywhere in the palace from here. "Where's Kavenlow?" I asked Captain Resh, and he winced.

The man took a breath, but I could tell it was to placate me, not to tell me what I wanted to know. Heather and Captain

Resh had been trying to get me to go to my rooms to be washed, combed, fed, and princessified. I wanted to talk to the brigandines, and Kavenlow was with them.

"Where is Kavenlow?" I repeated more firmly, and the man shifted his weight from foot to foot.

"Your Highness," he began, coaxing.

Heather took my hand in hers again, clucking and petting it as if it was a sick kitten. "Oh, look at what you did to your fingernails!" she said, and my gaze followed hers. My nails were torn to the quick, and there was dirt caked in the cuticles. Seeing my sun-darkened hand lying in the cradle of her perfect white fingers, something in me snapped.

The zephyr inside me chattered and chortled, the trees past the high windows swayed, and the wind in me swelled. My pulse quickened, and the tingle of venom spilled into me. Feeling it, my heart gave a hard pound, and steeling my face into a careful blandness, I pulled my hand from my longtime friend before I accidentally killed her.

The young woman blinked as my hand jerked from hers. She started, meeting my eyes. I would talk to Kavenlow before seeing to my needs, and she knew it. "In the solarium," she said, and I pushed into motion while Captain Resh started a soft protest.

"He's been there all morning!" Heather continued, almost jogging to keep up. She had been my best friend and informant since we had met when she had been eight and I six. She could tell me what I wanted to know with impunity, having been labeled a fool since having been caught with two different men in a single night.

"They look like scoundrels," she babbled, and Captain Resh's look grew pained, "but they smell like fish. One is downright handsome. Rings and jewelry. I've tried to get in there, but the guards won't let even a kitchen maid in with wine."

Heather pouted breathlessly: a rare skill in itself, but she could do it while panting to keep up with me. I slowed so she could do it more proficiently. Jeck was watching in undisguised fascination. "He's a pirate, Heather," I said dryly. "He tied me up and tried to kill me."

A small gasp escaped her. The woman stopped stock-still. Jeck came to an abrupt halt to keep from running into her; just as she planned. His elbow bumped her chest, and he dropped his head and apologized, turning a surprising shade of red. I never slowed, intent on gaining the solarium. There was the jingle of metal and the creak of leather as Captain Resh and Jeck lurched to stay with me.

My face was calm, but inside I was seething. They had been here all morning while my sister languished. Duncan wasn't with them, or Heather would have told me. *God, please let him be all right.*

"Tess!" Heather bewailed as she ran to catch up after disentangling herself from Jeck. "You can't be presented. You're filthy! Begging your pardon, but you *are*!" she exclaimed.

"Princess," Captain Resh interrupted. "I must protest."

"And I insist," I said, never slowing. Jeck had caught up, and Heather's brow was furrowed as she probably tried to find another way to get him to knock into her again. She was a very smart woman but badly in need of a husband. I would have to remember to tell her Jeck hadn't the capacity to care for anyone except perhaps in how he might be able to use her. That she wouldn't feel the security of his arms around her unless he saw a benefit to himself, that she wouldn't know the comfort he could give unless he was trying to wrest something from her that she didn't want to show him, that she'd never see how his smile changed him unless it was to lull her into misplaced trust. But seeing how attractive he looked in that uniform of his, all-powerful and foreboding, she probably wouldn't care.

"Your Highness," my sister's captain of the guard tried again. "You're in no condition to receive guests. I strongly suggest you meet with them at supper."

Anger surged through me, quickly checked. I stopped short, and Jeck sidestepped Heather. Captain Resh's eyes widened, and he halted before me. He knew he had gone too far.

"Those men are not guests," I said softly. "They are thieves and murderers. I will not be having dinner with them. They will be out of my palace in an hour."

"Yes, Your Highness," he said stiffly, his gaze fixed to a point over my right shoulder. I hated it when they did that. "Thieves and murderers. Which is why—"

I took an aggressive step forward, clamping down on the chattering excitement in my head. "Captain," I warned, "I have chased them from Yellow Tail to here in two days to talk to them. I would hope that you are confident enough in your men's abilities to keep me secure while I'm in my own palace."

"Yes, Princess," he said, his eyes never moving from the spot on the wall behind me.

Satisfied, I spun on a heel, gathered my filthy skirts, and stalked forward past the library, where I first learned there was a world beyond the capital's gates, past the secondary ballroom, where I discovered not all men could dance, and past the private sanctuary, where I didn't go anymore since Contessa had made it her place to be alone.

Jeck was snickering at my elbow. I didn't know what he was so amused about. If I didn't get in, he wouldn't either. My confident pace faltered when I saw the door to the solarium. This was where my parents had died. I would not hear of my sister's demise among the roses and caged birds. I wouldn't.

There were three guards outside the door, all in Costenopolie colors. Through the glass were three more. All of them were older and experienced. Suddenly unsure, I tucked a stray brown curl behind my ear, jerking as I found a sandbur. Hesitating, I looked down at myself.

My hands were dirty and still smeared with tar. My dress was torn to my waist and held together with string. My boots were not my own. How on earth had I been recognized outside the city? I looked like the beggar woman my mother had probably been.

Jeck flicked a glance at me, having moved closer to ensure he gained entrance with me. "The fire in your eye, the set to your jaw, your bearing," he said as if he'd read my mind.

I flushed in embarrassment despite my better judgment. "Captain Jeck will accompany me instead of you, Captain Resh," I said, knowing it had been flattery but finding myself more inclined to let him in on the meeting. Heather fussed with my skirts, ignored.

"Yes, Princess." Captain Resh sounded pained. "Allow me to announce you."

I smoothed my tattered dress from habit as the older captain opened the door and held it for me. The scent of warm earth and the sound of birdsong filtered into the hallway. I breathed deeply, and my shoulders eased to bring me to a royal bearing. The solarium had once been my favorite place for taking my lessons in sums, letters, protocol, and history. Not anymore.

Leaving Heather behind in the hallway, I entered first to halt beside the inner guards. Jeck was next in his clean coat and hat, smelling of sweat and the sea. Captain Resh closed the door, and after a hushed word of instruction to the sentries, preceded Jeck and me down the winding path through potted trees and climbing vines. We passed statues of Contessa, carved while she was growing up. I vowed anew that the entire crew would die if she wasn't all right when she returned to me. The scent of early roses brought the memory of Kavenlow shouting sums at me across the garden. My pace faltered, and Jeck went a step past me before he realized I had slowed.

How am I going to tell Kavenlow? Can I just leave with Duncan and never tell him?

Eyebrows raised, Jeck ran his gaze over me, undoubtedly taking in my cold, frightened face. Black feathers drooped across the back of his neck, and a new sword hung from his belt. Adjusting that awful hat atop his head, he took my arm in escort and pulled me into motion.

"Cold feet, Princess?" he said, when Captain Resh moved ahead to announce us.

I pushed the worry down to set my stomach. "I thought you didn't want me to touch you."

"You aren't angry at me," Jeck said, his voice preoccupied. "You're harmless."

I frowned, thinking we made an odd pair, both moving with grace and refinement, stinking of dirt and looking like beggars on parade. "What makes you think I want you to touch me?" I said softly, and he made a small noise.

"What you want never crossed my mind." His voice was casual, low, pleasant, and I hated that it had somehow gained the power to soothe the voice of the wind in my head. "I've got ahold of you so you don't do something foolish, like kill Captain Rylan when he prods you."

"If I want to kill Captain Rylan, you won't be able to stop me," I said boldly.

Jeck's grip tightened in warning, then eased. "My king's son is in jeopardy," he breathed so only I might hear as our boots thumped on the slate tiles behind the captain of my sister's guards. "Do anything to anger that man enough to harm Prince Alex further, and I may not be able to sway my sovereign from any warlike directions. You already drove his second son mad. If anything befalls Alex, he will assume the abduction and murder were planned by your queen."

My heart pounded, and I tried to calm myself before I filled my veins with venom. It had been Jeck and Kavenlow who had driven King Misdev's second son to appear mad, but it didn't really matter. And planned treachery sounded exactly like what the war-loving Misdevs would think. "What kind of player are you if you can't control your pieces?" I mocked softly, as the patter of Jeck and me being announced came from around a vine-hidden court.

Jeck stopped, leaning close enough for his breath to stir a wayward curl. "I may let my king believe what he wants in this case."

"You care what happens to Alex?" I asked, truly surprised. And I caught a flicker of emotion, seeing him hide it behind a grimace. I was slowly learning that was his way of divorcing himself from feelings he thought were useless or counterproductive. Emotions such as understanding, mercy, compassion, empathy, love.

The sound of chairs scraping came as Captain Resh finished announcing us. Immediately, Jeck shifted us into motion. "I've invested a lot of time in him. That's all."

Thinking, I let him pull me forward. It was more than that. After so close an association, he couldn't lie to me as easily as to everyone else. Could it be that Jeck, Captain of the Misdev guards and player extraordinaire, actually cared about the people he was responsible for?

But my musings vanished when we found Kavenlow, Captain Rylan, and Mr. Smitty standing at a parlay table beside the orchid pond. My eyes went to Kavenlow and stopped. I stared at him, feeling helpless. A thousand words rushed to be spoken, but I could say none of them, bound by rigid patterns of proper behavior. He looked shockingly relieved for an instant, then it vanished behind a shield of formality.

In a familiar gesture of worry, he ran a short-fingered hand across his tidy, black-and-gray beard. Shifting in graceful agitation, the thickset man looked more like a master of horse-men than a master of books, despite his fine clothes. A dagger rested on his hip in an obvious threat, enforcing his mien of hidden power. His blue-gray eyes, full of dismay and sorrow, took in my ragtag appearance. I flushed. I was a princess. Sort of. On my better days.

Mr. Smitty was staring, his mouth working as he crossed himself and backed up a step. "You're alive!" He clutched at Captain Rylan's sleeve, tugging at it as if in disbelief. "She's alive," the uncouth man hissed at his captain. "She's burning still alive. My God, how did she get here so quick? We left 'em—"

"Mr. Smitty!" Captain Rylan barked, almost cuffing the frightened, superstitious man. "Shut your bloody yelp hole."

Kavenlow seemed to have to tear his gaze from me as he fixed his hard gaze on the overdressed captain in his faded fin-ery. "Left behind, Captain Rylan?" he said, every syllable pre-cise and carrying a heavy anger. "You told me she perished with the crew of the *Sandpiper.*"

"That would be a matter of interpretation, Chancellor." My voice was smooth and even, surprising even me. The captain of my sister's guards had quietly excused himself and was gone, and I heard the door shut in the distance.

Kavenlow came forward, reaching out and taking my hand. "Princess," was all he said as he bent his head over my filthy fingers for the expected greeting. I almost cried. I wanted to fall into his shoulder and sob—and was reduced to this. Kavenlow's hand trembled as he let my fingers fall. "Captain Jeck," he said evenly, his gaze turning to Jeck. "I'm pleased to see you."

"Sir," the man said softly, never looking at Captain Rylan or Mr. Smitty, his hand still cupping my elbow. "I would speak with you at your earliest convenience concerning a matter of mutual interest."

A ribbon of panic slipped around my heart and tightened. Kavenlow saw it, his face going expressionless. A matter of mutual interest? With Jeck's hand still on my elbow, that could only mean one thing. Me.

I tried to pull away from Jeck, and he set his other hand atop my arm, preventing it. My pulse hammered, and though I tried to stop it, the wind swirled in my head. From outside came the patter of old leaves against the glass. Venom pumped into me, and my vision blurred. Frightened, I set my weak right hand atop Jeck's arm and sent a warning pulse of hurt through him. It was a fraction of what would kill him, but I knew he felt it, as he started.

Jeck casually took his arm from mine and moved me to a bench. I bent my weak knees and obediently sat where he put me, shaking inside. Saying nothing, he fell into a parade rest beside me, the arm I had touched hidden partially behind his back. As I composed myself and the leaves outside dropped to the ground, I could almost feel Kavenlow's unspoken question fall heavily on me as he looked first at me, then at Jeck's stiff posture. It was obvious he knew something had happened between us, but not what.

I felt sick. Hurting Jeck had been as easy as learning how to spit from the palace's tower. He hadn't been aware it was coming as before, and I didn't think he had the control I'd found. And where I should be pleased I had taken what he taught me and brought it a step further, it scared me even more. What had I become?

The two pirates, oblivious to the small drama, had retreated to their wood-paneled chairs beside the table. One was confident in his faded finery and ringed fingers, the other frightened and stinking of sweat because I was alive and sitting before them. The thought of my sister rose to the forefront of my mind, and I leaned toward Captain Rylan, smoothly, calmly, and with the grace of forgotten queens.

"If my sister returns to me less than when I left her, I will do terrible things, Captain Rylan," I said. My voice was cold, chilling even me.

Oblivious to the danger behind my threat, Rylan smiled as if he wanted to reach out and pat my hand. Mr. Smitty heard it though, and he paled, crossing himself as he stood and all but hid behind his captain. Kavenlow's expression was pained. Jeck remained impassive. If he had laughed, I would have slapped him.

Rylan smiled, clearly thinking he was still in control. He wasn't. The man was as dead as my parents. "That depends upon your tightfisted money handler," he said confidently. "He's rather reluctant to part with it." Making a soft sound of admonishment, he settled an ankle atop a knee. His fingers steepled, and he eyed me from over them, smiling. Behind him, Mr. Smitty moved from foot to foot, fidgeting.

"I can't tell you how pleased I am to see you alive and . . . ready to enlighten your chancellor that my threats are real," the pirate captain said, making my stomach clench. "It seems he's stalling while your guards are scouring the country trying to find them. You won't. I want a decision now, or I will send your royal couple back to you. One alive, one dead."

My face went white. He wouldn't.

"Oh, yes I would," he said matter-of-factly as he idly spun a thick ring with a blue stone on his pinky finger. It looked like a ladies' ring, and I wondered where he had stolen it. "I'm still in a quandary trying to decide which one. Who would you rather have? A live sister and a war with Misdev, or a dead sister and a broken kingdom?" He simpered, making my blood pound in my ears. "Or you could make it so much simpler by giving me what I want. I'll send them both toddling home with nary a scratch on them." He hesitated. "For the most part."

The leaves beat again against the glass, and I forced the chatter in my head to be still. My fingers were tingling with venom, and I had a despairing thought that in my worry, I was making my own situation worse, dumping more poison into me to raise my residual levels of toxin even higher.

"You'll have your ransom, Captain," I said, feeling breathless and unreal. "And I'll have my sister and her husband, safe and unharmed."

"Princess," Kavenlow murmured in warning.

Jeck was a lot more direct. "He's lying," he said, as if the man wasn't six feet away.

"I don't care if he's lying or not," I said hotly. "We will pay the ransom."

"Tess," Kavenlow protested, "may I counsel you for a moment?"

I flushed, suddenly aware I was arguing against my master's game. It was my sister's life, though, and Alex's, and probably Duncan's. My eyes dropped, and I whispered, "Sorry."

Jeck grunted in surprise at my quick apology, a soft sound that probably reached only me.

Kavenlow straightened and stood, tugging his simple jacket straight. "Gentleman," he said firmly. "We shall take a rest. Wine, if you will, and perhaps something from the kitchen."

"Do what you want," Captain Rylan said, waving a generous hand with his rings flashing. "But if I and Mr. Smitty aren't aboard our boat by sunset, word will go out, and they will die."

My throat closed, and my shoulders tightened. Kavenlow took my arm and pulled me to my feet. I rose numbly. Jeck was going to tell him. I was going to lose everything that meant anything to me, and my sister was going to die.

His grip supporting me, Kavenlow gestured to Jeck. "Sir? Would you care to accompany us?"

"No!" I exclaimed, then lowered my voice. "No," I said softer, when Kavenlow hesitated.

Eye twitching, Kavenlow looked at Jeck, clearly not wanting to leave him alone with the two men to possibly talk deals he would know nothing about. He took a firmer stance, his squat silhouette looking aggressive but the look in his eyes questioning.

"Please, Kavenlow," I begged, my voice barely above a whisper.

He grimaced, frowned, and vacillated.

Jeck wasn't helping. Smiling at Kavenlow's discomfort, he said, "Of course, please go. We can talk later. I'll stay with Captain Rylan and Mr. Smitty. We have much to discuss on our own." His face was pleasant behind his ragged beard, but I could see his hidden anger now that I had spent several days with him. It wasn't directed at me, but at the two pirates, and I wondered if he could read me as easily, now, too.

Kavenlow muttered a terse, "Gentleman," taking my arm and pulling me into a fast pace that quickly left them behind. My heartbeat grew fast, and I was glad I was in flat-heeled boots so I could keep up. My steps seemed loud on the slate pathway. I couldn't hear Kavenlow's at all. He moved quickly, his motions abrupt and short. My brow pinched, and I became pensive. He was angry with me. But I had to talk to him before Jeck had a chance.

We came into view of the door. The waiting sentries straightened and opened it for us. I felt unreal as Kavenlow escorted me into the hallway, now smelling empty and barren after the rich scents of the solarium. Still not having said anything, Kavenlow dropped my arm and beckoned one of the outer sentries closer. I stood like an errant child, woebegone and shaky, as the door to the solarium closed, shutting out the birdsong.

"Wine," Kavenlow said shortly. "Immediately. Until I return, I want two serving girls in there to keep the conversation to the weather and how big the crabs are this year."

"Yes, sir."

"And a plate of food as well," he said. "Something warm. I'll be in the sanctuary with Princess Tess."

He took my arm. My eyes fell upon his fingers. The tips were stained with ink as they usually were, his nails trimmed neatly and his fingers strong from reining in spirited horses rather than turning pages. He was angry with me. I could understand why. She had been in my care, and I had lost her. Twice.

With a quick, preoccupied gait, he pulled me down the hallway to the sanctuary. He was right in that it would likely be empty. No one went in there since Contessa had made it her refuge. I stumbled in after Kavenlow, seeing her everywhere in the familiar room: the low black ceiling, the one stained-glass window shining like glory itself, the simple altar, and the three short rows of pews. It was a very small room, comforting to her after having been raised in a nunnery.

He left me standing in the middle of the narrow aisle, going with an angry haste to check to see that the small anteroom behind the altar was empty. I heard the thunk of the door closing and the clatter of the bar being set in place.

"Kavenlow . . ." I said, low and miserable.

I gasped when he grabbed my shoulders and spun me around. Expecting a severe chastisement and lecture, I wasn't prepared when he took me in a fierce hug. My shoulder throbbed, and I stifled a cry of pain and surprise.

"They said you had died!" he whispered fiercely, his grip on me never loosening. I could smell the scent of leather and horse that ever lingered on him, and the pungent scent of ink. My breath was forced from me, and I belatedly returned his embrace. *He isn't angry with me,* I thought, in a wash of relief that brought a lump to my throat.

He pulled away, his hands remaining atop my shoulders. His blue eyes were dark and glinting with unshed tears, the wrinkles about them deep with emotion. "They said you had died, Tess. They told me you had died!"

My breath came in a sob. He wasn't angry with me. "Kavenlow . . . I—"

He gave me another hug, gentler this time but no less intense. "When I received Contessa's letter, I was so worried," he said, interrupting me. "I knew you would be all right. But they told me you were dead! Oh, Tess, I thought you had left me."

Left me, echoed in my thoughts. I couldn't bring myself to look him in the eye. A hundred things to say flashed through my mind. A hundred things to tell. A hundred lies to give him so I wouldn't have to leave. But what came out was a weepy, "I'm sorry, Kavenlow."

His hands dropped from my shoulders, falling to take mine in his. "Hush," he admonished, seeing the ruin of my hands. "It's part of the game. We'll get them back. One game lost doesn't mean the end of play. And if the danger brings the two of them together, which I imagine it has, then we have come out well."

"No," I said, forcing myself to meet his eyes. They dropped immediately, and my throat closed. "I'm sorry," I all but squeaked. "I can't be your apprentice anymore."

A sob escaped me, and I held my breath lest any more follow it. My head pounded. I wanted to stay his student so badly, I would have lied to keep the position. But I couldn't. Seeing him there with nothing but love in his eyes, I couldn't lie to him. Not for anything.

As he stood in a frozen surprise, I sank into a pew, my head falling forward to rest upon the back of the seat ahead of me. My life was over. There was nothing left.

I heard him take a slow breath. Leather and wood creaked as he sat beside me. I pulled myself straight as he took my hands in his, turning them over to look at my palms. "You learned to use your hands," he said. "Tess. I'm sorry. Captain Jeck said it would happen whether you wanted it to or not. I am so proud of you—"

"Yes, but . . ." I interrupted, my chest clenching with an unbearable weight.

"Did he let you think you had to be his apprentice if he taught you?" he questioned, a hard anger slipping into his quiet voice. His blue-gray eyes were narrowed when I brought my head up, my gaze swimming from unshed tears. "I bought his instruction for you in this matter. You don't owe him anything."

"It's not that," I said, the pounding in my head making my eyes ache.

He placed my palms together as if in prayer, his surrounding mine. "You willingly want to be his apprentice? Are you leaving my instruction for his? Tess—"

His voice was low and even, and I heard the hurt in it. "No!" I exclaimed, pained and distressed. "Kavenlow, please."

He pulled my hand up and gave it a squeeze. "Duncan," he said softly, his soft gaze full of regret and understanding. "You want to leave the game to be with Duncan. I understand. I told you that you could. The choice was always yours."

"Stop!" I cried, overwrought with guilt, the thick walls soaking up my outburst. It would be so easy to lie to him, and say that was it, but I couldn't. "I don't want to leave with Duncan. I want to be a player. I want to stay your apprentice. But I can't, Kavenlow. I can't!"

He waited while I took a shuddering breath, then another. "I lost my tolerance to venom," I whispered, unable to say it louder lest it break my soul to hear it. "It's gone. One dart will kill me. I can't be a player with that kind of risk. Jeck knows. He'll use it against you when he can." I looked up, not knowing what I would find.

Bewilderment shone from my teacher. "Did Captain Jeck—" he stammered. "Did he elevate your residual levels of toxin when he taught you to use your hands?" He turned to look behind us at the chapel door. "We will wait until the levels drop."

"They aren't going to drop," I whispered. "It wasn't Jeck. Please, Kavenlow. Listen. I'm trying to tell you."

His breath was fast and impatient as he turned so we were almost facing each other in the narrow space between the pews. My heart seemed to beat in my ears, and I didn't understand why the wind in my head was silent and still when I was so upset, but I was glad it was.

"The pirates tried to kill me by trapping me in a pit with a punta," I said. My face twisted at the awful memory of it: the fear, the thought that I was going to die, the melding of our thoughts, and the pain of his existence when I taught that great cat of death.

"Tess!" Kavenlow whispered, horrified.

I couldn't look at him, but I was fairly sure the warm drops of tears falling upon our hands were from me. "I tried to charm him," I said, keeping my voice low so I could force the words past the lump in my throat. "I thought that if I charmed him and showed the pirates that he wouldn't hurt me, that they would let me out of the pit." I glanced up at the new fear in his eyes. "I almost did," I said. "But they frightened him, and he broke from me, then he bit me. He was so frightened. All he wanted was to be out."

"You were bitten?" The wonder in his voice brought my gaze to his, and he ran his attention over me as if looking for it. "You survived a punta bite?" he asked. "My God, Tess. Where? How long ago? And you walked from Yellow Tail?"

I touched my shoulder, and his gaze sharpened in understanding for why my dress was being held together with cord and string as well as why it was rimmed with the brown stains of blood that the seawater couldn't remove. He reached out, hesitating until he saw the permission in my eyes, then unlaced the temporary fix with his trembling fingers.

"Jeck saved my life," I said, staring at the red triangle in the stained-glass window. I was numb and empty, having told my worst fear to Kavenlow. There were no decisions now that were left for me to make. I had only today to live for.

"He was there?" Kavenlow said, his fingers gentle as he undid the knots. "He was there and didn't stop them?"

"He wasn't there," I breathed, not caring when Kavenlow caught his breath in dismay when my shoulder came to light in the dusky gray of the sanctuary. I wondered what was different that Kavenlow could unfold my dress to bare my shoulder, and I couldn't let Jeck watch me do it on my own. "Jeck was on the *Sandpiper* trying to find us," I whispered.

Kavenlow was silent. I tensed when his fingers traced lightly beside the scars, evaluating how much they had healed. "Tess," he said softly, gathering the ends of my dress back together and settling back. "How could he have healed you if he was on the *Sandpiper*?"

"Through a dream." Of its own accord, my hand rose to cover my bite to hide it again. "I was dying from the venom, but it threw me into a prophetic dream."

"Are you sure?" he asked, his brow worried and pinched.

I nodded, remembering being tied to the mast of Jeck's raft, the emotions of anger and frustration riding high in me. "One came true already."

"There was more than one?"

"Yes," I whispered, remembering. "One wasn't a dream, though. I was Jeck, on the *Sandpiper*. And I pointed the way to the island through him. It was real, because he dosed himself on venom to try to maintain the link we had, and we landed together in the same dream."

"You shared the same vision?" Kavenlow went white behind his graying beard.

I ran my fingers over the grooves in the pew ahead of me, feeling the sharp smoothness of the lines. "It was the venom," I explained, though he had probably figured it out for himself. "And it wasn't like the first dream. He was as aware as I was. After I told him I'd been bitten, he tried to heal it." I felt myself blush, hoping it was too dark to see. "Of course we ruined any chance of seeing the future correctly," I said, trying for a flippant air. "But it worked. When I woke up, I was alive." My gaze went distant, remembering it.

Jeck had saved my life. For what? It was over except for what came now day by day. My hand dropped from my shoulder to lie still in my lap.

Kavenlow watched me with wide, worried eyes. "It looks well healed. How long ago was it?"

"I don't know anymore," I said softly, not caring, then realizing he did, I thought for a moment. The moon was almost full now. It had been a waxing quarter when I had gazed at it from the bottom of the pit. "Five days ago?" I said, surprised. It seemed like forever.

"It looks two weeks old," he said, and I nodded.

"If the last dream is anywhere accurate, I'll live long enough to have Jeck take me prisoner in the woods again," I said, telling myself I didn't care. "Shouldn't be too much longer, by the age of the scar. It almost matches that in the dream." My voice rose up high at the end, and I made fists of my hands. My right hand ached, but I clenched it as hard as I could, fighting the tears.

"Tess . . ." Kavenlow soothed, putting a fatherly arm across my shoulders and pulling me close. "Don't cry. Those dreams can't be believed."

"I'm not upset about the fool dream!" I said around a hiccuping sob. "I can't be a player anymore." I started to cry, hating myself for it.

"Listen to me," he said firmly. "We don't even know what your tolerance is. It might not be so bad."

"It was a punta bite!" I cried in frustration. "I should have died. I have so much venom in me that I almost killed Jeck in a flash of annoyance. I can't control it, Kavenlow!" I exclaimed, coming out with the worst of it. "It's fighting me. It's too much. And it's not going away. The venom fixed itself into my healing tissues. It spills out into me when I get angry."

I sobbed as Kavenlow pulled me closer and held me as he used to when I fell from a horse. "Shhhh," he soothed. "It's never as bad as you believe. Slow down. Take a step back. We'll go carefully until we know just what happened. Your tolerances will fall."

"They aren't," I said around my sobs. "It's replenishing itself. Jeck accidentally fixed the venom into my wound as it healed. It's there, replenishing itself just as it does in a punta. Even if I never taste toxin again, my residual levels won't ever drop. I'll never be rid of it. Never." The tears flowed freely now, and I let them fall. I had wanted to be a player. I abandoned a life with love in it to have it, and now . . .

He held me as I cried, knowing that the tears weren't just for Contessa and Duncan, knowing they weren't for the days of hunger and uncertainty I had endured, or the pain and fear of my death. They were for saying good-bye to what I had been promised, to what I had pointed my entire life toward.

Though Kavenlow had meant to be reassuring, I knew that I could never be a player. My life with him was over. He would take another as his apprentice to succeed him in the game. There was no choice to be made. It was done.

Twenty-one

❖

I pushed the food around on my dinner plate, the muted conversation between Jeck and Kavenlow all but unheard and uncomprehended as I sat in the small private dining room between the kitchen and the large banquet hall and pretended to eat. It had been designed as a staging area to prepare food for large gatherings, but those gatherings had been so far and few between that my parents had turned it into a casual dining hall. Tapestries decorated the stone walls, and torches lit the windowless room. My eyes lingered on the brightly lit fireplace where I had hid from Jeck a bare half a season ago, and I went more melancholy still.

In the few hours that I had been back in the palace, I had been brushed, combed, washed, dressed, primped, and fussed over until I all but shouted at Heather to leave me alone. I loved her dearly, but her unending prattle had seemed to incite the wind in my head instead of soothe it as Jeck's voice did, until it was as if the two of them were carrying on a rapid, excited gossip that neither of them were listening to.

Having been at my limit, I had told her in a very soft voice to please close her mouth and not open it again. She had pressed her lips together and not said another word, but my scalp still hurt from her yanks as she put my brown curls into my usual topknot.

There were no darts in it; Kavenlow had ransacked my room while I was bathing and removed every drop of toxin, even the small vial I had thought he hadn't known about tucked in the hole within the foot of my bedpost. It had left an aching hurt, as if he mistrusted me. In silent protest, I had fastened my second-best bullwhip around my waist—disguised under a filmy scarf of silk—and tucked my throwing knives away in various places. But I didn't need them. I could kill anyone but Jeck with a touch.

My gaze dropped to my hands, seeing them trembling slightly. They looked no different—browner and thinner than they used to be, the nails trimmed to nothing from Heather's trying to even them out—but they could kill a man more surely than darts. My stomach clenched, and I pushed my plate away to set my napkin aside.

Kavenlow met my eyes across the narrow table, his brow raised and his fork paused halfway to his mouth as he continued to talk to Jeck. Sighing, I replaced my napkin on my lap and pulled my plate closer, pretending to eat so he could properly finish his meal. Normally we didn't adhere to political niceties when in a setting as informal as this, but Jeck was here, and apparently Kavenlow wanted to follow the royal axiom that everyone is done when the ranking royal is. I didn't question why. Kavenlow had his own reasons for everything he did. It might be as simple as him wanting to force a few more bites down my throat, but I was betting it was to remind Jeck I was the ranking person here. Me, the useless apprentice.

The masculine murmurs of talk between bites of food had slowly calmed the voice of the wind in my ear until its buzzing and chortling vanished. Basking in the blessed silence, I closed my eyes and put my elbows on the table, ignoring Kavenlow's harrumph to remove them. My fork was dangling from my fingers so he could eat if he wanted. It didn't seem right to be dining on honey-soaked veal when my sister was choking down cold biscuits and muddy water.

Captain Rylan and Mr. Smitty had left long before sunset, the former confident and mistaken, the latter frightened and wise. With me safe and Jeck available to help effect a rescue,

Kavenlow had agreed to pay the ransom. I think he was planning to use the carrot of money to get closer to them. The pirates would be stupid to not suspect something, and though overconfident, Captain Rylan wasn't stupid.

The two pirates had left hours ago amid a bristle of guards, escorted back to their ship where they were now under the watch of young sentries, men too old to fish, and sly, clever street women well versed in using their wits and their powers of observation. We were just waiting now to hear when and where to take the ransom.

A sigh shifted my shoulders, and I jumped when my fork slipped from my fingers and clattered onto my plate. "Sorry," I said, frowning when Jeck and Kavenlow continued their conversation unabated. My frown deepened when I realized their talk had turned to me.

Jeck pointed a fork at Kavenlow, looking comfortable and relaxed in his clean Misdev uniform as he sat across from my teacher with his hair washed, styled, and smelling of cedar. "You can't even begin to speculate on her possible higher tolerance," Jeck said as if I weren't in the room. "It would be a great disservice to discount the possibility that it's lower than you think. She was performing high-venom manipulations shortly after being bitten. The prophetic dreams alone used a great deal of toxin and would have washed much of the poison from her body immediately, giving her an apparent lower dose. And I can't begin to guess how much venom was pulled from her to join our thoughts so closely that she was able to point the direction the pirates had taken them by shifting my arm."

Kavenlow hesitated, my gut tightening at the alarm in his eyes when he leaned over his plate to Jeck. "Possession?" he stammered. "As can be done with animals? She—"

"No," Jeck interrupted, and the knot of tension eased in me. Jeck took off his feathered hat, setting it down beside his wineglass, his fingers resting on the rim of black felt. "Her thoughts slipped into mine for an instant," he said carefully, his eyes flicking from Kavenlow to me and back again. "I allowed her to move my arm. It wasn't possession. I was always in control. I'm sure it was due to the high levels of free venom in her at the time."

I returned to the memory of our thoughts mingling when the pirates had taken the *Sandpiper.* The slight tightening of Jeck's brow told me to keep quiet about it. It hadn't been possession, either, but the fear Kavenlow had shown at even the suggestion kept my mouth shut.

The tip of my teacher's fork touched his plate. He was watching me, and I wondered if he had seen Jeck's silent admonishment for me to be silent and my acceptance to take direction from him: a rival player, not my master, a man who would play upon my fears for his own gain. I was so foolish.

"I've never heard of that possibility, even with the oldest players," Kavenlow said, and I tried to hide my guilt.

Seeing me quiet in indecision, Jeck turned away and frowned. "The point is that she used so much venom so quickly after being bitten that she may have brought her levels down to a reasonable limit, even if they are replacing themselves. You don't know unless you run a few trials. It would be remiss to waste the opportunity to explore what she can manage, to ignore the possibility to see what she is capable of, or to see what the retired players can do that they don't tell us. But to remove her from the game entirely?" He pointed his fork at me though his avarice-filled eyes never left Kavenlow's. "That is the move of a timid, foolish man."

My eyes went to Kavenlow at the insult. His suntanned brow furrowed, the only show of his anger. "I will not risk Tess's life to find out what she can do," he said tightly. "She's a person, not a dog or a horse. She's out of the game." His blue eyes finally met mine, full of a pity that made me nervous. "Temporarily, Tess. Your residual levels will fall. I don't understand why they haven't started to drop already."

Jeck set his table knife down with an excessive amount of force. "I told you why. It's fixed in her tissues and replenishing itself. Ignoring a fact because you don't like it is going to get her killed."

"And speaking to me like that at my dinner table is going to get you incarcerated," Kavenlow shot back, a lifetime of protocol keeping his voice soft and him unmoving in his chair, though his brow was tight with anger. "No player can renew venom."

Sighing in exasperation, Jeck settled back in his chair. "A

punta can. I didn't know fixing the venom in her tissues to
slow down its release into her body would result in it finding a
suitable home and allow it to reproduce itself. But if a punta
can do it, why can't a person?"

My gaze went between them, Jeck's horrible certainty
starting to frighten me. Kavenlow didn't want to accept it—
didn't want to believe—but I knew Jeck was right. My levels
wouldn't be dropping. Ever.

"I am sorry," Jeck said, his apologetic tone making me
miserable. "I didn't know this would happen. She was bitten,
and I tried to save her life. To make her unusable was not my
intention. That you yourself don't believe it possible is my
only defense."

Kavenlow's fingers on his glass were deceptively loose,
and I knew from his distant expression that he was starting to
believe. "We will proceed carefully until we know more," he
said, not looking at me, for which I was grateful. "Tess will
have no toxin, and she will not use her magic, allowing her
residual levels to drop."

The taste of honey in my mouth grew flat. From the corner
of my sight, I watched Jeck pull himself forward. "They aren't
going to drop," he insisted. "And if she were my apprentice, I
would find out what her tolerances are. Immediately. And go
from there with the appropriate precautions."

Kavenlow speared a carefully cut square of meat, equal on
all sides. "She was bitten by a punta. She isn't tasting venom or
performing any magic for at least six months. If careful testing
at that time puts her threshold higher than I like, I'll not risk
her further. I don't care if she can manage master-level manipulations or not. I'll not balance her life against the single dart
of a rival player. And her levels will drop if she shuns all toxin
and magic. They always do."

My throat closed, and I alternated my gaze between the
two of them. I knew more certainly than the sun would rise tomorrow that Jeck was right, but I couldn't bring myself to say
it, and I could feel Jeck looking at me, biting his tongue to keep
from demanding I do just that.

"She has been doing incredible twists of magic safely since
we got off that island," Jeck said instead, and my face burned at
my cowardice. "Did she tell you she manipulated the people at

the gate into a calm state after they recognized her and knew something had happened to the queen? The entire crowd?"

"She's been doing that since she was fourteen," Kavenlow said gruffly, not looking up from his plate as he pushed his food around.

"And the rays," he offered, an eager intentness in him I didn't understand. "She charmed them into following us, even up onto the beach. Even now, the harbor is full of them. It's because of her."

Fearful, I glanced at Kavenlow, but he shrugged. "Her ability to manipulate animals has always been high. It's one of her better skills. I'm not surprised that's happening if her residual venom levels are elevated." Kavenlow sighed, his brown eyes tired as he turned to Jeck. "I'm not arguing that her levels are high and she's doing incredible things. But I will not risk her life on a game, Captain Jeck."

"Risk is part of the game," he said, and tension filled me.

"Of course it is." Kavenlow's voice was hard, and I forced my jaw to unclench. "But hers is not an acceptable risk anymore; it's an extraordinary one."

"And so are her abilities." Jeck pressed his lips together. "Sir. Reconsider."

Kavenlow laced his fingers together and leaned over his plate. "Why do you care? She is *my* student. Not yours."

I didn't move, afraid they might remember I was here and make me leave.

Jeck hesitated, taking a slow, steadying breath. "Sir," he said softly, as if loath to say his next words. "She is able to regulate the amount of killing force through her hands, to give a nonlethal dose if she chooses. Even I cannot do that. If you insist on dismissing her out of hand—"

"I am not dismissing Tess out of hand," Kavenlow snapped, his fist beside his plate going white-knuckled. "If her punta bite endangers her life beyond the normal risk, she will not be a player!"

I took a deep breath, trying to find enough air. I knew that's what was going to happen, but to hear him say it made it irrefutable.

Jeck leaned forward, not backing down. "You're ignoring the larger picture. Yes, her tolerances have been pushed to what is likely to be an unsafe level, but so have her skills. I say go cautiously, but go! A player won't waste a dart on another unless there is a reason. She's in no more danger than she would be otherwise as long as no one knows of her elevated levels."

Kavenlow's eye twitched. He wiped his graying beard carefully and set the napkin in his lap. "You know," he said, his voice flat, angry, and heavy with the cadence of threat.

Jeck's face went still. Slowly he sat back. He never looked at me. "Yes. I do."

I swallowed hard, watching the tensions rise.

"I'd have to kill you to keep it quiet," Kavenlow said.

Frightened, I felt my muscles tighten. My pulse raced, and I felt a wave of vertigo. *Chull bait*, I swore, as my fear dumped a sliver of venom into my veins. I forced myself to relax, pulling on a lifetime of control. But Jeck only smiled, his eyes telling Kavenlow he wasn't going to make any sudden moves. "You could try," he said. "Or you could give her to me."

Shocked, my mouth dropped open. Eyes wide, I stared at Kavenlow, then Jeck. I didn't want to be Jeck's apprentice. I was Kavenlow's!

Kavenlow hunched like a bear over his plate, his short fingers trembling about the delicate stem of the wineglass. "She is my apprentice," he said, a shocking amount of anger in his soft voice. "You won't have her, Jeck."

Jeck leaned back in his chair and steepled his fingers. "If you tell her she can't be a player anymore, she'll come to me. The game is in her blood. She doesn't care about the risk."

Mouth dry, I couldn't move. Kavenlow stood in the harsh sound of his chair scraping, his shoulders tense and angry.

"Stop it!" I shouted, standing up as well. "Just stop it! Both of you! And stop talking about me as if I weren't here! I don't belong to either of you!"

His face quirked with an irritating confidence, Jeck eased back in his chair, his expression wry from behind his freshly trimmed beard to make him look both annoyed and amused. "Your apprentice seems to have something to say. You should teach her to mind her place."

I turned to him, face warm and knees shaking. "And what would that be, Captain?"

Kavenlow sat back down. His motions were still quick with tension. "Tess is a princess by law. Higher rank than both of us put together. It would do you good to remember that aspect of her is as real as her apprenticeship. If not more."

Jeck's eyebrows rose a bare fraction. "My apologies. I assumed that when talking of player matters, she reverted to an apprentice in full."

My legs shook, and I wondered why the wind in my head wasn't taking advantage of my shaky state, but there wasn't a whisper or chortle despite the trace of venom making my shoulder ache and my legs wobbly. "I am always a Costenopolie princess. Just as you are a Misdev captain," I said, hearing my voice tremble.

He nodded once, taking a drink of his wine and accepting that.

A soft cadence of boots on tile came distantly. Kavenlow flicked a glance at me, telling me to sit without saying a word. "Would you like more wine, Captain?" Kavenlow said, as I reseated myself. It was their agreed cue to change subjects in the palace, where interruptions were rampant.

"Thank you, no." He covered the top of his glass, hardly touched.

We all turned as the captain of my sister's guard entered, his attention going to me first, then Kavenlow. My heart clenched. Something had happened.

"Princess, Chancellor, Captain," he said in greeting. His face was both puzzled and pleased. "Ah . . . Duncan is here."

Twenty-two

❖

I rose in a sliding sound of silk, almost unaware I had moved. My pulse shifted into a quick pace, and I put a hand on the table until the dizziness caused from the venom it dumped into me passed. "Duncan," I said intently. "Where?"

"The main receiving hall, Your Highness." There was none of the hesitation from Resh I had seen earlier this morning.

Gathering my skirts, I ran in a skittering of slick-soled boots into the hall.

"Your Highness!" the guard protested.

Faint behind me came Kavenlow's voice. "Let her go. She can take care of herself."

Hope lifting through me, I continued down the torchlit corridor at a near run. Princess or not, I could get away with it. I'd been running in the halls my entire life. The staff was used to seeing me with my dress streaming and my hand to my head to keep my topknot from falling apart. As a guard, Jeck, too, might be able to get away with running in the halls, but he'd be with Kavenlow, and Kavenlow kept a more decorous pace—generally.

Feet skidding, I made a turn. At the end of the hall was the main reception room, unseen but for a small bit of tile floor and wall. I ran to it, lurching to a stop at the open archway.

Duncan had apparently heard my feet and turned from his crouch before the fire beside the dais, ever burning at coals. A guard was with him, his voice soft in conversation. Duncan's eyes lit up as he saw me, and upon standing, he held out his hands, smiling.

"Duncan!" Relief made my steps falter. Eyes fixed on his ragtag figure, I said breathlessly to the guard, "Leave us."

"Your Highness," the man in Costenopolie green and gold said, almost laughing when he turned on a heel and walked smartly away. The guards in the palace—especially the younger ones—liked Duncan. And they knew I did, too.

"Tess," Duncan whispered, and I finished crossing the large room, my footsteps sharp and quick. His hands met mine, and he pulled me willingly to him. I didn't care if the guard was gone or not. I put my cheek against his freshly washed shirt, taking in the smell of mint, salty mud, and the new scent of the ash on his hands.

"You're alive," I said, my voice small sounding. "You escaped them." I pulled my head up, my hand touching his shaven face. It dropped at a sudden thought. "Contessa! Is she all right? How did you get away?"

"Chu pits, woman," he said, smiling to tell me everything was all right as he tucked a curl of my hair behind my ear. "Shut up for a moment. Kavenlow is probably right behind you, and I've been waiting five days to do this. I own you now, you know."

Smiling roguishly, he tilted his head to mine. His arms went about my waist, and he eased me willingly closer. Breath catching, I leaned into him, the motion as gentle and familiar as it ever was. My eyes closed as our lips met, and my body eased.

His hand rose from my waist, curving around me. Not a hint of his scraggly beard was left, and I sent the fingers of my good hand behind his neck, approving of the lack. With a slow exhalation, our kiss became deeper, more tender. It reached an as-yet-uncrossed line and hovered. My heart pounded as I felt him hesitate, then reluctantly retreat.

I was a fool, I thought, even before his lips broke from mine and pulled away with a teasing slowness. Duncan loved me. I could be happy with him. I could live the life of a nomad, writing letters of correspondence or totaling sums for merchants not willing to do it themselves. I could make my own way without relying on anyone and live my life with someone who loved me. Wasn't that what was important?

The fire leapt when the wind from the bay scoured over the chimney top, pulling the small flame Duncan had stirred higher. A gust swirled in from a distant window. It went slack and slow upon finding the large room. A curl that had escaped my topknot shifted. Within my thoughts came a chattering of demand, easily overpowered.

Be still, I admonished the wind in my head, pulling Duncan back to me with a new feeling of abandonment. His eyes flashed open in surprise, then he responded. Again we kissed. His hand shifted hesitantly to the small of my back, the faint pressure becoming firmer when he felt my new acceptance. I reached upward, finding the nape of his neck, drawing him close. His breath quickened, meeting mine. Warmth tickled behind my closed eyes: tears for having decided to leave Kavenlow and all I'd worked my life for, tears for having said yes to Duncan.

A distant shutter banged, and I heard a distant cry of dismay, but here by the dais, all was still. Duncan pulled from me, and I looked up at him. He smiled, wiping a thumb under my eye. "I was so worried for you," he said softly, and my chest tightened with an unbearable weight that he cared for me so much. "I thought they had killed you. I should have known you were all right. But how did you get off that island so quickly?"

A dry rasp of boots scraping across the tile jerked me from Duncan. I stumbled back, my upbringing making a warmth come to my cheeks. I reached to check my topknot, then my skirts, though nothing needed adjusting. Jeck and Kavenlow were just inside the archway, watching.

"K-Kavenlow," I stammered, taking a step from Duncan though my fingers remained intertwined with his. "Duncan is here. He got away from them."

Duncan is here, I thought. *Chu pits, how soft in the head was that?*

"So I see," Kavenlow said thinly, his expression pained and full of acceptance.

I looked to the fire before he could see the heartache in my eyes. I couldn't be a player anymore, and I wouldn't make Kavenlow tell me to go. He knew it as well as I. Duncan, though, had a defiant gleam to his eyes that didn't surprise me. I'd often felt like a bone of contention between them. With that kiss, Duncan seemed to know that he had finally won. As did Kavenlow.

So why do I feel so miserable?

"Duncan," I blurted, turning back to him. "We're eating. Are you hungry? Come sit down, and you can tell us everything while you eat."

I took a step to the hallway, my hand slipping from his as he stood unmoving beside the fireplace. Duncan dropped his head, then pulled it up. In his brown eyes was a pained worry. "I can't stay," he said softly.

Understanding flashed over me, and I put a hand to my shoulder. "You didn't escape. They sent you," I whispered. "You're here to tell us where to take the money."

He nodded, his long face unhappy. "They knew I'd be recognized and thought I'd be less likely to be killed on sight. Not that they care," he muttered, scuffing his feet on the tile floor. "I think they'd just as soon see me dead, but it would give them an excuse to hurt Contessa or Alex if you did."

"We're not going to hurt you!" I exclaimed, taking both his hands again. "Duncan, you have to go?"

His bangs fell to hide his eyes. "I'm sorry. This isn't what I wanted to have happen."

Kavenlow pushed forward, his boots tapping as he came even with me. "You have an hour at least. Come and sit. How are Queen Contessa and Prince Alex? Are they well?"

"They're fine."

Fine? What was fine? Couldn't he be a little more descriptive than that?

Impatient, I let go of Duncan's fingers when he gave mine a squeeze, and he followed Kavenlow to the small arrangement of chairs and cushions before the fireplace next to the left of the official dais. My parents had usually kept court in the more informal seating arrangement, a tradition the modest Contessa had taken a liking to as well.

Duncan took my arm and pulled me into Kavenlow and

Jeck's wake. I sat on the long couch before the fire, shunning my usual spot set back and out of the way. Jeck dropped his black hat with the drooping feathers to the oval table before kneeling to build the flames higher. A member of the palace staff hastened forward, and Kavenlow waved him away so we could continue to talk without interruption or the spreading of rumors. Settling himself between the fire and the low table where he could see both Jeck and me, Kavenlow put his hands behind his back, waiting until the large hall was clear before nodding to Duncan.

"They're both fine, last I saw them," he said softly, well aware how voices carried and how servants loved to skulk about corners, as he was usually among them. "Though the crew was ready to keelhaul Contessa if she stayed on board any longer."

Still crouched beside the fire in his boots and black Misdev uniform, Jeck looked over his shoulder to Duncan as the cheat sat gingerly on the embroidered couch beside me. "They have divided the crew?" Jeck asked, his low voice seeming to rumble through me. There was more than a hint of threat in it, and I stifled a shudder.

Duncan leaned forward to put his elbows on his knees. "There's just what's needed to sail the ship left on *Kelly's Sapphire*. The rest are somewhere south of here between the capital and Saltwood with Contessa and Alex."

Jeck's motions to set a piece of wood on the fire hesitated. Dropping it to send up a flurry of sparks, he stood and turned, looking dangerous and dark in his leather jerkin. "Where?"

His eyes pinched and worried, Duncan ran his hand down his clean chin. "I don't know for certain," he said, his second finger rubbing his thumb in worry. "They don't trust me that far." He turned to me, seeing my hope burn to ash in my eyes. "I'm sorry, Tess. I haven't seen them since most of the crew left with them yesterday. They could be anywhere by now."

"Anywhere within a day's ride," Jeck said intently. "We can find them."

Duncan was suddenly pale. "Don't," he advised. "They'll kill them. I know it. I've been listening, and they have no reason not to. Some have even started currying the favor of Captain Rylan to be the ones to do it. Contessa . . . Contessa is being very difficult. She thinks you're dead, Tess."

I tried to swallow, failing. I stared at Kavenlow in fear, and he put a calming hand upon my good shoulder. "Duncan, can you give us any idea where they dropped them and the crew?"

"If I had a map, maybe."

Spinning, Kavenlow strode to the racks of charts tightly scrolled and shelved neatly. He chose one from memory, his gaze hazy in thought as he slapped the roll of parchment down onto the low table before the fire. My heart pounded, and I scooted forward when Jeck shoved his hat off the table and set the weighted boxes of sand at the corners to hold the map open.

"Where?" Kavenlow said tersely, his gaze riveted downward.

Duncan's brow creased as he looked at the detailed map. It showed a small section of the coast a day's sail in either direction. He pressed his lips together as he oriented himself. "Here," he said, pointing to a small cove where a river ran from inland to the sea. "Or maybe here," he added, pointing to a smaller rivulet closer to Saltwood. "I can't say for sure. But it was at a river."

Jeck leaned closer, and I forced myself to make my motion slow as I eased back from the smell of leather. He didn't notice, intent on the map. "You don't know?" he demanded.

"No, I don't." Duncan's voice was indignant. "It was late at night, and they had me working in the galley most of the time. But Contessa, Alex, and most of the crew dinghied to shore and didn't come back. The best I can guess is that we then retraced our path back to the capital and anchored in the harbor. That's all I know."

Kavenlow's motions were quick and sharp as his finger stabbed down to a third river. "That's where they are." Looking up, he fixed upon Duncan. "There's a shallow river that no one lives upon. But the cove it empties into is deep enough for a shallow-draft boat. At full tide, they could row a dinghy up to here." He pointed again, far inland. "Then ride the outgoing tide back down to the sea with the ransom. The road from the capital to Saltwood crosses it here. That's where they are. That's where they'll stay."

My heart leapt into my throat. "Are you sure?" I whispered.
Duncan's brow furrowed. "I didn't think it was that far

north, but it could be. And it goes along with what I was supposed to tell you about the ransom."

I put my hands on my knees to hide that they were shaking.
Duncan put his fingers atop mine, feeling them tremble. "I'm
sorry, Tess," he said softly. "They want the money in a wagon
headed to Saltwood tomorrow at sunrise before they leave to
rejoin the ones holding Contessa and Alex. They can see the
gate from the harbor, so they'll know if you don't. You're to
keep moving until they're sure no one is following, then
they'll come and collect it. After they have the money, they'll
tell you where your sister and Prince Alex are. No wagon tomorrow means one less royal. You miss the next sunrise,
they'll kill whoever is left and send you both their heads."

My stomach churned, and I couldn't seem to breathe. "I'll
take it," I said quickly. "I'll be the driver." The tingle of venom
coursed through me, pushed into my blood by my pounding
heart. Not a breath of wind stirred inside my head or out. I was
too frightened to wonder why.

Kavenlow's face was expressionless as he watched me from
over the map. "No," he said firmly. "We will find them while
the pirates are distracted by the promise of ransom and steal
them back."

"I agree," Jeck said. "We can put men on the wagon instead
of money."

"I'm taking the wagon," I repeated, louder, and Kavenlow
frowned. "And there will be money on it."

"Tess," Kavenlow said, the irritation in his voice tightening
my fear. "We know where they are. We'll get them back. And
we can't give the pirates what they want. It will only invite
other attempts. You know it."

"We'll retake the money after we get my sister safe," I
said, my knees going loose. "You don't even know if that's
where they are. Duncan hasn't seen them since they were
dropped off yesterday. They could be anywhere by now, even
the capital itself. And why would they send Duncan to us
knowing he might tell us everything he knew? If you go up
that river or road with guards and soldiers, you'll find nothing. And then they'll kill my sister for our having tried to rescue them!"

Jeck shifted back a step, his gaze on Kavenlow decidedly mocking. Seeing it, Kavenlow's frown deepened. "Tess," he warned, "that is enough."

"It's not enough!" I exclaimed, fear making me reckless. "I will *not* sit here and listen to you two plot and plan when all we have to do is give them the damned money and get them back. This is my sister's life, not some foolish game!"

"Tess!" Kavenlow thundered. *"Sit down!"*

My breath caught, and I realized I was standing. Duncan was staring at me, and Jeck's brow was raised as he leaned against the mantel, watching me find fault with my master's game and probably wondering how Kavenlow could control his pieces if he couldn't even control his apprentice. My jaw clenched, and I refused to be ashamed.

"Sit," Kavenlow repeated roughly, his face creased in anger as he pointed.

"Excuse me," I said abruptly. "I find I am in need of some air."

Flustered and angry, I gathered my skirts and fixed my gaze upon a dark archway. Duncan rose with me, and Jeck pushed himself from the mantel. Kavenlow was already standing, but I thought he would have remained seated in an unspoken rebuke that I had not been acting like a proper lady, shouting at him like that. Ignoring them, I headed to the archway that would lead to the palace grounds. My steps were loud in the tension-filled air.

"I need to get back," Duncan said, and I heard him start after me. "I've told you everything I know. They'll want a response. What do you want me to tell them?"

I paused at the archway, turning to see that Kavenlow had already bent himself over the map. Jeck, though, was watching me, which I didn't like at all. "Tell them we will be doing what they ask, though there will be nothing on that wagon but sand," Kavenlow said, and my heart seemed to clench. He had told Captain Rylan that the ransom would be paid.

Duncan hesitated, and when Kavenlow said nothing more in farewell, he turned and headed after me. His head was down in worry, and his pace was fraught with indecision as he came even with me. My throat closed when his hand slipped familiarly about my waist, and we continued down the torchlit hallway together.

Judging we had gone out of earshot, I dragged my feet and brought us to a halt beside a window yet unshuttered for the night. The moon was behind the low clouds threatening rain, and I kept my gaze fixed upon the lights of the city, glowing from the haze of a thousand cooking fires. They blurred and cleared as I forced the tears away. From the gardens below came a rush of wind in the green leaves of spring, then nothing.

It was chill by the window, and Duncan's hand was warm upon me. I could hear him breathe, and I longed to feel his arms about me again. But I couldn't bear it. He was leaving. My entire world was falling in on itself. "Do you have to go?" I asked, thinking my voice sounded very small.

"You know I have to."

"I know," I whispered, eyes closing as I swallowed the lump in my throat. "You'll come back?"

He put his arms about me, pulling me to fall back into his chest. His lips brushed my ear in a whisper as he said, "I'll try to help, if I can. When Kavenlow and Captain Jeck come to rescue them."

"I know," I said, my face resting against him so I could hear his heartbeat. I should have left with him the first time he asked. I should have told Captain Borlett to sail on past the island and risk the shallows at Yellow Tail. I should have never suggested we invite that foul man on board our boat, my beautiful boat now wrecked on the sandbars. My sister was in ropes and going hungry. My life was twisted and turned until there was nothing left.

"How did this happen?" I asked, wiping a clean hand under my nose.

"I don't know." His voice was a rumble through me. He didn't move, and we stood for a moment, just taking strength from each other. My eyes were on the lights of the city below us, and they flickered when a gust from the bay visibly flowed into the streets. The zephyr in my head heard it coming, and I held my breath and forced it to be still. With an excited chatter, the wind in my head settled.

"I have to go," he said softly, his grip tensing for a moment, then releasing. "If I'm not back soon, they'll become suspicious."

"What about you?" I asked softly, stifling my worry lest the wind escape me. "What happens to you when we steal them back, and they find nothing in that wagon?"

Fear flashed over him, quickly hidden behind a rakish grin that I could see through easier than springwater. "I'll be fine," he lied. "I'll be on the boat. How could I have anything to do with an empty wagon?"

"But they'll know you told us where they were," I protested, frightened. "When Captain Rylan realizes there's nothing on that wagon, he'll know you told us. He might kill you!"

Duncan pulled me close so I couldn't see the fear in his eyes. "I'll slip away," he said evenly. "Right before you steal them back."

"What if you can't?"

A sharp cadence of boots on tile pulled my eyes up to see Jeck. In his hands was a tightly rolled scroll of paper, and that awful hat was again on his head. His eyes met mine, and I fought the urge to push from Duncan at the disapproval in his gaze.

"Duncan," I said, as Jeck turned a corner and vanished, "what if you can't slip away? What then? What happens then?" *To you? To us?*

The wind from the bay finally reached the palace, flowing in a hush over the wall, across the gardens, and climbing the palace walls finally to slip in the window before which we stood. It brought the scent of fish and smoke to me, and a strand of hair that had escaped my topknot caressed my cheek. Heart pounding, I made sure the zephyr in me was silent lest it provoke a whirlwind.

Duncan put his hands atop my shoulders and eased me back until he met my eyes. The corner of his eye twitched, and his smile became forced. "I'll be fine," he said. His gaze went past me and into the night. "I need to go."

I could say nothing. Miserable, I pulled from him. Arms wrapped around myself, I stared out the window, not seeing anything as the salt-laden air pushed gently on me. From farther inside the palace, a door slammed. Kavenlow wasn't going to put any money on that wagon, and princess or apprentice, there was nothing I could do about it.

"Tess," he whispered.

"You'd better go," I said, bowing my head and pushing my fingers into my temple.

He touched my shoulder, and I didn't respond. If he tried to kiss me again, I would fall apart. Duncan's hand fell away, and I listened to his steps move away from me, slow and reluctant.

"Duncan," I said. My head pounded, and I refused to look at him. A thread of venom slipped into me. Outside, the wind soughed in the trees. Inside, the wind in my head promised lies if I would only let it go. It made it hard to think, but I knew if there was no money on that wagon, they would kill Duncan. It was that simple. I wondered if this was Kavenlow's plan, then dismissed it as being far too ignoble of him.

"I'll make sure that there's money on that wagon," I said softly, and the voice in my head fell to a soft, insidious chitter. "If they get their money, they won't care if you told them where they were and they are stolen back."

"Promise?"

The fear and relief in his voice pulled me around when nothing else could. Five steps from me, Duncan stood with his arms slack at his side. His red boots were ruined from salt, and the rings on his fingers glinted dully. The time spent at sea had left him thinner, the excess pared from him to leave a different man. He was stronger of body and will, but more vulnerable in his heart. More vulnerable because of me.

The fear in him for what he would be returning to was well hidden, but it was there. He was braver than I was—going back knowing he would be blamed when we stole them away. There was nothing keeping him from running away, from not returning to the ship as planned. He was putting his life in jeopardy for my sister and Alex. For me. *Money,* I decided, *is a small price to pay for the life of someone you love.*

"I promise, Duncan," I whispered, and the wind in my head gibbered to be free. "It will be there."

Twenty-three

❖

The wind that had been clamoring in my head when Duncan left was nearly gone. Whispering. Slumberous. Soothed into almost nothing by Jeck and Kavenlow's conversation. They were ignoring me, though I sat within fifteen feet of them. I didn't care. I had been arguing with them; I was lucky to be in the same room.

Jeck had taken my usual place beside Kavenlow as they pondered the chart spread atop the low table before the stone fireplace. It was lit more for the light than the warmth, and I curled up in my usual chair beside it, thinking how different everything was from just last night, when I had been shivering in the dirt. A wisp of worry went through me, and I hoped my sister and Alex weren't as miserable as I had been, but knew they probably were.

My gaze went to Jeck, his resonant voice catching my attention as he pointed down with a strong, sun-browned finger. I thought it odd that he and Kavenlow were working together as well as they were, their games meshing for the good of both of them, and a pang of jealousy flickered through me that Jeck was sitting where I usually would be, at Kavenlow's right.

"Here," Jeck was saying, silently tapping. "If you bring men in from the water and hold here at this cove until we're ready, you'll remain undetected. I will bring men in from the land and take what they have ashore. You can then bring the water force around when I signal with smoke, and we will have them all.

Kavenlow's bearded face was empty of emotion. "I'm not taking the water force. You are."

Eyebrows high at the resoluteness of Kavenlow's voice, Jeck leaned back and eyed him in question. "Why?" he asked flatly.

"I don't like the water," Kavenlow said immediately, and I nodded, curling my feet up under me though I had been told not to more times than there were leaves on a linden tree. Kavenlow abhorred the water. I think it was because he believed his father had been a sailor and was afraid he might find him—though his father would be an old man by now.

"You take the water force," Kavenlow said.

Jeck shook his head. "I'm going to have the men taking the area where the queen and Prince Alex are likely to be."

I pulled my knees up to my chin and clasped my hands about my shins. It was an inexcusable breech of protocol, but it was late, and even the servants had been sent to bed. And I didn't care if Jeck thought I was an uncouth woman with no manners. But he probably thought that anyway, after seeing me barefoot and tied to a mast, doused with oil and dripping, standing on a beach in my underthings . . . The list was endless.

"One of us needs to be in charge of the boats," Kavenlow said, not noticing my feet on the cushion though Jeck did.

"You do it," he said, as his eyes slid from me. "You're the master of the seas."

Kavenlow bristled. "Fine. I'll get a second guard detail to do it."

"If you think that adequate."

"I don't think it adequate, but seeing as you won't do it——"

"That's right. I won't."

They sounded like a married couple bickering, and I dropped my cheek to my knees to watch the fire. I was beginning to realize why two players working together was such a rare phenomenon.

"If you're so bent on it, I'll take the water," Kavenlow said with a poor grace.

"Good," he said, his annoyance tempered with a shade of satisfaction. "I'll take the wagon and put my men on it in hiding."

My head came up as unease pulled me straight. "Are you sure there will be enough room for them with the money and spice already on it?"

Jeck glanced at Kavenlow and away. Muscles bunching under his clean Misdev uniform, he stood and went to tend the fire. My eyes narrowed. Pulse quickening, I focused on my teacher.

"Captain Jeck will have the wagon," Kavenlow said, and my shoulders tightened at what he was not saying. "And I will take the water force. It will be close as it is, finding the best available men from those who are here and getting them into position without their being spotted."

"We're going to put money on that wagon, not men," I said, fear pulling me to the front of my chair and my feet to the floor. "I promised Duncan there would be money on the wagon."

Jeck poked the fire, his back hunched. Kavenlow stood. Drawing me to my feet, he took my hands and pulled me a short distance away to the dais, my skirts rustling in the absolute quiet broken only by the snapping of the fire. His eyes were pinched in what I recognized as heartache. "Tess," he began, and I pulled my hands from his.

"She's my sister, and there will be money on the wagon," I said, louder. My pulse rose, and I felt the tingle of venom rising. I took a slow breath, willing myself calm.

Kavenlow pressed his lips together to make his mustache bunch. "Contessa and Alex have forbidden it, but more importantly, it's my game, and there will be men, not money."

I looked to the floor, not seeing the bright-colored tile through the darkness. The venom made me feel ill, unreal. I wanted to shout at him, to rail against him, but if I did, the wind in my head would break free. Even worse, he would send me to my room, disgraced.

Forcing my fear down, I whispered, "You know they'll kill Duncan if something goes wrong. If you don't get there in time, they'll know he betrayed them."

"I'm sorry, Tess. He knew the risk. He went back willingly."

"He went back because if he didn't, they would murder

both of them!" I pleaded. "Did you coerce him? Did you use your magic to sway him?" I asked, ready to be angry, but he shook his head and ran a hand down his graying beard.

"No. It wouldn't have been right."

I glanced at Jeck, wanting to ask him the same thing, but I knew in my heart Duncan had willingly taken this risk. He had done it because I had promised the ransom would be on that wagon. "I have to sit down," I said breathily, my mind whirling as I returned to my couch.

"I'm sorry," Kavenlow was saying, his voice sounding hollow. "We will do all we can."

"But you won't put money on that wagon." The back of my knees hit a cushion, and I instinctively sat. I could see a corner of the flames past Jeck. The fire leapt and I watched, too numb to look away.

Slowly it began to take on meaning, making my heart sink to my belly. Duncan was going to die because he believed my promise. I couldn't argue with Kavenlow, and I knew I couldn't convince Jeck to side with me. Duncan was going to die. Because of me. I wouldn't let it happen.

Cold despite the fire, I watched the two master players return to brooding over the chart, arguing over who got how many men and how they should get past the city walls under the notice of the pirate ship still at anchor in the harbor. They'd argue until the sun came up and it was too late to do anything.

My stomach clenched, and I felt a sweat break out over me. I was going to take that wagon out, and it was going to have the ransom on it. Duncan's life depended on it. If I couldn't convince them with my words, by God, I'd do it by magic.

I listened to my breath slip in and out of me as I steadied myself, wondering if I could. Manipulating memories was a master's skill. Kavenlow hadn't even tried teaching me yet. But as Jeck said, I had been doing master twists of magic since being bitten. It would be the only good thing to come of it if I could.

Kavenlow was murmuring something, and I focused on him. *Forgive me, Kavenlow,* I thought. But I could see no other way.

I closed my eyes and felt the warmth of the fire on my face. Fingers tingling, I willed more venom into me, increasing my pulse and quickening my breath. I stifled a gasp when a rush of power flooded me. For a moment, I sat and did nothing, hoping neither of them looked up as I panted, trying to get ahold of it. I had no idea the strength that was at my thoughts to wield had been this strong. Pushing aside my fear, I reminded myself that it was to save Duncan's life.

Kavenlow, I thought, closing my eyes so I could find his presence in my mind easier. My chin trembled when I sensed his bird-quick thoughts, silver against the closed blackness of his character. It had to be him, as I sensed a great concern.

Aloud and in my head came Jeck's voice saying, "No, ten. More than that, and they'll be noticed."

My lips moved, and I realized I'd found Jeck's thoughts. My surprise melted into understanding; I had spent all winter practicing finding him by tracing his emotions through the palace. Of course I would find him first.

"Ten isn't enough," Kavenlow said, sounding peeved and jolting me from my thoughts. "You said there were at least forty men on that boat."

"And at least six of them will still *be* on the boat," Jeck said, and I found myself mouthing the words again. I had to find them both. I had to do this simultaneously, or it wouldn't work. Dizzy, I willed more venom into me, and Jeck's emotions came out of the blackness of my mind like a slap. My breath caught, and I held it for a second, then started breathing in time with him. He was irritated, wanting to act now, not waste more time on this old-man planning of movements. I knew the feeling.

"That leaves thirty-four men on land," Jeck said, not a hint of his bother showing in his voice, and I wondered how much was going on under his closed demeanor that I continually missed. "Ten men plus me will do it," he added. "Four if I use venom. They stole mine. I'll need some of yours."

"I'm not giving you any of my toxin," Kavenlow said, sounding insulted. "I cannot believe you asked."

Confidence joined Jeck's annoyance. "You need more men than we have to take the boat successfully as it is. Don't get your nets in a knot; I'll replace your toxin, old man."

The last had been a dark mutter, and Kavenlow sighed. Leaving a breath of my awareness in Jeck, I sought out Kavenlow. I floundered, his higher tolerance to venom making him harder to find. But it was his voice—ever familiar, ever the sound of security—that led me to him.

"Four men," I heard Kavenlow say, and I followed the echo of it in my head to fasten on to his thoughts. They flowed like gray silk amid the black, almost unseen, like smoke. "That's rather bold of you," he added. My hand rose to my chin, and the soft feeling of his beard rose through my tingling fingertips. I had them both.

Guilt tightened through me, though I hadn't done anything yet. It wasn't like reading their minds. More like standing too close and whispering into their ears, eavesdropping on their thoughts an instant before they had them.

A wash of bother flooded me, an emotion not mine. "I kill men for my bread and butter," Jeck's voice echoed in my ears and head, frightening the wind into a gibbering silence. "You do books. I only need four, and most of them will be for show."

Kavenlow's sour tone mixed with it, making me ill. "Four men with my toxin. Fine. But they won't be my best men."

"I don't care. I'll be the one doing most of it."

I waited for the opportunity to make a suggestion to put the ransom on the wagon as a precaution for not finding my sister and Alex where they thought they were. Four men would leave room for money. Why not put it on the wagon with the men just in case?

My hands were clenched in my lap as I tried to keep my own heartsick emotions to myself lest they pick them up. I knew this was wrong, but I had to do it.

"There aren't many men to choose from," Kavenlow said. I heard a rustle of paper, and his mood sifting through mine turned glum. "All but a few of my best are out ranging for them. We can't wait for their return. We need to move the land force at least within the hour so we can remain under the cloak of darkness."

There it is, I thought, clamping down on my excitement. It wasn't exactly what I wanted, but I didn't trust myself to remain undetected much longer. Getting them to put money on that wagon instead of men was going to be impossible, but if I could put off their attack for half a day, I could take the wagon of money in the morning, get my sister and Alex, and be back in the palace as they were starting to move. Once the pirates had their money, Duncan would be safe. He could slip away when the pirates were celebrating. Alex, Contessa, and I could be back in the palace before Kavenlow had sailed from the harbor and Jeck had left the city.

An hour? I thought more firmly, focusing on the pattern of Jeck's thoughts, melding my will with his until he whispered the words in tandem with me. Confusion flashed through Jeck, and I suggested it was because of what Kavenlow had said. Still he hesitated, and I almost passed out from the venom I drew upon. *It's sundown they want the wagon to pass the gates. Sundown, not sunup.* I imagined the cool breath of the hour, the red angle of the sun, the sound of leather creaking, and the smell of horse. *It's sundown. The fool of a chancellor wants to move too quickly. It would alert the pirates that not all was as it seemed.*

"An hour?" Jeck said hesitantly, and my heart pounded. My eyes almost flew open, and I forced them shut. "It takes only five hours to get to that river by way of boat or horse. Moving sooner will alert them of what we're doing."

The small sounds of Kavenlow rustling in the paper ceased. I could almost see his questioning look, the firelight glinting on his eyes as he peered at Jeck in disbelief. I turned my thoughts more fully upon the gray silk of him. My eyes warmed under my closed lids. Betrayal rose high in me, making my chest hurt. This was wrong. So wrong.

"Noon?" my teacher said.

I scrambled to find Kavenlow, but his venom-rich mind slipped from mine. My dread began to overshadow his confusion. I was losing him. He was too strong.

"They wanted the wagon to come out at sunset," Jeck said, sounding suddenly unsure. His doubt joined Kavenlow's, making my fear double, mixing with their emotions in a chaotic slurry that left me reeling and my head pounding. "That way we can bring whatever men out in the morning crush and the pirates would be none the wiser," Jeck finished.

For Duncan, I thought, trying to shield my desperation from them. I had to do this for Duncan, or he would be killed. I would have nothing. No game, no sister, no life with Duncan. Nothing.

Gritting my teeth and pressing my eyes tight to keep the tears from leaking out, I pushed aside my feelings of right and wrong, wrapping my will about Kavenlow's slippery, gray-ghost thoughts. This was wrong. I didn't want to do it.

Sundown, I thought. *The wagon goes at sundown. The men slip out with the morning crush and wait until noon to move.*

"That's right," Kavenlow said, his confusion wavering. He hesitated, and I felt his certainty strengthen. "Why did I think we needed to move that close so soon? And waiting until noon will give us more men back in the capital to choose from."

Jeck said nothing, and a tear made a warm trail down my face. I left their thoughts with a rush, floundering and holding my breath until I reclaimed the feelings that were only mine. I was loathsome and unclean. I was the filth scraped off the boats and left in the chu pits to rot in the sun. It had saved Duncan's life, and it was the most awful thing I had ever done.

"Sunset," Jeck said slowly. "Where's that list of men back in the capital already."

I'm so sorry, Kavenlow, I thought, taking a shuddering breath and holding it. *Please forgive me.*

I opened my eyes, wiping them on the back of my hand. Jeck and Kavenlow were just as I had last seen them. Kavenlow shuffled through the stack of papers that had come in with the latest reports of rumors from the city. "Here," he said, leaning close with a list of names. "If you have the land force, you'll want Jamie and Turlo. They grew up in Saltwood. They might even have an idea of where the pirates are holed up."

It was done. Shoulders hunched, I stood, wavering on my feet. Neither man looked up as I used the residual magic resonating in me to keep them from noticing me. It was easy as I was still sensitized to their individual thoughts. Hunched in heartache and dizzy from the venom, I walked slowly from the hall, working to keep my steps soft.

For the first time in my life, I had used my magic to deceive. *It will be the last,* I vowed as I made my uncertain way to the stables. But what could Kavenlow do to me for my deception? Cast me out? Make me leave him? He was going to do that anyway.

Twenty-four

✦

"One more, yet, Tess," Thadd said, pushing a heavy satchel onto the wagon bed and snuggling it up to the other three. The rare spice in their tight chests shifted closer to me, sending the exotic scent to tickle my nose.

I nodded, keeping my head lowered as I stood beside the driver's bench. In honor of my subterfuge, I was wearing a worn dress that was too small and dingy with grime. I had worn it while retaking my palace last spring—having to hide it from Heather so she wouldn't burn it—and I would wear it again to rescue my sister. I had been recognized at the gate looking much worse, but I'd wanted to be identified. This time, I didn't.

Thadd walked away, his slow ponderous pace and short stature keeping him unnoticed amid the bustle of men at the stables preparing for their departure in the predawn dusk. The young sculptor was fraught with worry, his shoulders tense and expression downcast, and I watched Contessa's first love with a heavy heart.

He had grown up with Contessa, and they had planned a simple life together before her world changed, and she went from foundling to princess in a day. Thadd loved her desperately, following her halfway across the kingdom to keep her safe from dangers he had no chance to protect her against, then showing his bravery further by changing his life to try to keep a place in hers. The simple but honest man was hurting more than anyone, and no one seemed to care as his status of "queen's advisor" was one politely ignored and often gossiped about. Depressed, I turned away, pulling Penelope's shawl tighter about my shoulders, and tried to stay unnoticed.

My fingers tingled with magic, and my cold nose itched with it. It ran through me in a thin, ever-present threat that was almost not there. No one would see me unless I drew attention to myself, but still, it made me nervous. The sun was almost up, and I was anxious to be away. I hadn't had but a catnap of sleep, and breakfast had been a roll I had stolen from the baskets brought out to feed the soldiers who had responded to the 'ware fire lit in the highest tower last night and returned. Between my lack of sleep and my worry that Kavenlow or Jeck would remember that the wagon was supposed to go out at sunup not sundown, I was anxious and nauseous.

Easing into motion, I crept back into the livery for my last horse. I'd spent the night there hiding from Kavenlow. I couldn't bear to look him in the face. I had broken his trust. I had lied and manipulated his thoughts. I didn't know if I would ever be able to make amends. He would never trust me again. *Not that it mattered.*

The smell of horse and leather brought a lump into my throat, reminding me of him. It was eerily quiet since most of the mounts were gone or in the yard. I went unhesitatingly to the last of the three mares that I had picked out hours ago. Fingers stiff from the morning cold, I saddled the remaining soft gray with a riding pad, leaving the cinch somewhat loose. Her bridle was already in the wagon with the rest, hidden in a rough sack smelling of fish. I draped a rude blanket over the riding pad, knowing it was a thin disguise but trusting my magic to keep me and my three horses unremarked upon. They would carry my sister, Alex, and me home.

I would have taken Duncan's horse as well in the hopes of finding him, but the gray gelding was gone, commandeered by the searching soldiers. It had been by luck and magic that these three and the one hitched to the wagon had been "overlooked."

Backing the last mare out into the aisle, I longingly thought of Jy and Pitch. Jeck had told me they had been moved to one of the slower warships before he struck out on the burned *Sand-piper*. The warships were still searching—unaware that we were back at the capital—and though I was glad my horses were safe, I missed them.

My eyes rose to the wagon when I came out from the gloom of the stables and into the chill light of the coming dawn. Thadd had loaded the last bag of coin and was sitting atop the driver's bench, his head bowed and patiently waiting with the reins in his thick hands, scarred from his profession. My shoulders slumped and my mood turned despondent. I said nothing while I tied the mare to the back of the wagon with the other two. He thought he was going.

Feet slow and reluctant, I came around to the front of the wagon. His strong jaw was clenched, as if he already knew what I was going to say. "Thadd," I said tiredly, and he turned to me, his brown eyes showing a hint of panic.

"I'm going."

It was soft, but heavy with determination, making me feel worse. He held out a hand, and I took it so he could help me onto the wagon. His grip was warm as he hauled me up, but I could feel the worry in it, the fear I would make him stay. I glanced behind me at the unwatching men before I sat beside him, knees together with my cold hands between them. It was a very unprincess-like position, but I looked like a street urchin and was cold. My well-made boots poked from under my ratty hem, and I pulled them under my skirt to hide them. *God, please help me find the words to tell him.* "Thadd—"

"I love her and I'm going," he repeated, the desperation he had been trying to hide creeping into his slow, methodical voice. Thadd was a big, heavy man, but his heart was as pure and fragile as new ice. His lovingly made plans with Contessa had vanished like a dream hiding between wakefulness and sleep.

Miserable, I looked at the light shining on the highest of the palace towers. It had turned the milky stone to a flaming red. *Red sun in morning, sailors take warning . . .* I thought, refusing to believe in superstitions. I had to go. I had to leave now. I didn't have time for this, but he, of all people, would come out of this the most wounded, no matter how it turned out. He loved her, but there was more here I had to address than his simply wanting to help rescue her.

"I know you love her," I finally said.

His feet shifted at the unsaid "however" in my voice, drawing my gaze to his boots. They were new, a gift from Contessa, along with whatever else he needed for his work and livelihood. I knew he had only accepted them so that people wouldn't stare and whisper at his bare feet inside the palace. He was a country artisan, and the last link Contessa had to her free, unfettered childhood.

"I need to be there," he insisted, a hint of panic in his serious brown eyes.

"And I need to have you here," I said. "In about three hours, Kavenlow or Captain Jeck will be looking for me, trying to make sure I don't go out with them and foul up their plans. You're going to have to tell them that I'm sulking in the garden."

"I love her, and I won't stay here and do nothing. Don't ask me to do that, Tess!"

It was a determined statement, and a lump came into my throat. I understood. I understood too well. "Please, Thadd," I whispered. "They said only one person. It has to be me. If you come, too, they'll assume treachery. I'm giving them exactly what they want so they have no excuse to hurt her. I lied to Kavenlow and betrayed his trust to keep her safe. If you come with me, it will endanger her."

His breath trembled. Thick, powerful hands shook as he gripped the reins. Worry creased his face, making him look twice his age. "Does she love him?" he asked. Surprised, I stared blankly until he rubbed his forehead, and added, "Alex. Does she love him?"

My heart seemed to clench. I didn't want to be the one to talk to him about this, but no one else would. I had a brief thought that this was the softer, but far more difficult side to being a player—manipulating people for a greater good they couldn't see. I consoled myself in that I would be telling him this even if it didn't fall within the span of the game, that the unfortunate tie between Contessa and Thadd had to be sundered or their entire lives would be tainted as polite society labeled their love with guilt and shame. But it didn't make me feel any better.

"I—I think she would love him . . . in time," I whispered, unable to look at him. "If she wasn't already in love with you

But she loves you, Thadd," I said, instilling my voice with a pained worry. "She won't abandon you for him. I know it." *And she needs to,* I thought, unable to say it. It was so unfair to him. God help us, it was so unfair.

Thadd dropped his head so that his long bangs hid his eyes. "That's what I thought."

"Thadd?" Worried that he might finally understand, I reached out. But he pushed the reins stiff with cold into my grip, and wood creaked as he swung down. Never looking back, he walked away, his head down and his back hunched. A soldier almost ran into him, the young guard's apology seemingly unheard as Thadd never shifted his slow, ponderous pace or acknowledged him.

Pained in my soul, I bit my lip and watched until the milling sentries came between us, and I lost sight of him. Thadd was suffering more than he let on: having already endured the heartache of seeing his love wed to another, knowing there would be a legal heir someday—and all that went along with that.

A sigh slipped from me. There was nothing I could do. We all had our own puntas to slay. And saying a quick pain was better than a long slow ache was a lie. It all hurt. They all left scars.

Turning to face the unseen sun, I pushed my feelings away and clicked my tongue to get the horse moving. It rocked into motion, and with my fingers tingling with magic, I trundled the clapboard wagon holding a kingdom's ransom unhindered through the palace gates and into the city streets when the gates opened to allow more returning soldiers entry.

The morning wind seemed to swell in the harbor to fill the streets with noise as I passed the palace walls and became lost among my people. The wind chattering in my head rose and fell in some private thought the zephyr didn't care to share with me, and I pushed it down, refusing to let it gain a foothold. Though it was early, the streets were noisy with merchants readying their wares, some doing a brisk business in the gray light. There was an unusual tension everywhere, words sharp and tempers quick.

I joined the steady stream of nervous people headed for the main gate. The snatches of conversation I caught revolved about the royal couple, and the frequent hails and questions shouted to the returning men in Costenopolie uniform had me on edge. There was worry, but no fear in them. A hard readiness, but no revenge. I had been right to tell them the truth.

My pulse quickened when I neared the manned exit, but I was let through without hindrance. The three horses trailing behind me earned a few curious glances and nothing more. The air freshened when I passed the gates and continued on straight down the seldom-used path toward Saltwood. Most of the outgoing people had turned north to the interior: carts and wagons, people with bundles on their backs. More people pushed past me, eager to get in and looking for news. The rising sun hit my face but gave very little warmth. The morning fog had risen, and, shivering, I sent my gaze down to the harbor.

Immediately I tensed. *Kelly's Sapphire* had her sails up and was riding the slack tide out of the harbor. My shudder of imagining the spyglass turned upon me turned to relief; I had been seen, and Alex and Contessa were safe for a few hours more. Someone would meet me on the road to Saltwood, and after I gave them the ransom, I would take them home. Then Kavenlow and Jeck could butcher whomever they wanted.

Slowly the sounds and stench of the lower city were left behind, replaced by the chill silence of wind and lusty songbirds when I passed under the old-growth trees. The clop of four horses was softer than I would have expected, the trail being damp with the last spring rain.

A confusing mix of numb inevitability and wire-tight tension filled me as I jostled along. My fingers kept returning to the braided leather whip about my waist, checking and rechecking that I had it and my three throwing knives. I had no darts, and to have asked Jeck for some after Kavenlow had cleaned out my room would have only aroused suspicion. Besides, Jeck had already refused me toxin once for the same reason Kavenlow had.

The sounds of the wagon and the horses behind me were hypnotic. I kept the pace slow, though I wanted to charge through the woods as if I were trailing fire. I quickly passed the few people on foot burdened with city goods who had left before me, keeping my head down lest I be recognized. There weren't many travelers since the road led only to Saltwood, and unless livestock was involved, it was easier to boat around the peninsula than travel across it.

I continued through the early morning, feeling the clammy dampness under the trees rise and turn to clouds. The farther I went, the more alone and guilty I became for having lied to Kavenlow. My stomach was pinching with hunger, but I hadn't brought any food and probably wouldn't have eaten if I had. I knew the creek Kavenlow had pointed out on the map couldn't be much farther ahead, and it was no surprise when I came upon a dubious-looking bridge made up of downed logs. It could by no stretch of the imagination hold a wagon, much less one as heavily laden as this one. I remembered it from my first run to Saltwood, but I had been on horseback at that time and hadn't given it a second thought.

Pulling the horse to a stop with my voice, I sat on the driver's bench and looked at the wide, oily-topped river. I had already rolled through several shallow creeks, but this one was larger, and the edges looked treacherous. It was a tidal river by the looks of it, brackish by the plants growing along them and too salty for the horses to like. The steep banks would be difficult for the wagon, not to mention they looked mucky, and we would probably sink to our axles. A thin trail ran farther upstream on this side, paralleling the murky river, and I wondered if it went to an easier crossing.

"How am I going to get past this?" I breathed, worried that the pirates wouldn't accept any excuses or my being late. But it was then I realized the horse was staring downstream, ears pricked and clearly interested.

Pulled by the sound of dripping water, I followed her gaze to a long rowboat making its slow way with the help of the day's second slack tide. The man had his back to me and I had a moment of panic. But with a small gasp, I recognized the hat.

"Duncan!" I cried softly. Fingers fumbling, I tied the reins to the front bench and lurched from the wagon. My skirt tore as I scrambled down the steep incline and stood with the mud covering my boot tops.

Duncan turned at the snapping branches, and he gave me a delighted wave before he bent his back to his work again, angling to me now. Feeling silly for having rushed to the edge, I backed up, fidgeting. The bow of one of *Kelly's Sapphire*'s long dinghies edged the shore. Fingers scraping the flaking paint, I pulled it up farther, eager to touch him and prove he was really here and all right.

Remaining seated, he spun on the bench to me, a relieved, truly pleased smile on him. He was wearing a new matched brown jerkin and trousers, the white shirt under it almost glowing in the soft light that made it past the pale green of the spring-fresh leaves. The rings on his fingers glittered, and he looked grand, newly shaven and washed. My thoughts went to the pirates. They couldn't hurt him. He was too clever. He would get away.

"Tess," he said softly, his eyes going from me to the wagon and back again. "I didn't think they'd let you bring the wagon. This is fantastic."

"I lied to Kavenlow," I blurted in confession. "They won't be here until after sunset. He wasn't going to put anything on it. I promised I would, and I lied to him."

"You're alone?" he said, his eyes widening. "You came out here alone?"

Wondering why he hadn't gotten out of the boat yet, I nodded. He smiled then, looking relieved when he took my hand, and he wobbled out of the boat. "My brave princess," he whispered, putting a welcome hand about my waist and pulling me closer. "That's why I love you, Tess. You make the impossible happen."

Feeling him press into me, I flushed and dropped my eyes, but only for a moment. "I can't get the wagon across the bridge," I said, not moving away. "I need to get the ransom to them." My gaze fell on his boat, not knowing if it was his escape or they had sent him to collect the ransom. "Where are my sister and Alex?" He said nothing, and a sliver of fear slid itself into my heart. From my thoughts came a faint chitter of wind, easily suppressed. "Where are they?" I asked again, softer but more intent.

"They're safe." Giving me a squeeze, he dropped his grip on me. "They won't move them until they know that ransom is on the cart and not men with swords."

My heart thumped at his words, and I soothed my conscience for having lied to Kavenlow. The pirates would have killed them if we had done it his way.

"I've got the money," I said, lurching to half climb the rise back up to the trail. "Come and see. I did what they wanted. Where's my sister?"

Duncan was quick behind me, blowing as he reached the top of the small incline. He took in the wagon, and said, "You brought extra horses?"

"They're to ride back on," I said, stopping stock-still and turning. The wind rose from my thoughts, inciting a small breeze down from the treetops to tug at my hair.

"Oh yes," he said distantly.

Seeing his eyes fixed to the lump of canvas, I eagerly flung it aside. "Look. See?" I opened a satchel and shook the heavy bag to make the coins slide. "The rest are the same, and there're two chests of spice." Spinning, I caught a rare look of awe on his face.

"Chu pits, Tess," he breathed. "You did it. You really did it!"

"Of course I did it," I said. "I said I would. Where are my sister and Alex? Is someone going to come for the ransom, or do I have to take it to them?"

I waited, heart pounding and breath held, watching Duncan shake his wonder off at the sight of so much gold. His motion smooth and unhurried, he closed the satchel without shifting a coin. The tarp was tugged back to hide them, and he turned to me, taking my elbows in his hands. "Tess," he said, his brown eyes earnest. "They're safe. They're safe and unharmed and will stay that way until someone collects them." He licked his lips and glanced over my shoulder and up the river. "Come with me. Now's our chance to run."

Shock clenched my stomach. "Now?"

He shifted from foot to foot, his eyes going to the trees when a sudden gust came and went. From my thoughts rose an accompanying chatter of mindless prattle. This was not what I needed. My excitement was causing me to loosen my grip on the wind, and my fear chilled me more than the cold early afternoon.

"It will be all right," Duncan said, his eyes pinched as he probably misread why my face was ashen. "I promise," he said, bringing his eager gaze to mine. "Bring a horse and come with me. Leave everything. We can do this together, Tess. It will be fantastic."

My knees went weak, and my heart sang as the treetops mirrored the song that the wind in my head chortled. My life with Kavenlow was over. This was what I wanted. But to leave now? When my sister's life was still uncertain? "Now?" I questioned, not believing what he was asking me to do.

"Now." He pulled me a step forward, his eyes alight under his dark bangs shifting in the growing breeze. "You and me. I've asked you before, but now it's time. And I won't be coming back. I want you to come with me. God help me, Tess. Say you will. We could be so good together. The things we could do. I know it!"

"Duncan." I shoved the guilt of having betrayed Kavenlow down where it mixed with the pain of abandoning him. "I want to go—"

His smile widened, and he drew me into a joyous hug that pulled my feet from the ground before I could finish. "I knew you would!" he said in exuberance as he set me down and the leaves swirled around us in a half-noticed whirlwind. "I knew it! We will live like kings. We can go far, far away. We won't ever come back, and we can go anywhere, do anything. Get your horse. This is better than I could have imagined, Tess!"

Moving with an obvious excitement, he dragged the nearest satchel off the wagon. It hit the ground with a heavy sound, and the nearest horse started. I watched in bewilderment when he tipped it over the edge of the bank and scrambled down after it. Red boots getting wet, he walked into the mucky river and, swaying with the unaccustomed weight, swung it with a clatter into the stern of the rowboat. Water splashed softly, and the boat sank into the mud. *He must be taking the ransom back to the boat before fleeing—now that there really was some.*

"Duncan!" I exclaimed, almost frightened when he came up to get another. "I can't go this instant! They still have Contessa and Alex!"

He jerked to a halt, his hand atop one of the wagon's sides. His face lost expression, making him look unfamiliar and almost threatening. Holding his breath, he pulled the second bag from the wagon. "They're fine," he said, dragging the satchel to the bank and sliding down with it. "I promise. She's fine and will be sitting before her fire in the palace before nightfall. You can write her later to tell her you're all right, but we have to leave now. She'll understand."

With a grunting heave, he tossed the second bag next to the first. He sloshed back to the mucky bank and took my hand when I extended it, pulling himself up and onto the path again. I watched in disbelief when he took the third satchel. "What about the pirates?"

He turned slowly, a hand on the third bag in the bed of the wagon. His eyes were bright, and his shoulders were tense. "It's all right," he puffed, clearly tired. "With the horses, we can outrun them if anything goes wrong. Your sister and Alex will be fine," he urged. "The tide is just about turned. We need it to get downstream fast enough for this to work. Come on, Tess. I could use a little help."

Dragging the bag, he stumbled down the slope and dropped it into the bottom of the boat.

"I can't just leave," I said, and he squinted at me in the wind that the laughing zephyr in my head had called down. "And you're the one that's in danger, not me. You take one of the horses and run. I'll take the ransom to them, and after I'm sure Contessa and Alex are safe, I'll catch up with you in Saltwood."

Duncan's shoulders slumped. He said nothing as he climbed back up the bank. Breathing hard, he took my elbows. His rings bit into my skin with an unfamiliar pressure. "No," he said softly. "No you won't. You'll never find me." He looked at the moving leaves, his grip on me tightening. "I promise it will be all right, but only if you come with me right now. It has to be now! It's me, or them. I can't risk waiting for you, and you'll never find me."

My heart pounded, and my knees went weak. The wind in my head chattered and chortled, driving me to distraction when the breeze it incited tugged at my hair and dress. I searched his brown eyes, not knowing why I couldn't see Contessa safe before I left. "Why can't I say good-bye?" I asked, my words a whisper over the rising wind.

His face went empty of emotion, and he dropped my hands. "I thought you loved me."

I felt as if he had hit me. Tears of confusion and frustration blurred my sight. The upper branches tossed, and I put a hand to my head to keep my hair from flying into my face. "I do," I said, my chest hurting as I tried to understand. "But I can't leave not knowing if they're all right. Why can't you wait, Duncan? Go to the palace. I'll take the ransom to the boat."

Duncan took a slow breath. He swung his head up to me, the light gone from his eyes and replaced with nothing. He dragged the last bag to him, grunting as its deadweight jerked his arms down. "Good-bye, Tess."

My mouth dropped open. He staggered away with the money, and I reached out after him, my hand falling. "Duncan . . ." I stammered, my voice sounding small against the wind in the new leaves. "Just let me say good-bye, and we can be together."

"I never say good-bye." Red boots in the muck, he half flung the bag into the bow of the boat. "If you don't come with me now, you'll never see me again."

His words took my breath from me. I looked at the chests of spice left behind, then back to him. "Duncan. I can't just leave!" I pleaded, but he put a foot on the gunwale. Muscles straining, he shoved the boat back into the water to leave a deep furrow that filled with a dark, oily water. He leapt after it at the last moment, pushing the boat out even farther. The water splashed and threatened to swamp the boat, then it settled.

"Where's my sister?" I cried, rushing to the edge of the bank.

"Upstream," he said, the clatter of the oars sounding loud. He wouldn't look at me. "In a shack. We could have been great, Tess. I wish you had said yes."

Bewildered, I stood by the wagon with my horses and watched him row back downstream with the outgoing tide. The wind tugged at me, rising and falling as I struggled to regain control of it and my chaotic thoughts both. The snickering lies in my head echoed and laughed. Not believing what had happened, I pulled my hair from where it was sticking to my face, only now realizing tears streaked it.

He just left. I didn't understand. He asked me to go with him, and when I asked him to wait, he just rowed away.

Twenty-five

❖

The horse pulling the wagon nickered nervously when I wrapped her reins about the rotting railing. I rubbed a cold hand down her bony face to try to soothe her, but she was picking up on my nervousness and would have nothing to do with it. Giving her a final pat, I stepped away, every part of me listening, tense for any noise that might come from the dilapidated shack.

The abandoned building's porch ran the length of the house, hanging over the tidal river in what might have once been pleasant but now only looked dangerous. On the other side, the chimney had fallen outward to leave a gaping hole. Bushes were growing in the opening, reaching past the rotting edges of the walls for the sun.

I straightened my raggedy dress and headed to the three steps, skipping the first as it was entirely gone. Duncan's behavior had me bewildered. I would have been angry with him if I understood. It was with an odd mix of confused hope that I edged cautiously from the steps to the porch, not knowing if I should call for Contessa or not.

A board threatened to give way, and I jumped to another. There was an obvious creak and thump, and with a horse nickering at my flailing arms, a masculine laugh came from inside.

Fear burned through me. Duncan had taken the ransom to the boat, and only honor would keep them holding to their end of the arrangement now. And there was little honor among thieves.

"Duncan, my lad!" came Captain Rylan's chuckle from inside. "You've outdone yourself. What did you do? Steal her horse as well as her heart?"

Skirts gripped tightly in one hand, I felt for the hilts of my three knives tucked in my waistband and loosened my bullwhip around my waist. Not knowing what I'd find, I stepped before the open doorway and looked into the rotting house.

The light coming in the broken ceiling was green with new leaves and dim. Lumps of the roof were scattered about, spindly saplings reaching for the sky around them. Squinting, I realized the humps weren't chunks of fallen roof but unconscious men. The sharp acidic smell of venom was everywhere. My lips parted when I realized the men on the floor were the crew.

For an instant I thought Jeck had discovered my trickery and gotten here before me, but then a jingling movement caught my attention and Captain Rylan rose to his feet from where he had been bent over the last pirate, fastening a knot tight. He turned, his wide grin vanishing when he saw me standing in the doorway to block the light.

"Where's Contessa?" I said, not understanding.

"You!" he barked, the bells on his boots chiming as he drew himself to his entire height. "What are you doing here?"

"Where's my sister?" I repeated, voice shaking as my fingertips touched my knife hilts.

"Where's my money?"

He took a step closer, and I fought to remain unmoving. My eyes had adjusted, and I shot a glance at the men slumped before me. Were they dead? I wondered, but then decided no one would tie up dead men.

"I said, where's my money?" he said, standing in his faded finery with the bells on his boots gently ringing.

Confusion trickled through me, tightening my fear. *He doesn't know?* "Duncan has it." Frightened, I stepped inside and out of the doorway, fighting the urge to retreat onto the rotting porch. My knees went weak, and my throat closed up. Captain Rylan's eyes narrowed, and I added, "I gave it to

Duncan. He's in the dinghy, taking it back to the ship. Where's my sister?"

"The ship?" he exclaimed, and a dove flew away from the rotting beams. "What the hell is he taking it there for?" Then he went deathly still in sudden thought, and I watched in alarm as emotions cascaded over him in a rapid fluidity. Question, followed by ugly realization, anger, and then fury. "The chull!" he said, and my breath came in a jerk. "The son of a chull!"

Legs trembling and wanting to run, I pulled a knife and showed it to him. Something was wrong. Something was terribly wrong. "I did what you wanted," I said, and his attention jerked to me. "Where's my sister?"

Captain Rylan ran his eyes up and down me. In an instant, I saw his decision. He was bigger than I, stronger. I had three knives and a whip that was of questionable use in such a small space. Breath coming in a quick heave, I spun to the doorway to flee. I could only pray he wouldn't use toxin to down me.

"No, you don't," he said murderously softly, and a shriek slipped from me when the bells on his boots tinkled and his hand fell heavily on my shoulder. He spun me around, and I flowed with it, swinging my knife. He cried out in shock as my swing thumped to a halt. Swearing, he shoved me away. I stumbled back, cold when I caught my balance. My knife had a sheen of red.

I've cut him. Oh God, he'll kill me for that. Frightened, I gathered myself to run when a panicked voice shrilled from a second room, "Tess!"

Contessa. I froze, then leapt past Captain Rylan fingering his white shirt where my knife had struck. He looked up as I passed him, his lightly wrinkled face twisting. I burst into a dark room, my bloodied knife still in my hand.

On the floor by the wall were the dusky shadows of Contessa and Alex. They were both staring at me, bound about the ankles and wrists. Contessa had worked her gag free, and Alex's eyes were hard with a frustrated anger. Stiffening, Contessa's fearful gaze darted over my shoulder. "Behind you!" she cried, but I knew Captain Rylan was coming.

A hundred ideas fell through my mind. I couldn't free them and escape both. It was them or me. The decision was easy.

Palming my last remaining knives, I leapt to my sister. Contessa screamed another warning, her gaze fixed behind me. My legs were pulled out from under me. I grunted in pain as I hit the moldy floor. My breath was knocked from me, and gasping for air, I pushed my knives at Alex. Pain pulled my eyes shut when he moved his black boots to cover them.

"You little dock whore," came Captain Rylan's voice, hot and heavy on my neck. His weight lifted, and I gasped for air as he yanked me up, and I hung from his grip like a rag doll. "Duncan and I are going to settle this right now," he said.

He encircled my wrist, squeezing until my fingers went numb, and he plucked the knife I bloodied him with from my grip. The other two were safe with Alex, the darkness of the room having hidden my actions. I met the prince's eyes for a fleeting second. "Don't come back for me," I mouthed, and my heart clenched when his face paled in understanding.

"Let her go!" Contessa shouted, ignored as Captain Rylan jerked me back into the green-shadowed outer room. "Tess!" she cried, voice going fainter.

I fought him, and the flat of his hand came out and struck a ringing blow across my head.

Gasping, I staggered, feeling myself yanked forward. I stumbled, almost going down when my foot found a hole in the floor. Pain lanced through my ankle, and he jerked me up. A cry of hurt came from me as my ankle flamed into agony, twisted.

"You'll be yelping more than that before I'm done with you," the captain threatened. "You best hope he's in earshot, or you're going to die for nothing."

"I gave you what you wanted," I panted, hunched and trying to see past my hair. "I did what you said. Let me go!"

"Stupid, stupid little rich woman," he said with a sneer, pulling me out onto the rotting porch. "Still don't understand, do you? I knew this was too good to be true. I broke my own rule and see what happened? I'll skin him alive for this. You aren't the only fool here. The difference is I'll be getting my money, and you'll be dead."

He spun me around, pinning me to him with a thick arm. His chest pushed against my back as he took a huge breath. The stink of green-slimed boards assailed me, mixing with the scent of salt and sweat. "Duncan!" he bellowed, making the horses at the railing start and shy. "Duncan! I have your palace whore! Give me the money, and I'll let her go!"

"I don't understand," I breathed, feeling unreal and dazed.

"No surprise there," he muttered, his eyes scanning the thick brush surrounding the slack river. The sun was lost behind new clouds, and the wind brushed the tops of the trees. "You've been duped by the best, missy. I taught that pup everything he knows, and this is what I get? Maybe I taught him a little—too—well!"

He jerked his arm with the last words, pinching my bitten shoulder. Pain pounded from my shoulder, and I moaned as a shimmer of black flitted before my vision, then cleared. My knees buckled, but he held me up, the arm of his faded dress coat chokingly under my chin.

"Yes," he breathed harshly into my ear. "Make some noise. Make sure he hears you. Call for him."

I won't, I vowed, then gasped when he dug his fingers into the newly healed wound. The dry rasp of my intake of breath was âlmost a scream in itself. "Duncan!" I shrieked, releasing the pain with my voice so it wouldn't drive me insane. "Oh, God, *Duncan!*"

"That's a good girl," he soothed, his raspy voice tight in anticipation. "Call him again."

"Duncan!" I raged, my throat hoarse and raw. I didn't understand, and I feared if I killed him with my hands I never would. Captain Rylan's fingers dug into me as if trying to meet his thumb on the other side of my shoulder, and I panted through the pain, almost passing out. A tickling trace of thought was forcing its way through the confusion and agony.

Duncan and Captain Rylan knew each other? The cold shock raced through me, making my legs all but give way. The wind whistled down from the trees, striking the ground and billowing up into my face with bits of earth and bark. *They already knew each other.*

"Duncan!" Captain Rylan shouted, jerking my hair to make me face the sky. "Hear her screaming? Don't do this to me, boy," he threatened. "There's enough money for both of us. I'll hunt you down. I know your hiding spots. I bloody well showed them to you!"

"You know Duncan?" I panted, feeling the venom spill into

me from where his fingers pressed my healing wound. My shoulder was damp and I could smell the metallic scent of blood. I think he had broken the new skin.

"Know him?" he snarled. "I all but raised him."

My eyes warmed as the truth hit me, heavy and crippling. "You're Lan," I whispered. "You're the one he took the thief mark for. You let them brand him for your crime and drag him through the street."

"He found me last summer," he muttered, his eyes searching the brush. "Told me he had the scheme of all schemes. A kingdom's ransom. All he needed was a little help from the master. Fifty-fifty," Captain Rylan said bitterly, pinching my shoulder again. His fingers came away red with blood, and my vision started to blur.

Captain Rylan filled his lungs. "This isn't fifty-fifty, Duncan!" he shouted, deafening my ear. "Talk to me, or her next scream will be her last!"

"He's gone," I said, dead inside.

"Then you'll be there to judge him at death's door when I catch up to him." Captain Rylan jerked me to the end of the porch so he could look down the river. "Duncan!"

"He never loved me," I said softly, the pain in my shoulder and ankle lost in a haze of heartache.

"No, you silly woman. He used you, just like he used me." Bells on his boots ringing, he turned to look behind him. "Duncan!"

He never loved me.

Muttering under his breath, Captain Rylan hauled me to the other end of the porch. The horses pulled back to the limit of their leads, frightened. "I'll skin him alive and make a purse out of it," he said. "I'll cut off his hands and feed them to the dogs."

He lied to me, I thought numbly. The wind in my head gibbered at the wind in the trees, inciting it to swirl down to find me. *It was a scheme, a play. He never loved me at all.*

Captain Rylan stopped his pacing and looked at the sky. The zephyr in my head howled joyously, and a blast of air beat down on the shack, sending the man to drag me to the back of the porch. I staggered in his grip, lost of will and empty of thought.

It had all been a lie. Maybe not from the start, but it had turned into one.

The wind chortled in glee, knowing it would win this time. It grew in me, calling the storm pushing on me to come and free it. "It was a lie," I said, betrayal soaking into me like acid to leave an empty hole. It grew slowly, insidiously, then, like a dam breaking, it flooded my soul. "A lie!" I shouted.

The wind gusted, pushing my hair back. The shack groaned, and Captain Rylan stumbled, gripping me to keep from falling down.

"What out of hell . . ." he breathed, staring at the clear sky full of wind. "Sweet mother of us all. . . ."

"He used me. *For money!*" I exclaimed, shouting to hear myself over the wind babbling in my head. It howled, it gibbered, it demanded release, but that would require a thought on my part, and I was dead.

I hung in Captain Rylan's grip. The toxin was pushed from my bite and flooded my body. My hands tingled. My legs shook from the poison taking hold and killing me. Raw force surged through me, and I flung my head back. "The foul bastard!" I raged, and a flash of venom-laced power raced through me.

Captain Rylan cried out, falling to crash into the railing. The horses scattered, the sound of their fear joining the ecstasy of the storm. Free and unencumbered, I stood on the porch. The wind in my head ran unhindered through me. Anticipation and fury raced each other to be the first to be acted upon. Bursting, I admitted to the heavens, "He never loved me!"

Flames licked at the sodden, green-slimed boards. The pines beside the house begin to smolder. The heat of anger and betrayal scoured through me. A distant roar echoed over the trees. It was the wind from the sea. It was coming to find me. It would take away my reason and sanity. And I welcomed it. God help me, I wanted to die from the hurt.

Sounding like a living thing, the angry soughing grew closer. I looked to the sky as the noise grew, and with the sound of lions, it crashed down upon me. I fell under the weight of it. Staggering, I pulled myself upright.

"He *never* loved me!" I exclaimed, and the nearby spring-sap twigs burst to flame. I fell to my knees under the blast of heat and dry wind.

The dry-rotted shack caught faster than light tinder. Heat washed over me, pushed by the wind and rolling over me like a summer-warmed field. The wind babbled and howled. It struck me and beat the flames higher, swirling with promise.

The air seared my throat, and I cried out when my breath was ripped from me and replaced with heat. The anger and hurt in me swelled, consuming me. With a whoosh, the nearby trees went up like an oil-soaked torch. The snapping and groaning of the shack burning behind me joined the tortured sound of trees waving and in flames. The heat of the burning walls behind me hit me anew, and I pulled my tear-streaked face up. My skin tightened from the warmth. Yellow with flames, the wall tilted and started to fall. It would crush me.

A part of me panicked, but the larger, broken part said no. I wouldn't move. I would choose to remain. I would end it. I had no life with Kavenlow, and now I had no life with Duncan. And how could I trust to love another? And without love, I might as well be dead.

I bowed my head, the soggy wood under my hands warm and steaming. I took a last breath, then another, burning my lungs with the sound of tearing paper. The wall creaked again. I closed my eyes, willing it to fall.

Something struck me, knocking me rolling into the railing and off the porch. I gasped, feeling the drop of air beneath me. Arms flailing, I struck the water. The roar of flames and wind was drowned out with the swirl of water. Cold shocked through me, my cry reaching the surface as a stream of bubbles.

I burst from the water in a cloud of denial and anger, finding myself sitting chest deep in the slurry of black mud and silt. Above me was the burning rubble of the shack. It had fallen in on itself without me. Beside me pulling himself up to sit in the water was Jeck.

"No!" I cried, hitting him as the wind clamored, angry that I was still alive. "You can't. You can't! Leave me alone!"

Lips pressed and hidden behind his dripping beard and mustache, he pulled me to him, wrapping his arms around me to try to contain me. I twisted and fought, helpless in the imprisoning strength of his grip, unable to accept there was compassion there, not believing it.

The shack slid majestically into the river, and a warm rush

of water cascaded past us. The trees above burned, a thick smoke coming from the death of the new leaves and old needles while the wind both inside and outside my head howled and tossed the branches.

My fury rose that he'd try to save me, fueled by Duncan's betrayal and my inability to accomplish even the simplest task of ending my life. The wind in me demanded freedom, and in a shared moment of loss, I looked skyward and called down its brother.

Screaming its defiance, it fell from the heavens like a stone, flattening the water and sending Jeck to bow his head against me. But he wouldn't let go, his voice within my ear saying that it would be all right, that I could survive this. I didn't want to believe, and I felt my hands warm with his coming death. He would let me go, or I would end it this way.

He felt it coming, and with the strength of the wind filling me, I stiffened when a surge of force pulsed through me. I screamed as it left me, burning my hands and my soul. Jeck shuddered, his grip slackening for an instant before it came back stronger, almost desperate. "No," he rasped, panting. "My hurt is as great as yours. I can take anything you can give. And I'm not letting you go. Listen to me. Listen to me, Tess!" he shouted over the tumult. "Let the wind go. Let it go for good."

"Please. I can't . . ." I begged, the water sloshing into a thick black silt as I struggled against Jeck with a faltering will. "There's nothing left. I've lost everything. . . ."

"No," he whispered, the pain I had heaped upon him making his voice a ragged thread laced with determination. "You're stronger than that."

The wind bent the trees and fanned the fire, sending smoldering bark to hit us. It was angry that I was still alive and held its brother hostage, but in my head, the wind cowered, frightened by Jeck's voice.

"I can't!" I sobbed. "He said he loved me. He lied and left me to die."

"Don't end it this way. Not because of him." It would have been unheard over the wind and fire but that his lips were brushing my ear. His arms pressed me into him, keeping me from moving. The smell of horse and leather lingering on him meant security, and the band crushing my chest eased. A choking sob broke free. I clung to the compassion I found in him, ignoring that he was a rival player. It was all I had. And I thought—I thought he understood.

"Don't let this kill you," he whispered, and I realized I was clutching his shoulders, crying into his shirt. The wind in my head faltered, falling into a soft muted complaint, sullen that Jeck had found a way to reach me, breaking its hold on me. The wind fanning the flames in the trees abruptly lost interest, lifting its head to look at the sea. With it went my anger, leaving only the crushing reality that Jeck had bested me again. Again I had failed. Again he had seen me weak and foolish. God help me, I couldn't even die properly.

"But he lied to me," I wept as I sat in the stream, the breath of reason sparking through me as the wind diminished. I was caught. Jeck had caught me and forced me to live. Leaning into him, I shook with my sobs. "He lied to me on the boat when he said he loved me. He saved my life only so I could bring him the ransom when I told him Contessa had forbidden it and I was the only one who could make it happen. I lied to Kavenlow!" I wailed, shamed and made into a fool by Duncan. "I lied to Kavenlow for him, and for what? This?"

"Shhhh," he breathed, his grip gentling when I started to shake. "It will be all right, Tess. Let the wind go."

"He used me," I said. "He only wanted money. He sent me here to die. He didn't come back. I called for him, and he didn't come back . . ."

"I know," he murmured, his fingers pressing against my head easing. "You survived it. You're strong, Tess. Don't let it break you."

I took a shuddering breath, smelling his leather jerkin and the briny stink of low tide over the sharp smell of burning. His arms were about me, warm and secure, giving me something real to fasten upon. Slowly, I realized the wind had slackened to almost nothing. Exhausted in mind and body, I let my head rest against the front of his shoulder and listened to the crackling of the last of the flames and the tinkling of slowly moving water moving out with the tide.

"Why?" I rasped, hearing the soft soughing of the burning trees as the wind forgot about me and blew out to sea to play with the stingrays. Around us was the reek of burning green, but here in the creek we were safe. "I thought he loved me," I said, my eyes on the filthy water swirling around us, my tears joining it freely. "Why did he do that to me?" I breathed, not expecting an answer. "Why?"

Jeck's arms around me tightened and released. "I don't know."

Twenty-six

❖

The soft thuds of our horses' hooves were a gentle cadence swallowed up by the leaf mold, and the sound of the wind soughing in the treetops taunted me. I sat without feeling, the reins slack and slipping from my fingers, balancing by instinct as we made our slow way back to the capital. In my ear was the unrelenting voice of the wind still trapped inside me, its message once blurred and indistinct, now obvious and painful.

It mocked me, telling me that Duncan didn't love me, over and over and over. First a whisper, then rising to a laughing chortle, then back to a sly burble, never ceasing. *Duncan doesn't love you.* It was a warning heard too late. I had blinded myself to it, not wanting to believe. No one had told me truth could be found in the voice of the wind, and now the truth was trapped within my head.

Before me upon a single horse were Contessa and Alex. The prince had his arms about her, the curve of his arms gentle and loving as he held her with her feet politely to one side of the animal. Their soft conversation was unheard but for the comfortable come-and-go of their intertwined voices. Jeck was half a horse length behind me on one of the three horses that had been tied behind the wagon. Alex, being an expert horseman, had caught them all after escaping the shack with Contessa.

Farther back was the creaking of the wagon and the loud voices of Jeck's men. There were far more than the four he had discussed with Kavenlow, and they were on foot as the wagon held semicomatose pirates along with the chests of spice. Most were awake now, not remembering Jeck pulling them from the burning building before finding me kneeling on the front porch. Of Captain Rylan, there had been no trace, but I knew he was too clever to have died in the fire.

I was exhausted, shamed in body and spirit. But it seemed I had changed the punta dream: I was not a prisoner upon a horse before Jeck; Alex and Contessa were with us, and the pirates were captured. Betrayal had made my heart a sodden rag, though, and the misery haunted me still. But my sister was alive and unhurt. I would not seek to change the future further but rather be content with what I had.

The voices of the men surrounding us grew louder as the trees thinned and the light brightened to early evening. Their voices were cheerful with the sound of anticipation. I pulled my attention from my fingers knotting in the horse's mane as we stepped out from the shelter of the woods and into the fields about the capital. The setting sun struck me, almost a pain upon my heat-damaged skin. I squinted and hunched deeper into my saddle, wanting to hide from it.

I had lied to Kavenlow. They must have realized it to have gotten to me so quickly. Not only had I lied, but I had been caught.

"Look!" came Contessa's cheerful voice. She was rescued and restored. Nothing could go wrong for her now. "In the harbor. They're back already! See? The pirate ship and the chancellor's."

My head came up, and I blearily focused. Far below in the harbor were the ships in question, their sails furled and their decks empty. A small group of soldiers on foot were headed our way, two men on horseback with them. One broke away and cantered to us. The man left behind reined his horse in to keep it from following, bending to talk to a man on foot. I could tell from his silhouette and black leather jerkin and cap that it was Kavenlow. My heart clenched. What would I say to him?

Distressed, I tucked a strand of hair behind my ear, noticing with an uncaring detachment that the tips were twisted and burned, singed from the fire's heat. I glanced at Jeck, who had nudged his horse up equal with mine now that there was room. He hadn't said a word to me since pulling me sobbing from the water when the first of his men on foot arrived. I knew he felt my gaze on him when his jaw clenched and his eye ticked.

My face flamed. I had cried in his arms over a thief, a man he'd warned me about if I had cared to listen. Jeck had seemed to understand at the time, his arms around me as we sat in the tidal river, him holding me together as my world fell apart and I realized just how foolish I had been. But now I wondered. Maybe I had just imagined his compassion. Maybe I had needed it so badly that I fostered the emotion on Jeck when it wasn't there. He certainly wasn't compassionate now, having returned to his usual stone-faced, closed-lipped self.

Ignoring me, he wiggled his heels into his horse's flank and trotted up to meet Captain Resh cantering closer. The captain of my sister's guard looked exuberant as he reined his horse to a four-posted stop, his back stiff and powerful arms tight.

"Captain Jeck!" he exclaimed, bobbing his head respectfully to Contessa and Alex. "We have the enemy's ship, sir. Duncan wasn't on it. Nor was the ransom."

I watched the play of emotions over the Costenopolie captain. Though he was excited, it was tempered with anger— anger at himself for having been played the fool. He, along with the entire company of Costenopolie palace guards, had trusted Duncan to a fault. I wasn't the only one to have been duped. It didn't ease the tightness of my chest, though, or the disgrace I felt. I wondered when his plan had evolved. Perhaps after having befriended the palace guards? During the time the plans for a nuptial voyage were discussed? Or possibly even as soon as when we had been fleeing Jeck last spring and he realized I had a claim on a royal title?

Jeck nudged his horse into motion as the rest of us caught up with them. "Take a regiment," he said softly. "Search the river for any trace of him. Both sides. Put four of your most even-headed men on horse and have them ride to Saltwood. I want a noninvasive house-to-house inquiry to see if he's been there and gone, then I want them to sit quietly in case he has yet to go through." The dark-eyed man turned to Queen Contessa and Prince Alex. "If that meets with Your Majesties' approval?"

He was playing his game with my pieces. I should care, but I didn't.

Her face grim, Contessa nodded, and Alex's grip on her tightened. "Yes," Alex said evenly. "That would meet with our approval."

"You'll never find him," I whispered, then coughed, leaving my throat feeling as if it were bleeding inside. No one heard me.

"I'll attend to it immediately, sir," Resh said. He gestured for one of the men with us to accompany him as he wheeled his horse about and started back to the city with a slow pace. The small group of approaching men on foot had already turned back to cluster about the entrance to the city, leaving Kavenlow to come forward alone. He sat straight and tall in the saddle, looking more at home there than in front of his books and ink. It grew harder for me to breathe, and I wished I could drop back and hide at the end of the line but knew any movement from me would only draw more attention.

My self-blindness had allowed Duncan to use us all: the nautical nuptial journey, the ship waiting conveniently at anchor captained by his old master, the lamp that fell to set the fire to my ship, the anchor line probably cut, the time such that only their ship could slip over the reefs. Believing he loved me, I had told him what Contessa's letter had said. *God help me, I was the fool.*

I wanted to believe that the punta bite had been unintentional, that he hadn't been trying to kill me. I wanted to believe his last plea that I leave with him had been an act of love, that he saw a life with me in it even if it was one fleeing the wrath of a betrayed master and a kingdom shunned. But I didn't know. He hadn't come back when I called him, in agony at Rylan's hand. Maybe that was my answer.

I kept my eyes down when Kavenlow's horse joined the line, prancing, neck arched. "Your Majesties," he said, his low voice full of relief and import. "You're well? Here, take my horse. I can walk."

"No," Contessa said, her voice bringing my gaze peeping from around my singed hair. "I'm comfortable upon my husband's horse. Stay. Captain Jeck has done justly by us. And it would do the people good to see us together and well."

Her accent was clear and precise, sounding like our mother. "As you will it," my master said, his gaze shifting from theirs to mine, trying to catch it. I wouldn't let him. His voice seemed as it always had, but I had betrayed him. I couldn't look at him.

"Chancellor," Contessa whispered, her affected noble speech falling from her. "Something's wrong with Tess. She won't talk to me. I think she blames herself solely for Duncan's betrayal of us all. You're close to her. Go ride with her. Tell her it wasn't her fault for me. Please?"

My heart clenched, and I hunched farther into my saddle. My fingers on the reins tightened. I wondered if it might be easier to bolt and run.

"Thank you, Your Majesty. You're as kind as you're observant," Kavenlow said, turning his horse in a small circle to fall back.

Heart pounding, I kept my eyes on my fingers when Kavenlow worked his horse between Jeck and me. From the corner of my sight I saw him nod to Jeck. Something unsaid passed between them, and I felt my heart crumble, the jolt of my horse's steps jarring me.

"Tess?" Kavenlow said, sorrow heavy in his voice. "Oh, no. He burned your hair? Are you all right? Tell me what happened."

I had betrayed him, and he was worried that I had been hurt? I shook my head, only able to bring my head up far enough to see his strong hands gripping the reins. The gold ring upon his thick finger glittered, catching my attention until the shifting of the horses broke my gaze. He had given the ring to me once as evidence that I was Costenopolie's legal player, entrusting me to win his game for him and give it back.

My shoulders tightened from an inner pain. It would never happen again. Even if I somehow lowered my residual toxin levels, I'd never be able to remain his apprentice. I couldn't be a player. I had broken the trust of my master.

"Tess?" Kavenlow prompted, and I flinched at the comforting hand he put on me.

"I can't," I whispered. "Kavenlow, I can't."

His hand slowly fell from me. "We'll talk later," he said softly. An uncomfortable silence took root. My throat tightened, and I forced my gaze up, focusing upon the towers of the palace, bright with light and promise. I took a deep breath, holding it for a long moment before letting it go shakily.

Alex and Contessa dropped back to force me into the coming conversation whether I wanted to be or not. "Chancellor?" Alex asked, leaning to look across Jeck and me. "What did you find at the pirates' ship? How many men were injured in the taking of it? Not many, I hope."

Kavenlow's eye made a single tic. His mustache and beard met as he pressed his lips together in worry. "Not a one, Prince Alex," he said. "We found *Kelly's Sapphire* at anchor with her crew unconscious and tied up for us."

"Duncan?" Contessa guessed, probably correctly. "He never intended to go back to the ship, did he? The pirates in the shack were poisoned as well. Captain Jeck told us how he pulled them from the flames."

Jeck's jaw clenched and relaxed. They had been downed by his toxin, stolen from him before they burned my boat to the waterline. And Duncan had known what it was capable of, thanks to me. The rival player visibly steadied himself. "I think we can be fairly confident that Duncan and Captain Rylan were working together, Duncan immobilizing the crew on the boat and Captain Rylan taking care of the crew that came ashore for the ransom."

"His name is Lan," I whispered, my voice sounding raw to me. "He isn't a captain. He's a thief. Mr. Smitty is the captain. Lan bought their services, fully intending to leave them with nothing. He didn't count on Duncan's doing the same to him."

No one said anything. The horses plodded forward, unaware and uncaring. Behind us the men talked among themselves, exchanging cheerful ideas of what they would do to Duncan should they find him alone in the dark one night. I felt sick and weary at heart.

Kavenlow made a soft sound. "He deceived us all, Tess. Don't take the entirety of the blame on yourself."

My intake of air caught in a rush of heartache. I had thought he loved me. The wind in my head laughed and gibbered. *He never loved you. He never loved you. He lied and used you. He never loved you.*

Head drooping, I held my breath, not caring that everyone could see my pain. I forced my emotions to dull. The voice in my head giggled and tittered, laughing at me for my foolishness, telling me it had warned me—but I hadn't listened. Around me, an evening breeze lifted off the bay, fluttering the horses' manes and shifting Contessa's green-stained dress before dying.

I blanked my thoughts, compelling the voice to go as empty and still as I tried to make my mind. There was an unexpected strength in apathy, and slowly the voice of the wind diminished to where I could ignore it.

"I'm sorry, Tess," Kavenlow said, seeming to be the spokesman for all of them. "I know you cared for him."

I thought he loved me, ran through my mind. I had been ready to leave everything for him, and it would have been for a lie.

"Captain Jeck," Alex said, stepping smoothly into the awkward breach. "We were there, but we missed most of it. How did the shack come to be on fire?"

I shrank into myself. It was going to come out. Not now, in front of other ears, but it would come out: how I had tried to kill Jeck, how I called the wind and couldn't control it, how I set the very wood and trees aflame with my anger and lack of control.

Despair soaking into me, I waited for what Jeck would say, not believing when he kept himself to a subdued, "The shack was on fire when I arrived. I would guess it was Captain Rylan's attempt to murder you and Prince Alex and keep his hands clean of it."

Contessa shifted before Alex to see Kavenlow better. "He was going to kill us, Chancellor Kavenlow, whether or not he got the money. Tess stopped him."

I did nothing, I thought.

"She gave us two knives without his seeing, allowing Captain Rylan to capture her so he would be distracted while we freed ourselves." Wide-eyed, she looked at me in pride. "She was very brave."

My chest grew heavy with heartache. *I was a fool.*

Kavenlow leaned to me. "Tess?" he prompted. I took a quick breath scented of leather and ink, holding it. I was dead inside. I was dead so I didn't have to hear the wind laughing at me.

My teacher pulled away, tightening the reins of his horse, and my tension eased. "I saw the smoke," he said. "I thought it was your signal to take the pirate's ship. Just as well I didn't wait. Too much longer, and the pirates would have been conscious and working themselves free of their ropes our good cheat had wrapped them in." He hesitated. "And the wind?" he asked.

I gritted my teeth. I could feel more than his eyes on me, wondering.

"Oh!" Contessa exclaimed, oblivious to the weight the question had. "Did you feel it, too? It was awful. It came out of nowhere and left just the same. It was as if I could hear the souls of the lost in it, come to take me with them if I didn't hold on to what was dear to me."

It was almost too much to bear. I held my head down and watched the track under us turn from flattened grass to dust and widen. A sudden swelling of noise cascaded over us as we neared the city. The sentries had temporarily closed the gates, but I looked up as they opened, and the people swarmed out.

The sun pierced my eyes, and I blinked the tears away. People cheered and waved bits of fabric, making the horses nervous. It was obvious the news of retaking Contessa and Alex had come before us. I numbly watched the smiling faces, the individual cries of well-wishing and approval lost in the tumult. I wanted to hide in shame. Had no one told them? Didn't they know that their beloved queen and prince would never have been in danger if I hadn't let my desire for love cloud my reason?

Apparently not, I thought, as they surrounded us. The crowd redoubled their noise upon seeing Alex and Contessa together. She rested easy in his arms, smiling and happy, looking like our mother despite the grime and that her snarled hair was tumbling about her shoulders.

A bittersweet pang went through me when she looked at Alex and whispered something to him, the love and caring obvious in her eyes. He gripped her more tightly, stealing a kiss to the delight of all as they crossed the threshold into the city.

My eyes lifted from the happy faces, lost in the joy and relief of finding their lives would continue unchanged now that their royal family was safely returned. The narrow streets echoed with them, spreading the news to those struggling to catch a glimpse. My hands automatically soothed my horse, and when a cheerful young soldier in the palace uniform took his head, I numbly let go of the reins. The noise was like a weight, and my gaze roved for a spot of unmoving color to stare at among the joyful commotion. I blinked as I found Thadd.

The squat sculptor stood high above the crowd atop a roof. His round, simple face was full of a raw despair as he watched the procession, his eyes riveted to his beloved Contessa. I thought of the kiss she had returned to Alex, knowing Thadd had seen it—knowing he had seen the caring and feeling behind it—knowing it had struck him to his core.

Shoulders bowed as if having been beaten, he stood with his arms slack at his side. He never moved, but I saw something in him die.

A spark of shared feeling lifted through me. I wasn't the only one hurting amid the combined joy swirling around us, leaving us untouched. *We are alike in that,* I thought as the tide of well-wishers pushed us round a corner and into the wide boulevard that led directly to the palace.

We had both loved the wrong person. Duncan had betrayed me, his soul lost to the greed of wealth. Contessa had fallen prey to a noble man who had seen her through hell and possible death. I wouldn't judge her. I couldn't. The thought that Thadd's love for Contessa wasn't any less because Contessa loved another lifted through me. Was my own love for Duncan, then, true and unsullied though he never loved me at all?

I didn't know.

I lost sight of Thadd when we went round the bend. The wind rose, filling my head with uncertainty. It laughed and snickered, and I pulled my hand up to hold down my hair though the pennants draped from the windows in celebration hung silent and still.

Twenty-seven

❖

After weeks at sea, just the stillness of the air made it seem warm despite the dampness. I sat on the stone bench in the garden, hunched and miserable beside my parents' graves. Banner, my dog, abided patiently at my feet, his head on my lap as I fingered the wispy, curly hair atop his head. The large wolfhound had joined me shortly after I found refuge upon the hard stone, skulking up behind me slowly with a drooping tail until he was sure his presence was welcome.

The heavy fog hiding the moon was chill, and the light from the candle I had brought with me glowed upon the flat expanse of the two slabs of polished stone embedded in the earth. It wasn't that I had anything to say to them, but this was the sole place I could get away from everyone where, if they saw me, they wouldn't dare approach.

And I was desperately seeking solitude.

I slumped, pulling myself straight when I reminded myself I was still a princess, even if I wasn't a particularly good one. Banner lifted his eyes to mine, never moving his head. When I remained still, he returned his gaze to nothing, content to offer what silent solace he could. The fingers of my right hand slowed their motion, and I rested my hand atop his head. The punta bite ached all the way down to my palm.

The damp wind lifted through the moonflower vine twining over the trellis arching over me. It stirred the slumberous zephyr in my head back to wakefulness, and I groaned. *Is this going to happen every time the wind blows?* Eyes shut, I willed the zephyr to go back to sleep. But it shook itself, whispering that Duncan never loved me. He used me. That I trusted him, and he never loved me at all, and wasn't I the *glorious* fool?

Teeth gritted, I forced my hands in Banner's fur to stay loose as I fiercely wrapped my will about the wind and forced it to be still. It laughed and pretended submissiveness, planning in a soft, audible whisper to drive me insane. The breeze in the vines died, and the candle flame grew steady in the damp night.

Relieved, I let my shoulders slump and looked across the expanse of damp garden and up the tower walls to the hazy square of light showing from Kavenlow's room. I could see the occasional shift of light from bright to dull. Kavenlow was there. With Jeck. Speaking of me, no doubt.

I'm sure their private conversation had begun with me helping Contessa and Alex to board the pirates' ship, making the natural progression to me having been bitten by a punta and surviving thanks to Jeck's healing powers. From there the talk would likely drift to the venom being trapped within my tissues, spilling out to make my magic violent and unpredictable when I grew angry. Jeck would tell Kavenlow that I had tried to call the wind and fallen prey to it, and I knew the rival player would make Kavenlow understand when he wouldn't believe me that my residual levels of toxin would never fall, making it impossible for me to take over Kavenlow's game when he was ready to retire.

My eyes closed against the new lump in my throat. *And it was because I let Duncan use us. I made it possible because they trusted my judgment, and my judgment was measured against the stick that I thought he cared about me.*

Kavenlow would never keep me as an apprentice. Not now. I was twice disgraced. And Jeck? Jeck thought I was a silly, foolish woman.

I caught my breath before I started crying, holding it. My head started to throb, and Banner whined. I pulled my gaze up and over the palace's wall, the fog glowing pink from the celebration fires lit in the streets. My fingers racked through

Banner's fur to reassure him. "It's all right, boy," I whispered, thinking lies were easy when no one but you could understand them. "It's going to be all right."

His eyes went soulfully to mine, then shifted away. His tail began to thump. It took on an urgent intensity, and I sent my gaze to follow his, seeing a white shadow flit across the tall black of the hedges and back behind the shrubbery. It moved with an awkward swiftness, and it was only Banner's calm anticipation that kept my hands from rising to remind me my dart tube and darts were missing from my topknot.

Banner's tail thumps grew louder, his head unmoving atop my lap. With a clatter of hard soles on slate, Contessa lurched from the fog and bushes behind me. She drew to a sudden, unexpected halt when she caught sight of me. "Oh, I'm sorry," she stammered. "I didn't know you were here."

The pitch of her voice and her utter lack of a noble accent told me she had been crying. We had all apparently been having a stellar evening. I silently slid down the damp bench to make room for her. Banner stood, waiting to see if I was going to leave.

"You want to be alone," she said, looking like a ghost as she stared at the long seat.

I glanced at our parents' graves. "I'm not alone. Sit. Unless you want me to go?"

"No." It was a quick-worded admission that brought a sliver of ease to me. At least Contessa thought no less of me. Somehow that made me feel worse.

She hesitated as if gathering her courage, then, after a nervous look at me, curtsied low and humbly to our parents. Silk rustled, and the faint scent of lavender and rock dust floated between us as she sat. Straight and stiff, she stared into nothing, her hands clenched in her lap as if she would fall apart if she dared loosen them. Banner sighed with a soft huff of air, lying on our feet so he could touch us both.

She took a shaky breath, and I readied myself for whatever Alex had done to her now.

"He's gone!" she blurted, her upright stance collapsing.

My mouth dropped open. "Gone!"

"Thadd," she blubbered, hiding her face in a hankie that

had been crushed unseen between her fingers until now. "He's gone!"

"Oh." My pulse slowed in understanding. The memory of his face when we had reentered the city passed before my mind's eye. Contessa shook with half-heard sobs, and I put a sisterly arm about her shoulders. Banner got to his feet, and the huge dog slunk to the shadows with his tail tucked, thinking this was his fault somehow. "Contessa, I'm sorry," I said, feeling her hurt though it had likely been my words to him that set his thoughts to leaving.

Shaking, she caught her breath, and my arm dropped from around her. "He took his nasty old horse," she said, the foggy candlelight showing a sheen on her face where her tears reflected it. "And his wagon, and all his tools. All he left me was this letter. See?" Making a small sound of dismay, she looked at herself as she searched for it. "Oh, here," she said, finding it tucked into her waistband and extending it. "He must have had someone pen it for him," she babbled, as I uncrinkled the crushed parchment. "I know he can't write."

Leaning closer to my candle, I held it so the light fell upon the unfamiliar handwriting. My first sense of relief that it wasn't Kavenlow's turned to worry as I wondered if it might be Jeck's. Lips pressed, I read, I LOVE YOU, AND I WILL NOT STAY HERE. A chill ran through me as I recalled it was the same thing he had said when he was going to force me to take him with me when I carried the ransom out.

"He didn't even say good-bye," she blubbered, and I looked up from the letter to the surrounding dark gardens, hoping no one could hear her. Yes, everyone knew they were lovers, but as long as there was no proof . . .

"I found it propped up on the statue," she continued. "The one he was making of my hands."

I stifled a cringe. It was supposed to have been a statue of her and Alex's hands intertwined. I was surprised he hadn't taken his hammer to it and broken it to dust.

"You don't think someone made him leave, do you?" she asked, her sudden thought allowing her to find a measure of control.

"No," I whispered, guilt thick in me. *Forced, no. Convinced, yes.* "You can tell by his words it was his own decision."

I probably should have said it another way, as Contessa renewed her tears, her last hope that he might return to her, broken. "He just left," she cried, sniffing and snorting like a jilted barmaid. Looking at her now, you couldn't tell that a kingdom almost fell because of her absence. "I thought he loved me," she wailed.

It was so close to my own raw feelings that I hunched in pain. "He does love you, Contessa," I managed, glad the moon was hidden behind the fog. I knocked over the candle before she could see my face, and it went out to leave the sharp scent of burned wick. "He saw that you were starting to care for Alex, and he left to protect himself."

"Protect himself," she scoffed, turning her tears into an unjustifiable anger as I knew she might. "Against what?"

"His pride," I said, then felt my face lose its expression. Maybe . . . maybe some of my shame for Duncan using me could be blamed upon my pride. I had been trained to be a player, to use my wits to manipulate people. Duncan had bested me using methods I had deemed too low to use. *How much?* I wondered. *How much of my pain was due to that, and how much was from my wounded heart?* I sat straighter when I realized I didn't know.

Contessa saw my new stance and eyed me in question. "How can you say he left because of pride?" she questioned carefully, wiping her nose on her sleeve.

I stifled a twinge of annoyance, knowing this wasn't the time to correct the backwoods manners that came out when she was stressed. "Contessa," I said softly, not wanting to hurt her but thinking she deserved the truth. "He saw Alex kiss you when you came over the city's threshold."

Her face went long, and her narrow chin trembled as it all fell into place. "He saw?" she warbled.

"It was a very sincere kiss," I added gently. "And you gave him one back."

"It was just a kiss!" she said belligerently, her emotions flying from one extreme to the other. Then she slumped, a faint gray shadow on the bench beside me. "And I meant it," she sighed. "Oh, chu pits, Tess. No wonder he left. How can it be wrong to love someone? I didn't want to care for Alex. I would have been happy living a lie if it didn't hurt anyone, but now, anything I do will hurt one of them. Why did Alex have to be so understanding, so nice? If he had been mean and ugly, this never would have happened." Her hands twisted in her lap as she wound the hankie tighter and tighter. "It's not my fault!"

"Contessa . . ." I cajoled softly. "He couldn't stay, knowing you might love Alex, even if that day hadn't yet happened. Could you ask him to remain where he would have to watch the love between you and Alex grow, always standing in the shadows, knowing he could never be with you openly? It would prey upon him. The life you had planned together would gather dust and take on the hue of childish dreams when held up to the life you and Alex would be sharing."

She sniffed, saying nothing, the haze of the newly risen full moon glowing dully behind her shoulder. Not wanting to be cruel but having to finish, I set my sun-browned hand atop hers. "Contessa, Thadd gave you a gift by leaving. Just as Alex did when he left his Rosie."

"Oh, don't," she said, catching her breath with a hiccup. "It was horrible. He thought I was her. He loves her so much. Didn't you hear it in his voice? How could he just leave her like that? He didn't even know me . . . then."

I glanced at the square of light coming from Kavenlow's room, thinking that even now I was playing the game, even now when it was lost to me. If I could convince Contessa that loving Alex wasn't wrong, then the kingdom would be strong enough to bear a hundred wars.

"Alex knew there might be a chance you might love him, and he, you," I said, telling myself that this was as much for Contessa's happiness as it was for Kavenlow's damned game. "And Alex would rather see his life with Rosie in the shadows shattered than see the chance you and he might find love destroyed because of a jealous woman. There's no right or wrong to it," I coaxed. "I can't give you an answer. Alex left her because he had to." Contessa sniffed, sounding ugly, and I added, "Just as Thadd left you. He knew you would never ask him to and that you would one day hate him for making you endure it. This way, the love you had for each other will never tarnish."

She was silent, emotionally spent. "I wish I could talk to him," she whispered forlornly. "Just one last time. I would ask him . . . I'd ask him . . ." She stopped, her eyes closing. The faint light from the tower glinted upon a new tear that slipped past her shut lids. "I don't know what I'd ask him," she finally said. "Maybe all I'd say was I was sorry, and that I love him and I always will."

"He knows that already," I whispered, thinking of Duncan. Had it all been a game to him or had he loved me . . . just a little less than he loved his money? The wind rose, rattling the leaves. I shivered, listening to it mock me. "Contessa," I asked hesitantly. "Could you tell . . . when you kissed Alex today . . . could you tell that he loved you? Like he loved Rosie?"

Her eyes dropped as she realized I had seen what she had done while playing Rosie under the deck of the pirates' ship. Shame showed in her slight motion. "Yes," she whispered. "It was the same. He loves me."

Contessa's eyes were wet as she turned to me. "I-I came to talk to them," she said, her gaze flicking to the flat gravestones atop the manicured ground.

"Do you want me to leave?"

She shook her head solemnly, and I settled back. I watched, somewhat uncomfortable as she rose, and with the grace of a saint, knelt before the slabs of stone to look like one of Thadd's heartfelt statues among the hazy ribbons of fog.

How could it be wrong to love someone? echoed her confused question in my thoughts. *How could it be wrong?* I turned my eyes from the sight of her lips moving in silent prayer. How indeed? But it certainly hadn't been right for me to have loved Duncan.

Had I loved him? resounded in me, and while my heart ached in *yes,* I found a new anger accompanied it, anger that he had used me for gain, anger that I had blinded myself to him using a weapon to manipulate me that I was not prepared to use. The anger felt better than the hurt, and I fastened on it, watching the petals of the moonflowers tremble in a soft breeze. From my deeper thoughts, the wind laughed, urging me on. If it could make me angry enough, it knew I would lose control and it would have its freedom. It would have had it this afternoon if Jeck hadn't brought me back again. Its wheedling, conspiring prattle checked my anger, but I still felt my pulse quicken and my muscles tense.

No one had found Duncan. The searching sentries had located his empty rowboat only a short distance from the shack, and a potent rush shook my fingers when I realized he had probably heard me call for him and never returned. There had been an obvious track of heavily sunken footprints where he'd staggered, carrying the heavy satchels to two horses.

The horses' deep prints had led back into the water, where the outgoing tide had washed away every trace of them. I imagined one of the horses had probably been Tuck, Duncan's gelding. It would account for the animal's absence in the stables. Duncan had undoubtedly taken the second horse from the stables as well, stealing it when he had come to give us Rylan's demands, walking past the palace gates and sentries with them unquestioned, secure in that they trusted he wouldn't have two horses unless someone in the palace knew about it.

My teeth gritted, and I held my breath. Duncan had twisted my emotions so easily that night, playing upon my feelings, letting me believe that his life was in danger, that he was making a noble sacrifice. And because of that, I had deceived Kavenlow, making sure the ransom that Kavenlow wasn't going to give made it into Duncan's thieving hands. And he had done it all so easily.

Stupid, stupid, I berated myself, but my heartache seemed to lessen as I accepted my failing for what it had been; I had been manipulated by someone using emotions I had thought were too sacred to sully with schemes. Never again. Not that it mattered.

The misty breeze lifted my singed hair, and I pulled my angry gaze away from the stark line the palace walls made against the sky. They were suddenly like the walls of delusion I had placed about myself to stay blind in my search for a happiness that I could never have. A wash of claustrophobia cascaded over me. I stood, heart pounding. From the shadows came Banner, pacing to me in a slow lope as he saw my need to move. I had to get out, get past the walls.

As I stared at the stone imprisoning me with an almost hungry fervor, I realized what Kavenlow had meant when he said I could make no lasting attachments. I had thought he meant that to do so would make me vulnerable as whomever I loved could be used against me. That the ones I loved would be in danger if a rival player knew they meant something to me and I would sacrifice my game to save them. But what it could also mean was that anyone I loved could use my emotions for his own gain. Just as Duncan had. "Bloody chu pits," I whispered, feeling my breath shake as I exhaled. I finally understood. But it was understanding come too late.

Contessa's bowed head rose at my mild curse. "Tess?"

I took three quick steps to her, feeling unreal. She looked at me strangely when I bent to take her hands and pull her to her feet. "I have to go out for a bit," I said, feeling the cold dampness of her fingers from the dew-wet grass.

Her eyes widened, almost unseen in the dark. "You're leaving the grounds?"

I nodded, giving her hands a little squeeze. "I can get past the gates all right, but I need you to tell Kavenlow or anyone who asks that I'm sulking somewhere and don't want to be disturbed."

"You want me to lie?" she stammered, pulling away and putting a hand to her face. "Why?"

"Queens do have to lie occasionally," I said roughly, anxious to be gone. "Otherwise, the world would always be at war."

"I know that," she snapped, meeting my ire with her own. "There's nothing wrong with a lie when it serves a good purpose and hurts no one, but I'm not going to do it unless I know why."

Taken aback—and not sure I was entirely comfortable with her philosophy—I glanced behind her at the surrounding shrubbery. My eyes rose to the familiar walls enclosing the palace, then up and over them to the moon-hazed fog beyond. "I have to find Duncan."

Twenty-eight

❖

Head lowered against the mist, I trudged to the city gate, immune to the joy rising from the spontaneous festival that swirled around me. It was well after sundown, but you wouldn't know it by the torches and fires that leapt in the very streets as people burned everything from tomorrow's cooking wood to straw from beds too old to be worth keeping in their celebration of the return of their queen and prince. The fog did nothing to dampen their mood, only serving to reflect the firelight and add a festive glow. Food and spirits were abundant and generously shared, but no one saw me. I felt disconnected, hearing but unable to share their happiness. I had to find Duncan. Until I did, nothing would have any meaning.

I had to confront him, had to tell him that I wasn't going to suffer because he didn't love me, that he had taught me I was stronger than that, that he was a liar and a thief, even if the only thing he stole was my trust. And that he couldn't hurt me anymore since his love was as worthless as a ladle of salt water.

Escaping the palace had been easy. I hadn't even needed to use my magic after I donned my too-short dress and Penelope's tattered shawl and boots to make the shift from the woman handing out sweets at the palace's front gate to the rabble taking advantage of the rare treat. My two black horses had come back earlier this afternoon along with one of the useless warships that had accompanied us on our disastrous voyage, and Jy's shod feet sounded comforting behind me as I led him through the streets.

A growing rattle and noise pulled me up short where the walk met the street. Jy blew nervously, and I clutched my cloak closer while people scattered. In a reckless swerve and shouting, a heavy coach draped with calling people thundered past, racing an overburdened city pony in a wild abandon. The surrounding people either cheered or cursed them before returning to their revelry. In six heartbeats, it was as if the coach had never existed, the street as full of people as it had been. Heart slowing, I shook myself from my numb mood before it killed me. Jy pushed his nose at me, shoving me almost into the street.

"Easy, Jy," I said, holding his head and taking strength from his mist-damp warmth that smelled of hay and leather. Steadying myself, I checked the street to cross, my heart freezing at the faint but familiar sound of bells.

It was Rylan, clearly angry as he pushed through the noisy throng, his long faded coat covered by an oilcloth cloak and a squarish hat on his head. By his tight pace, it seemed he was looking for Duncan, probably of the mind that the cheat had risked the autonomy of the streets to spend a coin or two of his ill-gained money.

I took a breath to call attention to him only to collapse back in on myself. My head hurt from indecision. If I spent the effort to catch him, I'd lose my chance to talk to Duncan tonight. By tomorrow, he would be too far to track.

I sank back against Jy, using him to hide should the man look my way. If Rylan hadn't found Duncan here, then I was right in my guess that he was past the city's gates.

As soon as Rylan was swallowed up by the noisy conglomeration, I swung up onto Jy, ignoring the hoots and ribald remarks of the nearby men with too much to drink in them commenting upon the way I was riding. Face warming, I spun Jy into a tight two-legged turn, giving him my heels and his head. He took it, racing up the street in the wake of the racing coach.

The enthusiastic cries of the men watching soon faded, leaving me with only a blur of alcohol-reddened faces and yellow glows surrounding open fires. Snatches of music and conversations rose and fell. Familiar buildings came and went. Jy was nimble-footed and clever, showing his warhorse training as he dodged people and carts without direction, eager for the chance to run.

Crouched low on his back, I leaned into the turn when Jy—his metal-shod hooves clattering on the cobbles—all but slid around the corner and onto the street leading to the eastern gate. It was open ahead of me, with the guards clustered about their warming fire in relaxed talk. I knew I could pass them with minimal effort if I stopped to talk, but I didn't. The need to find Duncan consumed me, and I raced past the guardhouse and into the night, trailing good-natured salutations and admonishments to slow down or I would break my horse's leg.

Free of the thousand voices the city sheltered, I felt my mind expand. The thumps of Jy's hooves were like my heartbeat. His lungs seemed to breathe for me. I was a spot of stillness atop his back, poised between yesterday and today, unable to live until I spoke with Duncan and settled in my thoughts what scar his betrayal would leave on me.

He never loved you, the voice in my head mocked, stirred to wakefulness by the wind of my passage. I shoved it down where I couldn't hear it, but it surfaced again, floating upward like bubbles slipping around my fingers. *He never loved you. You'll never find him. Never find him. Never find him.*

Jy carried me into the more certain dark under the trees, his hooves taking up the litany. I closed my eyes and rode with no direction, the wind laughing in a demented glee. It knew it had me. It was going to drive me insane. I was halfway there, riding my horse at a breakneck speed into the woods on a trail that led to nowhere.

Frustration tightened my chest, and my jaw clenched. The wind in my thoughts slipped my control, inciting the breeze in the branches to grow. "Then you find him!" I shouted at it, and Jy's pace faltered.

My breath caught at the wash of sly contriving the wind met me with. It could. It could find him . . . if I freed it.

Heart pounding, I sat straighter. Jy felt my weight shift, and we came to a jostling halt under the trees quicker than I would have imagined. The sudden lack of movement sent a rush of sensation through me as the trees and darkness closed in to become real again. The frog song seemed to burst from nowhere. The sound of Jy's breathing and the soft thumps of his feet as he moved in place were loud. Hidden behind the trees was a hazy spot of white, the only evidence of the moon.

Holding the reins tight, I sat on the riding pad and stared at the nothing that surrounded me. My lungs took the damp air in as if I were the one who had run here, not Jy, and fear slid its fingers about my heart and squeezed. I had to find Duncan. I was going to free the wind.

Jy sensed my nervousness and pranced in place. I sent a calming thought into him, reminding him he was a warhorse and to be still. Under me, I felt his body slip into a relaxed wariness. His hooves stilled and his head rose high. His body under me expanded and relaxed as he breathed, his nostrils flaring as he took in the heavy night and became still and unmoving.

The wind in my head picked up where Jy left off. It cajoled, promising everything, denying nothing. It gibbered in anticipation of its freedom, and I sat with my head bowed and fastened my will about it and squeezed with the passion of my anger.

It yelped and shattered into a thousand zephyrs that screamed like banshees as they whirled and flew about inside my head, battering me. *You,* I thought, grasping one with my will. *I'll free you. You will find Duncan and return to me.*

The tiny breath of wind agreed, burying me in giggling promises and false platitudes. I knew it would do as I said, though the sly confidence it coated its flattery with filled me with a black foreboding.

Yet I released it.

My hair swirled upward when the zephyr made a wild spiral about me and vanished. Jy started at the sudden gust, and I soothed him. The wind that remained imprisoned in me called plaintively after it, but the leaves had stilled. It was gone.

Heart fast, I waited for its return, feeling the heat from Jy rise to warm my fingers buried in the mane about his withers. The spring frogs sang from hidden pools, and the moonlight grew as the clouds thinned. Trapped within me, the wind complained, its attentions not on me for once as it pined after the part of it I had freed.

A distant rushing came over the frogs. Jy pricked his ears,

and I followed his gaze into the dark. Sweat broke on me. It was coming back.

Though the trees about me stood with a frozen stillness, the soughing of distant branches swelled. Like an animal through grass, it flowed, gaining strength, pushing everything before it into a protesting complaint. The wind in my head heard, renewing its demented delight. I held my breath and my zephyr—now grown into a breeze—crashed onto the path.

It swirled and danced, taunting me to catch it. It knew! it mocked. It knew, but it wouldn't tell me!

My hair swirled up like fall leaves. Angry and afraid, I made a blanket of my thoughts and snared it. Jy pranced and shifted under me, frightened but not enough to bolt. My zephyr howled in protest as I forced its obedience.

"Where?" I demanded aloud, forcing it smaller until it was a breath roiling about the prison my cupped hands made. "Show me."

It whimpered. It cowered. It agreed to everything.

I cracked my fingers, and a soft breath slipped out. Obedient and cloying, the zephyr played about my face, cooling the sweat of fear on me. It tugged my hair, then danced to Jy's forelock and tied it into a knot. Jy snorted and shied, and I couldn't blame the beast.

"Where . . . ?" I prompted softly, and it zipped away, leaving a rustling path of leaves. Tension filled me, and I nudged Jy into a fast pace. The leaves stilled. I had lost it already. But it came back with a soft encouragement, pushing behind me for an instant before darting off again to make the leaves quake in its wake.

Easier now, I followed, anxious with the knowledge that I had managed to chain the voice in my head, even if it was only this small whisper. The wind remaining in me had fallen into a soft sulk that part of it was under my control.

As the moon rose and the clouds thinned further, I followed the sound of pattering leaves through the damp woods. There might have been a trail, but the wind didn't follow it, going straight through everything. Ducking low over Jy's withers, I dodged low limbs and snagging vines, finding my way by sound more than sight. Slowly, I grew wet, as the earlier mist brushed and plinked from the leaves onto me. Through small rivulets and crossing ragged outcrops of stone, I followed my zephyr until Jy balked at a thorny impasse.

The thin cloud cover was almost gone, and the full moon made the spindly saplings into dark slashes against the silver expanse of the briar field. Behind me lay the heavier forest, before me was a large open area. Beyond that, the woods began again, and even farther were the shadows of mountains and a neighbor's realm. A strip of boulders lay to one side of the field, slumped in a ragged line. The light from the moon glinted wetly on it.

Here, the zephyr encouraged. *He's here, he's here, he's here.* The whisper prattled in my ear, setting the wind in my head to echo it until it threatened my balance. Shuddering, I cupped my hand about the zephyr, willing it to be still. It wouldn't, demanding freedom, racing about my hands with the coldness of winter. My hands began to ache from it, and I finally promised to let it go forever if it would be still and not say anything.

The breeze battering the insides of my fingers grew warm and soft. Taking that as acquiescence, I opened my hands. My hair shifted and swirled into snarls, then the zephyr was gone.

Relieved, though the rage from the wind still trapped in me made me feel ill, I slid from Jy. The horse dropped his head, and I held his massive face for a moment to gather my strength. I looked at the briar field with a feeling of weary hopelessness and betrayal. *Duncan.* He was in there somewhere, hiding among the boulders.

Leaving Jy to do as he would, I gathered my skirts and started to pick my way through the last of the trees. The clouds were gone to leave a bright ring of blue about the moon. Dampness from the rain rose, sitting heavy in my lungs. My anger at Duncan had fallen to a depressed sadness. I didn't even know what I was going to do when I found him. But I had to see him, to tell him what he had done was not going to hurt me forever because he wasn't worth it.

My wet dress caught, and my hair tangled. I stopped and tediously unhooked every snag and snarl, patently moving forward at a halting but steady pace, my fingers going cold and unresponsive. I was headed for the line of rocks, sure Duncan was among them and using the briars as a way to detect any one approaching. But I was one person using stealth, not several score using knives to hack and break my way to him.

The numbness was settling deep into me again by the time I found the line of rocks. I scrambled up onto the first, using them as stepping-stones to work my way to the larger boulders. Their shadows were deep enough to hide bears. The zephyr returned, urging me on and earning the disgust of the wind still trapped in my head. It set the tiny leaves of the raspberry canes to tremble beside me, laughing merrily at its freedom.

A sudden gust pulled my head up, jerking my attention to a soft glow emanating from behind a curved boulder. I suddenly realized the rocks I was walking atop had once been a tower, now fallen to stretch its length across the earth. And in the pit where the tower's base had been, was a fire.

My throat tightened. Willing the wind in my head to be still, I crept forward slowly, so I wouldn't cause a rock to slide and give me away. Breath held, I eased to the edge of the light and peered down.

Duncan. He hadn't seen me. Tuck, his horse, had his ears pricked and was watching me. A second horse stood beside Duncan's gray. By the tidy state of his spring coat, I would guess that it belonged to the palace.

Tuck put his ears back at me, and I admonished the horse to be still. He sneezed and stamped a forefoot, rebelling against thoughts not his. Duncan didn't notice. The man was crouched beside his worn pack, his back to me as he dug to the bottom for something. Beside him were a broken bundle of hay and four satchels partially covered by a tarp. He looked calm and relaxed, only the quickness of his motions giving any indication that he had a kingdom's ransom beside him in the dirt. The sheltering walls of the tower curved almost entirely around him to hide the glow of firelight. It was an excellent spot to hide.

And an even better place for a murder, the wind in my head whispered, jolting me. Its voice was clear, more clear than my blurring vision.

He sent me to Rylan to die, I thought, my heart pounding when the wind urged me to act, telling me it was my right to exact revenge. *He lied and used me.*

My muscles in my calves tensed. A flush of anger warmed

my face. The wind in my head whispered insidiously, *He never loved you. He never loved you.*

With no thought of what might happen, I asked my freed zephyr to whisper in Duncan's ear. The tendril of breeze obediently darted away. The fire leapt, and Duncan started.

Spinning in a scuffing of boots, he rose. His face was long in shock. His eyes met mine, and his lips parted. Emotions followed each other so quickly I couldn't read them in the dim light of moon and fire.

"Tess!" he blurted. "You found me!" Motions quick, he strode forward as if the last three days hadn't happened. Eagerness radiated from him. "I can't believe you found me," he said, his hand extended to help me down from my rock. "Where's your pack? Oh, this is fantastic! Did you bring a horse?"

My legs trembled, and my jaw clenched. He thought I was here to run away with him. "Did you hear me call for you?" I said, making no move to take his hand extended to help me from the collapsed wall.

Duncan rocked to a halt, his hand dropping. A closed look came over him, accented by the shadows on his face from the fire behind him. His silence told me everything. He had heard me call. He had run with the money, leaving Rylan to torture and kill me.

I watched his eyes as they roved over me, cataloging my lack of weapons. I hadn't brought my whip. I hadn't brought my knives. I had no darts, and my curls were tumbled down about my shoulders, lank from the wet of the forest. I didn't need weapons anymore; I was a weapon. His expression grew soft, placating. He believed I had come defenseless.

Duncan's second finger went out to rub his thumb. A surge of anger flooded me when I realized it was his tell for lying, not nervousness as I had thought. "No," he cajoled, confirming it. "Did you call me? Just now? If I had heard, I would have called back. Did you bring a horse? There's a narrow path to bring one in from the south if you're careful."

He turned to look behind him as if to show me. The wind came from nowhere, pulled into existence from my fragmented thoughts. It laid the fire low for a moment, following the inside curve of the broken tower to break upon me. It pulled my hair back and whipped my skirts. The chatter in my head surged, falling to an insidious murmur for freedom as the gust flowed past me and into the night. The voice was becoming clearer, telling me that Duncan had lied to me then and was lying to me now.

Feeling unreal, I jumped to the ground to keep the fire between us. "Did you ever love me?" I said, knowing I looked like a fool but needing to hear him say it.

Duncan's eyes were fixed to mine, carefully away from the bags as he lied, "Tess . . . How can you ask that? You know I do."

He never loved you! the wind screamed in my head, and a gust from the skies followed it down. It filled me, reminding me of the power of the wind and waves. *Let me go,* it urged. *Let me go, and I'll free you from the hurt and anger, from choice and decision. Let me go, and I'll end your pain.*

"You have the ransom money," I said flatly, wondering what his answer would be.

He glanced at it, his lips pressing tight as he thought.

"You lied to me," I continued, before he could say anything. "You endangered my sister and me for it."

His brow furrowed. "Okay," he said abruptly. "It's the ransom. I took it. But I knew Lan wouldn't hurt you or your sister. He's a thief, not a murderer. I did it for you, Tess. I took it for you. The palace owes it to you for ruining your life. They bought you and lied to you. But your sister is safe just like I said, and now you can come with me with a clear conscience. There's nothing to stop you!" His eyes were bright with promise, hurting me. "We can be away and into the next kingdom in a few days of hard travel, then we don't have to do anything ever again!"

He came closer, his suntanned hands reaching. I backed a step away, and he rocked to a halt. "I did it all for you," he coaxed, his brown eyes full of expression. "So we could be together, living the way you deserve to live. I couldn't do it any other way. I'm a cheat, Tess, not a prince. How else was I going to get enough money to be worthy of you? Didn't I ask you to come with me? *Didn't I beg you to come with me?*"

Legs trembling, I stood before his fire, wanting to believe. I wanted to believe it so badly. What if I had been wrong? What if it had all been my silly female mistrust? Thadd had left Contessa because he felt unworthy beside Alex. He had forsaken love, leaving her to learn to love another because he felt unworthy of her. What if Duncan was willing to fight for love? Willing to lie and cheat instead of letting his circumstances dictate what he could and couldn't have? What if he was willing to die in his search for love should he be caught? What if I was wrong?

"Tess . . ."

My eyes jerked open as he touched my shoulder. He froze, his brown eyes pleading.

"Kiss me, Duncan," I whispered, tension singing through me. *Prove you love me in your touch.*

A beautiful smile fell over him, turning him happy and content. "Oh, Tess," he murmured, reaching for me. Shoulders falling as he relaxed, he gently pulled me closer.

My breath caught as I put my forehead against his upper chest, breathing in his scent. His arms went about me, pressing me tight. I looked up, eyes wet. *Please let there be love in his kiss.*

"Don't cry," he whispered, bending his head to mine.

The wind screamed in my head as our lips met. It rose through me in a silent wave, setting my fingers to tingle. It whipped about us, making my ugly dress flap and my damp hair flutter. A harsh snapping came from the fire as the wood was consumed and Tuck whinnied.

I savagely pushed the wind in my head into submission, ignoring it, filling my thoughts with Duncan: his lips moving against mine, his hands firm against my back as his need kept me tight to him, my own willingness urging him to continue.

I sent my hands across his back, pulling him closer until our bodies touched. I willed my self-imposed barriers to dissolve, allowing my desire to wash from me in a heady wave. I had to know if he loved me. If I gave him my love and got nothing in return, then I would know.

He felt the shift in me and slid his hands lower, more insistent. A soft sound of acceptance came from him, and I closed my eyes and sent my desire out to find his own. Tears warmed my eyes when the familiar smell of leather and horse cascaded through me. The wind howled and screamed in defeat, shrilling in my ears that he never loved me, over and over. But I didn't listen.

Until the zephyr I had released brought a new scent to me: the biting smell of coin that lingered about Duncan's hands. He had been running his hands through the ransom the same way he was now running them through my hair.

His lips on mine suddenly went dead. They were warm, but the tenderness I felt was only in my mind. There was no spark in Duncan's thoughts for me. It was an act. The wind was right. He might have loved me, but he loved money more.

Gasping, I pushed away from him, falling back two steps before catching my balance. Duncan stared at me, standing with a wary caution in his simple clothes and mud-rimmed boots while he took in my cold face, as the hurt and pain crashed down anew on me. My eyes flicked to his hands, only now seeing Rylan's blue-stoned ring on his finger. He had won the wager. "You don't love me," I said flatly.

Duncan tilted his head and wiped his mouth with the back of his hand. "Well I'll be damned," he whispered. "You can tell from a kiss after all."

"You never really loved me," I said louder. In my head, the wind agreed, wildly demanding I free it. It whipped my thoughts into a frenzy, promising it would take the hurt and pain away if I would free it. It would solve all my problems if I would let it go.

Turning his back on me, Duncan went to the fire and calmly started to pack his things. Tuck stomped, his eyes wild at the rising wind in the trees at the outskirts, moaning like a living thing. "Love?" he said, folding his bedroll and tying it to the frightened animal with a frayed string. "I don't know, Tess. Maybe someday I would have. I did enjoy kissing you. Too bad you're so straitlaced." Rakish grin looking ugly, he pulled his second horse closer. "We could have had a lot more fun if that last kiss was any indication."

Free me, the wind soothed, hot and insistent. *I'll end your hurt and anger. Give me your will, and I'll give you justice. I can take his breath. I can still his heart . . .*

I took a step forward, my fists at my side. "You never loved me."

He glanced at me irately. "I like you, Tess. I really do whether you want to believe it or not. So if there's anything else you want to say, say it. I have to go." He took Tuck's lead, giving him a knee in his ribs to get the horse to exhale before he cinched the riding pad tight.

Angry, I stepped closer until the fire was at my toes. "You heard Rylan hurting me."

"Lan was ready to castrate me!" he said loudly, turning to show anger in his brown eyes. "I'm a cheat, not insane." He draped the tarp across Tuck's back, and the flighty animal shied. "And I knew you and your magic could capture him. See? You're here and all right."

Tears blurred my vision while the memory of the pain and hurt resounded in me. Around me, the swirling wind faltered. The need I had felt for Duncan to come and rescue me flooded back, making me feel stupid. I had made myself weak by expecting him to save me. I was a fool twice over. "Why?" I whispered, while the leaves stirred against the moss.

Kneeling by one of the satchels, Duncan shifted to put one foot flat on the ground. His elbow went out to rest on it. "Why did I do it?" he said, then chuckled. "The money. And it was easy, just waiting to be taken. You were easier to charm than a drunken barmaid. So hungry for love that you'd believe what you wanted to hear. And I gave you your fantasy, a clever man willing to sacrifice anything to please you. You should be thanking me. And this?" Straining, he stood with the first bag and put it on the unwilling Tuck. "This is mine. I earned it. You won't stop me from taking it; you love me."

I could do nothing, frozen, when he led Tuck closer and put on a second bag to balance out the first. "And you always will," Duncan said, his fingers slow as he tied the satchel to keep it from slipping. "You'll do anything for me. *You have* done everything for me. You got Contessa to jump to Lan's ship, you told me about the false letter, you even woke me up when Captain Jeck stole them. It took me forever to convince Lan to maroon you on that island instead of killing you outright, but I knew you'd find a way to get back to the capital to make that fool of a chancellor pay the ransom. I saved your life there."

"Kavenlow didn't pay the ransom." The numb feeling in my shoulder was creeping up to smother my thoughts. "I lied to him." A quick intake of breath cleared the fog from me. I had betrayed Kavenlow's trust for Duncan's false love. "I lied to him for you."

"That's what I mean!" Duncan exclaimed, the third bag going atop the unhappy second horse. "You did it all, Tess, just as I laid it out. And *that's* why you're going to stand there and watch while I ride out of here."

Wind pulsing in time with my heart, I came closer. *Free me* the wind soothed. *No more pain, no more anger. Only the sweet bliss of nothing,* it promised insidiously.

My hands felt thick, so full of power I couldn't feel them. My pulse had quickened, sending venom into me. "I believed you," I said as I took his arm, halting his next motion to put the last bag in place.

Duncan jerked to a stop, frowning as he looked at my hand on him. His face was harsh in the come-and-go light from the fire, flickering with the wind I was stirring up. I could feel the strength of his muscles beneath my grip. I could sense how it would feel to pour my hate and anger into him, stopping his heart and burning his flesh. How the clean wash of insanity would purge me of pain and shame.

The power swelled, and the wind screamed inside my head. My breath caught as I fought with my hurt, trying to find a reason. My legs shook, and my skin burned. The wind grew stronger with my magic. *Now,* it demanded, pulling my anger and sorrow together. The wind rose higher, beating at my will, demanding I free it so it could kill him. And I resisted.

I balanced on the cusp, wanting it, wanting to hurt him, wanting to see my emotions revenged. The wind in me howled in my head, taking my will and giving it direction, and with a gleeful surge of possession, washed my anger into my hands.

"No!" I exclaimed, jerking my hands from Duncan. Pain jarred through me as I fell to kneel beside his fire. My hands burned with the force of death, my hate rebounding upon me. It rolled under my skin, seeking an outlet. My eyes widened in fear. It had nowhere to go.

Kneeling in the dirt, my mouth opened, and I stared at the moon, realizing what I had unleashed. Inside my head, the wind sang in delight. It had promised me release, and it would deliver. It had won! It had won! I would die, and it would be free of me!

Panicking, I frantically twisted my thoughts, sending the burning hatred in me to fall upon the wind. The voice shrieked in agony. I stiffened, unable to scream when the strength of winter racked across my soul. An upwelling of heat flashed through me, an ocean tide of fire that rose and consumed.

From my knees, I fell to my hands. I struggled to breathe, feeling as if my mind was on fire. My hands clenched the dirt, and I ground shards of stone into me. Fire burned in my skull as the voice in me was burned to ash, hurting me in the process.

Tears blurring my sight, I took a gasping breath, then another. *I was alive?* Panting, I brought my head up, seeing past the ragged curtain of my stringy hair Duncan blissfully unaware of what had happened. *I was alive.* But the slow hum of chatter in my head was gone. *I was alive; the wind was dead.*

I wouldn't kill Duncan for my mistake of trusting him. I was hurt and betrayed, but *I* allowed it to happen. I could live past the hurt. Killing him would mean I couldn't and that he had beaten me. Letting him live would mean he hadn't.

"Silly woman," Duncan muttered, turning from fastening the last satchel, his once-pleasant face harsh and ugly. "Can't hear the truth without falling down in hysterics. You should have brought someone with you to cart you crying home to your fire."

My head was pounding, and I felt light. Cleansed. He didn't even know I had almost killed him. Head bowing back to the earth while I gathered myself, I decided it didn't matter.

"What makes you think she's alone?" came a masculine voice behind the horses.

Tuck shied, the ringing thorns the only thing keeping the flighty horse from running away. Shocked, I pulled my gaze up from the dirt, shaking in spent energy. My breath slipped from me in dismay. Jeck. He had seen. He had seen everything.

Jeck let go of the lead of his horse and mine. Coming into the round hollow of stone, he stood before Duncan and me. He was dressed in his usual Misdev uniform minus his captain's insignia, looking confident and comfortable. His arms hung loosely at his sides, and the fire glinted on his wet boots. A sword hilt showed, and twin throwing knives were tucked into his belt.

I knelt on the ground, drained and feeling every inch the apprentice that I was. He was a real player, sent to pick up my slack, able to make the hard decisions that I continually balked at. I was twice the failure. Slowly, I got to my feet, disgraced. My hands were raw and red, burned from within.

Duncan fell back to his horses, grabbing their reins and making them nervous. "It's mine!" he shouted. "I earned it!"

"She caught you," Jeck said softly. Not having even looked at me yet, he moved—a powerful arm jabbing out. Tuck jerked his head back in alarm as Duncan hunched over, gasping. "So you get nothing," Jeck finished, catching Tuck's lead before the animal could bolt.

Jeck smirked when Duncan fell back against the broken curve of the tower, still struggling to breathe. Nudging the thief's pack open, he shuffled among Duncan's things until he pulled out a familiar-looking tin and tucked it inside his jerkin. By the tightness of his jaw, I knew it was his source of toxin, stolen before they marooned us on my boat and set it burning.

Expression empty, Jeck reached for Duncan. I took a quick breath, pulling myself out of my stupor. "Jeck," I said, when he took his shoulder and yanked him forward. "Don't."

Surprise pulled Jeck to me, his hand on the unresisting Duncan, still gasping in an awkward hunch. "He's going back for his hanging. He's a criminal and a thief, Tess. I saw you spare him. I thought it was for wisdom." His brow rose, and he eyed me in the firelight. "You still care for him?"

My pulse pounded in my hurt hands as I stood before him. "You told me once there're ways to wreak revenge other than death, and some can serve a purpose."

His brow rose higher, and I would swear that a smile threatened to quirk the corner of his mouth. "I'm listening," he said softly—dangerously.

Duncan heard the threat in his voice, and he flicked a glance at me, taking his first clean breath. Blood slipped from the corner of his mouth, and I wondered if Jeck had broken something inside him. A devilish grin was on him, though a bit grim, and he eyed me sideways. He obviously thought I was going to plead for his freedom, believing I still loved him.

"Rylan is still free," I said, and Duncan paled, every ounce of confidence washing away to leave only a thin man in a dirty shirt and damp knees.

"You didn't capture him?" Duncan said, coughing as he

felt his ribs. "You were supposed to capture him. I sent you there so you would catch him!"

Clearly disgusted, Jeck pushed him down until his knees hit the dirt.

A flush of satisfaction warmed me, pulling me straighter. I hadn't danced quite the way he wanted when he pulled my strings, and now he was going to lose everything. A wicked smile came over me, and seeing it, Jeck's lips parted in question. "Rylan will find him," I said. "And until he does, Duncan will spend his every waking moment looking over his shoulder, expecting a knife in his side." I looked at Duncan with satisfaction. "It's not the life he thinks he bought with his lies. I saw Rylan in the streets. He's a day behind me."

Duncan went even paler. Seeing it, Jeck nodded once sharply. "As you will it, Princess. You are as gracious as you are clever."

I blinked at the dry sarcasm he laid on the word *gracious* as much as for the compliment that he followed it with. *He thought I was clever?*

"Wait!" Duncan lurched to his feet. Jeck pushed him, and he sprawled on his back.

Turning from Duncan, Jeck led Tuck and the second horse laden with the ransom out of the hollow of firelight. Jy and Pitch nickered a welcome.

"Leave him his horse," I said, and Jeck turned to look at me in exasperation.

"Thanks, Tess," Duncan said, getting to his feet.

"It will make you easier to track," I finished, and this time, Jeck did smile. Duncan looked from me to his horse in horror. He had trained the animal so well that unless he tied him down to starve, Tuck would follow him to the ends of the earth.

Grunting, Jeck flipped a knife from somewhere on his person, slicing through the knots. The sacks fell to the ground to make Tuck start and prance. "That's mine!" Duncan exclaimed when Jeck lifted one.

Jeck gave him a weary look. The firelight glinted on his sword's hilt as he took the bags one at a time and loaded down Pitch's saddle, then tied the remaining horses together. In a smooth, enviable motion, he vaulted to Jy's riding pad, extending a hand to help me mount before him.

My face lost all expression in shock. It was my prophetic dream.

I lifted my eyes to Jeck, and he nodded at my understanding. His eyes held a faint hint of respect, of appreciation for a well-played game, and the acceptance of my unique justice. Heart pounding, I brushed the last of the damp grit from me before I extended my arm. Jeck grasped my wrist instead of my burned hand, leaning to slip an arm about my waist and pull me smoothly into place. I sat before him, unsure and feeling unreal. *Oh God, it's the vision of the future drawn to life by the punta bite.*

"You can't!" Duncan exclaimed, taking a step until Jeck shook his head and pointed his foot to kick him away. The man looked small from the top of my horse, as he glanced between the horses and us heavy with ransom. "She owes me something!" Duncan insisted, licking his lips and gesturing. "She took my skills as a cheat with her poison darts. She owes me!"

"She owes you nothing," Jeck said, his voice disgusted.

"I *earned* it," he insisted, his upturned face ugly in greed. "I put up with her foolishness for almost a year." His face went desperate. "If I don't give Rylan something, he'll kill me."

My heart clenched at his callousness, and I felt as if I had been kicked. I had been such a fool, mooning over a man and letting my emotions chart my decisions. But Jeck only made a sound of revulsion deep in his chest, shaking the reins with his arms around me to get Jy moving.

"Tess!" Duncan pleaded, taking a step after us. "Rylan will kill me!"

I clenched my jaw to keep my chin from trembling. "Goodbye, Duncan," I said softly from atop my horse, not looking at him. "Run fast and hard. Don't come back."

"You sorry little whore!" he suddenly swore as we clopped out of the firelight and the clean glow of moonlight bathed us. "I won't forget this. You owe me. I'll be back!"

I thought of Rylan and his fast, angry pace in the street. Satisfied, I put a hand atop Jeck's arm, and he obligingly pulled Jy to a halt. "What did the wind whisper in your ear?" I asked Duncan. "When you first turned and found me watching you. What did it say?"

His dirt-smudged face went long and still. "It said I was going to die."

Fear trickled through me. The wind didn't know how to lie. "Then you won't be coming back," I said, turning my face to the thin track leading out of the thorns. *God help me. What have I become?*

"Tess!" Duncan called, as the clops of the three horses sounded faint on the thick moss. I closed my eyes, willing the heartache away. Jeck's arms were around me, the warmth of them reaching me even through my cloak. I finally recognized the source of my feelings of betrayal in the punta vision. They stemmed from Duncan, not the man whose arms now encircled me.

Not sure what I was feeling, I glanced at the two horses with their heavy satchels plodding behind us, twin shadows in the moonlight. "I don't remember the money," I said.

"It showed up after you left the vision." His resonant voice echoed up through me, and the faint hint of a deeper emotion brought me to a questioning stillness. Something tingled through me, almost like a healing force to soothe my battered soul.

We broke free of the brambles, and the horses walked faster when we turned to the east, knowing they were headed for the stables. The wind soughing through the moonlit trees held no meaning. I had killed the wind inside me. It was gone.

I closed my eyes in a long blink of relief. It was short-lived, though, as a laugh snickered beside my ear. It was the zephyr I had freed to find Duncan, and it whispered something I didn't hear before swirling my hair and dancing away.

Frightened, I held myself with a tense stillness, waiting for its return. Jeck said nothing about the brief whirlwind, for which I was thankful. "It's gone," I said shakily. "I killed it using my anger at Duncan."

"The wind?" he asked nonchalantly. His voice was as soft as the distant frog song, and I nodded. "Good. That will make things easier for you."

I swallowed, suddenly nervous for his arms about me. "Is there anything else different from the dream?" I asked hesitantly.

"No," was his quick reply, but by the hint of guilt in it, I thought he might be lying.

Twenty-nine

❖

It seemed I could feel the waves already moving under me as I stood at the palace quay and watched the final preparations for my new boat, the *Black Sandpiper*, to set sail on her maiden voyage. Having been commissioned even before I had lost the *Sandpiper*, it had only taken a month to finish. She was ten feet longer, had yards more sail, three inches less draft when riding empty, narrow lines to make her even faster—and was painted black. The hold had been converted entirely into living space, and I was eager to travel in the higher comforts the specially designed ship would have. There was even a tiny bathing room. Heaven.

Captain Borlett was standing with Contessa and Alex at the ramp, alive and feisty as he enthusiastically pointed at the rigging while explaining some point of nautical lore that they clearly didn't care about. He and his crew had been found in the hold of the pirate ship and freed the same day as Contessa and Alex, not nearly as injured as I had believed.

Though having gained a severe limp and pale from too many days away from the sun, he showed that his ability to bellow orders over storms hadn't been reduced at all. Seeing him dressed in his captain's best with shiny buckles and ornate braids made me feel tremendously at peace with myself. I again had my boat. Nothing could go wrong.

Filing onto the *Black Sandpiper* were several ranks of Misdev guards, their belongings on their backs and in small totes. They were returning to Misdev now that Alex felt secure among the Costenopolie court. A stir of nervousness quickened my pulse when I found Jeck in his official capacity come to a standstill behind Contessa and Alex while the prince said good-bye to a favored sentry. Jeck was leaving, too, and a small pile of his belongings waited to be loaded apart from the rest. Mine were apparently already aboard since I didn't see them on the dock.

Jeck's presence at the ramp was the main reason I was tucked out of the way while last-minute details were being remembered and dealt with. I wasn't afraid of him anymore, I was embarrassed. He had seen me at my worst—handing my charges over to pirates, getting bitten by a punta, alerting brigandines that we were escaping, trying to kill him not once but several times, fainting, crying, and generally acting like a silly woman over a man she thought loved her. God help me, it was the last that bothered me. I was a player's apprentice and might be excused for mucking my master's game up past repair, but crying over a man was pathetic.

I had taken to actively avoiding Jeck in the last month, and saw no reason to change anything. Heather had laughingly told me after I caught sight of him in the hallway, and took another, that I'd developed a healthy infatuation with him and that it was about time, as the man was so handsome he could make a dove swoon. I told her it was because he had seen me cry over Duncan, and I felt like an idiot. But the reality was I felt as though he had been judging me, and I was coming up lacking. Which was doubly painful as I was starting to wonder if Heather was right. About the infatuation part, not the dove.

Tucking a strand of wayward hair behind my ear, I watched him across the distance as he took off his gaudy hat and tried to lose it, smiling tightly when a helpful crewman rescued it before it rolled into the bay. Time had given me the chance to look upon the few days we had been forced into close association in a new light, and I wasn't sure yet what to make of it. After having seen his skills as a player and the deep emotion he was capable of, hidden behind cross words and empty looks, I had grown to respect him. At least that's what I told myself it was. It had the unfortunate result of turning me from a once-confident apprentice to a stammering, flushing seed-fluff-headed girl when he asked me anything. So I avoided him.

I was thankful the trip upriver would only take a few weeks. Then I'd be rid of him for good. He and Kavenlow had been having too many private conversations lately for my liking. It made me feel like . . . like an apprentice.

Alex's voice came faintly to me over the distance, and the populace watching from behind silken ribbons cheered. Contessa and Alex turned to wave, bringing an even more furious shout. The two of them shone without me, and I liked to watch their happiness. My eyes dropped, and a mix of melancholy and joy warmed my eyes as I was reminded of my parents. They, too, had been loved by the people they governed. Perhaps some of the people's love could be attributed to the stories of Alex's valor and Contessa's fight for his and her survival. It was easy to put your trust in two such honorable people.

My head rose, fastening on the distant blur of fluttering gray at the far end of the harbor. The pirates' bodies hung in warning to all that would enter. The vultures and eagles had been at them, not leaving much now but bones and scraps of clothing. I didn't agree with the action that had been taken to prevent another such attempt at abduction, and again I thought that perhaps my punta bite had been a blessing.

I wasn't made to be a player despite Kavenlow's assurances. I didn't have the moral fiber to carry out distasteful acts. I'd rather invent excuses to avoid them, like letting Duncan live by telling myself that his life would be hell with Rylan chasing after him. One more thing to convince Jeck I was not player material.

Shoulders slumping, I pulled my attention back to the happy throng of people on the platform. Kavenlow's somber tunic was a black spot toward which my attention gravitated, a restful place for my eyes to linger among the glaring whites and vibrant greens and golds. Why Kavenlow hadn't accepted that I couldn't be a player was a question that sifted through my sleepless nights.

He insisted on waiting six months before testing my resistance to the toxin, convinced an extended abstinence from venom and magic would allow my residuals to drop to the

levels where I could function on a limited, carefully struc-
tured apprenticeship. His stout avowal that I not give up hope
only strengthened after I admitted I had called the wind and
told him that I had managed to purge it from me before it
drove me insane.

Even that I had betrayed him using my magic hadn't moved
him. It had been Jeck who finally realized that I'd changed
their memories as to when the ransom was to have gone out,
bringing him to the burning shack in time to save my life. And
the discovery hadn't come on the heels of my not being able
successfully to change their memories; I had. The tides had
been wrong, and the incongruity had bothered Jeck until he decided that it was more likely I'd manipulated their memories
than that the pirates were going to row up a river against the
tidal current to take their ransom back out to sea.

My face warmed at the memory, and as if responding to it,
a stray vagrant of wind blew up from under the dock. I wasn't
sure if it was an extension of my new skills or not until the
breeze swirled my hair up in a whirl, letting it fall into a snarl.
Lips pressed in a mild bother, I carefully ran my fingers
through my hair as a comb.

Kavenlow was of the belief that I never *had* the wind in my
head, that I had mastered it the first time I had called it. He
said that the laughing, derisive voice in my thoughts had been
my subconscious trying to warn me that Duncan didn't love
me. Jeck seemed to agree. I was trying hard not to think about
it, not comfortable being able to do something that even retired masters were too wise to attempt.

As if drawn by my uncomfortable thoughts, Kavenlow
turned to me. Making a gracious bow, he made his escape
from the royal flurry and strode across the wide, sun-soaked
dock to where I sat atop a tarp-covered bundle of hardwood
slated for the next boat headed to Misdev. I wouldn't miss him
too badly. After all, it was only going to be a short trip. And I
only had myself to worry about this time, not a royal couple
trying not to fall in love.

My hair tangled again when a zephyr whirled it upward. It
was worse down here at the docks. I knew it was just my unconscious pointing out that I was lying to myself and that I

would miss Kavenlow sorely. But at least it wasn't trapped in my head anymore.

"What are you doing hiding back here?" Kavenlow asked as he came to a squinting, smiling halt before me.

I shifted down the rough tarp to stand beside him, being careful not to snag my dress. "Trying to stay out of the way until we're ready to go," I said.

He eyed me from under bushy eyebrows before turning to Jeck. Trying to stay out of Jeck's way was more likely, and I grimaced in embarrassment that he probably knew it. A sigh escaped him, and he leaned against the nearby rough-cut planks of wood. His gaze went out across the sun-laced harbor, then he bowed his head. "Tess . . ."

My heart seemed to stop. Something was wrong. I could hear it in his voice. Stiff with tension, I looked across the quay to Jeck. He was watching us, and my alarm doubled.

"I've been meaning to talk to you," Kavenlow continued. "Contessa . . ."

"What?" I breathed, frightened.

He curled his lips in upon themselves to make his mustache shift. Still not looking at me, he said, "It was decided finally today, or I would have told you sooner. You aren't going to be the ambassador to Misdev anymore."

My breath hissed in. I frantically looked at the *Black Sandpiper,* then back to him. Shame seemed to stop my heart. I had allowed them to be taken, and she no longer trusted me. "They don't want me to be ambassador," I said. "I—I understand. I'll get my things off . . . the boat." My voice rose to a squeak at the end, and I hated it.

"Tess, no," Kavenlow said, and he reached out, sounding embarrassed and worried all at the same time. "You're to be Costenopolie's ambassador at large, and that there"—he nodded to the *Black Sandpiper*—"is your boat. But you won't be on it when it goes to Misdev. Today or any other day. Misdev will have a more permanent ambassador, which is a polite term for willing hostage. Alex's father insisted on one after this latest fiasco."

He frowned, and my threatened tears hesitated. "I don't understand."

Letting go of my elbows, he put his back to the fuss and noise at the ramp to face me squarely. His hands took mine, and he looked at them, lying small and smooth within his rough grip. "Tess," he said softly, "I can't be your master anymore."

Panic flooded me, and though I had been expecting this, my heart beat wildly, and my throat closed. I was being dismissed. The long, private conversation he had had last night with Jeck took on a new meaning. I swallowed hard, keeping my voice low so he wouldn't hear it shake when I said, "I understand."

"Don't cry," he said, his rough voice pleading. "It's a matter of necessity. I wish it could be otherwise, but our skills don't mesh. Your tolerances have hardly dropped in the last month, and Jeck, knowing it and being a rival, would be forever a danger to the Costenopolie game. You understand I can't risk it."

I nodded, dying inside. "I understand." I couldn't look at him, and I pulled my hands from his.

Making a small noise, Kavenlow took a step back. "We've talked it over and have agreed that you will become Jeck's apprentice."

Shocked, my head came up. I blinked back the blur of unshed tears, feeling my face go cold. "Jeck's . . ." I stammered. Tearing my eyes from Kavenlow's patent, pained smile, I looked at the Misdev captain. The man stood stiff and uneasy beside Alex. He knew what we were talking about.

My knees went weak, and I struggled to form a coherent thought. "I don't want to be his apprentice!" I finally exclaimed, flushing at the memory of his arms around me, a single spot of comfort and understanding when my world had been falling apart. "I don't like him!" I lied. "He doesn't care about me at all. I'd rather . . . leave the game!"

"Slow down," he soothed, his hand landing on my shoulder. "You don't mean that."

"Kavenlow . . ." I pleaded, knowing I would rather die than leave the game voluntarily. "He's mean and cruel to me."

"He's not."

I stood in a panic, feeling unreal and ready to pass out. This could not be happening. "He left me on the island with the pirates," I said. "And he tied me to the mast on the raft like an animal. And then he just walked off and left me to find my way back to the capital alone, taking all the food! Please don't make me be his apprentice!"

"Shhhh," he said, using the inside of my expansive sleeve to wipe my face. *Chu pits, I'm crying.* "He did nothing to harm you," Kavenlow said. "He was evaluating you."

Breath catching, I met his proud, sorrowful gaze. His shoulders shifted as he gathered his thoughts. "There are things going on that you don't know about, Tess. Jeck did nothing to hurt you. By leaving you to be recaptured by the pirates, you might have saved Contessa's and Alex's lives. It was a good move, and if it had been me, I would have done the same thing, though I admittedly would have told you. If Jeck hadn't tied you to the mast, you would have either killed him or jumped into the waves and killed yourself."

My eyes widened. I hadn't known Jeck had told him all that. But there was no fear in Kavenlow, no shame that I had lost control of myself and tried to kill Jeck.

"And the walk to the capital alone?" Kavenlow said, bringing my attention back to him as he patted my hand. "His slowing to the pace you were capable of would have done nothing to help you at all. As it was, he went ahead and made sure you had a fire when you caught up. And by walking away in front of that old woman, it moved her to pity you. Not a bad emotion if used properly, which you apparently did. Angry at him for abandoning you, she gave you things you needed, whereas she might not have otherwise."

I stared at him, balanced as I tried to believe. Had I been even more blind than I thought?

"When he brought up the question of stealing you away as his apprentice last spring," Kavenlow said, "it wasn't only a matter of not wanting to expend the toxin needed to bring a novice up from scratch. It's expensive and risky, and he really didn't want a princess to succeed him, but a soldier. But you impressed him with your tenacity and resourcefulness in regaining the palace. He thought that only a soldier had the fortitude to become a successful player. You proved him wrong. You never gave up. Though you moaned and complained, you saw what needed to be done, and you did it. Your resourcefulness and daring salvaged a game played out and lost. You made hard choices, knowing you would have to live with the results. And when you were facing death, you carried yourself with the bravery of a soldier."

"Really?" I prompted hesitantly, and he smiled, his eyes darkening with moisture.

"Really," he affirmed. "And since the punta bite elevated your residual levels, I agree that Jeck is the only player who can survive teaching you. The only one who can best you. Not in power, perhaps, but in skills."

"You think I'm more powerful than Jeck?" I asked, a stab of fear taking me.

He nodded, his expression serious. "Yes. But be careful. Strength means nothing without the ability to wield it. He hides his skills almost as carefully as you hide your strength, and if you're anything but obedient, he will find a way to humiliate you in some way that can't be traced to him, so mind your manners."

"No," I protested, believing it. He made it sound like it was settled and sealed. *Don't I have a say in this?* "I don't want to. I don't trust him. It's a trick, Kavenlow. Don't send me away! I don't want to leave Costenopolie!"

He turned from me, a hand brushing his silvering beard smooth as he looked across the bay and into nothing. "You aren't."

Confused, I looked at my boat, then him.

"We agreed that taking you out of Costenopolie would be a mistake. Contessa relies heavily upon you, and inflicting you upon a new kingdom would be disastrous." His eyes darted to mine, and he touched my nose. "You do tend to leave a trail of destruction, and a population not used to it might be appalled."

"Kavenlow?" I warbled, my eyes going to the pile of trunks by the ramp. They were his, not Jeck's. I recognized them now.

"I'm leaving," he said, not sounding at all apologetic. "It's all arranged. I'm taking Misdev, and Jeck will stay here in Costenopolie."

Heart beating wildly, I grabbed his arm. "You can't! Why?"

Eyes pinched, he took my hands and held them in the comforting strength of his own. "Tess, forgive me for being selfish, but I'm bored. I've played all I can with Costenopolie. I want new pieces, new challenges. I'm not ready to leave the game, but there's nothing left for me here. It's become too easy. I'm becoming soft, complacent. And you?" Again he smiled, though I thought it was getting harder as the wrinkles about his eyes grew deeper. "Jeck can give you what I can't."

I looked over Kavenlow's shoulder to Jeck. I didn't want him as a master. I was starting to like him, whether it was a silly-woman crush or not. And the thought of taking instruction from him and trying to hide my feelings was going to be a nightmare of embarrassment. Especially when he figured it out. Which he would. If he hadn't already. Chu pits, I would not have him knowing his words of comfort and his quiet understanding had meant that much to me!

"He doesn't like me," I insisted, feeling it was a lost cause but having to protest. "Kavenlow, don't do this to me. I don't want to be his apprentice!"

"That's enough," he said sharply, the first hint of metal in his voice. "I can't teach you anything more. You've taken everything I can give you. You've gone past me. Jeck can do what I cannot." His eyes softened, and his hand touching my jawline trembled. "And I didn't just bring up a player, Tess. I raised a daughter, and I want her to be happy. You need love to be complete. You take your strength from it. And Jeck—"

I jerked my hand from his, covering Kavenlow's mouth, cold with the words he had almost said. The breeze off the bay swirled through my hair, tugging at it. Kavenlow smiled softly from behind his graying beard as he took my hand back in his own.

"He loves you, Tess," he said gently, but it scared me nevertheless. "I never expected it to shift from respect to love, but it did, and I can see it as clearly as you can see it between Alex and Contessa."

"No. He doesn't," I said, my mouth dry and my stomach in knots. But a zephyr rose, whispering and buzzing in my ear, laughing cheerfully. I didn't listen to it, afraid what my subconscious was trying to tell me.

"With him, you can be a player," Kavenlow said, and this time, his smile was laced with sadness. "He won't tell anyone about your punta bite if you're his apprentice. And God is my witness that I won't. You will have the ten years you need for your venom levels to drop."

"But I . . ." I stammered. *Jeck loves me? He hardly knows me.* "Kavenlow . . ."

A bellowing shout drew his attention to the ramp. It was Captain Borlett, berating the crew for smacking Kavenlow's trunk into a piling. Kavenlow moved from the stacked wood with a relieved quickness. "Excuse me, Princess. I want to be sure they don't damage my things.

"Kavenlow!" I moved to follow, frightened. He was leaving. Right now!

His arms went around me, and he gave me a crushing embrace. The air fled from my lungs, and my eyes watered. Behind him, Contessa was watching from Alex's arm, smiling at us.

"It's all arranged," Kavenlow whispered, seemingly unwilling to let go. "I'm going to Misdev under the guise of being the permanent ambassador as Contessa wishes. I'll be sending your ship back as soon as I get there. In reality, I will be taking over Jeck's game. Jeck's sovereign has permanently assigned him to the Costenopolie court in light of the recent abductions, and in truth he will be Costenopolie's player. We have a six-month grace period where no other player can interfere while we learn our pieces and settle in. Six months where you will go with absolutely no toxin or magic to evaluate how damaged your toxin tolerances are."

The gulls wheeling above us cried, sounding like my heart breaking. "You've both settled this in a nice neat package," I said, my voice harsh. "Don't I get a say?"

He pulled from me, his eyes tearing. "No. You can leave the game of course. But it would be a shame. The things you can do . . ." He hesitated, putting me at arm's length. "You will be one of the greatest players, Tess. I just don't know how Jeck is going to keep you under wraps as an emerging power."

Hope mixed with heartache. I was going to be a player. I had lost nothing. Except Kavenlow.

My joy crashed as he let go of my hands and stepped away. I stiffened, suddenly realizing Jeck was standing behind him— waiting. I eyed him warily, my pulse quickening as I saw him still wearing his Misdev uniform. Apart from when I had been crying over Duncan, my heart wounded and my thoughts trying to find a way to heal the pain, he held himself distant. He was brusque, short, and sarcastic. I would swear he went out of his way to irritate me. His eyes were always on me, and usually there was a tight look of annoyance in them.

Understanding fell on me, washing the warmth of the sun away. He didn't *want* to love me. That was why he was so disagreeable.

Kavenlow saw my cold face and nodded, knowing I finally understood. "Good-bye, Tess," he said, and my eyes widened. "I'll write you."

"Kavenlow . . ." I struggled to say something, but my mind was blank.

"Take care of yourself," he whispered, angling himself so Jeck couldn't see his moving lips. "And don't be too difficult with him. Give him time to figure out he can love and find strength in it, not failure. You can teach him that."

He pulled from my numb grip. Visibly steadying himself, he faced Jeck. "Captain," he said formally, nodding with a deep respect.

"Chancellor," he responded, his low voice calm and confident.

Lump forming in my throat, I watched Kavenlow twist a ring off his finger and give it to him as a token of surrendering his position as Costenopolie's player. Jeck shifted his balance and put it on his finger. He hesitated in thought, then with a smile quirking his lips to ruin his stiff demeanor, he took off his gaudy hat and gave it to Kavenlow.

Kavenlow took a breath to protest, his brow furrowed. Jeck cocked an eyebrow, and Kavenlow collapsed in on himself, accepting it. He turned to me one last time. My mouth worked, but nothing came out. Smiling, he bowed his head for an instant before he turned and walked confidently to the ramp, the gaudy monstrosity of a hat crushed in his grip.

I sniffed loudly, stiffening when Jeck slid up beside me. We stood shoulder to shoulder, and I wondered what was going to happen. Suddenly nervous, I glanced at Jeck sideways. *He loves me?* "Captain."

"Apprentice," he replied, not looking at me but at the sparkling waves. Falling into a parade rest, he laced his hands behind his back, his feet spread wide and his head level. "If you ever try to change my memories again, I will slap you into next spring."

I took a breath, knees shaking as I felt small beside him, my white dress brushing against his black trousers. Some women get flowers or poems from their suitors. I get insults and threats. Heather would laugh herself pink. "I still outrank you," I said boldly.

He shifted slightly, giving me a wry look before turning away. "I'll try to keep that in mind. You will join me in the stables tomorrow morning at sunup. Your horsemanship is appalling."

My eyes widened, and my pulse quickened in ire. "I can outjump you any day, Captain. I've been riding since I was three."

He made a comfortable-sounding scoff, a hint of anticipation in it. The desire for a companion that could meet him strength for strength? Skill for skill? Understanding for understanding?

"Then you won't mind showing up an hour earlier to prove it," he said, turning away when he saw my eyes go gentle in thought.

I took a breath to protest, then changed my mind. A small cheer rose at the ramp, and the ship cast off in a flurry of shouts and commands. Kavenlow stood beside the wheel with Captain Borlett, and the distance between us had already grown too far to jump. My heart ached, and tears blurred my sight.

My heart full of loss and hope, I sent my zephyr to grow and fill the sails to speed him on his way. With a surprising thump, the canvas snapped full. And though the crew scrambled to respond, Kavenlow gave me a little bow, his pride obvious even from the distance between us.

Jeck sucked at his teeth and rocked back on his heels, then to his toes. "Got it under control now, hum?" he asked softly.

The wind swung back to me, making the women on the dock cry in dismay as their hair blew to hit their faces. I reached up and pressed my hair down. "Sort of," I said, holding myself still as the wind tied my hair in knots and whispered very clearly in my ear that Jeck loved me.